Julie Caplin aka Jules Wake is an internationally bestselling author of over twenty five books including the highly successful *Romantic Escape* series which has been translated into over 24 languages. Her books have topped the charts in the UK, Germany, Austria, Switzerland, Iceland, Italy, Czech Republic and Slovakia.

After reading English at university, Jules Wake worked in PR where she honed her fiction writing skills on press releases and swanned around Europe taking journalists on gastronomic press trips. These visits inspired the locations of many of her books. She's now a full-time author and what better job is there than making stuff up! It certainly beats housework.

As an avid romance fan, she's written in several genres including historical romantic fiction, contemporary women's romance fiction and romantic comedy.

Instagram @Juliecaplinauthor
Website: www.juleswake.co.uk
http://www.facebook.com/JulieCaplinAuthor

Also by Julie Caplin

The Cosy Café in Copenhagen
The Little Brooklyn Bakery
The Little Paris Patisserie
The Northern Lights Lodge
The Secret Cove in Croatia
The Little Tokyo Teashop
The Little Swiss Ski Chalet
The Cosy Cottage in Ireland
The Christmas Castle in Scotland
The French Chateau Dream
A Villa With A View
A Little Place in Prague

As Jules Wake

Talk To Me
From Italy With Love
From Paris With Love This Christmas
From Rome With Love
Escape to the Riviera
Covent Garden in the Snow
Notting Hill in the Snow
The Spark
The Saturday Morning Park Run
The Wednesday Morning Wild Swim
Secrets of Latimer House

A Girl's Best Friend

JULIE CAPLIN

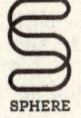

SPHERE

SPHERE

First published in Great Britain in 2018 by Sphere
This reissue published in 2026 by Sphere

1 3 5 7 9 10 8 6 4 2

Copyright © Jules Wake 2018

The moral right of the author has been asserted.

*All characters and events in this publication, other than those
clearly in the public domain, are fictitious and any resemblance
to real persons, living or dead, is purely coincidental.*

All rights reserved.
No part of this publication may be reproduced, stored in a
retrieval system, or transmitted, in any form or by any means, without
the prior permission in writing of the publisher, nor be otherwise circulated
in any form of binding or cover other than that in which it is published
and without a similar condition including this condition being
imposed on the subsequent purchaser.

A CIP catalogue record for this book
is available from the British Library.

ISBN 978-1-4087-3616-6

Typeset in Caslon by M Rules
Printed and bound in Great Britain by
Clays Ltd, St Ives plc

Papers used by Sphere are from well-managed forests
and other responsible sources.

Sphere
An imprint of
Little, Brown Book Group
Carmelite House
50 Victoria Embankment
London EC4Y 0DZ

The authorised representative
in the EEA is
Hachette Ireland
8 Castlecourt Centre
Dublin 15, D15 XTP3, Ireland
(email: info@hbgi.ie)

An Hachette UK Company
www.hachette.co.uk

www.littlebrown.co.uk

For Justine, the very best sort of friend
one could wish for.

Acknowledgements

I suppose I should really thank my husband for this book – he who announced one New Year's Day to our children's absolute delight that this was the year of Project Dog. Immediately visions of being chief dog-walker, pooper-scooper and general cleaner-upper filled my head.

Enter my cunning plan. To ensure that my enthusiastic family became a tad less enthusiastic, I volunteered us all to dogsit for Ash, a very handsome black Labrador, owned by friends of ours.

This backfired spectacularly as at the end of the week, I'd fallen completely in love – but we had to face the practical reality: it wouldn't be fair on a dog to take one on at that stage in our family life.

However, there is a bonus, as much of what I learned that week inspired the story that became *A Girl's Best Friend*. So thanks, Nick!

I'd especially like thank the Matthews family – Mel, Jay, Ben, Jacob and Olivia – for being brave enough to lend the lovely Ash to complete dog novices for one half-term holiday; and my children, Ellie and Matt, who were the most excellent dog-walking companions.

Heartfelt gratitude goes to local vet, Patrick Dale, in Tring, who let me spend some time at Springwell Veterinary Surgery, learning just what goes on in a veterinary practice. It was an absolute eye opener! One of the highlights, and look away if you're squeamish, was being allowed to watch a dog being spayed using keyhole surgery, about which Patrick is evangelical because it is so much kinder and less invasive to animals. I may also need to apologise to him, as he bears no resemblance whatsoever to the Patrick in my book.

Thanks also go to superstar pet-sitter and book-blogger, Ann Cooper, who read an early draft to check that I'd got my dog facts correct.

Last but not least, thanks go to my best writing buddy, Donna, who is always there for me with Prosecco and pep talks; my fab agent Broo Doherty and my lovely editor Maddie West for falling in love with this book as much as I did; and to Thalia Proctor for making the process delightfully painless.

And of course you, for choosing *A Girl's Best Friend*. Enjoy x

Chapter One

As the train rocked to a halt with a gentle thud, Ella rounded up nearly all her worldly goods. It seemed her life had come full circle, back where she started, except she really hadn't been that far. Like an overloaded tortoise, rucksack on her back, pulling two cases and juggling the variety of mismatched bags, she struggled along the platform, but had to give in and make two trips up the flight of stairs before rumbling along the bridge to the car park, every step feeling more leaden than the last.

'Ella, darling.' Her mother darted across the car park. 'Gosh, you do look tired. How are you?' Her eyes, bird-bright, gave Ella an assessing look.

'I'm fine.' Her terse, brittle response elicited a quick worried frown. Ella looked away. One slight crack in her determined defence and her mother would prise her wide open, like a reluctant mussel, forcing everything out.

'Let me help.' Despite her diminutive size, her mother tried to take the larger case. 'Good Lord, what have you got in here?'

'Everything,' muttered Ella with feeling, having dragged it from Shoreditch across London and then been wedged up against it from Euston to Tring for the last forty-three minutes. She'd packed as much as she could and brought along most of her art supplies and her clothes; everything else, not much at all, had gone into storage.

Her mother tutted. 'I don't know why you didn't ask us to come and collect you, it would have been a lot easier.'

Ella gave a vague smile and managed to refrain from pointing out that it would have been far too much like being picked up at the end of a college term. An admission of failure. She settled into the front passenger seat of the little runaround, as pristine as the day it rolled away from the showroom with its little pockets and gadgets to keep everything in its place. Mints, de-icer, cloths, spare air freshener. For some reason all that neat orderliness irked her and she longed to run a streak through the slightly misted windscreen with one finger, just to leave a mark. *Ella woz ere*. Ella was somewhere. Ella was still in here somewhere.

'Now,' her mother started brightly, 'your father's going to meet us there. Magda's left the house all ready for you and I've popped a few bits in the fridge. You're to treat the place as your own, help yourself to anything you want and of course there's—'

'Mum, I spoke to Magda myself.'

'Right. And how are you ... er ... you know ... feeling?'

'Mum, you can mention Patrick's name without me bursting into tears.' Ella tightened her mouth, schooling her face into an impassive mask. 'We're just taking a break, at the moment. Taking some time to assess things.' Even-toned, her explanation sounded perfectly normal. Well thought-out. Logical. A grown-up way to do things.

Ella winced as her mother swung out of the car park, narrowly missing taking off the wing mirror of an oncoming car. Conventional to the core, Mum and Dad had no idea about how relationships worked these days. Some days she wondered if she did.

Nausea rolled in her stomach as her mother speeded up along the straights, veered around corners and slowed to a snail's pace when the country lanes narrowed.

'Are you sure you'll be all right on your own out here?' Her mother jerked her head towards the village signpost as they passed it.

'Mum, after living in London, I think the crime rate in Wilsgrave is considerably lower, unless of course there's a serial killer on the loose that I hadn't heard about.' The first ribbon of small houses started to appear and Ella's mother slowed down.

'I meant being on your own. Not knowing anyone. You can always come back home.'

'I'll be fine.' This already felt enough of a defeat. Thank God, she'd have the use of Magda's car. She could be back within Central London in forty-five minutes at a push.

Her mother pulled smartly into a space right outside a pretty double-fronted end of terrace house.

'Here we are, then. I've got the keys. No sign of your father yet. He's going to miss Tess.'

Was that his new chiropractor? A tamer version of Miss Whiplash? Releasing herself from her seatbelt, Ella took the proffered keys and got out of the car. Daffodils, tulips, crocuses, and anemones danced in the dappled light cast by overhanging trees. They lined the narrow brick path leading to a front door painted in a tasteful National Trust shade of pale green, their scent perfuming the air.

For a moment Ella paused. Sunshine yellow contrasted with brilliant blue. If only she had the ability or the skill to capture the hope and promise of those spring colours, the shapes and textures, that fabulous fractured light or even the essence of the season, new life, new hope. A pang filled her chest, blooming with a fierce emptiness. Focusing on the front door, she averted her gaze and marched up the path.

Juggling with the keys her mother had handed over in the car, she stepped into a roomy hallway with a flagstone floor. She'd been to her godmother's plenty of times before to know that to her left was a big kitchen, pretty enough if your taste ran to French provincial, and large enough to house a huge central table. To the right a door led into the wood beamed lounge with its focal open fireplace which took up most of one wall and an eclectic mix of furniture which shouldn't have worked together but did, all of which made the room seem smaller than it was. Ahead steps led up to one large master bedroom, a second smaller bedroom and the bathroom. Beyond that the loft conversion, a long white room, almost bare of furniture, lit by skylights through which the light flooded, making it the perfect studio. This was just about the only reason she'd agreed to come and house-sit for six months. Well, that and having nowhere else to go. Work had been impossible of late, she was so behind. Incarceration in the country with nothing else to do might focus her mind and force her to address the blank pages of cartridge paper.

'Ah, your father's here.' Her mother's voice held a touch of nerves – or was it uncertainty?

Carrying what looked like his own body weight in a sack which read COMPLETE DOG FOOD on the front, her father shouldered his way in through the front door, straight into the kitchen.

'Phew, that was heavier than I thought,' he said, dumping the bag on the flagstone floor. 'Hello, love.' He gave her a cheerful smile now he'd released the load.

'What's that?' Ella's voice echoed in her head, sounding overly sharp.

'Dog food.'

'I can see that.' She hated herself for using the tone with Dad, ever the sweetheart and as laid back as they came. 'I meant, what is it for?'

He instantly looked sheepish and turned towards her mother for support.

'I thought you said you'd spoken to Magda,' said her mother, suddenly developing a fixation with rubbing away some mark on one of the kitchen counters. 'She said you wouldn't mind.'

'What? Storing dog food for people?'

Her mother flashed an over-bright smile. 'I'll just get the rest of Tess's things.'

With that, she bustled back out of the tiny cottage hallway.

'Mum . . .' Too late. She was already halfway down the long skinny garden to Dad's trusty Mercedes. Who the hell was Tess? Was Ella expected to run some kind of storage facility?

A clatter from the hall moments later made Ella jump, setting her heartbeat racing a thousand miles an hour.

'What the hell?' The angry snap escaped before she could stop it.

'Sorry, dear.'

Her mother's over-apologetic, sparkly isn't-everything-peachy smile pricked all Ella's guilt buttons as she watched her carry in some large oval of foam and fabric and a leather and metal chain-choker-dog-lead thing. At Ella's feet, the metal bowls she'd dropped were still rattling and vibrating to a final standstill on the floor.

'Here.' Her mother thrust the lead into Ella's hand. Definitely a dog lead. What the hell did she want with a dog lead?

Paws skittered across the stone floor and she heard the snuffle of excited dog.

'What's that?' Ella backed away, staring down at a tubby black Labrador, sniffing furiously around the skirting boards, its tail thud-thudding against the wall.

Mum tried to hide her snigger. 'A dog, dear.'

'I can see that. What's it doing here?'

'It . . . er,' – her mother and father exchanged a look – 'lives here.'

'No way on earth.' Ella folded her arms, her shoulders rigid as tension gripped them. 'You are not leaving that thing here.' Fear skittered in the pit of her stomach; she couldn't, absolutely couldn't be responsible for anything right now.

'She's not going to be any trouble.' Mum lifted her chin, standing resolute. 'Besides, it will do you good.' She gave Ella a sharp-eyed up and down, her mouth wrinkling.

Dad chipped in. 'She's lovely. Great company.'

'You have her, then.'

'We can't. You're at home all day.'

'Mum ...' Her mother wasn't paying a blind bit of notice. Instead she unloaded another bag in the kitchen.

'Poo bags.' She screwed up her nose. 'I brought you a scooper. Sorry, but I'm sure it's no worse than babies' nappies.'

Ella's head jerked up, panic-spiked adrenaline roaring through her veins.

'You'll get used to it.'

'And you would know, how?' Ella asked, spitting sarcasm like hailstones. They were not an animal family. She'd never even had a hamster. She was not a dog person.

The dog had moved away from the wall, head in the air as if scenting new prey.

Her mother ignored her, wearing an air of busy-busy like some kind of armour, impervious to Ella's objections. Dad had made himself useful shifting the bag of food to the pantry.

With the precision of an Exocet missile on target, the dog headed towards her, snuffling, and her hand received a fulsome wet slurp.

'Eeeuw! Seriously Mum, you can't leave it here.' Ella wiped her hand furiously on her jeans, itching to wash it immediately.

'It's a she and she's lovely, aren't you? She's called Tess.' To make up for Ella's obvious uselessness with dogs Mum patted Tess with a great show, although Ella felt pretty sure the pats were vertical, carefully pushing the dog away from her immaculate cream wool trousers.

'Mum,' she whined, with all the grace of a petulant toddler sensing defeat.

'It's easy, darling. You won't know she's here.'

'Mum, I can't have a dog.' She sighed, she certainly didn't want one. She didn't want anything, anyone. Was being left alone too much to ask?

'Of course you can. You're here all day. It's easy. Honestly, I don't know why you're making such a fuss. All you have to do is feed her twice a day. Once in the morning, once in the evening at six o'clock. One scoop only. Put water in the other bowl. Take her out for a walk once or twice a day.' Her pasty cheeks received another narrow-eyed look. 'Fresh air and exercise will do you good. You look so tired and . . .'

Ella waited to see how she might diplomatically mention the pounds she'd mislaid recently.

'And,' her mother puffed herself up like a pigeon, 'she'll be company for you and your father won't be quite so anxious about you being here on your own at night. We're worried about you.' Her mother's mouth quivered.

Ella sighed. 'Mum, I'm fine. Honestly. I've been busy, working really hard. I've got a deadline.' One that, currently, had as much chance of being met as her and this thing entering Crufts. 'I'm fine.'

Her mother tilted her head, turning away, but not before Ella spotted the slight sheen in her eyes. Shit. That's what mothers did. They worried. Cared. Maternal instinct pre-programmed. When did it kick in? Hard and fast, from conception? Birth? Or did it settle in with serene grace, bedding in as the mother–child bond grew?

Crossing the kitchen, feeling a tender whip of shame, she touched her mother on the shoulder. 'All right, I'll take the damn dog.'

'That's wonderful. It'll do you good, get you out of the

house. In fact,' she said brightly, 'Dad only took her for a short walk earlier.'

'Actually Shirley, it was—'

She shot him a look. 'A dog like this needs lots of walks – don't you, sweetheart?' She gave the dog another vertical pat. 'Why don't you take her to Wendover Woods once you've settled in?'

She watched as her parents in their separate cars – Dad in his faithful Mercedes and Mum in her nippy runaround – vied to let the other go first before they pulled away from the kerb. It took them a good five minutes of misplaced manners before her mother finally conceded and roared off in an irritated huff. Dad gave her a cheerful wave and followed in an altogether more sedate manner.

The minute they were out of sight, whatever backbone Ella had mustered to hold it all together upped and left without so much as a backward glance. Her inward breath sliced sharp in tandem with a half sob. Stumbling to one of the wooden chairs, she collapsed onto it, dropped her head to the table and cried. No-holds-barred sobs, tears running down her face – and she didn't give a shit when they mingled with her running nose or when she wiped it with the back of her sleeve, sniffing with pig-like snorking noises against the tidal flow.

It was so bloody exhausting trying to pretend everything was OK, and a bloody relief they'd gone and left her in peace. A gentle whiffle around her ankles reminded her she wasn't completely on her own. Not that a dog counted. She gave one last unladylike sniff and glared at the animal at her feet.

'And you're the last thing I damn well need.'

She pushed her hands against the table to shove herself upright and crossed back to the sink. Through the kitchen window, beyond the long front garden, the empty green and silent street seemed to mock her. Why had she let herself be persuaded by Magda? It might only be an hour back into town, but there were 24 hours in day, 168 in a week, 672 in a month and she had 4,032 of the buggers to fill over the next six months. (She'd worked that depressing figure out on the train on the way here.) With what? This place could have been the dark side of the moon, for all the similarity it had with London. There was nothing here.

The dog began another of its nosy explorations of the corners of the kitchen, snuffling with the gusto of a Dyson on turbo charge. As her gaze followed it, she spotted a navy blue envelope pinned to a floral fabric-backed noticeboard. Her name was written on it in Magda's distinctive script, the silver letters flowing like moonlight across the dark colour.

She released it from the pin. It looked like a party invitation. Although it was probably more instructions for the boiler or for locking up the house. Wearily she tossed the envelope down on the table.

'Don't look at me like that,' she snapped as the dog gave her what definitely looked like a disapproving frown, its brown eyes blinking, and furrowed lines appearing on its furry face.

Rolling her eyes at her own stupidity and for the prick of guilt that lanced her, she reached for the envelope.

Mother Nature has a wonderful way of healing. Repeat this blessing daily to find your peace and centre.

Oh dear, was Magda on some spiritual kick? That was new. With a wry smile, she read the writing written on a postcard-sized piece of heavy blue paper. Her godmother meant well but surely no one believed in this mumbo-jumbo. It was rather sweet, although she didn't imagine for a moment, it would make her feel better.

Under Spring's awakening gaze
Breathe Earth's bountiful fragrances
Enjoy slow lengthening days
Find peace among the blossom
the warmth of deepening rays
breathing life back
Pay homage to nature's beauty
and circle the blooms daily
And take peace as yours
Blessed be
Madga x

'She's nuts.' Ella shook her head. Definitely barking. Imagine a floatily dressed sergeant major and you had Magda. How on earth had the Women's Institute stalwart that was Ella's mum hooked up with her and stayed friends for thirty years?

Walk among the blooms daily. Yeah, right. About to throw it in the bin, Ella tapped the card thoughtfully and with a sudden change of heart pinned it back onto the noticeboard.

Chapter Two

'Do you have to do that? It's very unnerving,' Ella said to the dog, as she sketched the outline of one of her characters, frowning when the shape of the head didn't look quite right but not looking up from the heavy white cartridge paper. If she didn't look at the dog, it might get bored and stop watching her with that amber-eyed intensity. Annoyed that she'd been side-swiped by her mother's emotional blackmail, she'd deliberately put off the prescribed walk until later. She had work to do. Her publisher was waiting – with shortening patience, if the last email was to go by – for the latest in the series of Cuthbert Mouse books. And at this rate, she was going to have a long wait.

Ella had gone straight up to the loft and got out the bare minimum of art stuff. Pencils and paper. The rest could wait. If she just made a start it might ease the pressure.

The dog sighed and lifted its eyebrows in an amusingly quizzical way. She carried on pencilling in Cuthbert's tail, trying to ignore the definite snake-like aspects that weren't supposed to be there. The dog yawned, with a yowly sound-effect, before walking round to the other side of her chair.

'What?' Ella said after it had shifted and fidgeted its way around the room for ten minutes. 'It's hard enough trying to do this without you disturbing me.'

Damn, Cuthbert looked more like evil Yoda than happy dormouse.

'Oh, for goodness' sake.' With sudden slashes, she scribbled over the feral little face and chucked down the pencil. 'OK. We'll go for a walk.'

The weather outside didn't look promising. 'If I get drenched I won't be pleased.' Nature and she weren't exactly at one. In fact, she was pretty sure it hated her as much as she hated it at the moment. Rain ran in haphazard, maverick rivulets down the Velux windows. She didn't even own a pair of wellies. Snow boots or trainers? What had possessed her to pack either? Not that the process of filling her cases and every last bag had been anywhere nearing methodical. Trainers were fashion suicide – she wasn't even sure how she came to own a pair and certainly not these lurid atrocities. The bloody snow boots had cost a fortune, the one time they'd been skiing. Neither she nor Patrick had taken to it.

Day-glo pink trainers, then. What else though? It was so cold this morning and would be even colder up in the woods which crowned the Chiltern Hills. It'd have to be layers. Tights, baggy leggings and an ancient pair of cargo pants usually reserved for decorating. Might as well go the whole hog and look totally ridiculous. She topped the ensemble with a turquoise ski jacket. Lord knows it wouldn't ever be worn on the ski slopes again.

By the time her laces were tied, the dog was waiting by the front door, lead in its mouth, tail going like a windscreen wiper on full speed. At least one of them was glad to be getting out. Ella caught a glimpse of herself in the hall mirror and wanted to cry. Seriously? What did she look like? Thank God, no one round here knew her.

She drove, or rather trundled, the short distance up to Wendover Woods in Magda's funny little red car. The whole way she had to keep winding up the window because with each rattle it worked its way down again. As soon as the boot was opened, the stupid dog jumped out, knocking her flying into a puddle on the gravelled surface.

'Urgh!' Dark muddy water immediately soaked through her shoes, tights, leggings and trousers. The dog didn't so much as look back. No, the darned animal hit the ground running and was off, darting in front of a car just turning into the car park. Shit. An irate horn blared. Not even a full day and she'd nearly killed the stupid thing.

The dog came dancing back to her side and she grabbed its collar, trying to ignore the cold slap of wet material against skin. She was so not a country girl. Managing to successfully avoid the eye of the driver, it took Ella several attempts before she latched the lead onto the metal ring of the collar.

'Idiotic creature.' Her heart banged against her ribs. God, what would she have told Magda if she'd damaged her dog on its first outing? What did you do if a dog got hurt? Did you have ambulances for animals? Where was the nearest vet? Were they like doctors? Did you have to register with them? Did they have accident and emergency, like for people, where you sat dry-eyed, in bloodstained embarrassment, for hours?

She tugged sharply at the lead. 'Come on, let's get out of here, before that bloke spots us.' Semi-jogging to get away from the car park before he got out of his car, she hit a speed not managed since school days. As soon as she was out of sight, she had to stop. Clutching her knees, she bent over, desperately trying to suck air into tortured lungs. Her heart pounded so vigorously she could feel the pulse attempting to fight its way out of her temple. Any moment it might explode. Everything went black. Heavens, was she having some kind of heart attack?

Gradually catching her breath, she stood up, worrying she might be sick at any second.

Sucking in lungsful of air, praying no throwing up would be involved, she took a slower pace, cautiously letting the dog off its lead. Thankfully it didn't run off. Like a newly released prisoner, it sniffed and snuffled the verges on either side of the lane, criss-crossing backwards and forwards in front and behind, chasing some elusive scent of goodness only knows what.

The dank air closed in. Ella could hear the steady incessant drip, drip of water through the trees. Damp seeped into her layers, spreading fingers of cold, as she plodded along behind the dog, feet squelching in trainers which were not built for the uphill path down which streams of water chased their way.

Why on earth had her mother thought this would do her good? All she wanted was to curl up under a duvet and sleep for ever. Snuggle in with imagination and memory to keep her company, replaying the elusive imaginary conversation in her head where Patrick would admit he'd made a terrible, terrible mistake. That he'd changed his mind.

The hollowness in her stomach stopped her in her tracks and she looked around at the trees melting into the hazy air. If she kept walking could she fade into the mist too? Dissolve into the landscape. Not have to face the cold reality of what she'd lost.

She stared sightless into the gloom until a wet head nudged her hand. She flinched.

'Urgh.' She searched for a tissue in her pocket.

The dog wagged its tail and bounced away before coming back to waddle around her feet in circles, batting the back of her knees as if to urge her on. She moved stiffly.

The woods, perched high up in the Chilterns, outlined the contours like a thick pelt of velvet, softening the undulating hills in a tapestry of vivid greens. The air smelt of peat and grass, a musky, grubby scent that brought back images of muddy boots and puddles. Her footsteps were muffled by the mulch of years of leaf fall. Overhead, leaves just unfurling their shades of bright spring greens fluttered in a light breeze with the occasional rusty groan of tree branches rubbing together. As Ella listened, she realised that far from being totally silent the woods reverberated with sounds. Bird song, wood pigeons cooing, others whistling, the dog's heavy pants and the pad pad of its paws as it nosed through the undergrowth.

Some far-sighted soul had placed a bench on the top of the escarpment, from which one could take in the view of Aylesbury Vale stretching towards the distant horizon, if the weather was good enough. Not today, though. She sat, plunking herself down with an uncoordinated thud, the dog at her feet, as she stared into the drizzly plain below. The weather matched her mood. The ache was still there. The constant lead weight wedged under her ribs was definitely still there, along with the strung-out, stressed tightness which if she was honest had been there for much longer than the last month.

When had it become so much a part of her life? That horrid sense of being late for something all the time, something intangible that she couldn't see or touch but that made her incessantly anxious and worried. It had been there before Christmas. Bonfire night. Halloween. The holiday to Rome in September.

For some stupid, stupid reason, she started to cry. Bugger, she'd thought she was all cried out. As the tears streamed down her cheek, the dog – Tess – came and sat right beside her, leaning heavily against Ella's leg. Absently she touched one of her ears.

'I bet you think I'm mad, don't you, Tess?' Beneath her fingers, the dog's ear felt surprising soft and velvety. 'Humans are so complicated. It must be much easier to be a dog. Eat, sleep, walk. You don't have relationships. Don't have jobs. Big decisions. People letting you down.'

The dog watched her, the eyes soft and gentle, as Ella stroked her head. She shuffled closer as if she were listening to every word.

'You've no idea what I'm talking about, have you?'

The dog just blinked.

*

The cold had taken hold, seeping right into her bones, and it took her a minute to get her car keys out of her pocket.

'Come on, in you get,' she said, opening the boot.

The dog stood next to her, looking as pathetic and exhausted as Ella felt.

'Come on. In.' Ella tapped the car, as if that might help. 'The sooner you get in the sooner we can warm up.'

She leaned down and got a noseful of yucky wet dog smell as she looped her arms around the barrel belly and tugged.

Tess stood four square as if she'd dug her paws in and wasn't going anywhere.

'Oh, for crying out loud.' Ella opened the back passenger door. Maybe that would be easier for the dog.

She heard a crunch of gravel and turned around to see a man marching towards her with quick angry strides.

'What—' she managed to stammer, aware of his fury. Dark brows had drawn in two angry slashes about flashing eyes.

'Are you mad?' he growled.

'Pardon?' What was his problem? She peered up at him from underneath the hood of her ski jacket.

'Have you any idea what happens to a dog if you brake suddenly? Not just to you. On impact a dog can have the equivalent weight of a baby elephant. Imagine that going through the windscreen. You wouldn't have to be going very fast. And a dog this size could do a hell of lot of damage … if it survived.'

She looked at the dog and the car, about to explain that she was new at this but there wasn't a chance – a brief breath and he was off again.

'People like you make me sick. A perfectly healthy dog

and look at the state of her. Overweight and under-exercised. Not to add that you have no idea of how to look after her. She needs to go on a serious diet and get more exercise.' His mouth tightened and then he added, 'You both do.'

Ella's mouth dropped open. What?!

'You've given that dog less than fifteen minutes of exercise. Labs are gun dogs. Bred to be working dogs. Christ, you've got all this,' he spread his arms about, 'and you manage less than a quarter of an hour.' He huffed. 'Irresponsible pet owners like you make me sick.'

Ella felt so winded by the full-frontal tirade she couldn't seem to make her mouth work. She stood, stiff, her limbs frozen into wary shock, eyeing him.

Now he'd stopped he just stood there, looking back at her. What did he want?

The dog looked balefully at him. Ella touched Tess's head. See, the dog was on her side.

Suddenly the man turned and it looked as if he was about to walk away, but then he spun around, crouched down and lifted Tess up. He paused and looked at Ella as if he were going to say something and then thought better of it, as he gently placed the dog in the car. He carefully closed the boot, ducked his head and marched off.

She. Was. Not. Going. To. Cry. At least not in front of him. It was worse than being dressed down by the headmaster at school, not that she ever had been. As he disappeared into the gloom she still couldn't think of a single quick-witted comeback. *Bastard* didn't quite cut it.

'Wanky, pompous gitface.' Her back straightened. Saying

the words out loud made her feel better, even though she still would have liked to use a good put-down. 'Bloody men.' All of them were hateful.

From the back of the car, the dog whined.

'And you can be quiet. This is all your fault.' She could have been at home in a nice warm house, inside of being caked from head to foot in mud. 'I'm probably going to get trench foot.' Water seeped down her neck and her cargo pants were heading west, their sodden weight dragging them down. Diet and exercise. Ha! She glared at her padded coat and the bulging layers. She'd never been so underweight as right now.

The day officially couldn't get any worse.

Chapter Three

'Hi Devon, how're you going?' Bets, the first in for morning surgery, was opening post, being her usual cheerful self. Too bad she was the closest thing he had to a sister, as well as being an employee to boot. Wouldn't life be simpler with a nice uncomplicated woman like her?

'I bloody hope it's better than yesterday. You missed all the fun.' Rolling his shoulders, he tried to stretch out the tension.

'I heard you had a cageful of baby hamsters on the loose.' She giggled and then looked at his face. 'You look like hell. Do you want a coffee?'

'Coffee would be great.' He followed her into the kitchen area and watched as she spooned a huge heap of instant granules into a mug. 'Steady on, I'll be flying with that much caffeine.' Costing him another sleepless night.

'You look like you need it to get through the next couple of hours. Please tell me you're not on call again tonight.'

Devon pinched his lips together.

'Oh, for God's sake, what are you like?' She shook her head, her glossy curls bouncing.

Devon suspected that next to each other they created the juxtaposition of life and death: him, dark eyed, pale and washed out, her, rosy pink and bursting with vitality.

'Give yourself a break.'

'I'm fine.'

'You're going to work yourself into an early grave.' Her eyes softened. 'You need to look after yourself. When was the last time you had a proper night off?'

He shrugged. Locum work on call paid well, even if it could be traumatic. Last night he'd been called to a field of sheep, some of which were so badly hurt, he'd had to put them down. Literally torn limb from limb by some predator. Those were the calls he hated.

She poured boiling water in the mug and handed it to him with a wicked twinkle. 'Maybe you like delivering kittens and puppies in the middle of the night. Wilsgrave's ministering angel.'

Then she gave him an assessing look. 'No, more like disreputable gypsy. You need a haircut.'

'I'm too damn busy. Meant to go this morning.' He scowled. 'I certainly wasn't anyone's ministering angel when I had to put the Briggs' dog out of its misery.' He tugged at his sleeve under the white coat, trying to think of something other than the trust in the young dog's eyes.

'Oh, no.' Bets' face crumpled. 'Not Essie. Poor thing. Ethel and William must be devastated.' Bets worried at her lip, her eyes round with sympathy. Too kind for her own good.

Devon gritted his teeth, swallowing back the flash of fury. 'Maybe they should have thought of that before letting the dog get so bloody overweight. I told them over and over – that dog needed to go on a diet. With diabetes and arthritis, poor dog didn't stand a chance.'

Bets sighed and patted his hand. 'And they'll be feeling terrible about it, Devon. They're not bad people. Just not very bright. They did really love that dog and gave it a very happy life.'

Now he felt doubly guilty because he'd given them a hard time. They should have been told before. 'Yeah, and I had to take it away.'

'Maybe you should go see them. See how they're doing.'

He stared at her. 'What?'

'It's good patient relations.'

'Where the hell did you hear that? I'm running a veterinary practice, not a flaming District Nurse service.'

Bets looked innocent, or tried to. 'It's the sort of thing your dad would do.'

Shame Dad hadn't been tougher with them earlier.

She gave him an encouraging smile. 'And most likely Jack,' she added with a wistful look that suggested she was thinking of Devon's younger brother, currently away in the final year at Vet School.

'Yeah, neither of the soft-hearted buggers would charge them either.'

'Everyone in the village loves your dad.'

'I'm not surprised.'

'Not because he's soft on payment ... he's very caring, whereas you ... well, you're more logical.' Trust Bets to temper her meaning.

'You mean I'm aware I'm running a business here and there's no place for sentiment. And it's a bloody good job I am as otherwise when you come to marry my brother, there won't be a practice for him to go into. Businesslike is efficient. Making sick animals better.'

'Yes, but,' Bets looked dogged, 'you can be nice too.'

'I *am* nice.'

She raised one insouciant eyebrow. 'You hide it well. You can also be a bit grumpy and bad tempered.' She grinned up at him, her laughing eyes taking the sting out of her words.

'Any other personal comments before I open up for the morning?'

'No,' she paused as if considering, 'not today.' Her cheeky grin penetrated his misery, making his smile slightly genuine for once. It was hard work trying to pretend that you were normal when underneath there was a black morass just waiting to drag you back down.

'You do remember who the boss is, don't you?'

'Yup, but I'm indispensable and very good at making coffee.' She nodded to the mug in his hand.

She had a point. Bets was probably one of the best veterinary nurses he'd ever worked with and also incredibly willing. She'd done loads of extra hours without being paid. He'd have to make it up to her, but unfortunately for the time being he needed to keep costs cut to the bone. If the practice were his, he'd have introduced lots of changes which would improve efficiency but also make life easier for everyone, but at the moment he was babysitting the business until his dad was well enough to come back to work. There was so much that could be done here.

'I, er,' he winced at having to ask her yet another favour, 'don't suppose you'd—'

'Take Dex out for a walk today?' she asked without letting him draw breath. 'Course I will.'

'No, actually I'm planning to take him out after surgery later but I was wondering if you'd have him for me next week. I've got to go into London to sort out some paperwork and I thought I'd take in a lecture.' He might as well make the most of the day if he had to put up with an hour's train journey into town for another showdown with his ex, Marina.

A most uncharacteristic shifty gleam lit Bets' eyes. 'Yes, if you'll do me a favour.'

'What's that?' He took a long draught of coffee, knowing it would be difficult to refuse.

'You know the darts team ...'

Devon groaned. 'Really. I—'

'We're short because the Myers brothers will be on holiday and I don't want to forfeit the match.'

'You might as well, I'm no good.'

'It'll be fun and it doesn't matter. We won't win without Dave and Phil anyway, but Magda's left me in charge. I can't let her down.'

'All right, then. And you'll have Dexter?'

'Of course. No probs. We can go out for a nice long walk first thing and I can call in on the newbie.'

'Newbie?'

'I forgot, you missed the meeting. Remember, Madga's got her goddaughter house-sitting for her.'

'I do remember and I'm very grateful I missed it. The poor woman probably just wants to be left alone.'

'Magda just wanted to make sure she feels welcome. So I can kill two birds with one ... dog.'

Devon ignored the dreadful pun.

'Shall I swing by and grab him first thing? I've got the key. Or,' her eyes looked hopeful, 'I could pick him up the night before and he could have a sleepover.'

It wasn't as if he didn't owe her. 'OK, you can have your dog fix.'

'Yay!'

'Just don't let him sleep on the bed. You'll give him ideas above his station.'

Bets sighed heavily. 'It's only for one night ...'

'Tough. Dexter stays downstairs.'

'But I get lonely.' She sighed again, pulling a lovelorn and pathetic expression. Unfortunately, Bets' wholesome pretty face didn't lend itself to the attempt. 'I wish Jack were coming home soon. It's ages until the end of this term and he's so busy with exams he doesn't want me to go down.'

Devon rolled his eyes. 'It's not for ever.' Personally, he thought the two of them were far too young to settle down but then he had a pretty jaundiced view of relationships right now.

'True.' She bounced up, her face brightening to its usual sunny wattage. 'And there's always the welcome-home sex-in-every-room marathon to look forward to.'

'Too much information,' he groaned, 'about my brother. And images I'd rather not have next time I set foot in your place.'

Chapter Four

Ella clawed her way back to consciousness from sleep, her heart pounding, a mournful howl echoing in her ears. What the...?

She lay in the unfamiliar room, her chest about to explode. The scent of lavender tickled her nose. Magda had hung heart-shaped pouches of the dried flower heads on either side of the brass bedstead. A radiator creaked and ticked, the noise heightened by the pitch black darkness of the room and the silence outside. This cocoon-like feeling of nothingness unnerved her. Where was the rumble of traffic, the rattle of the windows when buses lumbered past, drunks shrieking at kicking-out time and the constant cry of sirens in the distance? This wasn't natural.

Even though sleep had been elusive for weeks, bedtime had become the highlight of the day. Ella looked forward to that time in bed where all the bad things in life ceased and she could go back to life how it was before.

Awoooo. Aw Aw Awoooo.

Damn dog. Another heart-rending wail hit the air. Ella closed her eyes tighter, hoping it would stop.

It didn't. After five minutes of the sort of howling which would have put the hound of the Baskervilles to shame, she grabbed her dressing gown and stomped down the stairs.

She'd shut the dog in the kitchen with its bed by the radiator, so at least it would have some residual warmth. She had no idea if that was what you were supposed to do. Did dogs feel the cold? When she opened the door the dog was there, tail wagging, looking bright-eyed and bushy-tailed.

'It's the middle of the night,' she hissed. 'Go to sleep.'

She walked over to its bed and pointed. 'Bed.' She vaguely remembered seeing something on TV about alpha dogs and showing who was boss, so she said it in a fierce, I-mean-business tone which apparently worked because the dog clambered into the bed, curled up and looked up at her, with an innocent expression as if to say, *Who me? Making that noise? Never.*

Praise. That was another thing Ella vaguely remembered or did you do that with children? The familiar pang gripped her stomach. Children. She didn't know much about them either but people learned, didn't they? 'Good girl.' The dog lowered its head onto its paws.

See, this dog-owning lark was a piece of cake. Easy.

'Right, goodnight.' Ella snapped out the light and with relief climbed back up the narrow staircase to her bedroom. Had she just said goodnight to a dog? Seriously, she was losing it.

The minute, to the very second, that her toes were nicely toasty and her body snuggly under the cocoon of the heavy-weight feather duvet, the howling started again. She buried her head under the pillows hoping they would silence the dog's cries, but to no avail. Dratted animal sounded heartbroken. Getting out of the nice warm bed was purgatory.

'You're having a laugh,' she growled, but the dog just grinned. Definite latent signs of smiling on its happy little face. 'Bed, *now*.' The dog slunk back to bed, climbed in again, and lowered its head, those crazy eyebrows lifting and separating with puzzlement.

She shut the door firmly.

'Vets On Call, Devon Ashcroft speaking.' There surely should be some law that when a phone rang before six in the morning, coffee was automatically dispensed. He rubbed his eyes and looked at the digital clock's numerals glowing orange in the dark. Four a.m. calls were bitches, rousing you from that deep deep sleep. At least he'd managed a straight five hours in his own bed. 'How can I help you?'

'Hi, thank God, Dr Ash— are you a doctor? Do you call vets doctors? Or is that just for people?'

He smiled to himself, amused in spite of the ridiculously early hour. 'I'm fine with Mr Ashcroft.'

'But you *are* a proper vet.'

The woman sounded anxious, but he was used to that at this time of day.

'Yes. How can I help?'

'I just don't know what to do. I've ended up with this dog ... it's not mine ... and I think there's something terribly wrong with it.'

'OK. Can you describe the symptoms?'

'Symptoms?'

'Yes, does it appear in pain? Has it vomited? Had diarrhoea? When did it last eat?'

'Pain, definitely pain. It won't stop howling.'

'OK. Are there any other signs of pain? Is it writhing, moving about as if it were in pain?'

'No, it's fine when it stops howling.'

'So the howling is intermittent? How long has it been howling?'

'Off and on since about ten o'clock last night.'

'And does anything appear to trigger it?'

'The minute I go up to bed.' She let out an indignant huff down his ear.

'Pardon?'

'Whenever I leave it on its own in the kitchen and try to go to bed, it starts again. I'm absolutely shattered.'

Devon took in a deep breath, wanting to shake his head, hoping he'd heard wrong.

'When you go up to bed? When you leave the dog? On its own?'

'Yes.'

'And where is the dog?'

'What, now?'

'No, when you leave it to go upstairs?'

'In the kitchen.'

'And is that where it normally sleeps?'

'I've no idea. I told you I'm just dog-sitting. Its owner's away. Every time I drop off to sleep it starts howling again. There's got to be something wrong with it.'

Devon slumped back against the pillow, resisting the urge to put voice to the words *God give me strength*. He was a professional. The woman was an idiot. 'So the dog's not howling continuously?' He tried to keep his voice level.

'No, only when I leave it on its own.'

Devon gripped the phone tighter. 'So more like crying? Like a child might, if it were frightened of a new situation? Lonely perhaps? Left on its own?'

'It's a dog.' She sounded cross and indignant now.

'Yes, but funnily enough they have feelings ... ' Devon could feel his jaw tighten and his back teeth meet as he ground out the words, 'which for obvious reasons they can't voice, so they might, I don't know, howl or bark or whine.'

'Well, how I am supposed to know that? I don't speak Dog. What am I supposed to do?'

Devon closed his eyes and counted to ten.

'Are you still there?'

'I'm still here.' He'd been told you should smile even if people couldn't see you to ensure you conveyed the right tone.

'Do you think you could come out and see it? Check it's all right? Do vets make house calls?'

'We do when it's an emergency.' Devon snapped. 'However, I think you'll find that this is perfectly normal behaviour. The dog is obviously lonely and scared. They're social animals. In the wild they live in packs – howling is their way of connecting with other dogs. You need to reassure it.'

'Right and how I am supposed to do that? Read it a bedtime story?'

'Keep coming back, so that it knows you are there. Reassure it. Be firm. It may take a few days but after that you'll find that he'll get used to the new routine. You need to impose a good routine. It's a bit like having a baby, really. They can't talk either.'

There was a resounding silence down the line. For a minute he thought she'd gone.

'A few *days*?' The plaintive, wailed words made him adjust the phone to a position away from his ear. 'I can't sleep through that racket. How do people do it? I've hardly had a wink of sleep.'

'Welcome to my world.' Damn, the words just slipped out.

The woman hung up.

Thank God neither Dad nor Bets had heard that exchange. He was crap at this community vet stuff.

Warm breath fanned over Ella's face and she turned, her heart leaping. *Patrick*. Sighing, she snuggled closer, her eyelids fluttering, until something at the back of her mind stirred in mild alarm.

'Aaaagh.' Catapulted into consciousness, she was greeted by a foul smell and a wet lick right across her left cheek. She sat bolt upright, almost falling off the sofa. 'That was gross. You horrible creature.'

The dog, totally unrepentant, placed its rump firmly on the floor beside the sofa, tail thumping happily.

Ella squinted at the digital display on the television. She'd ended up dragging the dog's bed in here, hoping the damn creature would go to sleep and she could sneak off upstairs. Fat chance. Her back felt crimped and stiff after a night on Magda's two-seater sofa. 'Half past bloody six!' She glared at the damn dog. 'You're having a laugh.' She slumped back onto the cushions, letting tiredness pull at her eyelids, only to find Tess snuffling and nosing at her hand.

'Leave me alone; it's far too early.' Outside, the birds were creating an absolute racket. Who knew they could make such a din?

Nudge, nudge, nudge. The shiny black nose was like a woodpecker, determined to drill through until it received the attention it wanted.

'What do you want?'

The dog whined.

'Oh, for Pete's sake.' Ella grabbed her robe. The dog jumped to attention, its tail switching back and forth at warp speed, and trotted eager-beaver behind her to the kitchen.

Keeping her eyes blearily half closed, she shoved the dog into the kitchen and shut the door.

When she woke again it was nearly nine. From the other side of the kitchen door, the dog whined softly. In need of coffee, she headed to the kitchen. As soon as she opened the door the dog whined again, shriller this time, running backwards and forwards to the back door. Ella might not speak Dog, as she'd told that horrible, unhelpful vet, but even she could pick up on that signal.

Crossing to the back door, she let the dog out. It went straight to the shrubs in the bed on the right and crouched for a pee on a par with Niagara. Ella winced. Oops, maybe she should have let it out earlier. She left it to an excited exploration of the garden, sniffing eagerly at every leaf and branch within nose distance. Honestly, you'd have thought the garden was uncharted territory and it had never been out there before in its life.

As she crossed the flagstone floor to put the kettle on, her foot squelched squarely in something lukewarm and slightly slimy. It oozed, with tenacious thoroughness, between each of her toes. 'Bloody bloody bloody hell. Yuck. Yuck.' Searching frantically for the kitchen roll, she hopped towards the kitchen sink, finally grabbing the floor cloth to wipe her foot. Flaming hell, the smell was disgusting. Her foot was covered in— 'Oh God. Oh God. Oh God.'

Her skin itched, reinforcing the sensation of being unclean down to the very last pore of her being. Filling the kitchen sink, she rifled through the products under the sink. WD40. Ant Powder. Screen wash. Brass cleaner. Surely to God there was some disinfectant. Ecover rubbish. No! She needed heavy duty, kill-every-last-bug-on-the-planet stuff. Ah – thank God. Domestos!

She filled the sink with hot water and squeezed half the bottle of bleach into it. Dragging a chair across to the sink, she hopped up onto the chair on her good clean foot, and dropped the unclean one into the hot bleachy water. Ouch! Too hot but hopefully it would kill the thousand zillion germs. The chair wobbled frantically as she started to scrub. She found it far easier to stand upright on the draining board crouched over the sink, taking a nail brush and using it over every inch of skin.

The dog had finished its Marco Polo exploration of the garden and had now come in, Ella was convinced, to laugh at her. At that moment, she would have been hard pressed to deny that the dog had an amused expression on its face.

'Don't even speak to me, Dog.' She growled. 'God knows what's in your poo. Toxi- something or other. What if I get dysentery or go blind?' Her position wasn't that comfortable so she stood up, one foot on the drainer and the other in the bowl, but she was going to soak her foot in the water until she was absolutely convinced that every last germ had been zapped.

The splattered pile of dog mess on the tiled floor drew Ella's gaze. 'Look what you did.' The dog did at least have the grace to lower its head. 'Bad dog.' Big brown eyes looked back. Her eyes slid across to the kitchen clock. Ten past nine.

Aw, cripes. The poor thing must have been crossing its legs for hours. Remorse crept in. 'OK, so maybe you're not. Although you did keep me up all night. That sofa is not built for sleeping on.'

The rattle of the postbox made Ella turn, her foot twisting and slipping in the bowl. At the bottom of the path, the departing postman grinned and gave her a very cheery wave. What did he have to be so ... Oh hell, standing right in front of the kitchen window, she'd just flashed him a full moon.

Heat rose like a tidal wave, turning her whole body beet red.

She'd been working for two hours and achieved sod all. Cuthbert, his brothers and sister, Catherine, looked like marauding rodent vandals instead of cute, winsome, mischievous mice with their own individual characters. At the moment the cast list could be Vampire Mouse, Zombie Mouse and Mouse Who'd Most Like To Do You Harm in the Middle of the Night. Ella lowered her head and banged it lightly on the table.

The dog appeared in the doorway, its head tilted as if trying to figure out what this strange woman was up to. 'Don't bother, mate,' snapped Ella. 'I've lost the plot completely.' She looked back down at her drawing board. The light was wrong, that was it. With a huff of annoyance, she stood up. The dog bounced up, its tail batting at her legs.

'Don't get your hopes up. I'm busy.'

Maybe if she moved the drawing board to the right under the skylight, it might be better.

Ten minutes later after faffing about with the desk angle, the chair height and the positioning, she sat back down and picked up her pencil again. She held it poised over the paper, staring at her fingers. Cuthbert's image wouldn't come.

She threw down the pencil and stood up again. The dog, which had wandered off to the corner, suddenly darted back towards her, barrelling past a small side table and knocking it flying.

'Oh, for God's sake.'

As the contents of the table tumbled down, sliding across the floor in a kaleidoscope pattern, the scent of lavender and rosemary perfumed the air. Stooping to gather up the scattered bags of herbs, another one of Magda's more recent eccentricities, her foot nudged a navy blue shoebox-shaped package tied with a silver-grey ribbon. Across one corner, her name stood out, silver against the darker background.

For a second her heart lifted. A parcel.

The dog shadowed every footstep, nudging her legs as she carried the package back to the drawing table and put it in the middle of the stark white cartridge paper, her fingers smoothing along the ribbon.

'I'll take you out for a walk soon.'

A long-forgotten frisson of excitement sizzled in her fingertips. Memories surfaced, taking flight like butterflies. Peeling back gossamer-fine tissue paper to find a silver necklace edged with tiny dragonflies, opening up a box to reveal a pretty bracelet of twisted wire, amethyst and aquamarine crystals, unwrapping a filigree compact mirror and pulling a tiny framed paper silhouette of a tree against the moon from a gift bag. Magda had some secret intuition when it came to finding and giving the perfect gift. One you often had no idea you wanted. Her whimsical and thoughtful presents were things Ella would never have considered buying for herself but instantly fell in love with. The mirror was still in her bag. The necklace, bracelet and picture, which Patrick had quite liked, mainly because it was valuable, were all somewhere downstairs in one of the still-packed suitcases abandoned in Magda's bedroom.

Gifts when you were a grown-up never had quite the same magic about them, not like this one shimmering with promise.

She tugged at the ends of the silver-grey bow, watching as the silk ribbon slithered free and pooled on the table. Lifting the lid, she parted the glitter-spangled tissue paper. A sheet of navy blue paper rested on top of the contents and like the one downstairs, contained a few brief lines in Magda's slanting script.

> *Open your heart and you open your eyes*
> *Letting go will loosen the ties*
> *Free your mind and your talent will soar*
> *Let in the light to open the door*

With a shake of her head she put the piece of paper to one side. It was sweet of Magda and she appreciated the sentiment but it didn't work like that. If only. She delved into the tissue paper and brought out several tubes of paint.

Nice thought, Magda. Sadly, she put everything back and

firmly closed the lid, surprised by the little lump in her throat. It had been such a thoughtful gift, so typical of her godmother. And it was a terrible shame. Guilt tugged at her – Magda must have spent a fortune on all these Newton & Windsor tubes. There were some expensive pigments in there. She wasn't to know that painting with watercolours was a bit naff.

Beside her the dog nudged her again.

'OK,' she snapped, decisively. 'We're going.' Anything to get out of here and away from her stupid up and down emotions.

Chapter Five

The stupid dog lay on the doormat waiting for her, leaping to attention as she hobbled up the path. Today's walk had been a complete disaster. With some effort she peeled off her filthy jeans, abandoning them on the doorstep to examine the damage. A livid bruise, purple with a smaller red centre, crowned her knee.

'Oh dear, had an accident, have we?' a hearty voice hailed her from the other side of the fence.

Startled, she looked up, tugging down her jumper to mid-thigh. At this rate if she wasn't careful, she was going to get a reputation as the local flasher.

'Something like that.' Ella gave the man leaning on the fence a terse smile.

'Your mother popped by, left you a few things. They're in my fridge, I'll just get them.'

Suddenly the man reappeared, walking down the garden path with a Waitrose carrier bag in one hand, the other awkwardly tucked behind his back. 'Here you go,' he said. 'Your mother dropped it round earlier. I'm George. I live next door. You have been in the wars. Smell a bit ripe too.'

'I fell over.' And landed in possibly the biggest cowpat on the planet after which the bloody dog had run off.

Forcing her fascinated gaze away from his virulent mustard-yellow cardigan, Ella took in the features of the older man. Extremely tall and thin, his lined nut-brown skin reminiscent of bark, he made her think of one of Tolkien's Ents, a real-life tree man.

'I keep an eye on the place when Magda's not about. Take in parcels.' He paused and then with a grin that brought all his wrinkles into furrowed life added, 'And deliver parcels.' From behind his back he produced a box wrapped in the familiar navy blue tied up with a silver-grey ribbon and held it up in one hand with a flourish, bringing to mind a basketball player.

With rather gentlemanly formality he held out his other hand, the shopping bag dangling awkwardly from it. She shook it. He had a firm strong grip.

'Thank you. I'm Ella. Magda's goddaughter.'

'I know who you are. Magda briefed us.'

Ella stiffened.

He leaned against the door frame as if settling in for a chat and then with a little start remembered the parcel.

'Here – for you.'

She took it from him and ignoring the avid interest in his eyes decided to open it out of sight.

'Pleased as punch she was that you could come. I'm going to miss her cakes, always brings me a few slices. Do you bake?'

He looked so hopeful, Ella almost wished she did. 'Sorry, not my area of expertise.'

'Ah, well. I'm sure you'll soon pick it up. Now, would you like me to bring you a paper in the mornings? I normally pop and get the milk as well.'

'No, thank you.' The automatic response, polite and immediate, popped out. She didn't know him from Adam, this effusive helpfulness seemed a little ... well, pushy. She couldn't imagine her neighbours in London making such an offer or her wanting them to.

He looked a little crestfallen. 'You sure? Magda does get through the old milk with her frother thing and Nespresso machine. Makes a mean cappuccino.' His face fell. 'She quite often brings one round for me.'

Ella gave him a perfunctory smile. There'd be none of that on her watch. 'Well, I must get on.' She glanced down at her knee.

'Looks nasty. Best get an ice pack on it. I've got some Arnica indoors. Shall I bring it round?'

'No, I'll be fine, thanks.'

'OK then, ducks. Well, if you change your mind, you know where I am.' He finally turned to potter down the path of his own garden stooping every now and then to pull up a weed.

Magda's super-duper coffee machine did indeed make fabulous coffee, even if it did take Ella a few minutes to figure out how the milk frother thing worked. Now that she'd showered and got rid of the methane-rich smell of cow poo, she could almost imagine she was in civilisation and forget the awful morning. Mum's bag of Waitrose goodies was stashed away, although quite what her mother thought she was going to do with that lot, she had no idea. Chicken breasts needed stuff doing to them, and she didn't have the energy or the inclination. At least she'd put a couple of bottles of Pinot Grigio in there.

Ella took her coffee and sat down at the table, hugging her mug between hands insulated by the sleeves of the cosy outsize sweater she'd pinched from Magda's drawers. In her haste to get cleaned up, she'd forgotten all about the parcel.

Putting down her coffee, she tugged at the wide ribbon, a renewed sense of excitement flickering as the fabric slithered down the side of the midnight blue box with sinuous grace into a soft pile.

Inside the box, there was more navy blue tissue paper and a sheet of paper. With a half-smile of recognition, Ella pulled it out to read the words.

They say food is the best way to a man's heart
but baking is the way to your own heart

Frustration sizzled in her fingertips as she delved into the box. Magda was definitely barking up the wrong tree. She pulled out a selection of sugar paste oblongs that reminded her of the Plasticine she'd had as a child, then an assortment of icing nozzles, a pack of icing sugar and a series of rounds of plastic which she realised were moulds and templates. At the very bottom was a battered notebook. Curious, she pushed the other items to one side to peruse its tatty pages. It bulged with recipes cut from magazines and newspapers, as if the pages were intent on bursting out of the confines of the hardback covers. On each page in a rainbow of colours, Magda's neat italic script handwriting annotated recipes with notes, added ingredients and fierce scribblings out, including on one page a shouty recommendation in large bright blue capitals, *DO NOT EVER ATTEMPT AGAIN!!!!*

Ella shoved everything back in the box and pushed it to the back of the kitchen counter. She didn't bake, wasn't about to start baking and that was final.

Chapter Six

'Morning!'

Ella took in a flurry of bouncing curls, lots of freckles and a wide, smiley mouth. After four of the most boring days on earth, the unexpected interruption was quite welcome.

'Sorry to arrive unannounced but I promised Magda I'd call in. Have you heard from her? Is she having a fab time? Isn't she amazing, going off on an adventure like that at her age?'

Ella blinked at the barrage of questions and then braced herself as Tess knocked her sideways in her enthusiasm to say hello to the stranger on the doorstep.

'Sorry, I'm Bets and this is Dexter.' She bent to pet Tess who was already nose to nose with the brown pointer on a lead at her side. 'Aren't you a darling?' she grabbed her collar and read the brass tag, 'Tess. I love Labs, they're so friendly. Dexter's very handsome but he can be a bit snooty.' She gave his ears a quick stroke. 'But he's lovely really, aren't you, sweetie?'

All Ella could do was nod. Her brain hadn't caught up yet.

'So how are you settling in? Sorry, I should have called in earlier but I thought I'd give you a bit of time and I've been so busy and then . . . ' she pulled out a dark blue envelope on which could be seen Magda's familiar silver script.

Ella's heart sank. Now what?

To Ella's surprise and faint annoyance, the girl didn't hand it over but slipped out a piece of paper and read it, before giving Ella a beaming smile.

'You're on the rota for the last Sunday of the month which is ages away but I thought you'd like some warning. You'll want plenty of time to prepare. And you might want some help.' She folded the paper back into the envelope and put it in the pocket of her rather hideous anorak that style had not so much forgotten but turned its back on. Then the girl grinned, her whole face lighting up and for a moment Ella forgot how irritating and loud and busy the girl was, in the sudden desire to capture all that energy and rosy cheeked openness. Form and shape, in an abstract way. Her fingers itched to pick up a paintbrush. Ironic when she'd spent the last two days trying to paint and failing miserably.

'Have you done flowers before? Magda said you were arty so wouldn't mind.'

Ella was so busy imagining painting that she wasn't really paying attention. She'd tried watercolours of flowers in the past, maybe she could have another go at them. 'I have tried, but they always look a bit rubbish.' She took another look at Bets' face. Lovely rose and cream complexion. Gorgeous luminous skin.

'Oh, the vicar won't mind, he's grateful they get done at all.' Bets turned around, trying to untangle the lead which had become wrapped around her leg as the two dogs weighed each other up, circling and sniffing, tails wagging furiously.

'The vicar?' Ella blinked again. Was this girl completely mad?

'Yes. Reverend Richard. He's a bit scatty but he has all the old dears running around after him, keeping him on the straight and narrow. Between you and me, I think he cultivates it a bit.' She tugged at the lead as Dexter tried to follow Tess down the garden. 'Although I did wonder if there might be something going on between him and Magda. He seemed quite keen on her.'

'Sorry, you've lost me.'

'The vicar at the church. He's very nice but he can be a bit disorganised.' Bets said it slowly, eyeing Ella with doubt.

'No, back up a bit. The flowers.'

'Magda put you down on the church flower rota. To arrange them. In the church.'

Ella straightened. 'You have to be kidding! I'm twenty-nine, not seventy-flaming-nine. I'm not doing bloody flower arranging.'

Bets gave her an irrepressible grin. 'Well, I did wonder when Magda said it, but she was very insistent. She said you'd surpass yourself – or maybe she meant surprise yourself. Don't worry, I can give you a hand. We'll muddle through.'

Before Ella could open her mouth to explain that she really, really wasn't doing the church flowers, Bets had moved on.

'Do you need anything? Came down from London, didn't you?'

Ella tensed. Did this girl know everything about her?

'Have you been out yet today?' Bets laughed. 'What am

I like?' She nodded towards Ella's pyjamas. 'Of course you haven't. I'm just taking Dex out now for his walk. You can come and bring Tess.'

'I haven't even got dressed or showered.' And she had work to do.

'No worries, I'll sit in the garden and wait.'

Short of shutting and bolting the door, which seemed rather excessive, Ella decided there wasn't a lot she could do but dress and join the slightly annoying Bets. She was the type of person who would just keep knocking at the door until you answered it. Besides, the dog needed a walk. To Ella's shame it hadn't had a proper one for a couple of days. Not after the cow pat fiasco. She'd got into the habit of going to the park around the corner, sitting on a bench and letting the dog charge about the field. It seemed happy enough.

Once dressed, Ella stepped out of the front door to find that Bets had been joined by George.

'Ella, this is George. He lives next door,' said Bets.

'We've met, old friends we are,' announced George addressing the whole garden. 'Morning, m'dear. How's that leg? All better now? I must say you're a quiet one. Not a peep out of her,' he said to Bets. 'Have a nice walk. I'm just off to pick up my paper. Do you want anything from the village shop?'

'That's kind, but I'm all right thanks.'

'Jolly good.' He saluted the pair of them and snapped his garden gate shut.

'He's such a sweetie,' observed Bets. 'Always on the go. You wouldn't believe he's nearly eighty.'

Ella looked back at the sprightly figure trotting down the path. Eighty? 'Really. He looks good.' Although probably because the pace of life was so much slower out here; he hadn't had a chance to wear himself out.

'So, Magda says you're an artist. What kind of art do you do?' They left the cottage garden and turned right along the high street, if you could call it that. With both dogs on leads, they strolled past the pub which looked quaint and villagey, not really Ella's kind of thing. Give her a wine bar any day. 'Magda didn't say, so there's been lots of speculation. Do you do portraits? Will we see any famous celebrities trooping up your garden path? That was Doris next door-but-one's idea.'

'Portraits? Why would she think that?' Ella shook her head.

'Bless her, she's partial to the odd copy of *Hello*.' Bets laughed and rolled her eyes. 'I think she had visions of David and Victoria Beckham popping by for a sitting.'

The mind boggled. People around here clearly didn't have enough to do.

'I told her that was wishful thinking. Then Greta, she runs the pub,' Bets nodded her head at the building they'd just passed, 'said you probably do those horrible daubs that pass for art.' She grinned. 'She's hoping you're a bit of a hippie with plaits. Shake up the place a bit.'

'God, no.' Ella had always rather hoped she rocked the chic, sophisticated Sam Taylor-Johnson look, if a slightly dishevelled version at the moment. With a sigh she realised just how much she'd let herself go in the last month.

'This way.' Bets wheeled off the road, following a public footpath sign. Once through the gate, she unclipped Dexter's lead. 'They'll be fine down here.'

'George was hoping you might do structural stuff. I think he had ideas about a spot of welding. And Devon, my boss, said you'd probably be very ordinary and not an artist at all but someone who does graphic design.'

Devon sounded disagreeable and uncomfortably close to the mark.

'Having a quiet day, were you?' asked Ella with withering sarcasm, or at least she hoped it was. Didn't they have anything better to do with their lives?

'Erm ...' Bets' peaches and cream complexion turned scarlet, 'not exactly. Magda likes to ... well, you know. Hold gatherings and ...' she scanned the sky as if an answer might burst forthwith from the clouds. 'It just came up. Parish council meeting. Yes, that was it. Dull old meeting.'

Ella ducked her head, hiding her expression from the other girl as she bent and tried to unclip the lead.

'Sadly, they're all going to be very disappointed, I'm not an artist. I wanted to be,' she turned her head but not before she caught Bets' surprisingly candid gaze, 'it just didn't happen.' A heap of canvases, piled like collapsed dominoes, testament to her failure, currently languished in storage. She had no idea why she paid good money to keep on storing them.

Bets sighed. 'That must be disappointing. Trying, wanting and it never happening.'

Ella shot her a startled look, surprised by the other girl's insight.

'I wanted to be an actress once.' There was a hollowness in Bets' voice completely at odds with her open, candid personality. The brilliant lightbulb personality dimmed for a moment and then she was off again with her runaway questions.

'So what do you do, then? Just so that I can reassure the hotbed of gossip that is Wilsgrave.'

'I'm an illustrator. Children's books.'

Bets put her hands on her hips, the loose lead chinking against her thigh, amusement dancing around her eyes, the earlier moment of melancholy completely banished. 'That sounds pretty artistic to me.' She gave a self-deprecating laugh. 'Crikey, I can't even choose the right colour wall paint.' The dramatic shudder she gave hinted at past decorating disasters. 'What sort of things do you draw?'

'Mice, mainly. Children's books about a family of dormice.'

'Not Cuthbert Mouse and all his brothers and sister in the shoe?' Bets' eyes widened, her mouth opening in a gasp.

'Yes,' Ella said warily. Patrick had always preferred her to keep the whole mouse thing low key.

Her eyes widened. 'Seriously? Wow. You mean you're her? You do those drawings. Get outta here. Why didn't Magda tell us that?' She punched Ella's arm. 'That's seriously cool. I love those little fellas. My nephews go nuts for those books.'

'Oh.' A vivid blush rose up her cheeks and for a minute she didn't know what to say in the face of such obvious and rather surprising enthusiasm. No one, apart from her parents and her publisher, had ever been that fulsome and of course they were all biased. 'Thank you.'

'Wow. I can't get over it. You really do all those little drawings. The hats. I just love those little hats.'

Ella couldn't resist all that vibrant enthusiasm and grinned back at Bets. 'Cuthbert's just got himself a fez.' Although she hadn't quite managed to capture one decent drawing that brought to life the little mouse's delight with his latest hat.

'Aww, how cute. I'd love to see that.'

'Why don't you pop round?' The words just ran out of her mouth. She'd never showed her drawings to anyone before they went to the publisher, but people weren't usually this interested.

'Really? Can I?' Bets' delight was so infectious there was no way Ella could retract the offer.

'Er, yeah. Why not?' Ella shrugged, crossing her fingers in her pocket.

'Just wait till I tell Fred and Harry. My sister's kids. They're going to be so jealous.' She punched the air. 'You made my day. Now let me show you around the village.'

'Village hall.' Bets pointed to the timber-clad building to the right of the green that was sporting a rather vivid pair of purple wooden doors. She saw Ella's surprise. 'Local company did one of those community days. The managing director was colour blind. Tarted the place up a bit, but weren't able to do much about the roof. We've got a fundraising drive on to pay for the repairs. On a wet day the toddler group has to slalom around the buckets on their trikes. But there's always loads going on there. Rehearsals. Yoga. Line dancing. Jumble sales. Brownies. Scouts. The allotment society. I tell you, you won't be bored living here.'

Ella almost stopped dead. The other girl had to be kidding.

They circled the green, the dogs stopping to mark their route with annoying frequency. Surely they were all peed out.

'Church, obviously. Some bits are quite old. We get the occasional coachload of tourists, although they're more interested in the duck pond. Makes a nice picture. They don't realise that Martha, the local witch, was drowned in there.'

'Local witch?' Ella's voice was scornful. She tugged ineffectually at the dog's lead, as Tess had suddenly decided to investigate a shrub they'd just walked past and have yet another pee.

'Magda discovered her. She's been tracing her family tree. Richard the vicar has been helping her by going through the church registers. They found all these records going back to the 1750s and that her great, great, great well however many, grandmother, Martha, was tried for witchcraft by being ducked in the pond.'

'That explains a lot,' muttered Ella under her breath, the herb bags and wannabe spells suddenly all making sense.

Bets in full flow didn't stop to draw breath. 'Of course she didn't survive. Well, she couldn't because if she had they'd have said she was a witch and killed her anyway. Lose–lose situation.' She paused. 'But a bit sad.'

Ella gave the pond a second glance. With its fringe of reeds and white Aylesbury ducks floating on the surface, it looked too innocuous to be associated with anything that grim.

Bets waved her hand. 'Cricket club. I expect George will have you on teas. They like their Victoria sponge.'

Ella pinched her lips together but didn't say anything. Her cooking skills stopped at the door of a microwave.

'And that's the shop, with the bow window and Georgian panes. Sells everything you could possibly need. It was going to close but we set up a community trust to run it and we all take it in turns. We'll have to get you on the rota. Oi Dexter, stop that.' The dog was nosing at a discarded crisp packet and half a bar of chocolate in the middle of the road, closely shadowed by the black Labrador. 'Don't let them near the chocolate.' Bets shot her a quick look. 'You do know chocolate is poisonous to dogs.'

Ella, with her work cut out trying to haul the dog away from the revolting melted mess, nodded, not sure if Bets was serious or not.

She put out a hand and stopped Bets, feeling a lot like Alice in Wonderland.

'I can't be on the rota – I've got to work. I haven't got time.'

'But you have to,' said Bets with a pugnacious tilt to her chin, looking rather surprised. 'Everyone does. Otherwise the shop won't survive. Lots of people rely on it. It's not something you can pick and choose to do.'

'Really,' said Ella with haughty disdain. With her village pronouncements, this girl was starting to get on her nerves. Well, they could forget it. Ella had work to do and she planned to keep herself to herself.

The footpath they were on opened out onto a stretch of water.

'I had no idea there was a river around here.'

Bets let out a gurgle of laughter. 'There isn't, this is the canal. Goes all the way to Birmingham. Oh, Dexter! Do you have to? You dreadful animal.' She shook her head, her curls bouncing with suppressed laughter, as with a huge splash, the pointer bounced into the water and Tess went in straight after him.

Ella stopped dead, unable to see through the sudden spray of water. 'Oh God, can they swim?'

Bets tutted. 'Of course they can.'

Ella blushed. She hated feeling stupid and wrong-footed. Her worst nightmare was being laughed at. 'Can they get out again? Should we get them out?' Ella stood on the bank feeling faintly alarmed. How did you get a dog out of the water? Would she have to go in after Tess?

'They'll be fine.'

'But the sides are quite steep.'

'They'll scramble out, don't worry.'

'Really?' Ella didn't believe her.

'Yes – come on, they'll follow us when they get bored. Or give them a call.'

Yeah, right. 'Tess! Come here.'

Nothing. Ella gave Bets a look.

'Pitch your voice a bit higher. Like this: Tess!'

Of course Tess immediately looked up and came splashing towards them, her tail spraying drops of water.

'Dogs hear things on a higher register.'

'Oh.' Ella felt more useless than ever. She cast a look back at the two wet dogs with dread.

'You'll soon get the hang of it, a bit like living here. Magda said you were going to fit in just like magic.'

Ella had no idea why Magda would think that.

'There's plenty going on for you to do. Although word of warning. The WI are always on the lookout for new members. If Audrey comes anywhere near you, make a run for it.'

'And how will I know who Audrey is?'

'You'll know, believe me. You'll know. Think Barbara Cartland crossed with Margaret Thatcher and you'll be sprinting faster than Usain Bolt.'

Ella suspected that she'd be barricading her door once she got home and not venturing out into the village again.

By the time they'd walked what seemed like the entire length of the Grand Union Canal and returned to stand by the small gate at the front of Magda's cottage, Ella's legs were doing a fair impression of jelly and her knee ached while Bets was still full of beans.

'Now, is there anything else I need to tell you?' mused Bets, running her hand along the top of the gate.

Surely not? Ella almost shuddered.

'I must go,' she said quickly before this girl thought of anything else she had to get involved in.

She opened the gate and let the filthy dog pad a few steps ahead of her. With a look over her shoulder, Tess paused and then let loose with an almighty shake of her rounded barrel belly, sending spatters of water arcing up into the air.

'Yeuw,' Ella screeched as gritty drops hailed across on her face and covered her pale pink jeans in muddy splodges.

Bets burst out laughing. 'You gotta love 'em.' She ruffled Dexter's ears affectionately. 'Pains in the butt and just adorable.'

Hmm, the jury was most definitely out on that one. Gritting her teeth, Ella tried to make it appear as if being drenched in stagnant smelly water was an everyday occurrence while fighting hard to block the easy tears that threatened. What was that hideous smell? Eau de Canal mixed with the odour of wet sweaters. Avoiding breathing through her nose, she grabbed Tess's collar, intending to drag the dog straight into the kitchen.

'This has been great. I enjoyed having the company. I'll knock again later in the week and we can go out with the dogs again. Oh, and there's a darts match coming up. You must come to that. It'll be a great way to meet some of the people in the village.'

Ella gave her a weak smile.

She was never answering the door again.

Chapter Seven

'Will you keep still?'

Tess wriggled out of reach before doing a neat about turn, right under Ella's nose, as she made another grab to towel dry the last muddy paw. They'd been out for their daily walk, a quick circuit around the village – and so far Ella had successfully avoiding running into Bets again.

It was like trying to do the cha-cha-cha with the blinking animal. 'I did not sign up for this.' Good thing Magda was on a boat in the middle of the ocean, far out of reach. At that moment, Ella would happily have pushed her overboard.

As the dog danced backwards again, her back leg skidded on an official brown envelope.

Ella picked it up, puzzled to see her name in the window of the envelope. Then she remembered that Gavin, her old boss at the art supplies shop where she'd worked part-time, had asked for her address to send on her P45.

As she took the stairs up to the loft room, she ripped open the envelope, glad that she'd had the sense to get her mail forwarded here.

Reading it, she took her seat at the easel table that she'd set up. A Statement on Account. A request for seven thousand pounds. She tossed the letter to one side. That was a laugh. She barely earned enough to pay tax. There had to be some mistake.

A beam of sunlight brightened the desk, reminding her rather appropriately that she needed to get some work done. Cuthbert's delight in his new fez just about came across in his dancing antics. A rare burst of enthusiasm after Bets' fangirl moment had produced this but it still wasn't right. She sighed. It would have to do. Her deadline loomed. She might not be much of an artist but she was at least professional.

What to do about Englebert? His character still eluded her. The antithesis of his naughty brother of many hats, he was supposed to highlight the difference between the two but without being a self-satisfied do-gooder. So far he looked like a smug rat bastard. There had to be something she could do with him. Oh God, this was such hard work!

But not quite as much hard work as trying to paint proper pictures. Over the last few years, she'd tried so hard it almost hurt. The ideas were there but formless and floating like spiderwebs out of reach, too flimsy to capture. Frustration tingled in her fingers. Why couldn't she do it? It had been so easy years ago, fresh out of art college. The ideas came thick and fast, and like making candyfloss it had been effortless to take a slender tendril of an idea and whip it into shape.

Those early canvases shimmered in her head: the night of her first and, as it turned out, only show. The night Patrick first kissed her.

When had it all gone wrong? The early promise that had split the critics in two camps fizzled out. Taking a paid job in the art supplies shop had been a necessity and then ironically her silly illustrations of mice took off.

She jumped when a wet nose poked into her thigh.

'Urgh! Don't do that!' She unpeeled herself from the chair, a muscle in her shoulder screaming as she straightened up. She'd achieved sweet Fanny Adams, apart from yet another wastepaper basket brimming with ripped up sheets of cartridge paper. Today had not been a productive one. She couldn't afford to lose another day. Bloody Cuthbert and his bloody fez and smugly annoying Englebert.

She rose heavily and went downstairs into the kitchen, with Tess trotting behind, and went straight to the fridge and hauled out a bottle of Pinot Grigio. The dog whined and scratched at the pantry door. Clearly if Ella wanted a drink in peace she was going to have to feed Tess first.

The first mouthful slipped down a treat, without her even checking the time on the clock. Five o'clock be damned. She deserved this. And sod it, she reached for the packet of Marlboro hidden out of sight on the shelf with the cookery books.

She sat down at the kitchen table and pushed the cigarette box around with her index finger. She had willpower ... she didn't have to have one ... but she wanted one, so she was going to.

Lighting a gas burner, she ducked her head towards the flame, careful not to singe her fringe again. As the end of the cigarette glowed, Tess began to growl. 'What,' Ella looked down at the stupid creature with a scowl, 'you're the nicotine police now?'

The dog jumped up, barking. Ella waved the cigarette in the air. 'If I want to smoke, I will.' Honestly. 'Did my mother put you up to this?' Tess gave her a look and slunk off, tail between her legs, casting reproachful looks as she padded out of the room.

In defiance Ella took a long deep drag of the cigarette and promptly choked. 'Bugger.' Coughing and spluttering, she stubbed the rest of the fag out on the nearest thing and the butt smouldered straight through the cigarette packet.

Jeez, what was the world coming to?

The dog had better not be on Magda's sofa. She jumped up and went to check the lounge. As she walked in, Tess slithered off the cream linen cushions, not meeting her eye.

'Bad dog. You're not allowed on there.' Ella didn't care if Magda let her, she didn't want dog hair all over her clothes every time she sat down. The dog slunk into the corner, casting looks up as if to say, *I still think I should be allowed on there.*

Suddenly the strident beep of the smoke alarm cut through the air, the dog began barking furiously and Ella could smell burning.

'No!'

As she rushed back towards the kitchen, smoke curled up and out of the door. She'd only gone and set fire to the whole bloody cigarette packet. The alarm screeched in her ears, so she threw the front door open to let some fresh air in, wafting it towards the alarm situated in the centre of the hall ceiling. Smoke carried on swirling out of the kitchen and she ran in coughing as she was wreathed in cigarette smoke.

The box on the table belched nicotine-infused smoke, bringing water to her eyes. Ella grabbed the nearby bottle of wine and poured the whole thing over the fag packet. The smoke stuttered and died, leaving a soggy pile of cardboard and tobacco. What a waste of money and virtually a whole bottle of wine.

She looked up to find Tess in the doorway with the closest approximation to a doggy grin that she'd ever seen.

Chapter Eight

Devon's image of a homely middle-aged lady who drew pictures of cutesy mice for a living was pushed straight out of the window when he spotted the rather neat backside in jeans, long legs and blonde hair cropped in a gamine style.

He pushed his way through the pub, towards the dartboard, managing not to spill his pint. Mouse Lady still had her jacket on and the sort of stance which suggested she might bolt at any second.

It looked as if she and Bets were getting a quick bit of practice in as she held a dart experimentally, weighing it up. Practice? Not the right word. It suggested some level of experience that was being honed. God help them, they were going to get absolutely slaughtered.

'Devon, there you are.' Bets strode over and tucked a hand under his elbow, pulling him closer into the small circle – her usual mother hen, making sure everyone was included. 'I was beginning to think you'd double-crossed me and signed up to be on call.'

'I wouldn't dare,' he drawled. 'Not that me being here is going to make a blind bit of difference.'

'Being so positive keeps you going! How do you know Ella here isn't a ringer?'

'Is she?'

'No,' admitted Bets with a sad little moue to her mouth. 'But we're quorate or whatever the technical term is for a full team. The vicar's just finishing his tea. Not that either of you could hit a barn door with a rocket launcher if you tried.'

'Ella,' Bets tapped the other woman on the arm just as she was about to launch her dart. She threw it wildly, the dart bouncing off the board with a thud. 'Oops. Sorry. This is Devon, my boss, landlord, brother-in-law to be and,' she shot him a cheeky look, 'friend, on a good day.'

'Be careful, otherwise I'll get my rocket launcher out, you cheeky mare. Hi,' he stepped forward with a smile. 'Nice to meet you.'

As if a cloud had covered the sun, the expression on Ella's face closed down. Her lips thinned and her chin lifted as she studied him with what he would have said was barely veiled disgust, but maybe he was being paranoid.

'Yes,' she said ignoring his outstretched hand and turning back to the dartboard on the wall. With one fierce, brutal throw, she speared the dart into the board. He winced.

This was going to be an interesting evening. It looked like Bets' new friend was some kind of man-hater. He wasn't on Marina's Christmas card list at the moment but he'd never had the impression she wanted to nail his balls to a dartboard. Although there was still time, he supposed.

'We've met,' said Ella giving him a pointed, almost triumphant look.

'We have?'

Her fierce expression darkened further.

He didn't remember but he could tell that admitting that was only going to make matters worse. This girl radiated brittle anger. Any moment now she might breathe fire all over him.

Bets watched the two of them, amusement dancing in her eyes. 'Come on, you can buy me a drink,' she said to Devon, already heading towards the bar.

'Would you like one, Ella?' asked Devon politely.

'I'm fine, thanks.' Her clipped tones had bite to them.

'Be right back.' Bets tossed the words over her shoulder as she led him to the bar.

'What's her problem?' he asked. 'You'd think I'd insulted her or something.'

Bets' eyes widened a shade too innocently and her gaze slid away. 'I might have told her that you thought she'd be ordinary and not an artist at all. But it's all right,' she added hastily, 'because what Greta said was far worse.'

'Ah, if I've upset her artistic sensibilities that might explain it.'

'I think she's just a bit sad at the moment.'

'Sad? And you surmise this how?'

'There's just this look in her eye sometimes and I get the impression she might burst into tears at any second. Magda didn't say what the problem was. You need to be nice to her. I had to force her to come out this evening. I think she's lonely.'

'Lonely! I'm not bloody surprised.'

'No, seriously. I think she's lost.' He shook his head and took his pint. 'Please be nice to her, Devon.'

'All right then, as it's you.' Bets was usually a pretty good judge of character.

Greta, the landlady, nodded at them as they approached the polished wooden bar, brass pulls gleaming in the low light, tugging at the denim straps of her ubiquitous dungarees. Apparently, she modelled herself on eighties band Bananarama, which also explained the red and white head scarf tied around her bird's nest of bright hair, pink this week.

'What are you having, Bets? Nothing too strong. You're our best bleedin' player.' Greta shot Devon a dubious look. 'Unless Mr Vet here has hidden talents.'

He put up his hands in surrender. 'Not a one. I'm just here to make up the numbers.'

'Christ alive. You and the vic, the dream team of disaster.'

'And Magda's goddaughter,' chipped in Bets.

'Ah, yes, the artist. What's she like? Is she a lesbian?'

Devon exchanged a look with Bets and raised an eyebrow.

'She doesn't like men, that's for sure.'

'Bacardi and Coke please.' Bets ignored them both. 'And no, she isn't. But guess what? She's the Cuthbert Mouse illustrator lady.'

'Is she now? And can she play darts?'

Bets shrugged. 'Of course not, I just invited her. She doesn't know anyone—'

'And you needed the numbers.' Greta shook her head with a knowing smile. 'Although to be fair it's brought a few extra bums in. Having the vicar is a real bonus. The blue rinse groupies are out in force. I had to send young Barry out to stock up on sherry and dust off the schooners.'

Devon sat down on the opposite side of the table to Ella. Unfortunately, Bets had been waylaid by the late arrival of the vicar. The minute he eased himself into the seat, he watched her stiffen. Ella's body language spoke fluently. Some perverse instinct made him push for conversation.

'So I hear you're staying at Magda's.'

'Yes.'

'Have you heard from her?'

'No.'

'I guess it's tricky when you're at sea.' OK, he'd officially bored himself to death with this conversation but she wasn't making it easy. Not like Marina, who sparkled in front of an audience, held them spellbound with every word and tilt of her lovely head and smashed his life apart.

A sense of bleakness cast its familiar shadow and his diaphragm clenched in response.

He looked at his watch. Please God, let the other team turn up soon. This was excruciating.

He should have given up then, but he had a habit of flogging dead horses.

'Bets says you're an artist. What sort of art do you do?'

Cold unfriendly eyes turned his way. 'I'm an illustrator. I draw pictures of mice for a series of children's books. Small. Fat. Chubby. Rotund mice.' She enunciated each with word with a dart of venom.

'Right.' Nothing wrong with fat mice. This girl was lining up to be the queen of crazy town.

'So how long have been you been here?'

'It feels like for ever.' Her mouth twisted and for a moment sheer unhappiness illuminated her face. She looked so lost and alone in that second. And he knew exactly how it bloody felt.

'God, I wish Bets hadn't roped me in for this. I'm bloody hopeless at darts,' he said.

'So why did you agree then?' She stared hard at him.

'Community spirit. And you know Bets. Besides,' he shrugged, 'the other option was Gerry, who has about as much control over his right arm as a boom on a boat in a force nine gale. I thought me making a complete dick of myself was preferable to spending the evening having to tend to people's injuries. People around here tend to value their eyesight.'

She looked up and for the first time met his gaze, her teeth worrying her lip as if trying to bite back any semblance of a smile.

'I thought you were a vet?'

'I am but people automatically assume I can deal with humans as well as animals.' He gave a self-deprecating laugh. 'I usually volunteer the information about how I take an animal's temperature and they quickly change their minds. Although obviously if it was an emergency, I'd help if I could.'

'Unless it was four in the morning.' Ice filled her voice.

'Sorry?'

'I phoned a vet recently. He wasn't very helpful. It was the middle of the night, I was desperate. I didn't know whether it was an emergency or not. I've never looked after a dog before. I was looking for help from a professional.'

The beer he'd swallowed seconds before stalled in Devon's gut.

'Ah.' Now that explained things.

She stared at him, an eyebrow quirking in dangerous question. Foreboding gnawed at him. He was in quicksand up to his neck. Even though it was far too late to save himself, he tried anyway.

'It was four o'clock in the morning. You woke me up.' That sounded pathetic.

'It was four o'clock in the morning because I was worried sick I was doing something wrong with a dog that I don't how to look after.' She shot him an oddly superior look which wasn't right because he was the professional and he'd told her the facts, albeit a tad sharply. 'Plus, it's not my dog. I'm looking after it while Magda's away. So if it's overweight, which you so kindly pointed out the other day, that's not of my doing. However, if *I'm* overweight, in your opinion, not that it has anything to do with you whatsoever and I couldn't give a ... what you think, that's my business.'

What the hell was she talking about now?

She tilted her head to one side, assessing. The silent study, as if she could see beneath the surface of him, made him want to squirm.

'You don't remember meeting me the first time, do you?'

Oh God. Cold panic flashed. As far as he knew, he'd kept track of every woman he'd slept with or tangled tongues with and there weren't that many of them. Admittedly quite a few drunken fumbles at university and two unmemorable one-night stands which had reinforced his view that fleeting sex left a nasty taste and a yearning for something more. 'I'm sorry ... no.'

'Up in the woods, a couple of weeks ago.' She looked ready to punch him, her chin lifted with all the pugnacity of a boxer. 'Told me I was fat. The dog too.'

A hot wave of shame washed over him but it didn't stop his eyes doing that bugging out thing, which immediately he saw pissed her off even more. The woman sitting in front of him now looked nothing like the drowned rat slash bag lady he'd torn a strip off that day.

'With that and the phone bedside manner, I'd say you copped the double whammy.' She sat poker stiff, her mouth twisted in bitterness, but it was the veil of misery he could see in the hunched set of her shoulders and the weary distance in her eyes that held his attention.

'Aw shit, I'm so sorry.' He winced in self-deprecation. 'I was bloody rude. If it makes you feel better, I felt bad about it afterwards. I'm not normally like that. Honest. I'm a nice guy really. Would it be any justification if I told you I'd been up all night and had to put down a dog that morning?'

Her eyes narrowed as she thought about it.

'I shouldn't have made the personal comment, although...' He racked his brain trying to remember exactly what he had said. He was pretty sure he hadn't come out and said she was fat. The dog, yes, but not her. 'Look, the dog I had to put down was in agony. So overweight it had developed diabetes. I'd warned the owners so many times... they didn't listen. That dog didn't need to suffer or be put down.'

Her eyes started to soften. Fractionally.

'I don't normally lash out at complete strangers, I was just feeling sorry for myself and took it out on you. I'm sorry. Really.'

She eyed him carefully, her nose scrunching ever so slightly as if she were weighing him up with the precision of a set of scales. Tension took hold of his shoulders, vicelike in its grip. Why should it matter what she thought? It wasn't as if she'd be alone in having a low opinion of him. Since taking over Dad's practice he seemed to have upset more pet owners than pleased them. If it wasn't for Bets keeping him going in the surgery, he'd have slung his hook weeks ago. Dad was still pretending to be at death's door but it was time to call his bluff. He'd give it a couple more weeks and then he'd be out of here. Start afresh elsewhere and no woman was ever going to derail him again. From now on he was going to focus on his career.

For a minute it was tempting to slump, let the depression break in and have its way with him.

Sheer boredom was the only reason Ella had come tonight. That and the realisation that Bets would have just kept knocking at the door until she answered. She sighed and narrowed her gaze at Devon.

One of her worst faults was this grinding inability to let a grudge go. Second only to the desire to go back to the seat of an argument and niggle at it like a tongue going back to a mouth ulcer over and over. Seeing Devon tonight was like manna from heaven, it gave her the opportunity to let out all her internal shittiness. Except he went and spoiled things by apologising and being human about being rude before.

She hated herself for the horrid small-minded meanness which seemed to have seeped into every corner of her soul. She hadn't always been like this. Seeing that bleakness in his eyes, the sudden blankness almost devoid of emotion, made something inside her pop like a balloon. She knew the expression. She'd seen it in the mirror every day for the last few months. Abject depression. Misery. Self-loathing. The sight of it punched into her so hard it almost took her breath away. Knowing the feelings so well she couldn't not acknowledge it.

Funnily enough, touching his hand made her feel better. His head shot up in surprise and they stared at each other. Probably the same surprise echoed in her eyes. Blind instinct. Wanting to dispel that darkness haunting his eyes made her want that human connection again for the first time in a long time. When had she become so cold and brittle? Remote and isolated from everyone? Stupid questions, because she knew the exact moment. No wonder her mother was so worried about her.

Of course, now she'd done it, it felt a bit weird. She pulled her hand back hurriedly and they both looked away, pretending the brief moment hadn't happened.

She swallowed. So maybe he wasn't all bad. 'I'm sorry too. A bit all over the place at the moment.'

'I know that feeling. Shall we call a truce?'

She nodded as they exchanged wan half-hearted smiles. Not that they'd probably run into each other that often. Before either of them could say anything more Bets bounded into view.

'Ella, Devon, this is Richard the vicar.' The sandy-haired vicar beamed from behind round glasses as Bets completed the introductions. For some reason, Ella immediately sat up straighter. She'd never met a vicar before.

'Richard the Vicar. Sounds rather noble, doesn't it?' he said noticing her posture. 'Bit like Richard the Third. Not, of course, that he was terribly noble. Quite the contrary. Rather ignoble. The princes in the tower and all that.' He beamed again and Ella couldn't help smiling back at him, not quite as happily. She noticed Devon smile too. Maybe the vicar was a spiritual miracle worker – he'd already lightened the atmosphere. In his checked shirt and sensibly styled jeans he reminded her of a rather beatific country singer, John Denver's younger brother. An image popped into her head. Startled, she sat wide-eyed for a moment. Then she grabbed her handbag.

'Sorry, I digress. Nice to meet you both. I'm sincerely hoping that one of you knows one end of a dart from the other, metaphorically speaking. Because of course it's quite obvious. The sharp pointy end ... you know.'

He mimed throwing a dart as Ella finally managed to pull a pencil out of her bag. A beer mat would have to do. With sudden energy, she peeled away the top layer of the beer mat, leaving the blank card beneath and rapidly sketched. Excitement fizzed and popped in her system as an angelic-looking mouse complete with wings and a halo took shape. With a breathless, 'Oh', she stared down. Englebert. It was Englebert. She hadn't been able to get a feel for his character for weeks. He didn't get much of a look-in. Always the quiet, serious one. With the pencil she shaded his eyes and added a blissful smile to his little mouth.

'Very nice to meet you, Ella. I hear you'll be doing the flowers for the church one weekend.'

'Yes? What?' Aware again of her surroundings, Ella looked up, her brain now computing what the vicar had said.

'That's wonderful news. It's always gratifying when people get involved in the community and doing the church flowers may seem like a small inconsequential thing but it's all part of the bigger make-up of village life. Magda's very good at that sort of thing.' He paused and looked out of the window. 'I don't suppose you've heard from her.'

Ella's shook her head as her heart sank. It was just as well she hadn't heard from her godmother, she might have a few choice words to say to her. Seriously, flower arranging? What had Magda been thinking? And now she'd missed a perfect opportunity – she should have told him she was far too busy. But you couldn't lie to a vicar, could you?

'And, how lovely, you're an artist. I shall look forward to your floral creations. It must be truly wonderful to have a talent like that. Sadly, mine run to much more practical things. Well, I say practical, but not in a plumbing or putting up shelves sort of way. So probably not terribly practical at all.'

Unsure of what to say to his stream of consciousness chatter, she nodded again, her eyes sliding to the quick sketch she'd done.

Devon peered down at the beer mat, took a sidelong look at Richard and then back at the picture, his mouth curving in sudden amusement. When she looked up again, his eyes danced with mischievous delight. For a second her breath caught. Was he going to rat on her? It hadn't been a deliberate caricature. He gave her a conspiratorial wink.

'I'm sure you're good at loads of things, Vicar,' piped up Bets, quite unaware of the silent exchange. 'I'm hoping for a bit of divine intervention. Or you could do a prayer or two.'

'I tend to do that with regard to somewhat weightier matters.'

Bets gave a cheerful shrug. 'Just a thought. Right, we're playing 501 to zero. Devon, you can score. You're better at maths than me.'

'And I have a calculator on my phone.' Devon held up his mobile.

'Even better. Here they come. Alan, Fred, Bill and John. Welcome.' Bets introduced everyone and the four men, who seemed to be a set of quadruplets in a general uniform of khaki chinos and chambray blue shirts, sat down with their pints at the table opposite.

Ella was amused by Bets' assumption that she was likely to be the weakest link. She was down to play last after Devon and the vicar.

Neither Devon nor Richard had lied about their skill. The vicar missed the dartboard completely with two of his throws and the third dart hit a three. Devon was no better and managed to hit a ten and the part of the board outside of the numbers. Alan, Fred and Bill threw their darts with quick efficiency. One. Two. Three. Insouciant confidence radiated from them as they stepped up to the oche with self-assured strides instead of shuffling about on the line the way Devon and Richard had done.

At last it was her turn. She weighed the darts in her hand as she took the set from Devon. The tiny bit of practice she'd had earlier had given her a feel for them again.

With her right foot just up to the line, she narrowed her eyes, focused and let the dart fly. Twenty. Double Twenty. Twenty.

'You've played before!' screeched Bets, leaping up and looping her arms around her waist.

'Once or twice.' Ella shrugged and tried to sound nonchalant, unaccountably pleased by Bets' delight and the look of surprised admiration on Devon's face.

'Why didn't you tell me you could play?' Bets indignant face made her giggle. 'Magda never said.'

'For starters, you never gave me a chance. I did try but you kept interrupting me.'

'She does that a lot,' said Devon drily to no one in particular.

'I do not... OK, sometimes I do. So how come you can play?'

'The double was probably a fluke as I'm a bit out of practice but I used to live over a pub when I was a student.' She flashed a superior grin towards Devon. 'Men tend to assume girls, particularly blonde girls, can't throw straight.' She winked at Bets. 'Kept me in paint and brushes while I was at college.'

Devon burst out laughing. 'That's brilliant.'

Richard tried to look however a vicar should look and after a few expressions crossed his face, he clearly gave up trying. 'Good for you. I'm sure there's a scripture in there.' He nodded his head and muttered to himself. 'Perhaps Colossians 3:23.' He lapsed into thought.

'So have you got any tips for us?' asked Bets.

'Yes, your throwing technique is dreadful.' She mimicked Bets' throw. 'You need to be side on and twist your upper body. Keep your body still. Aim, bring the elbow back a little and then throw and let your hand follow through.'

'Show me again.' While Bill took his turn, Ella took hold of Bets' arm and elbow.

'Like this, feel it.'

This time when Bets threw her dart, she scored a far more respectable eighteen, a one and a twelve.

'Yay!' She swivelled her hips, chanting, 'Go me. Go me. Go me.'

Stepping up and skirting around her smartly, Fred made short work of three throws scoring twenty, twenty, twenty.

Bets, her face a picture of petulance, muttered, 'Show off,' as Devon, Ella and Richard burst out laughing.

Ella noticed how quickly she cheered up when Richard's improved throw delivered three darts, all of which hit the board. Despite the fact none of them scored anything he received a hearty round of applause from the group of ladies sipping drinks behind them. Maybe she should take a few lessons from the ever-cheerful Bets. Nothing seemed to slow her down for long. In fact, now she was very unsubtly celebrating John's surprisingly inept score of three.

'Not very sporting,' teased Devon, nudging Bets.

'I know, but it makes me feel a lot better.' She smirked and rubbed her hands, waggling her eyebrows in pretend villainy. Ella smiled and tried not to laugh at her silliness. It was very childish, but it was impossible not to laugh when she realised the vicar, who should never ever play poker, was doing his utmost to look suitably disapproving while distinctly unholy glee danced in his eyes. Bets' unsportsmanlike delight was infectious.

'Right, my turn again. Let's see if Miss Midas here can give me the darts touch.' With his dark brows screwed in concentration, almost meeting in the middle, Devon stepped up and took his time, mirroring Ella's technique. Letting his darts fly, he scored two twentys and a twelve.

Bets leapt to her feet and high-fived him with a loud whoop. 'Yee-ha!'

Ella took a deep breath as she stepped out of the pub into the chilly night, immediately aware of the quiet. Ahead, her solitary shadow loomed tall and thin in contrast to the bright lights behind her. When she looked back she could see everyone inside, laughing and smiling, action and noise, in ambers and golds. With a leap of her heart she stood stock-still, taking note of the angles and planes of faces, the light and shadow between, the colour and shapes coalescing in her head.

She turned sharply and crossed the street in quick, impatient strides. Devon had offered to walk her home but she'd refused. The place was so tiny compared to London, any hint of danger was laughable unless she was likely to be mauled by a passing hedgehog.

When she opened the front door, the dog bounced up and down in the hall with her usual ridiculous excitement. You'd have thought she'd been gone for three days instead of three hours. With a small sigh, which might almost have been contentment, Ella hung up her coat.

The dog butted her head at her legs gently as if to say, *hello, remember me. I'm still here.* The evening had turned out far better than she'd expected. She'd had fun. Bets had been a lot less irritating than she remembered. The vicar rather sweet and Devon, well, he wasn't so bad after all, but one to steer clear of – she couldn't cope with another lost soul.

Chapter Nine

Spring sunshine dappled the route as Ella made a sudden decision to head for the reservoir.

She walked along the road, Tess trotting alongside, her paws pitter-pattering on the Tarmac.

Once she and Tess had left the road, crossing at the right bend, she followed the footpath through to the reservoir and let Tess off the lead. Her tail wagged joyfully as nose down, she zigzagged back and forth across the gravel path, in hot pursuit of some exciting scent.

Ella followed slowly and stopped on the bank high above the water, unexpectedly charmed by the moorhens who pootled this way and that, their legs scurrying madly beneath the water with no obvious aim or direction. She watched them go round and round in circles. They seemed happy enough. Her mouth crumpled in a bitter smile. That's what Patrick had accused her of – losing her direction, her artistic ambition, of wanting to settle down. But what was wrong with wanting what other people had. Families? Children? Wanting those things didn't have to be at the expense of art, did it?

A heron swooped by on impossibly long wings, its body and legs a long straight line at odds with the curving sweep of its flight. She followed its progress, the huge wings dipping and rising with mechanical precision. Sunlight sparkled on the water like glitter and the trees at the water's edge arched with the grace of ballerinas in front of an audience of brilliant green reeds. She studied the arcs and curls of the foliage and the rainbow of greens before being distracted by a gaggle of ducks over to her right who turned up-tail in quick succession in a feverish hunt for breakfast. That would make a picture. She stood for a moment. Looked closer at the trees, Degas' dancers emerging from the shadows. She looked deeper. There it was.

The idea grew like unfurling blossom, spreading out. Her heart soared. Acrylic paint to give it texture. Brilliant spring greens lit with gold. Intense white and silver. Ideas raced and for once it was easy to grasp them. Hold fast to them. A long slender canvas mirroring the elongation of the water, the trees and their reflection.

She blinked. It wasn't her style at all. Could she even do it? The ideas were there but could she ever capture them properly?

She looked round for Tess. But what if she could? There was something that called to her, elemental and insistent. It brought back a wave of emotion, a dizzy headiness of excitement. Ella picked up her pace. She needed to get home. Needed to paint. Now.

Where had Tess got to? She'd forgotten all about her. There was no sign of the wagging tail scything through the undergrowth.

'Tess!' She pitched her tone a little higher, the way Bets had told her.

She stood at the top of the reservoir wall, her eyes casting left and right, looking for any sign of the dog. Below her the water lapped at a gravel beach. Had Tess wandered down there or off the path around the corner into the trees?

'TESS.' Now she bellowed. Bloody typical when she wanted to get back. Where was the damn dog? 'Tess!'

Suddenly there was an aggrieved yell from one of the fishermen's tents pitched on the water's edge. Tess galloped towards her as a man strode out, his gait wide and awkward in waders, shouting and red-faced. Oh God, what had she done?

With Tess dancing around her heels, looking particularly pleased with herself, Ella had nowhere to hide. She grabbed the dog's collar and tried to put herself between the man and the dog.

'You stupid bitch. Can't you control your effing dog?' His red face burned with fury as he clambered up the steep bank.

Her hand tightened on the collar and she put the other hand on Tess's head. Fright-induced adrenaline whooshed through her, leaving a sensation of light-headedness and wobbly legs.

'I ... er, I ...'

'Your fucking dog just ate my fish.' With broad shoulders, close-cut hair and a dirty complexion, the man loomed over her. What could she say, apart from sorry which even she could see was not going to cut it?

'What you gonna do about it, you dumb bitch?' He took a step forward. It took all her nerve to stand her ground, and not give into the urge to run away as fast as her shaky legs could carry her.

As she stood there gawping uselessly, probably like one of his ruddy fish, cold at first and then hot, she straightened. OK, so he had a right to be a tad pissed off that her dog had run off with his breakfast, but it was a fish and it wasn't exactly up there in the statute books.

'I'm really sorry but—' her voice came with a shaky squeak.

'Sorry!' he roared, hot fetid breath washing over her face. Tess froze and Ella heard the deep rumble that came from her chest and its attendant vibration against her leg. The dog took several steady steps in front of the burly man.

Ella's legs began to shake. Whoa, this was getting serious. Surely Tess wouldn't attack him. Praying she could hold her, she grabbed the dog's collar and laid what she hoped was a calming hand on her head and murmured, 'It's OK, Tess. It's OK.'

What if Tess bit him? Or went for him? She wasn't sure she was strong enough to hold her. It wasn't even her dog. If Bets were here, she would know what to do.

'Oi!' came a shout from behind them.

Ella turned. Devon the vet. Out running. With early morning stubble, dark angry eyes and a baseball hat crammed onto his head, he looked an unlikely rescuer but very welcome all the same. He whipped off the cap to free just-got-out-of-bed tousled hair. He had a magnificently mean air about him. Angry sparks flared in his eyes.

'John Wilkinson, what the hell do you think you're doing?'

'This dumb bint's dog nicked my fish. Ate the lot. Swallowed 'em down whole, little bastard.'

Without any fanfare or fuss, Devon insinuated himself

between her and angry John, one gentle hand pushing her discreetly to one side. For the first time she noticed the breadth of his shoulders and just how tall he was. With the dark shadow dusting his chin he looked a lot meaner and harder than she remembered. And much more attractive. And where had that thought come from? He so wasn't her type. Not with that dangerous edge to him. The way his chin jutted out as if daring the man to take a pop at him surprised her. This was a far cry from the man in the pub.

'Fish, plural? And where were they?'

There was power in his stance and the testosterone in the air sizzled until Wilkinson suddenly seemed to deflate, shrinking in size, his voice becoming a mumbly growl against Devon's taut, ice-laden words.

'I think you owe the lady an apology, don't you?'

The man nodded and grudgingly muttered 'Sorry,' in Ella's direction. As apologies went it was hardly handsome but it was so unexpected she could hardly complain.

John Wilkinson marched back to his little tent on the shore, with one narky scowl over his shoulder.

She sagged in relief, realising how tense she'd been and how near easy tears were.

'What was all that about?' Her words only held the slightest quaver. 'You the local Godfather or something?'

So he couldn't see the sheen in her eyes, she looked down. A mistake. Up close, the tight thigh-length running shorts emphasized sleek corded muscles, biceps femoris, and outlined the full glorious definition of his gluteus maximus. Her mouth tightened and she swallowed. She'd done enough nudes to notice that he was well put together in a purely muscle, skin and bone type of way. That was all. But she couldn't resist taking another peek.

'Something.' Devon grinned, the dark and mean pirate of seconds before vanishing in a flash of white teeth. He leant down and patted Tess. 'Good girl.'

Ella's heart did an unnecessary little skip which had her clenching her hands in denial.

'Well, it's an impressive something. Black belt in karate?'

'No, just an understanding of fishing bylaws. On the reservoir here, you are supposed to put the fish back. Most fishermen catch them and put them in keep nets in the water. The fact that John had fish, plural, that Tess could get hold of, suggests perhaps he wasn't playing by the rules. I think getting more than one fish out of a keep net without being spotted would be a tad difficult.'

'Well, he got pretty angry.' She bit her lip and reached for Tess, patting her on the head.

'Are you OK? You look a bit shaken up.' His eyes met hers, assessing, gentle. She'd missed that before; he had kind eyes. 'I'm sorry about John, he can be a bit of a thug. We're not all like that round here.' He winced. 'Shouting at complete strangers.'

She raised an eyebrow. He blushed before his face blossomed into a disarming rueful smile and as she smiled back, their eyes held for a fraction longer than normal. A fraction where they stared at each other, as if seeing something completely new. A fraction that made her heart flip just a tiny bit and her lungs stutter out a breath.

'Er ... I ... are you OK or do you ... want me to walk back with you?' Confusion marred his forehead.

'I'm fine. I've got Tess. I'll be fine. I'm OK.' Her words tumbled out in haste.

'If you're sure.' He touched her arm. 'Take care. I'd better get going before I cool down too much.' He looked across the reservoir, flexing his knee in a quick lunge. 'Well, try not to get into any more trouble and take care.'

'You said that already.'

'I did, didn't I? Right.'

With another smile, he gave her a wave and took off running in the opposite direction.

She watched as he covered the uneven ground in strong strides. From a purely artistic point of view, he was a pleasure to watch. She didn't do manly men, they were normally too intimidating, but she could definitely admire his physique.

Was it her imagination but did Tess's long sigh sound like appreciation?

'You and me both.' Who knew knights still existed, even if their armour was a tad on the tarnished side? 'Come on. Let's get out of here before you cause any more trouble.' But Ella patted her head and gave her silky ears a fuss to show Tess that she didn't really mean it.

Chapter Ten

In her mind's eye she could see the paints she'd use. Raw Sienna, Burnt Umber, Sap Green. She fizzed with a sense of anticipation that she hadn't felt for years. Wedgwood, Fluorescent Blue, Prussian Cyan, Deep Violet, Pale Olive Green.

Ella took the stairs two at a time. Since the walk around the reservoir, her mind had kept circling back to the ideas but this morning something had clicked. Now she paused eager but a little too scared to make the first brush stroke.

There was none of the nervous trepidation that had gripped her for the last couple of weeks. She knew exactly what to do and it felt such a relief. This was for her, so it didn't matter what anyone else thought. No one need ever see this picture. It was all hers and she could make it whatever she wanted. It felt like a liberation. Total freedom.

She picked up her paintbrush and slipped a sidelong glance at Tess, who'd crept in and had settled down in a patch of sunlight with a heartfelt sigh as if to say, *I know this could take some time, so I'll just take me a little nap.* Unaccountably, the sight of the dog, snoozing and so trusting, made her smile. The two of them in harmony up here in the attic, filled with sunshine and light, so close to the sky.

Sure and confident, she made the first stroke and then the second. She painted and painted and painted. The light dimmed but she carried on. It was only when a cramp in her calf seized the muscle with vicious fingers that she finally stopped. She'd been painting for nearly three hours.

When her leg eased, she stood back to look at the canvas. And then took another step back. She'd poured her heart and everything else into it. She took another step back.

Closed her eyes and then looked again.

The trees were well executed. Light shone on the water. The bowed branches extended their limbs like dancers. The reflection mirrored the static image.

She swallowed hard and tossed down her brush. With clenched fists she rubbed her knuckles at the seams of her jeans. Technically it was adequate but she'd failed to capture the essence beneath the surface. There was no movement, no sparkle and none of that otherworldly sense of magic and secrets she'd sensed. It was crap.

She stomped down the stairs, her limbs stiff. Bugger, bugger, bugger. Who was she kidding? As she stepped off the bottom step, hell bent on a serious caffeine fix, her foot skidded and she almost went down. What the heck? A random cardboard sleeve from last night's ready meal sat innocently in the middle of the hall floor.

As she bent down to snatch it up, she caught sight of the kitchen.

'Oh my God!'

Tess stood, legs four square, next to the upturned dustbin. Like washed up debris on a beach after a storm, the floor was strewn with lettuce leaves, an empty coleslaw pot, polystyrene meat trays and the remnants of a plastic pack of pâté. There was a hangdog expression on her face as if to say, *I've been a bad dog but might you still love me, just a tiny bit?*

Ella stormed over to the bin, her feet crunching on random bits of carrot and onion.

'For Pete's sake,' she spat, and marched over to the back door and wrenched it open. 'Out.' She pointed. The dog ducked her head and slunk out of the door. 'You know you're in big trouble, don't you?' Tess looked back with a mournful expression and then carried on with the long slow walk of a condemned dog.

'Bloody hell.' What a mess.

With a roll of her aching shoulders and a heavy sigh she pushed up her sleeves and pulled out a black bag and a pair of rubber gloves from under the sink. It took a while to round up every last bit of carrot, some of which was now smeared on the blue card which must have fallen from the pin board onto the floor at some point during Tess's rampage. Wiping off a chip of cabbage, she was tempted to throw it away but as she re-read Magda's words, she decided against it and pinned it back on the board.

It took half an hour to put the kitchen back to rights but afterwards she suddenly felt a lot better. Venting all this anger had helped her earlier crushing sense of disappointment.

Tess had decided that her banishment to the garden had lasted long enough and now had her face pressed up against the door, a halo of condensation ringing her nose where it touched the glass, although clearly she didn't have the nerve to whine or scratch.

Ella glared at her. 'I should leave you out there ... for ever.'

The dog stared at her, tilting her head slightly. Ella looked more closely. Tess was definitely quieter than normal, subdued.

'Oh, for crying out loud.' She threw open the door. 'Come in but stay in your bed. You're still in trouble.'

Guilt radiated with every movement as the dog sloped in and went straight to her bed, giving Ella sorrowful glances.

'Don't try making me feel bad,' snapped Ella.

Tess ducked her head and looked up, the amber eyes sad.

'No, I'm not buying it. You're a bad dog.'

How could a dog look reproachful?

'Hello, is it possible to speak to Bets?'

'Who's calling?'

'It's Ella.'

'Hi, it's Devon. How are you? No more walk mishaps? Bets is wrestling with an irate Chihuahua at the moment. Can I help? Or can I take a message?' In the background Ella could heard short snappy barks.

He was the last person she wanted to share her latest dog foul-up with. 'I'm not sure. I need some advice. Tess has eaten something and I'm a bit worried it might give her food poisoning.'

She explained what the dog had done with a quick run-down of the menu.

'You really don't have to worry on that score.' Devon replied with a restrained laugh. 'Her nose is a lot more sensitive than ours. She wouldn't have eaten it if it was really really bad ... Actually scrub that, she's a Lab, she probably would. They eat anything. All that food, dodgy chicken and rich pâté, might upset her tummy. Could affect either end.'

Marvellous, another thing to clean up. Ella had never been on such good acquaintance with rubber gloves.

'You should keep an eye on her.'

Just peachy.

'But do call if you're worried about her.'

Ella let out a small sigh.

'I mean it, Ella.'

His reassuring tone made her feel slightly better and she couldn't resist saying. 'Even at four in the morning?'

He laughed. 'Even at that time. Although if I have to come out to make a house call, make sure there's a good supply of coffee.'

She shook her head and glanced at Tess, who had her eyes closed and looked pretty sorry for herself.

'That bit I can do, but what should I be looking for? I don't want to call you unnecessarily.'

'Ella,' the gentle chiding tone he used hit her somewhere in the chest, making her feel suddenly warm. 'Look, if you need to call, just call. After that lot, I would probably expect her to be sick or have diarrhoea. I'm sure she'll be fine, but the one thing you should look out for is if her stomach looks bloated or feels hard. That can be the sign of something more serious. So call if that happens. But the foods you've described, I think she's going to be OK. A bit windy and smelly possibly.'

'Thanks, Devon.'

'No problem. Oh, hang on.' Ella heard muffled voices in the background as if he'd put his hand over the receiver. 'Bets wants a word.'

'Hi. How are you? Well, that was a bloomin' performance. Don't ever believe anyone, especially not your boss, who tells you it's much easier to get a worming tablet down a small dog. Now, I meant to ring you today. You haven't forgotten about the church flowers, have you?'

Chapter Eleven

Ella couldn't believe she'd agreed to this. There had to be better things to do than wandering along a muddy footpath, slipping and sliding all over the place at half past nine on a Saturday morning. At home she would be at the Hackney Grind, eating delicious eggs Benedict, sipping a flat white and scanning the arts pages of *Time Out*, with Patrick debating which exhibition they should see. She hunched deeper into the North Face coat she'd pinched from Magda's coat rack. She was turning into the woman style had forgotten.

'Woo hoo!'

Ella spun round to see Bets charging along the path towards her, two branches brimming with white hawthorn blossom held up to her head like antennae. Dex and Tess raced around her, almost tripping her up with wanting to join in the fun but she just laughed at them.

'What do you think?' Bets waggled the foliage comically. She looked totally ridiculous, rather like an overgrown ant, but clearly she didn't care. Her giddy uninhibited silliness stopped Ella in her tracks and, unable to help herself, she burst out laughing.

'You're mad.' She giggled as Bets continued to wave the branches about. 'But they'll fill the arrangement up. Thank you.'

'My pleasure. Let's see what else me and my trusty hacksaw can carve up for your delectation today.' Bets did another energetic twirl, leaving a flurry of petals in her wake.

They'd amassed quite a bit already on the short walk this morning. Both dogs seemed utterly perplexed by the women's sudden interest in the hedgerows.

'Lots of this would be good.' Ella pointed to some white flowers.

'Common mouse-ear,' said Bets. 'It's a weed, I think, but I always think it's so pretty. I wouldn't mind it in my garden. I wonder what makes it a weed. Maybe because it grows like one. There's loads of it.'

Weed or not, she agreed with Bets. The delicate white flowers hidden among the green stems were rather lovely. Her eye was caught by another shrub, glossy leaves just about to unfurl like emerald-backed beetles. Above her head the branches of a sycamore spread, like arms extended to embrace the sky. Her eyes traced the limbs, their arterial divide reminiscent of biological sketches of veins and blood vessels. Funny how these things in nature seemed so interlinked. She'd not noticed it before.

They continued walking and passed under an overhanging bough, bushy with plump catkins. Ella reached up and touched them. 'Some of these would be good.' They were reminiscent of the lambs' tails in the field they passed earlier. To her amazement, the tiny white creatures had actually gambolled, just like they did in cartoons. They were quite cute although the parent sheep looked like grubby old tramps with their shaggy coats encrusted with mud and other unmentionable stuff.

'So do you know what you're doing? Or is it a question of get enough stuff and pray?' asked Bets. 'Is it going to be like the darts night? You have a hidden talent you didn't tell me about and you've been doing that Japanese ikebana for donkey's years?'

'I've never heard of that.' Ella looked quizzically at the other girl who pulled a mournful face.

'Audrey. Women's Institute. I get roped in to do all sorts of things, especially when numbers are low.'

'Ever heard of saying no?'

Bets raised an eyebrow and looked pointedly at the pile of flowers in their arms.

'I didn't feel I could,' Ella said defensively. 'Not after I met the vicar.'

'With Audrey, you definitely can't, she's a force of nature. It's easier to roll over and say yes.'

It was Ella's turn to raise an eyebrow.

'I'm not as bad as her,' protested Bets. 'You enjoyed the darts in the end. And the church flowers are down to Magda, not me. Anyway, if it turns out badly, just think they'll never ask you again.'

'Again? I thought this was a one off.'

Bets gave her a pitying look, shaking her head. 'You've got so much to learn about village life.'

Finally, satisfied with the haul of greenery, Ella suggested they head for home.

They walked along the path, the dogs making sudden appearances bursting out of the undergrowth, circling each other – and then one would dive off the track, the other dog bouncing along in its wake.

'They're having a great time,' said Bets patting Dex as he bounded past, did a quick about turn and went back the other way, Tess doggedly following in his footsteps. 'Two dogs are definitely better than one. When Jack and I get married and he takes over the practice we'll have two.'

Ella didn't know much about Jack, apart from that he and Bets were childhood sweethearts and he was away at Bristol University studying to be a vet like his older brother.

'What about Devon?'

'Devon's had his own practices for the last few years. He's only back at the moment because Geoffrey, their dad, hasn't been well. And he split up from his girlfriend, Marina.' From the petulant way Bets emphasised the consonants, Ella guessed that the ex-girlfriend wasn't *persona grata*.

'You don't like her?'

'Can't stand her.' The words burst out, then Bets paused, her face telegraphing confusion as if disturbed by her own uncharacteristic venom. 'Sorry, that's not fair. I don't really know her that well. She's not exactly one for family gatherings. Since Devon met her, he's kind of separated himself from us.' Bets rammed her hands into her pockets, her pace picking up as if matching her frustration. Ella couldn't imagine any of her friends being this irate on her behalf.

'Bloody Marina's always been too busy to come with him. Filming here. Interviews there. I'm probably biased. She's got this fabulous, exciting career. I see how much it hurts his parents and pisses Jack off. If she'd made Devon truly happy, maybe none of us would have minded, but he hasn't seemed very happy for years. Not that he ever said anything. Far too much of a gentleman.'

'What does she do?' Ella was intrigued. Devon seemed an unlikely boyfriend for an actress or a model.

'She's a celebrity vet. On the telly. Every morning. An absolute cheesefest. *Making Pets Well with Marina.*' Bets put her fingers in her mouth and mimed gagging.

A devil of mischief popped into Ella's head. 'What? Treating celebrity bitches?' She thought she might have caught the show once.

Bets let out a shout of laughter and held her hand up for Ella for a high five.

'Bloody brilliant!'

As they neared Magda's cottage, which Ella now thought of as home, both dogs slowed their pace, panting.

'Let's have a cup of tea before we go to the church.'

With the dogs lapping thirstily, Bets explored the kitchen.

'I love the colour scheme in here,' she said, looking round, 'it's gorgeous.'

Ella smiled. 'Magda wanted colours that would distract from the cobwebs. We spent a fortune on paint samples to get them right.'

'You did it?'

'I helped. Magda knew she wanted French Provincial and Cath Kidston. We just went from there.'

'It's lovely. You've got a good eye – but then you are an artist.'

Bets stood next to one of the duck-egg-blue walls and stroked the soft matt paint. 'I stand in Homebase, look at the colours on the tins. Then I think "that's the one", buy ten litres and then when you start putting it on the walls it looks like cat-sick.'

'No, you can't do that. You need to get samples. Try them out on the wall. Light. Textures. They can affect the colour.'

'I realise that now, when I've got enough sodding paint to cover the whole bloody flat five times over and I've done two walls and it looks hideous.'

'I have to say I'm not familiar with cat-sick. What sort of shade would that be?' Ella teased.

'Believe me, you don't want to know. Bilious, mauve-cum-beige-cum-puce. Not nice. The tin said Mushroom.' She pulled a morose face as Ella burst out laughing.

'Sounds hideous.'

'It is. Bloody tin lied. And at the moment I can't afford to buy more. And it looks so dark. I feel like I'm living in a cave with a mood lamp set permanently on angry.'

'There's still loads of this left.' Ella pointed at the pale blue kitchen wall. 'I'm sure Magda wouldn't mind you having it. I could give you a hand if you liked.'

'That would be awesome. Let me know when you're free.' Bets' eyes widened. 'Oops, you're free a lot at the moment. So what's the story?' asked Bets, suddenly turning her way. 'Sorry I'm nosy. No filter, remember. If you've got some terminal illness, you don't have to tell me.'

'Not a lot to tell. And nothing special. My boyfriend, Patrick, and I . . . we've just sort of split up at the moment.'

'Sort of?'

Instead she shrugged and fell back on her usual explanation. 'It's complicated.'

'Pants, that's horrid. Are you OK? Was he a bastard? Or do you still love him?'

Delaying her answer, Ella took a long look at the unshaded grey expanse of sky.

He certainly wasn't a bastard. But he'd damaged something which couldn't be repaired.

Ella gave her a non-committal shrug.

'So how long have you been together? And when did you break up?'

'We haven't broken up.' Ella's words sound terse and defensive. They hadn't broken up. Not officially. They were officially taking some time apart.

'I met Patrick straight out of Art College. He's a bit older than me. I met him at the end of year show which was a big deal. He loved my work. He'd just opened a gallery and he wanted to show my pictures.' Ella flinched, remembering the golden promise of those early days, both of them poised for take-off, the world theirs for the taking.

'Wow, you must be really good.'

Ella shrugged, kicking at a sod of mud on the kitchen floor. 'I was OK. The first show went well.' It had been a sell-out. She'd been critically acclaimed. Patrick had fallen in love with her. 'After that I lost my mojo and had to get a proper job.'

'But you do those brilliant books. The illustrations are gorgeous.'

Ella blushed. 'Thank you. The books are just a bit of a sideline. Not exactly what I had in mind when I was going to be an artist.'

'No way, Jose! They're so clever.'

'Clever?' Ella stared at Bets. 'No one's ever said that to me.'

'Well, you've been talking to the wrong people, then. The expressions you manage to convey on their faces. I love them.

This is a bit cheeky but I was wondering if you might donate a picture for the silent auction at the Spring Fayre. For the new roof for the village hall.' She twisted her hands nervously. 'I mean it's a big ask because I know you could sell something instead of giving it to us. You can say no.' Bets screwed up her face. 'I'm sorry. I always do this. Devon's always telling me I'm too impetuous. I just thought of it.'

Ella was amused by Bets' sudden discomfort. 'Bets, it's fine. Of course you can have one.' She smiled. It was quite flattering. 'I've got enough of the bloody things, although they're all in storage. It's not going to raise much, though.'

Bets snorted, 'Yeah, right.'

Ella shrugged. 'They're just drawings. Not even technically that good, if I'm honest.'

'Blimey, I dread to think how much they'd go for if they were,' Bets bookmarked quotes with her fingers, '"technically good".'

'They're just not what I thought I'd be doing.'

'So what were your real pictures like?'

'Not like Cuthbert, that's for sure. I did urban abstracts. The city in decay.' Ella gave a half-laugh. 'Gloomy. Miserable. Angsty. Ironic really. I come from a nice middle class family. I think Patrick would have preferred it if I'd come from a migrant family living in a grim northern town.'

As she gazed across to the field out of the window, thinking back to some of those early abstracts, the elusive tail of a thought darted through her mind.

'Earth to Ella. Are you listening?' asked Bets nudging her.

'I don't suppose you know where I might get some barbed wire?' asked Ella. 'I've had an idea. I need to get some tulips from Magda's garden too.'

Chapter Twelve

Ella took a step back. The finished arrangement looked a bit of a dog's dinner. No, it was a complete dog's dinner. Make it a four-course extravaganza of a dinner.

'Shit, this is a disaster.' The coil of barbed wire which she'd thought might add an edgy touch looked like what it was, a bit of abandoned wire fence, upon which drifting blossom had caught without great effect.

It was supposed to represent the dichotomy of nature, fresh and pretty on the surface and its darker undercurrents with the deep red tulips symbolising the blood of innocents. Unfortunately, that idea hadn't panned out.

Bets tipped her head to one side. 'It's not that bad ...' She wrinkled her nose, her freckles dancing. 'It's not that great either. What if you ...'

Ella waited hopefully.

'Nope.' Bets plunked down into the front pew. 'I can't think of a single thing you can do.'

Ella sat down next to her.

'In fact,' said Bets, her cheeks moving as if she were working really hard to keep a straight face, 'it looks bloody awful.'

Ella winced. 'It does, doesn't it?'

'Y-yes,' said Bets still trying to look serious but starting to lose the battle. 'I suppose you c-could say it's quite ... quite, um ... eye-catching.'

Ella bit her lip, as she looked at the drunken display. 'It's t-terrible.' She sniggered.

'Yup.' Bets nudged her in the ribs.

'Truly terrible.'

Bets nodded and snorted. Then the two of them caught each other's eyes and burst into laughter.

Finally they calmed and leaned back against the wooden pew. Ella considered the arrangement, tilting her head from one side to the other.

'Doing that isn't going to help,' observed Bets.

'I know,' sighed Ella. 'I think I might have to nip down to Tesco to—'

'Good afternoon, ladies. It looks like you've been rather busy here.' Ella turned to see the vicar striding down the aisle, his black cassock flowing.

'Afternoon.' She found herself almost wanting to nod or curtsy.

'Goodness gracious. That's quite monumental.'

He came to a halt in front of the first pew and peered over his round glasses, studying the arrangement before taking several steps to the right to look at it from a different angle.

Ella stiffened, mortified and ready to apologise.

Richard prowled another few steps and tilted his head.

'Well, I must say, this is one of our more dramatic pieces.' He stepped forward, tentatively touching one of the tulip heads.

'Hmm.' He folded his arms and stood in silent contemplation.

Behind his back, Bets began to snigger again.

'It's really rather symbolic, isn't it?'

Ella opened her mouth but didn't get a chance to speak.

'I must say it's a very interesting arrangement. I'm assuming as we approach Easter, the tulips represent the blood of Christ and the wire the thorns on the crown, and combined with the green and white foliage you could say it represents the rebirth of nature during Spring.'

Bets covered her mouth with her hand and looked up at the wooden rafters in the ceiling. Ella could see her shoulders shaking with mirth.

'See, Ella,' she called managing to compose herself, 'I told you Richard would get it.'

'Well, of course,' said Ella, fighting to keep her face straight, thinking of what Patrick might say when he was at his most pompous. 'I'm delighted that you understand the quintessential philosophy behind this piece.'

'I'm not sure what our ladies are going to say, though.' He shook his head and turned to her and then she saw the wicked twinkle dancing in his eyes. 'I'm looking forward to tomorrow.'

Chapter Thirteen

There was something so comforting about a hot bath and slipping into a fleecy onesie, even if it was covered in glow-in-the-dark pink, green and yellow elephants. You couldn't lose her in a hurry, that was for sure. It was a forgotten – make that deliberately forgotten – stocking filler from last Christmas from Ella's mother, who had never quite got the concept of stocking fillers being small enough to fit in a stocking. Ella had unearthed it when she'd finally unpacked one of her cases.

Pouring herself a glass of red wine, she guiltily sneaked a look at the blue card on the pinboard. The flower arrangement still bothered her. Taking down the card, she crossed to the French doors. Through them she could see a pink-streaked sky as the sun started to set.

A gentle fragrance filled the air and she followed its scent to a small tree, its branches laden with plumes of lilac. Only when she reached it did she realise that the garden extended further than she'd initially thought. Feeling a little foolish, she read Madga's words.

No one could see her. She ducked under one of the branches

and stopped dead. Like a secret bower, this second garden was almost completely surrounded by feathery leafy trees that seemed to bow inwards as if trying to protect it from the real world. Crocus, periwinkle, bleeding heart, clematis, spring beauty and grape hyacinth created a gorgeous spectrum of pale blues, pinks, mauves and white. The flowers filled a series of beds surrounding a soft sandstone circular patio at the centre of which, picked out in tiny weather worn bricks, was a star shape. Delicate heads swayed like dancers in the gentle breeze, nodding with elegant grace. Unthinking, she reached out to stroke the velvet softness of the petals fluttering with the fragility of butterfly wings, as if they might take flight at any moment. Scents of bluebell and hyacinth tinged the air, subtle and heady coming in bursts as she passed slowly doing a circuit of the patio. When she came back to her starting point, she realised she'd almost followed Magda's instructions to the letter. Well it hadn't done any harm and certainly didn't mean she believed in any of that Mother Earth rubbish.

Relishing the peace of the tiny bower, she sat down on a stone bench fringed by bluebells and sipped at her red wine, gazing around lost in thought. With a sudden gasp, her mouth dropped open. 'Oh.'

Now she could see it, the flowers had been grouped to create shade and shape like multi-hued clouds on a blue sky, creating a painting in three dimensions. It made her white and red monstrosity in the church seem horribly vulgar and obnoxious.

Her eyes scanned the flowers, an idea taking shape in her head. She jumped up. She knew exactly what to do.

*

'Interesting outfit,' Devon drawled. Ella jumped and almost dropped the armful of flowers she clutched.

'What are you doing here?' She looked horrified as he stepped out from behind the hedge which Dexter had been busily watering for the last few seconds.

'You're asking me that when you're attempting to sneak across the green in a pair of pyjamas that are probably visible from the moon with a florist shop in your arms?'

'It's a *onesie*,' she said, pulling herself up with a dismal attempt at gathering her dignity. 'And it's a free country.'

'True, but I can't help thinking it's a bit out of character.' He eyed the fleecy trousers with their lurid cavorting elephants with a grin. Even in the rapidly fading light he could tell she'd turned a brilliant shade of pink.

She shrugged and then winced before answering with surprising honesty. 'It seemed like a good idea at the time.'

'Riight. And the flowers?'

It was comical watching her face as she searched for an answer. He decided to help her out. 'Fresh impetus? A late addition? I hear the vicar already called it monumental.'

She let out an annoyed huff. 'Did Bets tell you?'

His lips twitched. 'She might have mentioned it.'

'Great.' She scowled, her eyebrows almost meeting in the middle. Some of the flowers slipped and she shifted trying to hold onto them. He wanted to laugh at her but felt that it would be most definitely the wrong thing to do.

'Want a hand?'

'No, thank you.' She lifted her neck with an imperious sniff at which point several stems tumbled out of her arms and Dexter gleefully pounced on them.

'No!' she cried and promptly several more rained down on top of the ecstatic dog who snapped at them as if it were a great game.

'No, Dex.' He grabbed the dog's collar. 'Sit.' With a brief hesitation the dog obeyed.

'How do you do that? Tess doesn't pay a blind bit of notice to me.'

'Practice.' He bent to pick up the flowers. 'Come on, I'll help you carry them over. I take it this is a last-minute rescue operation.'

She stood there, several contrary expressions flitting across her face until with a resigned purse of her mouth she said, 'Yes, thanks. I had ... well, I'm hoping to simplify things a bit.'

He took some more flowers from her, the petals tickling his chin as he tried to grasp them.

'Thanks for the advice the other day,' she said hesitantly.

'My pleasure.'

I take it as you didn't call back there were no ill effects from her bin binge. And no more fish episodes?'

'No.' She groaned. 'You always manage to turn up at the wrong moment. I'm getting quite good at this dog-owning malarkey.'

'So no more dog disasters?' His mouth quirked.

Ella wrinkled her face. 'Apart from the wind. Dear God, it was awful.'

He laughed. 'I thought it might be.'

'Not to mention the mess. She threw up all over the kitchen floor, luckily just once but I had only finished cleaning it two minutes before. So I had to start over. Honestly, I think I spent nearly all day tidying up after her. Who knew dogs could be so time-consuming? I'm going to have words with my mother. Two meals a day and walks, she said.'

They'd almost reached the doors of the church in the porch and she turned her head towards him, suddenly formal again.

'Thank you. Do you want to leave those there and I'll come back for them?'

He shook his head, looking at the dark windows and then back at her. 'I'll wait with you.'

'You don't have to. I'll be fine.'

'You might be fine but my mother would skin me alive if she thought I'd left you here on your own.' Wilsgrave might be a peaceable small village but there was no way he was going to leave a woman alone in a dark church.

'You're going to be very bored.'

'You don't know that. I might find half-naked flower arranging fascinating.'

'I'm not half-naked,' she snapped but he noticed her lips curled in embarrassment as she glanced downwards.

The pyjamas weren't exactly flattering but they were kind of cute and odds with her usual prickly demeanour. He quite liked them. 'No, but you're not exactly dressed for . . . '

'For what?'

'For anything.' He smiled.

He sat in a pew watching Ella move, her quiet determined grace belying the baggy fleece all-in-one thing, which was growing on him. Flat refusal had met his initial offer of help and at first he'd assumed it was out of pride or the ever-present prickliness, but as she worked, he realised it was because she was so focused. She knew exactly what she was doing. With quick sure stabs, she placed each flower head in position. A quick tweak here, a snip there with her secateurs, measuring a length against another flower and all the time, he could hear her muttering to herself, in between humming.

'Yes that's it. Dedee da da. Yes, there. And there.' It was rather like watching a conductor with an orchestra in the palm of his hand.

Within minutes, he could already see a shape emerging. Every now and then she'd step back, tilt her head and then dive forward again.

She was so absorbed she didn't hear the occasional squeak of the door and never once turned around to look his way.

There was a strange satisfaction in watching someone at work who was not just oblivious to but totally disinterested in their audience. What a contrast to Marina who played to the camera, constantly aware of her audience and the nuanced effects of every move she made. A consummate actress.

The thought sliced at his heart. Had Marina ever really loved him? In that single-minded, give-everything-up-for-someone-else way? The way that he had loved her. Had it all been an act?

He had no idea why he made the sudden comparison but it struck him that willowy Ella was a complete contrast: private, reserved, her face usually shuttered apart from the rare occasions when she let the emotion leak out. Like now, when an aura of quiet confidence and serenity surrounded her, quite at odds from her usual demeanour.

He'd never been particularly interested in art, but he could appreciate the talent involved. Watching Ella, he was intrigued by her absorption and commitment to the task in hand and surprised by how similar it was to his own approach to work, although she might come to regret her single-minded dedication when she realised that in the last ten minutes, several members of the choir had amassed in the aisle in readiness for their weekly practice.

With a low voiced exclamation of triumph, she stepped back one last time and nodded. He had to admit the finished display was a thousand times better than the previous incumbent.

Colin, the leader of the choir, winked at Devon before raising his arms and launching the thirteen strong chorus into a rousing verse.

Nellie the elephant packed her bags and said goodbye to the circus...

Devon smiled as rich baritone voices filled the church, singing one of their regular repertoire that he'd heard before, but that was perfect for this situation. Amused, he shook his head. Colin was almost as mischievous as the badly behaved German Shepherd he owned. Ella whipped round, startled.

He waited for her to relax into the moment. Smile along. See the ridiculousness of the situation.

His disquiet grew second by second as she remained as if struck by stage fright in a spotlight, her limbs jerky almost like a robot and her face a rictus of consternation.

It quickly became clear she had no idea what to do. And he knew that Colin and Co had settled in for at least a full verse and chorus. And knowing Colin, probably a full three verses.

If she found the situation excruciating, it was even more so for him to witness.

He jumped up and crossed to her, taking her arms and forcing them into a dance pose, her right arm out and her left arm around him.

'What are you doing?' she hissed, her eyes flashing at him, stiff still and unyielding in his arms, her feet stumbling over one another behind time.

He lifted his shoulders. 'I'm not sure,' then he grinned at her, 'but it seemed like a good idea at the time.'

The words elicited a blank stare, so he pulled her along in a jaunty dance which he vaguely thought might be a polka. It took a good few bars of singing before she gradually relaxed into the steps.

They cantered up the aisle as the choir, now with even more gusto sang, *with a trumpety trump, trump. Trump, trump, trump.*

As they galloped back down the aisle, he could pinpoint the exact moment when she loosened up and the fluidity returned to her muscles. Suddenly her feet matched his step for step.

'You're mad,' she laughed up at him breathlessly, her face lively and alight, as they danced back down the aisle, skirting Colin conducting away like a ringmaster.

'You're welcome.' He smiled broadly back at her, relieved that her haunted, mortified expression had been banished.

Feeling oddly protective of her, he brought her back to the front of the church just as the final notes of the song died away. With a final flourish Devon held up one arm to give her a twirl before bowing to her with a wink. A rueful smile touched her face as she dipped her head.

The chorus began to clap and she turned to them and with a regal tilt to her head dropped into a deep graceful curtsy, holding out the baggy legs of her onesie as if it were a glamorous ball gown.

Chapter Fourteen

She carried on sketching, outlining a new, rather sumptuous hat for Cuthbert. It was possibly the most flamboyant hat he'd ever worn, but he, the most debonair of the brothers, deserved it. Very Cavalier. In fact, she might give him a Charles the First wig and buckles on his shoes. She inked in a purple plume for good measure and sat back to admire her work.

'Looking good, Cuthbert, my young man.' She nodded, so caught up she almost expected him to nod back. 'Quite the dude.' Which of course he would agree with and doff his hat with a courtly bow. She drew another quick rough sketch of Cuthbert sweeping his hat off, the plume dusting the floor. Just so she wouldn't lose it.

She ended up doing several different versions and before she knew it, another hour had elapsed.

Over the last three days, she'd taken to having her morning cup of coffee in Magda's secret garden when she let Tess out for her morning wee and although she felt a bit silly stroking the flowers and inhaling the scents, she couldn't seem to help herself. She'd got into a really good daily routine and her deadline worried her less and she even had ideas for a new book with three alien characters who'd happened on an English village.

Englebert with his mouse angel wings and decidedly skewiff halo had come to life. He wore an endearingly dopey expression rather reminiscent of a certain vicar. Ella bit back a smile. Hopefully no one, least of all anyone in the congregation, would ever spot the likeness, with the exception perhaps of the sharp-eyed Devon, who since his rescue act in the church had been popping into her thoughts rather too frequently.

Tess appeared, the lead in her mouth. Ella rolled her eyes, laughing in spite of herself. The dog was a pain but kind of cute with it.

'Is it that time already?' She checked the time on her phone. 'How do you do that? Bets will be here any minute.'

Following the flower arranging, Bets had taken to calling for them for a morning walk before the vets' surgery opened. Ella looked out of the window. Yes, she could get used to the walking, especially when the weather was like this. Bets had shown her a couple of different walks.

At the sharp knock of the door, Tess raced in circles almost tripping over her own legs and then went charging down the stairs, the metal link on the collar *thump*, *thump*ing down on every wooden step.

Ella ran down the stairs, trying to dodge the thoroughly over-excited dog to reach the front door.

'Won't be a mo.' She opened the door, Tess's tail beating a happy tattoo against her leg.

'No problem,' said a gruff voice.

'Oh, I thought you were Bets.'

'I decided it was high time I walked my own dog for a change. But Bets said you'd be expecting her, she said I had to call in.'

'Right.' That told her, then.

'Are you coming or not?' His face didn't look particularly inviting. What had happened to the man who'd been so charming the other night? He had cross written all over him. Was it because Bets had probably forced his hand, insisting that he called in? She seemed incapable of believing that people actually liked being on their own.

She wasn't sure wanted to go for a walk with this Devon. An impromptu dance was one thing, but what on earth would she have in common with a man who, if the James Herriot books she read as a teenager were correct, spent half his life with his arm up the backside of various farm animals?

With rabid excitement, Tess's body squirmed as she tried to rub up against both their legs, her tail slicing the air with the finesse of a rolling pin.

Ella's mouth pursed as she looked down at the dog wriggling with ridiculous over the top excitement. She could hardly say no. The poor dog had been cooped up all morning.

'I'll just grab a jacket and some shoes. Is it cold outside?'

Devon wrinkled his face as if giving the question serious thought. 'It's bright but the wind's a bit chilly. You'll need to wrap up warm.' He paused and she fixed his face with a warning glare, which of course he ignored. 'A onesie won't cut it today.'

'Haha! Very funny.'

'I thought so.' It was a relief to see the disarming smile replace the furrowed lines on either side of his mouth.

She tied on her trainers, grabbed her jacket and followed him out of the door and down the path.

Wrestling the lead from the dog's mouth, she hooked it onto her collar and did her best to hang on as Tess threw herself forward, frantically pulling to catch up. In a half run, Ella followed the crazy racehorse-under-starters-orders plunging gait which was par for the course every single day. You'd think the damn dog had never been out of the house in her life.

'For goodness' sake, you need to show her who's boss,' said Devon, giving Tess a stern glare.

Ella rolled her eyes, thinking of the constant ache in her shoulders from having to hang on for dear life. 'You think I haven't tried?'

'Here, let me.' He grabbed the lead from her. 'She needs to learn some manners.'

'Be my guest.' Just when she'd started to think better of him, Captain Grumpy was back with a vengeance.

He held out Dexter's lead for her to take over. Immediately she could feel the difference as the handsome pointer walked beautifully alongside her, matching her pace.

Tess started to pull ahead and Devon stopped, pulling gently on the lead but not yanking the young dog back.

'I don't think she's ever been trained properly. That's the problem. But you can teach her a few good habits.'

The stop, start, stop, start took for ever but Devon's earlier grumpiness seemed to vanish, replaced by an infinite well of patience as he talked soothingly to Tess.

It was slow progress and a massive relief when they turned

off the road to take the footpath down to the canal. The two dogs charged off the minute they were released from their leads, joyfully leaping through the almost waist-high grass of the open field. Devon and Ella wandered along in silence for a good fifteen minutes. His mood seemed to have improved.

'Sorry.' Devon lifted his head and looked up at the sky. 'I was in a really shitty mood this morning. Getting out always puts things back in perspective. Realigns things.' He picked up a loose branch and scythed at the grass with it. 'Gets rid of the City blues.' He thrashed at the foliage again, this time a little more viciously. 'I was in London again yesterday.'

'Don't you miss it?' asked Ella, curious rather than challenging as she might have been a week or so ago. 'Living in London? Bets said you lived there until recently.'

'Not really. You can be there in under an hour. In fact, when I get back here, I realise how little I miss it. The only thing I miss is knowing what the future holds. I'm in limbo at present.'

'I know that feeling.' She dug her hands into her pockets.

'You missing London?' Devon didn't look at her, just continued to walk by her side.

'Yes! Of course I am.' Was he stupid?

'What do you miss?' he asked, his voice tinged with scepticism.

She paused for a moment. 'Well ... I miss ... I miss being able to nip out for a decent cup of coffee and ... ' She frowned. There were heaps of things she missed, nothing precise she could put her finger her on. 'The buzz. You know, lots going on.' It sounded feeble but she couldn't identify one particular thing.

Devon let out an incredulous laugh. 'Don't let Bets hear you say that. There's plenty going on here. She'll have you roped into things quicker than you can find a coffee bar on Islington High Street. There's always some event happening: the Village Hall fund raisers, the Spring Fayre, the Christmas Fayre and local charity events, the Muddy Run, the Santa Run and the Chiltern Peaks Challenge, and then there's the Canal Festival, not to mention the action-packed programme of the WI and the primary school events plus all the things at the theatre, the pantomime, comedy festival and there's talk of a literary festival. It's never-ending.' He gave a wry smile. 'And I get roped into most things. I don't see why you should escape.'

'I've done the church flowers!' she said, indignantly. 'That's my bit for village life.' All those other things sounded hideously dull.

'Not quite. Don't forget the chance to play shopkeeper.'

'I've been trying to. Hopefully they'll forget about me.'

'I doubt it, everyone has to take a turn. It's written in the village bylaws.'

'Really?' She raised a disbelieving eyebrow.

'Well, I'm sure if it isn't, it should be. And if I have to, you do too. And sometimes you get free stuff.'

'Like what?'

'Out-of-date Swiss roll!' He grinned at her.

'Marvellous, I can't wait. Although I could give it to George. He refuses to believe I can't bake a cake for him now and then. He's a right pest.'

'George? He's all right. Just lonely, I suspect. Magda used to keep an eye on him, although she lets him think it's the other way around.'

Ella cringed. Not nosy at all. She felt a touch ashamed now. Perhaps next time she saw him, she might offer him a homemade cappuccino from Magda's machine. Although she drew the line at baking anything, despite Magda's magic box. That was never going to happen. He'd have to go homebaked-cake-less.

They reached a stile, the path left continuing along the canal and the other way looping away through a field.

'Which way do you want to go?'

Ella lifted her shoulders. 'No idea.'

'If we go along the canal it cuts back to the other reservoir and we have to cut across the fields to get back. If we go across the field now, it loops back and brings us back to the village behind the church.'

Devon's face looked a touch too innocent.

'And what's the time difference between the two?'

He gave her a sheepish twinkle. 'Busted. The first one will take us another hour. The second twenty minutes.'

After the last few weeks, she had built up her stamina, so an hour's walk didn't faze her. If she had to, she could.

'Which would you prefer?'

'As it's a nice day and I had a skinful of the city yesterday,' his mouth tightened, 'I'd like to head over to the Northern End reservoir. Have you been there?'

She shook her head. 'Left it is, then.' She followed him over the stile, and on the other side, he waited and took her hand to help her climb down.

'Thank you.' She smiled and raised an eyebrow. 'Very gentlemanly.'

'Or sensible – those wooden planks can get a little slippery.

Gentlemen around here know it's a smart move if they don't want to have to carry maidens in distress all the way home.'

'Oh.' She'd been impressed by his thoughtfulness.

'And it's good manners,' he teased.

'In that case, thank you again.'

'Are you one of those types who doesn't like doors opened for them?'

'No,' she said with a twist of her mouth. 'Although I do have a couple of friends who don't approve.' She'd heard the arguments plenty of times. 'Apparently it's benevolent sexism. The type of paternal and protective behaviour that perpetuates the view of women being incompetent beings who need to be cherished and protected.'

'Bollocks,' said Devon. 'I think my ex would have disagreed with that. At the risk of sounding bitter, Marina loves nothing more than being cherished and protected, but I'd like to see the person that calls her an incompetent being. Ha!' He let out a mirthless shout of laughter. 'She'd chew them up and spit them out into very small pieces before stomping on them with her very sharp pointy stiletto heels.' He sobered for a minute, before shaking his head. 'Yeah, you don't mess with Marina.'

He looked rueful.

'Bets said you'd split up recently.' Ella chose her words carefully. The tone in his voice suggested a certain amount of admiration for his ex. 'That must be ... '

'Difficult, very difficult. Trying to detangle two lives.' He sounded resigned and weary. 'I had to go and see her this week. She's decid— she wants us to put our house on the market. Except it's not going to be that straightforward.'

He scowled. 'Not straightforward by any stretch of the imagination.'

Ella screwed up her face. 'Don't tell me that.' She sighed. She'd been desperately trying to avoid thinking about the practicalities.

'Bets mentioned that you ... well, she mentioned that you were having problems.'

She liked Devon's diplomacy, appreciated that he didn't want to pry out her secrets.

'We're taking some time apart ... but if we go our separate ways, there are all those decisions involved in detangling, as you put it.' They'd have to sell their flat. But neither of them could afford to buy one another out individually. Where would she go? If she made the decision to split from him, she was making a far bigger decision which would impact on what she did in the future.

'You have to do what's right for you, detangling complications or not. Ours is complicated by the fact that our property is in negative equity. So we can't sell.'

'Ouch. That's one thing we don't need to worry about. We bought our flat ages ago. We split the mortgage and the gallery that Patrick runs is doing really well.' Amazing really, considering other friends in the art business weren't doing so well. Patrick had the golden touch when it came to sniffing out new artists. Shame his scouting ability had failed him so badly with her. 'What if one of you wants to sell? To get out for good? What do you do?' asked Ella, wondering what she'd do if she found herself in the same situation.

'Find the money to pay back the negative equity or stick together.'

Whether it was because she turned to try and gauge his expression or the slipperiness of the muddy bank, but when Tess came bounding up, barging past with Dexter following at full pelt and hitting Ella's legs, she lost her footing.

In a heart-stopping moment, her feet scrabbled precariously for purchase, to no avail. Like some cartoon character with windmill arms, she flailed about, grasping at nothing but air. Then just like in all the cartoons, with an inexorable trajectory she started to pitch head first into the canal and there was nothing she could do to stop herself except wait for the inevitable splash and hit of cold enveloping her body.

'Aaargh!' Screaming was a big mistake. Her mouth filled with pond soup, her head went under and water rushed up her nose. 'Nggghnnn.' She started to splash about, the weight of her clothes heavier than she could have imagined. Furiously swimming, she got her bearings.

Tess and Dexter were perched on the bank, barking furiously, and behind them stood Devon, his mouth twisting suspiciously.

Grimly she splashed towards the canal edge, tears of mortification stinging her eyes. How the hell was she going to haul herself up out of the water? Devon's lips were now pressed together and he'd assumed a bland expression which didn't fool her in the least. Bastard was laughing at her.

She reached out to grasp the side and her knee bumped something.

Shit. Both knees bumped. The bottom. She closed her eyes. This wasn't happening to her. Slowly she rose to her feet, water pouring out of her coat sleeves, her hair plastered to her face and her feet squelching with each step. She looked down, staring the final indignity in the face. The water level came to just above mid-thigh.

Devon had turned away but she could see his shoulders shuddering.

Wiping at her slimy face, she waded the final metre, her jeans clinging heavy and wet around her crotch. Her nose felt full of bits and bringing her hand to her mouth, she spat out a mouthful of stuff, feeling sick as something slippery dislodged itself from her teeth.

The treacherous toad on the towpath had composed himself enough to turn around and offer his hand to help her step up and out. She took it and didn't say a word.

'Are you ...' Apparently there was some problem with his breathing or he appeared to have a terrible stomach complaint, from the way he kept almost doubling over. 'Are y-you ...'

'No, I'm not.' She refused to cry in front of him. Instead she brushed past him, heading along the towpath.

'Erm, Ella,' he called.

She stopped, took in a deep breath. 'What?'

'Er ... it's this way.'

Ignoring the rushing in her ears, she wheeled around and stomped past him, water oozing in her trainers with every step, her jeans chafing and the heavy coat releasing yet more bloody reservoirs of water at regular intervals.

She hated this horrible muddy path. Hated the pissing canal. The stupid hedges. The fact that they were still miles from the village. No bus. Taxi. Gritting her teeth to keep in a howl of frustration, she marched on. Her fingers were freezing and she couldn't even put them in her pockets. Probably find a couple of frogs in there or something.

Devon did try to talk to her but she quelled every attempt with icy hauteur. The walk back to the village seemed interminable and at least by the time they hit the green, she was too chilled to give a toss what anyone might think. With her head held high, she stalked past several dog walkers, all of whom were stunned into silence by her silent deadly glare which dared them to say one word, just one word.

When they reached the cottage, she was surprised to find that Devon had followed her up the path. Did he have some kind of death wish? She was about to reach boiling point and if she didn't get inside, away from everyone, she might just explode right in his face. And she never exploded. Never lost her cool.

Her fingers were so cold and pinched she couldn't get the key in the door. When Devon took them from her and opened it, she couldn't look at him.

'Why don't you strip off here and go up and have a hot shower? I'll sort Tess out and make you a hot drink.' The calm, reasonable tone almost ripped the lid off her control.

Fuck it. She mustered a baleful glare and slipped off the coat, letting it fall at her feet.

He gave her an approving nod.

Approving nod. She'd give him flipping approving. Stamping her foot down, she toed off one soggy trainer and kicked it across the room narrowly missing him. He jumped and she gave him a grim smile, setting to work on the second. This time her aim was better, although not perfect.

'Oi, careful.' From his sudden wariness, she could tell he

wasn't so sure of things now. He glanced down at the damp footprint on his thigh and then up at her.

Fuck reasonable. Fuck everything. She peeled off her T-shirt and jumper in one go and flung them on the floor and furiously yanked down her jeans, quite a feat as the beggars had glued themselves to her legs, and hurled them on the floor at Devon's feet.

His eyes widened and he had that oh-shit-what-have-I-got-myself-into-here-look, which gave her a smart slap of satisfaction. See how you like being discombobulated, Mr I-have-all-the-answers.

In bra and knickers, both decorated with pondweed, her skin red and chafed, she stormed across the hallway, her dramatic hauteur somewhat spoilt by the squelching of her soggy socks which left puddles in her wake. Stomping up the stairs, she wheeled into her bedroom, slamming the door for good measure.

That was it. She'd made up her mind. She was going back to London as soon as she could pack her bags.

Chapter Fifteen

The red paint looked angry and vivid on the canvas, but Ella kept going, dogged and furious. She'd woken from a dream at the ridiculous hour of five o'clock, her head full of a startling image of her falling in the canal and crawling her way out with blood flooding down her legs instead of water. She gradually came to, unravelling herself from the dream, disorientated and dazed with furious emotion, tears streaming down her face.

She'd come straight up here, knowing the exact shade of colour she needed. It oozed into the china palette, her wide flat brush dipping in with haste to smear the canvas. Without thought or planning she dived in, covering a section with instinct driven strokes, the thick paint glistening with horrible reality. Like a bloody pool, the overladen area began to run, drips slipping down the white in horrible mockery, but she carried on, feeling the pain again. Anger and outrage filled her, like a cup under a running tap, overflowing over and over again, as she remembered the cramping sensation low in her belly and the vicious disembowelling sense of being utterly on her own in this. Her hand translated with slashing rips at the canvas, the helpless anguish at the unfairness of it, that awful sensation of having something wrenched away. She added another colour, oxygen-rich red, deeper and darker, to shadow the oval shape that had emerged. Grabbing another shade, rusty-tinged brown, she added that too and then another and another.

Finally, exhausted and angry, she pulled back to look at the painting. Except it wasn't a painting – it was nothing more than a childish, fury-fuelled daub that left her feeling shaky and shocked. Pure emotion and nothing else; no finesse, no style. It was a mess. She closed her eyes, her shoulders slumping. Numbness filled her limbs, heavy with the adrenaline hangover.

With shaky hands she laid down her brush and looked critically at the picture. It summed things up rather too well. A cruel parallel with her life. Utterly crap. It had been a terrible mistake coming out here. But she couldn't go back either.

With a loathing look at the painting, she left the studio.

As soon as she opened the kitchen door, the idiotic animal bounced around her legs with delight, her excitement translated in the feverish wag of her tail.

'Blimey, Dog, you'd think you'd been locked away for fifty years instead of overnight.'

The dog carried on weaving around her, as if to say *where've you been? I really, really, really missed you. It's so lovely to see you.*

'OK, OK, calm down.' Despite her gentle chiding, Ella's heart lifted, the furious explosive emotion somehow starting to dissipate. She opened the back door and the dog dived out, a blur of speed, careered around the garden like a lunatic, weed several times and then came charging back to nuzzle at Ella's legs.

'You're wet,' she said, brushing the dew that clung to the dog's coat. Tess's tail flapped furiously, beating Ella's legs as she wove round and round as if she just couldn't contain her sheer happiness.

Ella bent to stroke her head. 'You are daft,' she said with a rueful smile as the dog continued to dance around her.

'Starving, are you? No wonder I've got a rock star's welcome this morning. And listen to me. I'm talking to a dog.'

With sudden resolution, Ella pushed her shoulders back and gave herself a shake. 'Come on, then. Let's feed you. What do you fancy? Lovely smelly biscuits or lovely smelly biscuits?'

This almost felt normal, getting the biscuits out, filling the bowl, putting water in the other one.

'Honestly, calm down. I can't see what you're getting so excited about. I'm glad I'm not a dog.' She laughed as Tess almost knocked her over, jumping and nosing at the bowl as she tried to lower it, biscuits spilling over the side to rain and bounce all over the floor, which Tess thought was a great game.

Before she'd even made her coffee, the dog had inhaled the biscuits like a turbo-charged hoover and then started nosing around the floor sucking up the stray crumbs until her paw slipped on something on the floor. Ella frowned. That bloody card had a mind of its own.

With a clatter Tess gave the empty bowl another hopeful once-over with her tongue and then tilted her head, looking at Ella with a beseeching expression.

'That's your lot, Tess, and you know it.'

The dog gave a mournful sigh, still gazing at her with hopeful longing.

'Now I know what puppy dog eyes are ... and it's still a no from me.' She gave the dog another stroke on the head, the blue card still in her other hand. A shaft of sunlight slanted in through the French doors, warming her hand where she stroked the soft silky texture of the dog's short fur. It was rather hypnotic and she felt her breathing calm. After the earlier fierce burst of emotion she felt a little wrung out. Something drew her eyes to the words on the card. With a self-conscious glance around the room, which was completely crazy as there was no one there to see, she stepped outside and headed for the little stone bench in the garden.

Several bluebells had burst into flower overnight and the buds on the tree had unfurled into leaves. She studied the vivid blues. The rich deep colours stirred something in her brain.

Sinking down onto the stone bench, she looked around the gorgeous garden with its profusion of colour, light and shape. The bright morning sunshine touched her skin and something inside blossomed, that earlier pinching tension seeping away like a thief in the night taking its leave. It was rather lovely to be able to sit and daydream for a while. She closed her eyes and tilted her face upwards like a sunflower. An image drifted into her head and she let it settle, her mind's eye wandering across it, lightly touching here and there.

The sweet notes of a blackbird pierced the air and she opened her eyes, her heart thudding with sudden excitement.

With a sudden warning cry the bird on the tree opposite took flight as Ella jumped up.

She raced up both flights of stairs. There it was: Magda's box. She couldn't believe she hadn't thought of it before. Actually, yes she could. She never painted with watercolours – it hadn't occurred to her to use them, but maybe they were right for this. It certainly couldn't hurt to try.

Without any of her usual prevarication, she grabbed a sheet of cartridge paper and a selection of paints, oozing them hastily onto a dinner plate. Misty blue first. Her fingers tingled with impatience. She dived in, the colour bleeding into the paper.

The rest of the morning passed in a blur of colour, desire and emotion as the images began to appear. Seamless, the picture came together, layer by layer, the shadows beyond the trees hinting at secrets, the willowy branches redolent with the movement of dancers in the foreground and the dappled light trickling through behind.

At some point she was aware of Tess getting up, yawning and wandering away, her paws pitter-pattering down the wooden stairs. Later, she registered the birds under the eaves of the south side of the house cheeping furiously.

It was the searing pain cramping the muscle in the back of her shoulders that finally brought her back to earth and the hunger pangs that rattled her stomach. Standing and stretching to release the pain, she glanced at her watch. Bloody hell. Two o'clock. She'd been painting non-stop since this morning. The dog had long since abandoned her post and gone downstairs.

Ella forced herself to put the brush down, turn around and

walk five paces back. She stopped and steeling herself as if she were in a duel, she took a breath and turned.

Her heart almost stopped. It was perfect. Quite simply perfect. A sense of absolute satisfaction and wonder filled her. The secretive warmth of the trees, the glittering water, the shadowed trunks and the texture of the bark had all been captured to perfection. So much and so little. Her heart almost burst.

Giving into the growl of her stomach, she headed down to the kitchen to make herself a drink. A flash of mustard outside caught her eye as she stood drinking her coffee, feeling drained but happy and she raised a hand to wave to George. He looked a little stooped and stiff when he returned the wave. What had Devon said? George was lonely? Without thinking she opened the window.

'Hi George, would you like a coffee?'

Before she had time to regret her spur of the moment invitation, George was ensconced in the kitchen, Tess's head resting on his knee with a look of adoration on her face.

'Here you go, one cappuccino.' She placed the mug in front of him.

'That looks grand, love. So how are you finding life in the village? Quite different to what you're used to, I expect. Must be a bit of a relief after London.'

'A relief?' It was a funny way to put it, but he was right. She hadn't realised how much effort she'd put into keeping up a façade all the time. She might not like it here, but yes, it was a relief.

'I can't bear the place. Everyone's always in a hurry. No one ever talks to you.' His eyes twinkled. 'I can tell you're going to fit in just fine here.'

Ella had no idea how he'd come to that conclusion. Ready to deny it, she asked curiously, 'Why do you think that?' He clearly hadn't seen her dripping her way home yesterday.

She was pleased to see he looked a bit nonplussed. 'Well,' he blustered. 'Once you've settled, there's so much going on, you won't have a minute to call your own. The Spring Fayre's coming up and it's all hands on deck. I've got to put some posters up around the village. I've just had them from the printers. And a lovely banner.' His face brightened and he sat up as if he'd just had a light bulb moment. 'Next year you can design the posters, with you being an artist.'

Ella gave a tight polite smile. 'I don't think I'll be here then.'

'Course you will, Magda said so. Now, you've got to take this handsome hound out, so why don't we kill two birds with one stone and you can give me a hand with putting some of these posters up. And I'll round up a few chaps for the banner.'

He drained his cappuccino, leaving a milky moustache around his mouth. 'That was grand. Thank you very much. Now I'll just get my coat.' He beamed at her, his face wreathed in wrinkles as his faded eyes twinkled. 'Not often an old codger like me gets to escort a beautiful young lady.'

She had to turn away to hide the sudden sheen in her eyes. He really was rather sweet.

When she returned from a surprisingly brisk walk – George had twice the energy of most people half his age – it was very easy to slip back up to the studio and get some work done on her mice pictures, sneaking the occasional glance at her new painting. She was completely absorbed in inking in the colour of Cuthbert's bright red fez, of which he was inordinately proud, when her mobile buzzed into life.

'Hey, doll! How's it hanging?'

'Britta.' Ella tried to hold her surprise in check. Britta had always been Patrick's friend rather than hers.

'So you're still alive, then. Not atrophied yet.'

'I'm just about managing.' Ella tucked the phone under her ear. Giving Cuthbert a satisfied nod, she got up and wandered downstairs through to the kitchen where Tess dozed in the corner, one eye opening and shutting as if to double check she wasn't missing anything.

'With all that time on your hands I'd have thought you'd have rattled off another six of your little fluffy bunny books by now, babe.'

Ella frowned. She should be used to Britta's casual dismissal but this time it stung. She stared out of the kitchen window, her attention caught by a flurry of activity on the green. There was George with a couple of other men, two of them unfurling the large banner, which he'd been very pleased with, and another banging in a big fence post.

'I do put quite a lot of effort into them,' she quietly rebuked.

'Yeah, yeah, whatever. So are you bored out of your brains? What on earth do you do all day?'

'Well ...' Actually, the days were flying past.

'Want me to come and cheer you up?'

Ella almost dropped the phone.

'What? You come here?'

'No, babe,' Britta drawled. 'Send a hologram in my stead. Of course come there, you dumb broad. Everyone's going to the Saatchi reopening and I didn't get an invite.'

'Didn't get an invite?' She frowned, realising she was paying too much attention to the activity outside. How many men did it take to put up a banner? Oh dear, yes, it needed a design overhaul. That shade of yellow was horrible.

'Yes, me. Didn't get an invite to the Saatchi gig. I always get invited to everything.'

'Oh.'

'I pissed off Giles, the curator of that dumb Noodle in a Field installation. For crying out loud, it was unadulterated A1 audience porn. Crowd-pleasing crap.'

Britta here in the cottage. Ella's stomach clenched in sudden nerves. Was that a good idea?

'A quick break will do me the power of good. I can fill you in on all the latest goss including the lowdown on Patrick. Much as I think you're crazy burying yourself in the sticks, I think the treat him mean, keep him keen strategy is working.'

Ella's lips twisted in wry disbelief. When she'd left London, she hadn't had enough energy to plan a trip to the toilet, let alone a strategy. All she'd wanted to do was hide from view, lick her wounds and avoid having to do anything or make any decisions.

Tess opened both eyes, lifted her head and watched her with uncanny intensity, eyes zeroing in on her movements as if she was worried about Ella. It was funny how in tune the dog seemed to be with her, almost as if Tess could read her emotions. 'It's OK,' Ella murmured in reassurance. The dog blinked owlishly, yawned and rested her head back on her front paws.

'What?' asked Britta.

'Sorry, B, I was ... I was thinking out loud.' Britta would think she'd gone barking, talking to the dog or even thinking the dog understood her thoughts.

'Yeah, I think he's really missing you. Seems what they say about absence is paying off.'

'Oh.' Ella didn't know what to say. 'I've not heard from him.'

George was talking to someone else on the green now as he hung onto his end of the banner. Oh, hell, it was Devon. The heat of yesterday's embarrassment flooded over her again.

'Well, duh! Isn't that the whole point of being on a break?'

'What?' She prayed Devon wouldn't turn around and see her.

'That's the whole point, I said.'

'Oh, yes, I guess so.'

Patrick wasn't known for his patience but she had said she'd be in touch. She was surprised he'd managed to respect her wishes this long. Had he put Britta up to this?

'Shit. I've ... ' Devon had suddenly materialised at the bottom of the front garden. He gave her a wave. Damn, she couldn't pretend she hadn't seen him. 'I've just seen the time. I must go.'

'Go! Go where? Don't tell me you've got a hot date with a couple of cows, a few horses, a sheep and a pig.'

'An ... er ... appointment. Dentist.' That was it. 'Toothache. Bad toothache.'

'Off you pop, then. I'll look up some trains. Let you know when I can make it.'

'Right, fine.' Typical B, to assume that Ella would have no other plans.

'What's the name of the station in this one-horse place you're in?'

'Tring is the nearest station.' Ella was already in the hall, ready for the knock at the door.

'Tring? OMG, seriously. Sounds horribly quaint. Do they still have steam trains? Will it take six years to get there?'

'No, it's a commuter line from Euston. Quite a lot of people round here work in London. You'll be just fine. Believe it or not, they run pretty frequently.' Ella didn't understand why she needed to defend the place. 'Look, I'm going to be late. Text me when you're coming and I'll pick you up. Gotta run.'

Tess stared balefully at her. Ella pulled a face. 'So I'm a liar, sue me.' With a decisive click, she switched the phone off, shaking her head.

In the meantime, she had to face Devon. What on earth did he want? She yanked open the front door.

As usual he had that ruddy healthy outdoors glow about him and his unruly hair was well and truly windblown.

'Hi, I came to see if you were OK. I ... er ... felt a bit bad about leaving you yesterday. You seemed a bit ... '

She blushed, the tide of heat sweeping right down to her toes.

'I'm fine. Thank you.' What else was there to say? She'd made a complete fool of herself.

'I'm really sorry.'

She looked up at his sincere tone. 'For what? It's not like you pushed me in.'

'Well, for not being more sympathetic.' He shifted on the spot, his hands pushed deep into the pockets of his jeans.

She raised a candid eyebrow. 'For laughing, you mean.'

'Yeah. That.' He did look rather contrite. 'I shouldn't have laughed. I wasn't laughing at you, it was the situation, but it wasn't very nice of me. You were clearly upset and I should have . . . ' He shrugged helplessly.

It was quite endearing.

'Should have . . . ?'

'I don't know. Been more . . . ?' Again that little shrug. He was nothing if not honest.

Honesty won the day. In truth, perhaps she could have handed the whole situation with a little more dignity. She squeezed her eyes shut tight, trying to block out the memory. It didn't work. The words *toddler*, *temper* and *tantrum* all came to mind.

'Apart from the laughing,' she fixed him with a stern look, 'there wasn't much you could have done.' She paused, took a deep breath and then said in a rush, 'I didn't give you a chance. I'm sorry, too. It was just so embarrassing. I took it out on you when you were trying to help, sort of, and thank you for cleaning up Tess, and feeding her and wiping up after her.'

The dimple in his left cheek gave him away. She'd seen it before when he was trying not to smile.

'It was the least I could do. So no ill effects. No pond fever.'

'Is that even a thing?'

'Probably not,' he said gravely.

She nodded.

'Right then. I'll be off.'

'Right.'

They stood looking at each other.

'Right,' he said again. 'Bye.'

For a moment she was almost tempted to offer him a drink. Just to say thank you.

He turned to go.

'Bye.'

He turned back, the dimple loitering. 'I don't suppose you fancy going for another walk sometime? One that doesn't require water wings. There's a nice one up the Beacon, well away from any body of water.'

She smiled, she couldn't help herself. 'OK.'

Chapter Sixteen

Ella could have predicted how the visit was going to go when she picked Britta up at the station. Britta let out a startled bark of laughter. 'My God. A dodgem.'

'It gets me from A to B,' she replied, equably determined not to let Britta's comments get to her. 'And none of us have cars in London. This little Citroën is fine and pretty essential.'

'I know, but,' she looked pained, 'it's ugly, like a washing machine on wheels.'

With great show, Britta gathered up the folds of her trademark white culottes and elegantly slid into the passenger seat. Ella turned on the ignition and sent up a silent prayer that nothing was likely to transfer onto the pristine white of her clothes.

'Here we are. The cottage on the end.'

'Quaint,' said Britta, warily eying the street. 'Is this it?'

'This is it. Wilsgrave. The pub. The shop's down there and we passed the church on the way in.'

'I thought you were kidding about there not being anything

here. What the hell do you do all day? You must be going out of your mind with boredom.'

'It's not that bad. I've got lots of illustrations for the new book done. And I've started,' she paused, 'a new style of work.'

Britta's eyes gleamed with avarice. 'Ooh, you kept that quiet. I'm dying to see that.'

Ella swallowed, suddenly not sure that she wanted anyone to see her new painting.

What would Britta think of her shadowy abstract landscape? It wasn't edgy or urban, but hinted at secrets in the landscape, something hidden beneath the surface. Nature was beautiful but also cruel. Her hand crept to her stomach. Very cruel.

She led the way up the path, tension in her shoulders as she prepared herself for Britta's comments about the cottage.

'You've got mail.'

'What?'

'A parcel on the doorstep. Someone's trying to impress you.'

Ella frowned. Another navy blue box, like the others, perfectly tied with the silver-grey ribbon.

She snatched it up wondering who else Magda had got in on the act and what well-meaning gift was in there this time.

Unlocking the front door, Ella paused for a second, meaning to warn Britta, but it was too late, an excited Tess burst through the door, tail wagging, running backwards and forwards in animated delight, her whole body quivering with happiness.

'Stupid dog, I've only been gone for half an hour. Honestly, anyone would think you'd been locked up all day.'

Britta gaped at her. Ella bit her lip and smiled apologetically.

'Sorry, don't mind me. This is Tess ... the dog.'

Britta gave her an icy glare. 'I can see it's ... a dog. And since when have you had *a dog*?'

'She's not mine. I sort of inherited her with the cottage but don't worry, she's all right really, aren't you, you stupid animal.' Ella shook her head as Tess continued to bounce about like a lunatic.

'All right?' Britta's lip lifted in disdainful disbelief, bending to brush her hands down the white culottes now speckled with black hair.

'Sorry.' Ella grasped Tess's collar. 'Behave. Britta doesn't want you jumping all over her. Calm down, you daft thing.' She stroked Tess's silky ears.

Britta backed away and put her purple carpet-bag back down. Ella held on tight to the collar, feeling Tess start towards it. Knowing Britta it probably cost an absolute fortune and she'd go mad if it became covered in dog slobber.

Britta shot another unfriendly look at the dog and then lifted her head to take a good look around the tiny hall. 'Well, this is cottagey.' Her foot tapped on the stone flag floors. 'Real as well.'

'Let me just shut Tess in the kitchen and I'll show you round. Not that there's much to see.'

Britta wrinkled her nose. 'Shouldn't dogs live outside? In kennels? It can't be very hygienic having one in the kitchen.'

Ella thought of the recent cold and misty mornings. Tess wouldn't like being outside at all. 'No, she's very good,' she lied. Britta didn't need to know about rubbish bins being savaged, being pitched head first into the canal, irate fishermen or early morning presents on the kitchen floor.

As soon as Ella shut the door, after dumping the latest parcel on the table, Tess began to whine and scratch at the wood. She wasn't used to being locked in during the day. Ella gave the door a worried glance. It wasn't for long. Britta would soon get used to her.

The tour didn't take long and she saved the best til last.

'What do you think?' asked Ella letting Britta enter the room ahead of her. Britta stood and considered, her head tilted as she paced the length of the room underneath the pitch of the roof. At last she nodded, her face non-committal. 'Big windows. Good light. Plenty of space. Not bad.'

'Not bad?' Ella echoed, feeling as if Britta had stuck an unnecessarily large pin in her balloon. She looked around the room, seeing it with fresh eyes. Even on a grey, dank day like today, light flooded in through three large skylights, which were bare of blinds or curtains so that nothing encroached to stop maximum light entering. Her feet had grown accustomed to the grooves and dips in the marked and scratched wooden floorboards which diluted the impact of the stark white of the walls and she knew to avoid the splintery board which needed some sanding so that it wouldn't catch at her socks when she got down from the high stool at the draughtsman's table. Apart from a faded blue sofa bed, piled with white and grey cushions which added colour and comfort to the simplicity of the room, there was nothing else in here. It was the perfect studio.

Britta shrugged. 'It's OK. Have you seen Xander's studio? You'd struggle to do any kind of serious installation in here. Unless you were filming. Although can you imagine how much it would cost to get a crew out here? Remember how much that video installation cost, the one that Bryce did. I think the location fees for a week alone were more than a grand.'

'I'm not aiming to do an installation,' said Ella, a little shortly. 'This is perfect for my work.'

Britta pulled a conciliatory face which Ella knew from experience heralded anything but.

'Exactly. Perfect. That's shorthand for settling. You don't want perfect. You want to be challenging. Settling is ... settling for what? You're limiting your horizons.' She pursed her mouth before bursting out. 'Seriously, Ella, what are you playing at. You shouldn't be messing around with this stuff.' She tossed a contemptuous arm towards the draughtboard and the makeshift washing line to which Ella had pegged pictures of Cuthbert and Englebert.

Ella bit back her words. Her fingers stiffened into angry fists.

'Excuse me ... ' Her heart beat a little faster; she didn't like confrontation. 'That's my work you're talking about. It might not be to your taste but ... '

'Ella, babes. Taste doesn't come into it. You're talented. That stuff's,' she lifted a shoulder in stylish dismissal, 'beneath you. You can do so much better than these silly little illustrations.'

If Britta thought that a backhanded compliment was going to take the sting out of her words, she had another think coming.

Ella straightened.

'Actually, I find that quite offensive. Plenty of people like my books. Just because something is popular doesn't mean it's no good.'

Britta pursed her lips and gazed away out of the window.

Ella was suddenly glad she'd tucked her new painting behind the stack of blank canvasses and the red monstrosity was under her bed. She didn't want to know what Britta would have made of the misty blues and greens of her fairytale glade at the edge of the water ringed by her fanciful tree dancers.

'Now this is more like it.' Britta advanced to the corner of the room, a tiny almost forgotten alcove under the dormer window. 'This I like.'

Ella frowned. What the hell was she on about? She watched Britta stalk into the corner with stately grace, like a tiger circling its prey. With a whirl she rounded on Ella.

'You beauty! This is brilliant, babes.'

Ella followed her to look down at the coil of discarded barbed wire and dead tulip petals, some of which hung from the bared points of the wire.

'This is so interesting.' Brita put a hand on her right breast, reminding Ella of a Roman emperor making some important declaration, and said, 'This speaks to me.' Her eyes flashed with enthusiasm and fervour. 'Absolutely fan-fucking-tastic. Patrick will bite your hand off. I can see this as the centrepiece in the gallery.'

Ella stared at her. Solemnly she tugged at her lips with her teeth. She didn't dare say a word or even open her mouth. She swallowed hard.

'Blood on a wire.' Britta declared as she circled the coil of barbed wire in a long loping mince which teamed with the white knee socks and flared culottes suddenly struck Ella as utterly ridiculous. She stared at the ribbed socks, which were more than ridiculous. Britta was a grown woman. Ella pinched her lips together even harder, doing her best to maintain an impassive expression. It was very hard.

'Babes, I thought you were mad coming out here but this … this is genius. I knew you could do it.' Her ice blue eyes softened as their gaze shifted from the mess on the floor to Ella's face with a slightly patronising smile.

Ella still couldn't say anything.

'I need the loo.' With that she bolted and fled down the stairs to lock herself in her bathroom where she sat on the edge of the bath trying to decide whether to be angry with Britta's rudeness or amused by her pretentiousness. She let out a snort worthy of a pig in truffle heaven. Laughter bubbled up. She sniggered and then the giggles burbled out, she couldn't stop them. Tears streaked down her face, but she could barely lift her hand to wipe them away as she clutched her stomach which ached from laughing so much.

Her shoulders shook. She needed to get a grip. The wire and flowers had been dumped in the corner after she'd come back from the church after dancing with Devon. Putting her hands over her mouth she tried to contain herself but every time she thought she'd calmed down, another gale of laughter would surprise her. What would Devon make of it? She pressed her lips together, screwing up her eyes. It was too ridiculous for words.

After splashing cold water on her face and taking lots of deep breaths as well as pulling admonishing faces at herself in the mirror, she finally pulled herself together. Britta was nuts. Once again she felt a million miles away from her old life but this time it didn't feel quite as bad. She no longer felt exiled.

How could anyone think that was art? But with a sudden forlorn insight, she thought of all the galleries and exhibitions she'd been to over the years. What was art? Maybe you could palm 'Blood on a Wire' off to an audience but if it didn't mean anything to her, then it was cheating. It wasn't real. Not in the way her new painting was. The secret world she'd tried to capture felt real, a glimpse of an alternate nature. Painting it felt right. As pretentious as it sounded, it satisfied something inside her soul, even though it would never garner artistic acclaim.

Straightening her shoulders, she left the bathroom and guiltily started as she heard Tess whine downstairs.

'Britta, fancy a drink?' she called up the stairs, unable to go back into the studio.

When everyone's head in the pub turned at the exotic vision of Britta in flowing white palazzo pants, a long white shirt and yards of white chiffon wrapped around her neck and trailing down the length of her body, Ella tried hard to ignore their avid gazes. Britta looked exotic anywhere.

'You sit down and I'll go get some drinks.'

Leaving Britta at the table in the corner slightly tucked out of the line of sight of the row of regulars lined up at the bar, she went up to order.

'Hi, can I have a white wine and a gin and lime, please?'

'Coming right up. What sort of wine?'

'What have you got?' asked Ella as Greta pushed over a menu.

'And I've just added a French Viognier which isn't on there yet. And do you want fresh lime in the gin?'

That would please Britta no end. Ella nodded. 'Yes, that would be great and I'll try the Viognier.'

'Good choice.' Greta grinned. 'Good job on the flowers by the way. Magda will be pleased you kept the side up.'

'Really?'

'Oh yes, the flower arranging thing is very competitive. Rather you than me.' Greta worked with easy competence, gracefully swiping glasses from the overhead shelves, sliding the wine from the fridge and with an easy twist yanked out the cork. 'Got roped into the salsa dancing yet?'

'No.'

Greta grinned. 'You will be.'

Ella smiled politely.

'Here you go, one gimlet.'

'Thanks.' Ella's eyes widened giving away her surprise.

'We're not complete philistines out here, you know,' admonished Greta with a sharp look. 'We've just opted for a better quality of life. You'll learn,' she added with an almost pitying smile.

Wrong-footed, Ella offered her a vague nod as she paid half the price she would have done for the same drinks in London.

'So, babes.'

Ella didn't like the sudden sharpening of Britta's features, as if they were being schooled to go into attack, especially not when she took what looked like a steadying sip of her drink. 'Whoa! Fan my little tush.'

Britta's unexpectedly enthusiastic response allowed her to breathe more easily.

'This is bloody marvellous. The good landlady knows her onions. I'm impressed.' Britta examined her glass and looked towards the bar, where Greta gave them both a mocking salute. Ella lifted her glass in a slight toast. Despite Greta's prickliness she rather liked her combative attitude. You knew exactly where you were with her.

The respite was brief.

'About you and Patrick, come on, you've punished him enough with this break business. Stop pratting about with the "I vant to be alone" crap. I'm no young romantic but you two, come on, you guys fit. The smart art team. Patrella.' With a sudden lightbulb bing moment, she sat up. 'You should so name a gallery that. I can see it now. Somewhere in Hackney, lots of brick walls, fractured lighting and the last word in installation art. A vision of your combined talents. The two of you merged. The ultimate creation.'

At this, Ella looked down into her glass. Britta's words couldn't have been more ill-chosen. They *had* created something together. Far greater than a stupid art gallery, and Patrick didn't want it. Her heart twisted at the utter irony of it all. A couple of months ago she'd have been giddy and excited at the idea of a new gallery linking their names.

'Hello – come in Ella.'

She swallowed and focused back on Britta. 'Can we just not talk about this, please?'

'That's the problem. You won't talk about it. Not to me. Lord knows not to Patrick. Poor guy, he doesn't understand. What went wrong? One minute everything was hunky dory, I saw you that night at Gallery 99, the next thing I know you've packed up and moved out here.'

Which just showed what a brave face she'd managed to put on while dying inside.

'I just need time to think about things.'

'He wants you back, you know.'

With sudden insight Ella looked at her friend across the table. 'Did he put you up to this?'

Britta stilled, her eyes unable to quite meet Ella's.

It all made sense. Britta's uncharacteristic desire to visit.

Ella sighed and then almost sagged with relief at the sight of frantic waving through the window.

Bets burst through the door, her happy smile at a lower wattage than normal. 'Ella! Hi. How are you? Crikey, what a day, I'm dying for a drink and I brought old Grumpy Git with me.' She tossed her head of curls over her shoulder towards Devon bringing up the rear.

'Hi, Ella.' Devon shook off his coat.

'Devon, Bets, this is my friend Britta. She's come up from London for a visit.'

'Hi, Devon.' Britta's voice appeared to have dropped several octaves and had acquired a chocolate depth that Ella had never heard before. Oh Lord, it wouldn't have occurred to her in a million years that Devon might be Britta's type. She normally favoured emaciated artists whose facial hair outweighed their bodyweight and who rarely ever took their hats off. With his lush almost too long curls and broad shoulders, Devon made Britta's previous conquests look like the living dead. With incredulous disbelief, Ella watched Britta.

Thankfully Devon seemed oblivious, but then he'd never met Britta before and had no idea that this was a far cry from her usual cultivated languid, indifferent air.

'Nice to meet you.' He stood awkwardly in front of them.

'Who wants a drink?' asked Bets, giving Britta a cheery

smile to which the other girl responded with a cool nod. 'After today, I need a very large one.' She shot Devon a disparaging glance.

'Just got one, thanks.' As always with Bets, Ella felt as if a whirlwind had just passed by. Seconds later, Bets had abandoned her coat on top of one of the bar stools at their table and sailed off to the bar, cheerily hailing people as she went. A bit too cheerily. There was an almost frantic edge to her voice.

Devon smiled fondly after her and shook his head.

'Do you mind if we join you?' Despite the fact that it was a done deal, Ella liked that he bothered to ask. She gave him a rueful smile. 'No, it's fine. Looks as if Bets has already decided.'

His face dropped. 'She's a bit disappointed. Jack cancelled at the last minute. He was due home this weekend.'

'That's a shame.' Bets had done nothing but talk about him the other morning as they did their usual walk.

'So what do you do, Devon?'

'I'm a vet.'

'Oh! How interesting,' lied Britta. 'Lovely. Gosh, it must be so complicated. Knowing the insides of all those different animals. If Damien Hirst hadn't got there first, you might have just given me an idea for an installation. It must be so fascinating dealing with them all day.'

Ella thought of poor Tess who'd been shut in the kitchen since Britta's arrival in order to protect the purity of all those white clothes. Britta's fascination had been in short order then.

'Every day is different, especially compared to when I was in London.'

'London? Where were you?'

'Islington.'

'Do you know the Green Bean bar?' Britta almost batted her eyelashes at the mention of London. 'Ella, they make the most amazing decaffeinated coffee. It's *the* place to go for brunch at the moment.'

'What happened to Frankinelli's?' asked Ella.

'That's so last year, darling. Honestly, you are so out of date already.' She shook her head and smiled conspiratorially at Devon. 'So will you be going to back to London?'

'Not sure.' The familiar bleakness descended on his face but Britta missed it.

Ella wished she could have clued Britta in to spare Devon the obvious pain that her subtle probing dredged up.

'I think you should. I can't imagine there's a lot round here to entertain a man like you. It must be quite limiting.'

Ella imagined that life with Marina must have been more than entertaining and wondered if maybe he'd had enough of that. Like her, he was looking for a period of respite.

Devon shrugged. 'I've been quite busy running the practice for Dad.'

'And trying to update some of his systems,' added Bets as she came up behind him and handed over his pint of beer. 'Poor Geoffrey isn't going to be able to find a thing when he comes back.'

Devon laughed. 'But it's all right, because you'll be there to find it for him.' He shook his head. 'Bets has taken complete advantage of me being here and has introduced all sorts of systems and new software while Dad's not looking.'

'You know they've improved things, so don't try and

pretend they haven't.' Bets defended herself, waving her hand airily at him. 'Admit it, you even said how good the new stock management system is. You're not a complete luddite.'

'No, technology is great but I'd rather spend my time helping animate objects that respond. Stock control leaves me cold but new equipment – that would be brilliant.'

'You're so right,' chipped in Britta, her eyes widening in appreciation. 'Personally I refuse to have any sort of relationship with anything that contains a chip. I can't bear it that all these corporate conglomerates are introducing all these devices, which are all immediately obsolete the minute they come out, and are sapping our nation's long history of cultural brilliance and innate creativity.' She turned to Devon. 'You don't rely on a silly computer to diagnose what's wrong with a suffering animal. I'm sure it's intuition and gut feel. You're in tune with your world. In your own way, you are an artist.'

She grabbed one of his hands and held it up. 'Yes, these hands that tend to the animals are the hands of an artist. I can see it.'

'He's not flipping Mother Teresa.' Bets rolled her eyes and smirked at Ella.

Ella smiled back. Devon looked slightly uncomfortable as Britta traced her pale long fingers across his palm and up to the broad tips of his fingers. Ella shifted in her chair, wishing Britta would let go. It was all wrong. She didn't know him. He was a kind man, too kind to snatch his hand away, but Britta was barking up the wrong tree with the artist tack.

His hands she knew were slightly rough, with a callous on the third finger of his right hand, possibly because of the way he held his pen. She'd seen him writing, his biro clamped oddly between those two middle fingers. From seeing him running, she knew the length of his strides came from long well-muscled legs and from walking next to him, she knew he was tall and broad.

Despite their rocky start, he was a nice man. A very nice man. Warmth bloomed in her cheeks as she watched him. When he smiled, tiny lines crinkled around his eyes. Too nice for Britta. Far too nice, in fact. Ella watched as Devon responded to something Britta said with a bark of laughter. She wanted to wade in and protect him, which was ridiculous. He was a grown man, but she knew his heart had been left bruised by Marina and Britta didn't.

They left the pub crossing the road to the cottage. Britta gleaming like a ghost in the dark.

Tess, of course, was delighted to see them, and leapt about with enthusiastic affection bordering on the hysterical.

'Good God, what's wrong with it?' asked Britta doing her best to fend off Tess's flypasts and keep the black fur from her trousers. 'Is it having a fit or something?'

'No,' Ella hid her face, smiling at Britta's stick insect antics, 'it's just her way of making sure we know how pleased she is to see us and that we really shouldn't ever leave her again.' She stroked Tess's head, trying to contain her and keep her away. 'Should we? You are daft.' She gave the dog's head another ruffle before turning back to Britta. 'She'll calm down in a minute. Do you want a coffee?'

'Lord, yes. With the exception of the rather divine Devon and surprisingly well made gimlets, it was a touch tedious in that place. I don't how you do it. That is what passes for civilised entertainment round here?' She sniffed. 'Last Friday we, the gang,' she shot Ella a look, which made it clear that Patrick had been there too, 'went to a brilliant opening at Hoxton Arches, that fabulous gallery under the railway arches, to see a show entitled Retrospective of Perspex, which was quite good and they had sublime canapes and red wine served in little pewter buckets. Then we decided to try out that hot Mexican place down by the old Hackney Empire, except it was rammed, honestly no tables before eleven, so we ended up in Bar Esmerelda, which is still a dive.'

Ella frowned, suddenly remembering all those nights, darting from here to there in a constant hunt looking for the social equivalent of a pot of gold, most of which was spent travelling either on the Tube or some godforsaken bus route.

'That's what you're missing out on, here.' Britta sighed. 'Although Devon can entertain me any time. I bet under that outdoorsy big man jumper there's quite a body.'

Ella's mouth tightened. The thought of Devon naked brought a sudden flush to her cheeks.

'Coffee,' she said decisively and marched into the kitchen.

Britta trailed after her. 'Aren't you going to open this baby?' She tapped her glossy nails on the parcel which Ella had forgotten all about.

Ella hesitated, unwilling to share the magical whimsy of one of Magda's gifts.

'Secret admirer?' asked Britta, prodding the box, openly curious now, tugging at the ribbon. 'Shall I open it for you?'

Ella wanted to snatch it away but instead, she eased it out of Britta's hands and undid the ribbon.

To lose yourself in the dance
is to live the dance of life
Dance on and free your heart.

'What does that mean?' Britta tilted her head, considering the words.

'It doesn't mean anything. My godmother is quite the spiritual type.' Ella didn't even want to begin explaining that Magda had decided she was the descendant of a witch.

Britta cast the blue note aside and pushed into the tissue paper. 'Holy Moly, call the fashion police!' She waved a strappy red satin-covered shoe with a stacked heel at Ella. 'Heinous shoe crime. And look,' with horror she pointed to the diamante trim across the ankle strap. 'She bought you these?' Incredulity stretched her voice out to a Minnie Mouse pitch. 'What the hell are they?'

They were dancing shoes, Latin dancing shoes – and the exact pair she'd hankered after when she was fifteen. Magda had remembered all this time later. Yes, they were naff, loud, vulgar and ... perfect for dancing.

Ella shrugged and rescued the shoe and box, putting the lid firmly back on and stuffing the box on the seat of one of the chairs under the table.

Ella made two coffees and Britta took a suspicious sip before saying,

'Thank fuck you have decent coffee.'

Britta settled into one of the kitchen chairs, crossing her legs and sitting up straight.

Ella looked at her watch. 'I need to take the dog out in a minute.'

'God, what a fag. Do you have to do that every night?'

She shrugged. 'You get used to it.' And she rather enjoyed the solitude of that last walk of the day. Tess pattering at her feet, the stars in the huge open sky. It always grounded her. Reminded her she was part of something so much bigger.

'Don't you find it a bit creepy?' asked Britta, casting a suspicious glance towards Tess watching them from her bed. She'd already collected her lead from the hall table and had it in her mouth.

'No, to be honest. It's quite comforting having another...' Ella laughed, 'I was going to say person, but then it is like having someone else around. I quite like it now.'

'How on earth do you cope? It's worse than having a child.' Britta shuddered.

'Do you think you might have children one day?' The question just popped out of Ella's mouth before she could stop it. Trying to look guileless she traced a knot in the wood on the table.

Britta took in a sharp breath. 'No.'

'Really?' Ella asked. How could Britta be so certain and decided?

'Kids don't do it for me. Commitment. Homes. Routine. Being tied down. Can't think of anything worse.'

All the things that scared Patrick.

'So were you serious in the pub about staying for the whole weekend?'

Britta gave a calculating smile. 'Only if Devon the hottie was on the cards. I could spend a bit of time with him. But seriously babes, no!'

'I think he might be on call this weekend,' Ella lied, knowing full well that on Sunday he was picking her up to take the dogs to Ivinghoe Beacon for a walk. 'You could come for a walk with me and Bets.'

'You have to be joking. Far too bloody Pollyanna. She would drive me insane with her pinky perky ways.'

A wave of shame rolled over Ella making her snap, 'She's all right. She's been very kind.'

'Oooh! Kind, eh?' Britta taunted.

Heat burned in Ella's face. 'Well, she has.'

Britta rolled her eyes. 'Ella, babes. You need to get back to the city. Seriously, the girl has not got a sophisticated bone in her body.'

She suddenly gripped Ella's arm, her blue eyes intent and almost frantic. 'No disrespect but . . . you're letting yourself go a bit. Going native. I tell you, it's not pretty. Your hair, those jeans, and I saw *trainers* in the hall. Make it up with Patrick. Come home. You could even, if you had to, kip on my sofa for a few days while you sort yourself.'

A few weeks ago, she'd have packed her bags and boarded the next train without a backward glance, but now she sat silently for a moment, rigid tension making her limbs stiff and awkward. She looked at Britta, the ice-white hair and the floaty scarves, and thought she looked just like bloody Ophelia or the Lady of Shallot. Too studied. Too false.

It was as if she were stuck between two worlds, neither of which had a place for her.

Tess yawned, stood up and shook herself, rattling the choker on the lead.

'I think someone's dropping a hint. I ought to take her out.'

Although it was tempting to take the cowardly way out, Ella couldn't bring herself to do that. 'And I think you're being very rude about Bets – she might not be to your taste but she's not done you any harm and she's really helped me.'

Ella stomped along at a furious pace. Shame and anger burned together. It was as if someone had taken away blinkers. She almost winced. Had she really been that pretentious?

She screwed up her eyes, acknowledging her guilt in that department. Yes, she had. Just like that. Art for Art's sake. The 10cc lyrics ran through her head mocking her. Oh, yes. Definitely Art for Art's sake. A memory surfaced: she and Britta at a small niche gallery opening gushing about a white basket of nuts painted black with a red plastic fish on the top. What the hell had that been about?

She couldn't even claim that it was a one-off. And then there was the way they treated other people. One of their friends had ditched his new girlfriend when Britta had berated him long and hard about being seen with someone without an ounce of style or originality, because the poor girl had worn a branded T-shirt. Patrick had joined in and Ella hadn't said a word in her defence. Just like she hadn't said a word about how much she loved her new red shoes.

Ella completed her usual nightly route but rather than turn at the edge of the green to return home as she always did, she carried on with a second circuit, reluctant to return. Her earlier furious burst of energy had left her and she dragged her feet with sluggish steps, a sense of discontent dogging her. Her centre of gravity had shifted and suddenly she wasn't sure of her bearings any more.

Tilting her head back as far as it would go, she looked up

at the stars. There were thousands of them, like pinpricks piercing a black veil. Her neck ached as she considered the hugeness of the sky. Even when she circled her head, she could see only a tiny part of the panorama spread out above.

Funny, those same stars could be observed from the London pavements and she'd never seen them properly. Had city life, like light pollution, prevented her from seeing what was in plain view all the time? Was going back to London really what she wanted? Suddenly she wasn't so sure.

Chapter Seventeen

Watching the brindle pointer bounce up the lane with Tess in tow, Devon felt the guilt loosen. This was the first time he'd been out with Dexter for a decent walk all week. Quick circuits of the park didn't count. He was a vet, for Christ's sake, he knew how important it was to exercise a dog this size.

He welcomed the earthy tang of the fresh air with its sharp breeze assaulting his senses and the lighter floral scent of Ella by his side. She seemed subdued today, thoughtful rather than cross or resentful. They'd both lapsed into silence on the short car journey here and she seemed quite happy not to talk.

Until he'd started the steep climb up the Chiltern hills towards the Beacon high above the village of Ivinghoe, he hadn't realised how much he needed this to scour out the fug of the week. That last trip into London had cost him dear, tempting him back to the edge of depression. The size of the debt hanging over him seemed insurmountable, dogging his waking thoughts for the last few days. Not having a run for a while hadn't helped either. Running had become essential.

Exercise had clearly paid off for Tess; the black Lab was

looking so much slimmer as she trotted up the chalk strewn path ahead. Ella looked brighter and healthier too, a touch of roses in her cheeks compared to her sallow complexion the first few times he'd seen her, although something wasn't right about her this morning. Too much like how she'd been when she'd first arrived, shuttered and reluctant to let her real self out.

Maybe his own blackness made him aware of hers today? Her face, shuttered like a building with the windows firmly boarded up, gave nothing away.

'Was it nice seeing your friend?'

She shrugged.

'Are you OK?' The words came out a little blunter than he'd meant them to and she turned and stared at him, stopping on the incline. 'Sorry, you just seem ... '

Indecision warred on her face and when he thought she'd ignored the question, her mouth firmed and she started to walk again, stepping over the uneven tussocks of grass dotting the area like a mogul field. Then she stopped, let out another of her heavy sighs, and to his surprise began to talk in a low unemotional voice.

'Seeing Britta brought everything back. I thought I wanted to go back to London when Magda gets back, but now I'm even more confused. I don't know where I belong or what I want any more.' Her eyes moved across the horizon. Despair, bleak and anguished, filled her face as she looked ahead of him towards Ivinghoe Beacon. 'I do know I've been an idiot.' In a quieter voice, she added, 'About so many things.'

'Welcome to the club,' he said touching her arm, with a self-deprecating smile. He could take the prize on idiocy.

'Idiots Anonymous. The first step is recognising you've been an idiot. Hi, my name is Devon.'

She smiled although it didn't quite meet her eyes.

'Hi, my name is Ella.'

'Want to talk about it, Ella? When did you first realise what an idiot you'd been?'

A range of expressions crossed her face as if she were trying to pick out her reference point, where the best place was to start.

'I'm not sure about the first time,' she pulled a face, 'it's been creeping up on me but this weekend with Britta ...' She raised her hands, 'it didn't go well. Although I'm not sure she realised.'

'Ah, yes. Interesting character.' He felt he was being super circumspect.

'I've known her for years. She's Patrick's friend, really,' Ella said the words softly and to his relief, she clearly hadn't taken offence. 'But ... she's kind of symbolic of everything that went wrong.' She stopped abruptly and looked appalled. 'I've been a complete ... idiot. And – this sounds pretentious, but – not true to myself, not true to what I really, deep down believed in and I don't mean things about art and style and taste, which were all we ever talked about. I mean important things, about values, how we live our lives, family, love.'

'It doesn't sound pretentious; it sounds as if you need to let your real self out,' he said, suddenly realising that was what he'd seen about her from the start. Someone hiding in there.

Ella frowned. 'I realised I was every bit as bad as Britta. I've been too scared of being laughed at ... by God knows who ... to be myself. To have a single original thought of my own; I was too reliant on what "they" thought. And half the time I don't even know who "they" are.' She let out a bark of mirthless laughter. 'Do you know what the crunch point was? When she told me I could do *so much* better than my mice. For years I've been outwardly agreeing with people like Patrick and Britta when they say those drawings aren't real art, but do you know what?' Her face filled with indignation, slightly red as she puffed up like an irate pigeon. 'There's a little piece of me in them, in each of them. Those characters, Cuthbert and Englebert, they're like my ba—' she faltered, 'they're mine.'

'Those drawings looked pretty skilful to me. So what *is* art?'

She turned to him, her expression sceptical.

'Seriously, how do you define *proper* art?'

'It's ... it's ... ' She glared at him. 'You wouldn't understand.'

'I don't need to understand. If you want my opinion, a lot of what I see is a load of bollocks. Messy beds. A load of blue carrier bags.' He couldn't even bring himself to mention dead animals which he found wrong on so many levels. 'But you must understand all that. What does art mean to you?'

The sudden confusion on her face was really rather cute. She considered the question for a minute, her breath even again as if she'd walked herself into her stride. 'The expression of emotion through artistic medium that has an impact on another person, a shared ... experience.'

Devon understood that. 'Don't you enjoy drawing the mice? They looked like a lot of fun.'

A range of emotions ran across her face and she sighed, her mouth curving into a secretive smile which grew as if with dawning awareness. 'Actually, they're coming a lot easier.' An unexpected glow of satisfaction lit her face. Everything softened like a filter over a camera. Her cheeks filled out, a dimple appeared and her mouth ... he shelved that thought quickly.

'This last few weeks I've really enjoyed working on them. It's like someone's ... ' she shot him a sudden, unexpected mischievous look, 'to be artisty about it, unlocked a treasure chest of new ideas.'

She lapsed into thought, her teeth worrying at her lip. 'When I first started drawing them, it was so easy. I didn't even have to think about it. Then after a while, it got hard.' With a slight start, she tilted her head. 'Now it's easy again.' Her smile held a touch of the eureka moment, as if it hadn't occurred to her before.

'Your books bring happiness to lots of people.'

'I don't know about lots.'

'Well, I don't know about your book sales but the mice themselves are certainly very popular. They're everywhere.'

She frowned. 'What do you mean?'

'The merchandise.' At the posh stationers that Marina liked to drag him to, the shelves had been full of pencil cases, glasses cases, bags, rulers, pens and pencils featuring the cheeky antics of Cuthbert and his brothers. 'Both Bets' sister's kids have Cuthbert pencil cases, rulers and I'm sure I saw a pair of wellies with them on.'

'Are you sure? I know I signed a merchandise thingy but Patrick said it wasn't worth very much.'

'Well, someone's making some money.'

'I'm not sure who.' Her face sank back into a gloomy

expression and he found himself wanting to touch her face, lift the corners of her downturned mouth and take away the residual sadness etched there. Did his face look like that, lined with the weight of misery?

'I know that feeling.' He gave her a half-hearted smile, forcing the muscles to work a bit harder. Maybe if he smiled a bit more, it might encourage her to.

'I thought vets earned a fortune.' Her eyebrow quirked in question. 'Everyone complains about vets' bills.'

'Yeah, they don't know how much it costs to run a veterinary practice. We're running a tiny hospital with all the same sort of medical overheads. Drugs, oxygen, anaesthetics, plus the staff to manage all that.'

'Ouch, no wonder you have to do so much locum work. Have you resolved anything with ... with Marina?'

He snorted, 'Let's just say hell hath no fury like a woman denied her exchange of contract.' He tried to avoid bad-mouthing Marina to other people but frustration got the better of him today. 'I understand why she's desperate, but I can't conjure up money I don't have.' He pushed a hand through his already wind-blown hair. 'The TV production company is getting rather twitchy.'

'What's it got to do with them?' He couldn't help but smile as Ella's voice peaked with indignation on his behalf.

'The TV series is filmed in her consulting rooms, which are in the basement of our house. We knocked through to accommodate the production crew and equipment. Marina says they need to know that they've got a secure location for filming for the next series. Apparently if I don't sell my half to her, her career could be hanging in the balance. But if I sell, the negative equity situation means I'll owe her nearly twenty grand. I've an appointment with my bank in a couple of weeks. I'm praying that with the additional work I've been doing, they'll give me a loan.'

'What about your job here?'

'I got conned into it. Dad had a health scare. I said I'd stay to cover for him for a few weeks and suddenly he's talking about needing more time to recuperate. Which is bollocks. I know what he's doing.'

His vehemence drew a startled frown from Ella.

'I'm a thirty-two-year-old man. I don't need my parents rescuing me.'

'I . . . ' She lifted her hands in mute surrender but it was like a cork had been popped and it all came spilling out.

'I don't want anyone rescuing me. I'm quite capable of sorting myself out. It drives me crazy that everyone wants some kind of input. Bets trying to rehabilitate me, like I'm some drug dependent crackhead who needs to be weaned off his addiction, because she thinks I'm hung up on my ex and that I'll find redemption by becoming the vet with a heart of gold. Dad's protracted recuperation. He's training for a marathon; how does that make him too ill to work? And Mum trying to save me from boredom by finding me things to do all the time. I don't need any of them. I just want to draw a line and get on with my life.'

'Me too.' Her quiet words silenced his rant.

The anger and resentment simmering inside him whistled out like a slow puncture as he paused and looked around him, sneaking extra glances at her profile as they marched in tandem up the steep gradient. His irate words seemed a bit silly now in comparison to her quiet, calm acceptance, but he didn't need or want any help.

Any further conversation died as they focused on reaching the triangulation point topping the Beacon. They had the hilltop to themselves and both of them naturally gravitated to the stone-built platform with its map of the ancient Ridgeway on top. Leaning against it they contemplated the view spread out before them, stretching away to the distant horizon.

'On a clear day, you can see the spires of Oxford from here.' Despite this fact, he'd never actually seen them himself. Perhaps you also needed binoculars.

She didn't say anything but conversation seemed superfluous. It was quiet, apart from the buzz of two gliders circling and vying for the wind in the sky above them.

His eyes scanned the view, picking out local landmarks: the Pitstone Windmill, Grim's Dyke, the Whipsnade Lion. Despite being away for so long, it all seemed so familiar, as if he'd never been away. Taking a deep breath, he sighed. Maybe he had missed this. Maybe it was good to be home. He glanced over to Ella and spotted a single tear running down her face. Her throat convulsed but she remained ramrod straight, as if refusing to acknowledge it. Not wanting to intrude, he diplomatically turned away to study the contours of the Dunstable Downs where more gliders swung and dipped with the thermals.

'Actually, I lied earlier – the crunch point wasn't with Britta at all.' Her sudden words, almost lost on the wind that battered the hill, were laden with sorrow. 'It ... came when I was in London. That's when everything broke.' She lifted her chin higher. 'I came out here to try and work things through. Find a way to go back. A way to go back to my life with Patrick and all that it is, but I can't go back.' Another tear slipped down her face. 'There's nowhere to go back to.'

She remained still, not turning towards him. Remembering the brief touch of comfort she offered him in the pub, he wove his fingers between hers and gave them a squeeze. Somehow he knew she didn't want him to talk. He recognised that point where the dam burst. It didn't matter who he was, he just happened to be there when the water came flooding out.

'I found out I was pregnant. Not planned.' Her voice held cynical heaviness.

He stilled; that wasn't what he was expecting at all. What the hell did you say to that?

'Definitely not planned. Patrick was even more shocked than I was.' Ella turned her head, giving him a bleak twisted smile, before turning back to the vista before them. 'I figured that at our age it was probably the next step. I hadn't given the children thing a lot of thought, I just assumed that it would happen one day.

'One day turned up out of the blue. Completely out of the blue, but the minute I thought I might be, God, I was so excited. Funny – I was on my way to work, grabbed my usual mochaccino, took one sip and thought I'd throw up, which was really weird. I've been drinking them every morning for the last five years. You don't suddenly go off something without a very good reason.'

A wistful expression lit her face. 'I couldn't quite believe it, because it wasn't planned. I didn't tell anyone, just in case I was wrong. In case it tempted providence. I remember going to buy the testing kit.' She held up a hand. 'I was shaking like a leaf when I opened the packaging.'

She gripped his hand tighter. 'When the line turned blue, I thought my heart would burst. The enormity of it seemed so huge. Me, having a baby. I couldn't wait to tell Patrick.'

She swallowed hard. 'It never occurred to me that he wouldn't feel the same. Even though it was a bit of a surprise, I thought Patrick would think like me, that it was the next step. Logical.' Her eyebrows creased, meeting in a dark frown. 'He didn't. Said it was bourgeois. Not us. People like us didn't have children. It would *limit* us.' Her mouth twisted with terrible weariness. 'Spouted a whole load of stuff. I presumed it was just the shock at first. That he'd come around. He didn't.'

Ella turned to Devon, her face haunted with sadness, and then she looked up, watching the gliders for a minute, as if trying to contain her emotion before she went on.

'He wanted me to have an abortion.' Her lips quivered. 'Get rid of it. That's what he called our baby – "it". As if the baby were nothing to do with him.' She shook her head, still in disbelief. 'When I tried to talk to him about it, when I said I wasn't sure I could go through with an abortion, he,' her breath hitched, 'he told me I was "being far too emotional about it".'

With his thumb, Devon rubbed her hand. She held herself so still, he was worried that if he put his arm around her or even tried to offer any other comfort, she might shatter like ice.

'I thought maybe he was right. It was the hormones. So I went for the first appointment.' Her face creased as if in pain.

'Except I couldn't get through the door. I couldn't do it. I froze. I knew then I wanted to keep the baby.

'Luckily for him, I miscarried.' The words, spoken without emotion, cold and blank, dropped like stones.

The grip of her fingers on his tightened but she faced away into the headwind. He could see her swallowing but the words had dried up for a moment. He didn't know what to say, didn't want to offer platitudes. Then, she spoke again.

'It was only the size of a bean. Who'd have thought there'd be so much blood?' She laughed mirthlessly, dry and heart-wrenching. 'No wonder Lady Macbeth got into such a tizz. I had to throw away my favourite pair of jeans.'

He could tell by the tightening of her jawline that she was working hard to hang onto her control. 'I r-really miss those jeans.' She winced, her other hand going to her stomach. 'When you have something, it's only when it's gone you realise how much you wanted to keep it. God, I miss those jeans.'

Tears stung his eyes at the heartbreak in her voice, at the way she worked so hard to keep her emotions in check, pretend that she was unharmed by it all. He resisted the urge to pull her into his arms and offer comfort. It took a lot of effort putting on a face that brave. He knew how damn hard it was and how easily the façade could shatter if someone was kind to you. Staunchly he hung onto her hand as the two of them stood motionless gazing out over the view.

Standing straight and tall she leaned into the headwind, imagining herself like the prow of a ship cutting through the waves. His hand in hers anchored her, when she felt as if her emotions might take flight and leave her rudderless.

The fingers interweaved between hers gave her strength. She could weather this, make it through. Patrick's casual dismissal, so cold, emotionless. Uncaring. How could he not care? For her that loss had slammed into her, leaving her adrift.

With the strong breeze whistling around them on the summit of the Beacon, picking and tossing at her hair, awareness shimmered through her. There was land ahead. The ever-present lump of misery lodged just beneath her heart was still there but it had lost its malignant presence and the threatening sensation that it might overpower her one day.

With a grim twist to her mouth, she tossed her head back, welcoming the fierce slap of the wind. When Patrick had suggested they had a break, she'd clung to that idea as if it might save her. It gave her enough distance to not have to think how much she hated him for not caring. It made her believe that in a few months' time she could go back and everything would be normal again. She'd have grieved. Her hormones, which Patrick had patiently explained were all over the place, would be righted. She'd see things differently. She'd realise that they were all right as they were. The two of them.

With heartsick sorrow, the knowledge came to rest like a feather gently but surely coming into land: there was no going back. She could never forgive Patrick for not wanting their child. Or forgive him for being able to forget so easily about it once she'd miscarried.

And she would never forget.

It was like trying to get those jeans back. She'd never find a pair quite like them. There'd be others but not the same. She hadn't wanted a baby but it didn't mean she didn't want one at some point in her life. She knew that with a fierce certainty. One day she wanted a family.

She closed her eyes. Despite the eddies and swirls around her, she'd resolved something, achieving close to some sort of equilibrium after being out of kilter for weeks.

'You know, he didn't even come to the hospital when I lost the baby. I didn't tell anyone else. I was ashamed.'

'*Ashamed*?'

'Yes. Ashamed that I'd even considered an abortion and that this was my punishment. Ashamed that he felt like that. Ashamed that I didn't know that his reaction would be like that. Ashamed that I loved someone so ... so heartless. That I'd got it so wrong with him.' Her mouth twisted. 'His relief was palpable. We'd had a lucky escape. He didn't even try to pretend that he wasn't relieved. I put on a brave face, I did pretend. Made out it was OK. But it got harder and harder.'

'But he must have been sympathetic.'

'Not really. That makes him sound like a bad person. He wasn't. Just didn't understand.' She closed her eyes, suddenly wanting to spill the horrible dirty truth. 'He got fed up with me feeling sorry for myself. I couldn't help myself. It finally dawned on me that he had no idea one night when we went to a new gallery opening. Gallery 99.'

It was a horrible night. She'd wandered around the gallery in a haze of misery, barely registering, in fact almost tripping over, the frankly ugly metalwork contraptions dotted around the floor. The only thing she remembered about them were that they were hard and sharp-edged when all she wanted was softness and warmth.

She'd tried to talk to Patrick before they went out. Her

stomach contracted now at the memory and she put her hand on it, pressing lightly as if that might take away the dull ache.

'I don't think I'm up to going to the show tonight,' she'd told him as she'd tried to pull on knee-high boots and losing the battle when what little energy she had ran out with the suddenness of the last sand grains in an egg timer.

'Ella, I get that you're feeling rough.' He'd pulled his sympathetic face. The one where his mouth under his sandy moustache stretched wide in an encouraging smile but the eyes stayed watchful. Just thinking about his mouth gave Ella a pang. Once she'd loved kissing it, feeling the bristles skating her lips, his beard brushing her chin.

'But seriously... this is going to sound harsh, but I'm doing it for us. You need to pull yourself together. You have to start acting normally again.'

Ella had gaped at him. His words were like physical blows. She wanted to clutch her middle to protect herself from them. He watched as she wrapped her arms around herself, nodding and smiling with patronising sympathy.

'Your body's been through a bit of a storm. But it's over now. Done. We've got to move forward. You'll feel better soon. In the meantime, why don't you try and harness the experience, paint it, sculpt it. It would make a dramatic installation. Think of it as an experience. Use it. Create a series of work. It would make a great selling point. We could say they're a manifestation of the artist's angst at losing an unborn child. It would have a lot of traction with the media. A great human story.'

'A story?'

He nodded.

But it wasn't a story, she wanted to say. *It was real. I, we, lost our unborn child. It was a real child, Patrick.* But if she put voice to the words, she'd have started to cry and she wasn't sure if she could stop.

That was when she'd given up trying to talk to him about it. That night she realised that Patrick couldn't understand what she'd lost and worse still, she couldn't bring herself to make him understand. It was almost as if she wanted to spite him for his lack of empathy.

In stark contrast, Devon moved closer and slipped an arm around her shoulders.

Unable to help herself, she nestled into him. He smelt of outdoors and life. The shield she'd battled to keep in place for so long, so that she could function day to day, slipped. Stripped back, all the vulnerability and longing to be safe again came flooding through with a piercing sense of relief. When was the last time she'd done this? Let someone else be there for her. Lean on them. Trust them totally to hold her up. The storm of emotions that she held fiercely in check for the last few weeks loosened. As she started to cry, Devon's arms came around her and it seemed right to lean into his chest and feel the rise and fall of his steady breathing. Silent tears ran down her face, tucked into the heavy Guernsey sweater. Devon held her closer and let her cry, a soothing hand rubbing her back.

Cocooned against him, like a ship protected in harbour, she closed her eyes. If she kept them closed she could pretend all the other things didn't exist. She could stay in this moment, savouring his warmth and strength. The moment stretched out. She closed her eyes tighter, focusing on the sound of the wind whistling around the hill top and the rough feel of wool against her face and trying not to think about the proximity of Devon's thighs against hers. A low level ache of desire snaked through her. She wanted to nuzzle into him.

The gentle hand on her back stilled. Oh God, she was about to make a complete fool of herself. Had he felt that tiny shift of weight? The last thing he needed or she did for that matter. She stiffened, schooling her face, and stepped back.

'Sorry. I didn't mean to unburden on you like that.'

'Don't apologise. I'm glad you were able to tell me. It sounds as if you've had a tough time.'

With his stern face in profile, his shoulders rigid, she had a feeling he'd been duelling his own demons up here in tandem with her. Whether he'd won or not was not her place to ask, but then he turned to face her.

'I know about crunch points,' he said quietly. 'I keep wondering about going back to Marina.' He sighed. 'It would make life easier. Solve all my money problems.'

He shrugged, lifting his shoulders up to his ears, his voice slightly hoarse. 'If I went back, everything would just go away. I loved her once, why not again? The truth is, I caught her in bed with the film producer. Skinny little guy, nearly twice her age, married as well. Rick. Looks like the weasel he is. Wish I'd punched the little git. We were already on the rocks, that was my crunch point.'

'Ouch.'

'I haven't told anyone else that. Pride more than anything else.'

'I don't know that it's pride. It's such a horrible thing to happen. I can't imagine it but I can imagine why you wouldn't want to tell anyone.' She looked at his worried face, guessing that he now regretted saying it. 'I wouldn't dream of telling anyone.'

'Thanks. Come on, you're getting cold. I think we both need a hot drink. Let's round up those dogs, they're probably halfway home without us.'

Whipping her head round, she scanned the hillside below – sure enough, there in the distance, she could just make out the two dogs criss-crossing the path. Her heart lifted at the sight of them. 'They don't ask for much, really do they? Life is so much simpler. Walks and food.'

The car journey back to the cottage passed in silence, as if each of them was worn out by the excess of emotion. The two dogs panted happily in the back, steaming up the windows.

When they pulled up outside, Devon got out and opened up the boot to release Tess. Ella got out of the car, suddenly tongue-tied. So much had passed between them, and she wanted to say something but didn't know what. She was on the verge of asking him to come in for a coffee when Tess began to bark.

She stood at George's gate, nudging at it with her head, her barks increasing in volume.

'Tess, stop that.' Ella went over to grab at her collar but the dog danced away. 'What's the matter with you? Stop it.'

'Probably spotted a cat or something,' said Devon, trying to close the boot of the car, but Dexter had now joined in and before Devon could stop him, he too jumped out and joined Tess at the gate, barking furiously.

Tess's head butted the wooden fence, poking her head

through the wooden posts and then Ella caught sight of a flash of George's favourite virulent mustard yellow on the path leading to his front door.

'George!' she called out, and ran over, fiddling to unlatch the gate. He lay crumpled on the path. 'Oh, my goodness.' Ella ran to his side and bent down. His face had a doughy grey cast with a slight clammy sheen to it. Too scared to touch him, she crouched down next to him.

'Can you feel a pulse?' asked Devon, pushing her out of the way and crouching down beside her.

Ella gave him a helpless look, hating feeling so useless. 'I . . .'

He placed one hand on the old man's chest, the other one with unerring accuracy homing straight in on George's pulse. 'He's breathing. Just. And there's a pulse.'

Now she was beside him, she could hear short rasping breaths.

Devon began to tap George's sallow face very gently.

'George, can you hear me? Hello, George. It's Devon. If you can hear me, give my hand a squeeze.'

Ella watched, dry-mouthed, as Devon picked up the lifeless arm and took George's hand in his, holding her breath until she saw the older man's fingers move in a feeble attempt. George let out a weak, breathy, incoherent moan.

'OK.' Although Devon's face looked grave, he managed to give Ella a reassuring but grim smile. 'He's alive. Breathing, conscious and has a pulse. All good signs but we need to get him warm and comfortable. Can you get blankets and a pillow and I'll call an ambulance?' He fished his mobile out of his pocket.

Relieved that she had a practical task, Ella jumped to her feet and raced back to the cottage.

When Ella returned, Devon was on the phone talking to the emergency services. He nodded towards George's prone body and then at the duvet.

She knelt and tucked it around George, biting her lip. He looked so uncomfortable lying on the hard path but she guessed they shouldn't move him. Thank God Devon was here otherwise she wouldn't have known what to do.

Even now he was giving the person on the other end of the phone concise information about George's breathing, pulse and age.

'The ambulance is on its way,' he said tucking his phone back in his pocket. 'Well done.' He leant over George and took his hand again.

'George. Can you hear me? Don't try to talk, just squeeze my hand to say yes.'

Ella stared at the wrinkled brown hand, dotted with liver spots and the joints gnarled through years of use, cushioned in Devon's larger capable fingers. Something shifted in her chest at the sight of Devon's broad masculine hands. Capable, strong and still gentle. They'd offered her comfort earlier. It was easy to imagine him at work, in command, dealing patiently and calmly with his patients. Animals and owners would trust him.

'We need to keep him conscious if we can,' said Devon in a very low voice. 'I'm going to run inside and just check if he takes any medication and grab some things for him.'

Taking a sharp breath, she nodded and watched Devon leave.

'Hi George, it's Ella.' She took his cold hand in hers and

rubbed the back of it, feeling the bones just beneath the skin. His eyes were glassy and unfocused but every now and then she felt his fingers move beneath hers. 'You're going to be fine. There's an ambulance on its way. So it looks like it's my turn to keep an eye on your place. Don't worry, I'll make sure it's all locked up properly.'

Another gentle squeeze butterflied against her hands. What would have happened if they hadn't come back when they did? And how long had he been lying there? Ella looked over at Tess. Clever dog. She and Dexter, for once, sat side by side at a respectful distance, watchful and still as if on bodyguard detail. How did they know to do that, when normally they were racing and bounding about like idiots?

'Tess found you, George. She's a bit like Lassie. I bet you remember Lassie.'

Quite where she dredged it up, Ella couldn't recollect later, but she chatted inanely to George for the next ten minutes.

In the quiet of the village they heard the siren coming way before they spotted the blue lights of the ambulance speeding down the road.

At last the paramedics loaded George onto a stretcher, an oxygen mask strapped to his face.

It was only when they went to shut the door, something snapped inside Ella. It felt all wrong, the vulnerable figure tightly wrapped in the red blanket all on his own.

'Wait. Can I go with him?'

'Are you family?'

She hesitated. She couldn't bear the thought of him going on his own and being alone in hospital. 'Yes, I'm his niece.'

Chapter Eighteen

Good God. Ella regretted putting the TV on. Dr Marina Scott was as absolutely blooming gorgeous this morning as she had been the morning before and the one before that. Each time Ella tuned in, she hoped that she'd remember wrong, but no, this woman had star quality written all over her. Her white coat stopped just above the knee, not too short to be tarty and just the right cut-off point to show off the shapeliest, most elegant legs Ella had ever seen.

From her shiny brilliant teeth to her long graceful fingers tipped in fuchsia pink to match her lustrous wet-look lipstick, she exuded polish and gloss. There wasn't a single feature Ella could find fault with. Even her walk, in stylish but sensibly heeled black court shoes, was sinuous. The camera loved her and she talked with friendliness and vivacity into the lens. She treated her guests with great charm, immediately scooping their pets up with enthusiastic exclamations. It was obvious why she was such a hit, she had so much warmth and empathy.

Ella could see that for some it might be addictive viewing

as Dr Scott talked to worried pet owners with an authoritative air, dispensing her expertise in a kind, reassuring manner.

Tess wandered in and stood right in front of the television and let out a gentle fart, just as Dr Scott introduced a chocolate Labrador called Larry.

'That's my girl,' said Ella, thinking it rather appropriate, even though poor gorgeous Marina had done absolutely nothing wrong to her.

The good vet gave the camera a particularly winsome look that made Ella mime gagging.

'Except, as regular viewers will know, Larry's a girl dog. She just looked like a Larry, so the name stuck.'

An off-camera interviewer interjected with a coy, 'And we hear you have news regarding Larry this week.'

'I certainly do,' gushed Marina.

OK, now Ella had gone off her. The format and delivery were too cheesy for words but then again this was daytime TV. Thank God, the curtains were still closed and no one could catch her watching this drivel.

'Larry is going to have a litter of puppies in the next month and we're very excited because we will be streaming the birth live as it happens.'

'And how can people find out when Larry will be having her puppies?'

'We've got a special Twitter account for Larry and a Facebook page. So people can follow from the first twinge. It's very exciting.'

Ella glared at the screen. It sounded awful to her. She bet Marina Scott wouldn't like to be filmed live in childbirth.

What if something went wrong? Did dogs miscarry? Did

they know they'd lost their babies? Did they grieve for them like humans did? Did it cause that awful hollow ache in the pit of the stomach?

With a vicious snap at the button on the remote control, she silenced Marina. The cottage suddenly felt claustrophobic and she was horribly conscious that the cottage next door was empty. Poor George – leaving him all alone, watching them wheel the hospital trolley away to the ward had been horrible. Perhaps she should go and visit him.

Underfoot, her shoes squeaked on the floor as she walked the length of the corridor, checking off the ward numbers. In one hand, she clutched a bag of books, fruit and biscuits, while in the other a cup of George's favourite cappuccino. Visiting hours had just started and she picked up her pace – she didn't want him to think no one was coming.

Once she'd decided to come she'd collected a few of his things, feeling uncomfortable as she went into his bedroom to find pyjamas and toiletries.

'Morning, duck. Well, you're a sight for sore eyes. Magda said you'd come.'

He was obviously a bit confused and had forgotten Magda was in the middle of the ocean on the other side of the world but she didn't like to remind him.

'Morning, George, how are you today?' His colour looked much better but he looked tired and was clearly confused.

'I'm absolutely fine, just had a funny turn, but they want to do all sorts of tests. Gives those doctors something to do. Don't suppose you brought me a paper?'

'I did.' She handed over the *Express* she bought at the

League of Friends shop downstairs. 'And,' she lifted the bag, 'PJs and bits. I'll put them in your locker. And,' she lowered her voice, 'cake.'

'You never. You baked me a cake.' George sat up straighter, his hospital gown sagging on one side to reveal a thin, bony, liver-spotted shoulder, reminding her how frail he really was.

Ella let out a peal of laughter. 'You never give up. No, it's one of the shop's Swiss rolls.'

'Hasn't Peter Reynolds got rid of that stock yet? At this rate, they'll be covering 'em in chocolate and selling them as Yule logs throughout December.' His thin arms reached out to grasp the offering. 'Oooh, that's grand. Will go nicely with my cup of coffee. Here, hand it over before the Sister comes round. I'm not supposed to have any stimulations.'

'Or stimulants.'

'Them too, but I'm not risking them taking this away.'

He took a long sip of coffee and gave a happy sigh. 'I think I should have been born Italian. They know how to make coffee.'

'You'd better make sure you wipe your mouth before the doctor does his round,' said Ella pointing to his milky, chocolate-spotted mouth.

George grinned.

When she stood to leave she asked, 'Can I bring anything else?'

'No, lass. I'll be home tomorrow.'

'Will you?' Ella asked in surprise.

'Yes,' he nodded before adding darkly, 'or you'll be helping me plan my escape.'

'If they think you should be here...' Ella bit her lip. When had she turned into George's keeper? She wasn't even family.

But, she felt responsible for him. There wasn't anyone else.

'Yoo hoo. Hello. Yes, you.'

Ella stopped, unable to pretend any longer that this woman wasn't talking to her, quite possibly because she was the only person in the hospital corridor.

'Ella, isn't it? The artist.'

Ella nodded.

'I'm Audrey.' She announced this in a forthright manner as if Ella should know who she was, which of course she did, thanks to Bets. Unfortunately, there was no chance to run as had been the fervent recommendation.

'Hi,' said Ella in faint voice. The famous Audrey looked completely harmless and nothing like the ruthless Attila the Hun type that Bets had warned her about. In her smart low-heeled shoes, a mid-length skirt of a definite Marks & Spencer persuasion and a very smart little nipped-in jacket, she looked more like a friendly, glamorous granny. Behind gold-framed glasses, big blue eyes, guileless and friendly, twinkled with warm but decided mischievous intent.

'Have you just been to see George? How is he? I heard he'd had a funny turn.'

'He's—'

'I had to stop you to say hello. I've been very remiss not calling in, although young Bets has been doing a good job. And I did promise Magda I'd look after you. I've been so busy these last few weeks.'

From a capricious but very ugly handbag, Audrey whipped

out a spiral bound diary. 'Now let me see, we've got the final meeting for the village Bake Off, the Village Hall fundraiser, the Spring Fayre. Not a minute to call my own. But there was something, Magda was most specific ... ah, here it is. Salsa. She said you'd love to join in.'

Ella just bet she did. When she finally got hold of Magda, she was going to wring her neck.

'Next Tuesday in the village hall. It's a shame you missed the flamenco, now that was a lot of fun.'

Ella schooled her face and tried hard not to look at Audrey's plump hips.

'Lots of stamping and attitude.' With a twist of her hands, she held them back to back above her head and with slow steps she circled Ella, like a cheetah its prey. Then she gave two quick claps and stamped her feet, completely oblivious to the fact she was standing in the middle of a hospital corridor.

'We do like our dance sessions. So we've got salsa coming up and much as the old dears all have a go, it would be great to have some young blood for a change.'

'I don't think it's—'

'You're going to love it. All you need is a pair of shoes with a bit of a heel. And it helps if you've got a skirt with a touch of swish in it, helps you get into the mood. Although some of our ladies get a bit too much into the mood. Old Beryl, who is nearly ninety, Lord, I thought she might put her foot through the floorboards, she was stamping with such gusto. Goodness, is that the time? So Tuesday, five-thirty in the village hall. I'll see you there.' She gave an impish grin. 'Tell Bets she should come too. I know she's been avoiding me. Surgery finishes early on Tuesdays, so no excuses.

'Oh I nearly forgot. One of our speakers has cancelled on me. Do you think you could come and do a little talk and a demonstration of your rather wonderful mouse pictures? I thought you could tell us how you started out and how you got published. Quite a few of the WI ladies are aspiring writers and then a few paint lovely watercolours. So, who better to come and talk to us than our resident artist. It'll be such fun. That's two weeks on Tuesday and there's . . . Joyce! Oh Joyce! Sorry, must dash.'

Audrey darted off leaving Ella slightly punch drunk. What had just happened there?

Salsa? In the village hall? With a bemused shake of her head, Ella continued back to her car. She'd have to catch up with Audrey and explain that it wasn't something she did.

Tess was delighted to see her.

'Stupid dog, I've only been gone for an hour. Poor old George is looking much better. He says you can have a big bone because you saved him. Clever girl. Although I might never leave the house again. It's too damn dangerous. Let me at least have a cup of coffee and do some work. Bets is coming over soon with Dex and then we'll go out for a nice long walk.'

Now that she was a lot fitter, she rather enjoyed their joint walks. The lure of spring sunshine was an added incentive. These bright sunny days lifted her mood.

Taking a steaming mug upstairs, she went up to her studio and quickly reviewed the week's progress. She could get an hour's work done before Bets arrived. For once she was actually well ahead and had enough ideas for the next book and possibly a series about her little alien characters. Her publisher would be pleased.

With a smile she surveyed the mice. Perhaps she should... flamenco. That was it. Grabbing a pencil, she started to sketch. Cuthbert would love one of those Cordoban flat black-brimmed hats and his sister Catherine would look rather swish in a bright red frilled and flounced dress and little red Latin dancing shoes.

Dropping her pencil, she ran back downstairs, scooped up the shoe box and taking the stairs two at a time hurried back.

Latin shoes with socks looked quite odd but they were perfect and they twinkled as she swivelled her foot at the ankle to let the light catch the diamonds. They'd been diamonds in her head at fifteen and they were still diamonds now, she decided with a happy nod of defiance.

She needed music. A quick YouTube search and she had the Gipsy Kings playing. Yes. With her shoulders rocking and her feet tapping to the music, she added a guitar-playing Englebert.

'*Bamboleeeeo, bamboleeeea*, lalalala.'

Her fingers flashed across the page, the drawings flowing from her fingers. When the music stopped abruptly, she clicked to play the track again but this time stood up. Shoes like these needed trying out. Up here in the attic with the skylights facing to the brilliant blue sky, no one could see her. With a wry smile at her own silliness, she stood up and started to dance.

Tess thought it was a great game and as Ella swivelled her hips and raised her hands above her head, she tried to join in, weaving in and out of Ella's legs and jumping up and down.

'Crazy dog.' Ella laughed. They probably looked totally ridiculous but no one could see her. When was the last time she'd danced? When she was in her early teens she'd done Latin and Modern. At college, she'd gone regularly to a local salsa club. With a sudden sense of sadness, she realised it was another thing she'd got out of the habit of doing. Patrick wasn't much of a dancer.

This time when the music stopped, another track began before she could get to her iPhone. *'Baila, baila, baila, me.'* She joined in the refrain, making up the words she didn't know. Whirling around the room, her heart full of lightness and joy, she danced through several tracks. Eventually Tess got bored, the initial excitement wearing off, and she wandered out of the room but Ella, relishing the feeling of her heart pounding and her pulse beating furiously, carried on dancing.

'Er, excuse me.'

Startled, she whirled round to find Devon standing in the doorway at the head of the stairs to the loft conversion, an apologetic smile full of sympathy on his face and right on cue the music stopped.

A fierce blush fired up her cheekbones.

'Crikey, you scared the life out of me,' she said. 'What the hell are you doing?' The aftershock of fear made her sharp. Tess bounded over to him and gave his hand a welcoming lick.

'Great guard dog, you are,' she snapped, irritated by the dog's complete lack of loyalty. 'You do remember that this is the man who called you fat?'

Devon rolled his eyes. 'I'm sure I didn't use the word "fat". Although she is looking much better.' His eyes slid to Ella's waist where her shirt had become untucked.

'Don't you dare say it.' Ella gave him a mock glare and shook her head in warning.

'Nice shoes.'

Automatically she went to cross her feet at her ankles as if that might hide them and then thought better of it, lifting her head to say with a regal nod, 'Thanks,' as if they were her finest footwear.

'Sorry, I didn't mean to startle you.' He gave her an unrepentant grin.

'Well, what did you mean to do?' She put her hands on her hips, a smile playing at her lips. There was a sense of freedom in talking to him today. The shared misery of the other day on the Beacon had seeded a tentative friendship. 'Do you make a habit of breaking and entering?'

'The door was open and I could hear the music – I did call up several times.' His eyes sparkled with wicked humour. 'Bets said you might be working.' He looked around. 'This is a great room.'

'Yes.' She ran a hand through her hair. What on earth did she look like? Slight sweaty and a bit breathless and very scruffy, apart from the shiny new shoes. He was used to super-sophisticated Marina with her immaculate white coat, perfect tanned legs and trim ankles. He probably thought Ella was a lunatic. Deranged. So uncool. And terminally clumsy.

'The light's good.'

'I imagine it is. So this is where you work.'

'Yes.'

Now she sounded stupid but she couldn't think of anything to say. In jeans and a big navy sweater, he made a larger than life contrast to the stark white brightness of the room.

His dark curly hair was a little too long for her taste and his clothes too casual but something about his confident stance made her heart jump and her mouth go dry. He looked solid and reliable. All man. More masculine than she was used to. It made her feel small and the strangest thought popped into her head. How lovely it would be to be encircled in his arms. Like she'd been when he'd comforted her on the Beacon yesterday.

Shaking her head as if to dislodge the unwelcome thought, she folded her arms as if that might keep any further fanciful notions at bay. 'Did you want something?'

'Sorry, I didn't mean to disturb you.' He nodded towards her drawing table. 'Bets is tied up and asked me to come instead. I assumed you'd be working, not ... dancing.' His mouth twisted with a wry smile. Ella blushed again. There was an awkward silence as she tried to gather her thoughts.

Ignoring her discomposure, he moved across to her drawing table.

'Mind if I take a look? I've never seen a real artist at work.'

'Then you'll be disappointed.'

He raised one eyebrow and she couldn't decide whether to be grateful or irritated as he took a measured, assessing look at her drawings.

'These are really good.' He sounded genuinely impressed but then most people thought a picture was good if things were in perspective. He continued to study the pictures with a thoroughness that Ella hadn't expected. 'I feel as if I could touch them and they'd spring to life.' He smiled, a half-hearted thing of a smile, as if surprised by his own fancifulness. 'In fact I expect them to move at any second. It must take real skill to draw like this.'

Seeing the pictures with new eyes, she gave a hesitant answering nod. Gentle pride bubbling up for the first time in a very long time. 'Thank you.'

'Now I understand the music.' He pointed to the female mouse in her red flamenco dress. 'Cute.'

He turned another page and burst out laughing, a wholehearted uninhibited gale of laughter she hadn't thought him capable of. He shook his head in amusement. 'Priceless.' With a broad gin, he pointed to the picture of Englebert clutching his Spanish guitar, an expression of extreme seriousness on his whiskered face. 'Do I recognise him?'

Ella's eyes widened and she put a hand over her mouth. 'Oh Lord, do you?'

With dancing eyes, Devon nodded. 'Yes, I think I do. If I'm not mistaken, he bears a decided likeness to our esteemed vicar.' Devon flicked through a few more of the pages lying on the table, his lips pinched together, cheeks dimpling as if trying to hold back his amusement.

Ella ran over and put a hand on the pages. 'Damn. I thought no one else would notice. Is it really that obvious?'

'Probably not. It's only because I saw the sketch you did in the pub.'

'Do you think it's . . . too much? I'm going to have to change him. Shame, Englebert, that's the character's name, has only just come into his own.'

Devon shrugged. 'I wouldn't worry. I doubt anyone else would pick it up. Besides, Richard would probably think it's quite flattering. It's not as if it's a malicious or unkind representation.'

'Yes, but people might laugh at him.'

'I think to be a vicar these days you have to be fairly thick-skinned and I'm sure Richard would see the funny side of it.'

'All the same.'

'People will laugh *with* him, not at him and if they're laughing at him, that says more about them.'

'What do you mean?' Ella couldn't comprehend his view. Being laughed at was horrible. When he'd said laughing was his way of coping with things at work, it was different. They were situations that were beyond his control. She lived in dread of people laughing at her work. Ridiculing the things that she'd put her heart and soul into. Perhaps that's why in recent years, she'd held back. Fear had a great way of stifling things.

'Don't you think that if someone laughs unkindly, it means they're mean-spirited? It's deliberate. Small-minded.'

'I guess. I'd never thought of it like that.'

It came to her with a sudden rush of freedom, like a lance bursting a boil, releasing the poison. No wonder she hadn't been able to do anything truly creative, she'd been bound by fear of what others would think.

Chapter Nineteen

'Oh God, you weren't kidding. This is truly awful.' Ella stared at the horrible colour on Bets' kitchen walls. 'I'm not sure I can even describe this colour. What were you thinking?' The awful walls notwithstanding, Bets' living space was wonderful. 'Thank God you didn't paint the lounge.' It would have taken for ever to redo, with those high walls reaching up to the wooden rafters.

Bets' home was part of a series of converted barns which had been split into several properties. Hers was the smallest of five.

'The kitchen aside, this place is lovely. I had no idea from the outside.'

'Thanks.' Bets giggled. 'The paint looked different in the shop, it was only when I started, I realised how awful it was and then it was too late to stop. I figured if I kept going it might not be quite so bad when it dried. I was wrong.'

'Good job you've got me then. Look, I even brought you your own painting overalls.' Ella had found two pairs when she was sorting through Magda's shed and was already wearing a set.

Bets' idea of a paintbrush was a semi-bald, sad-looking thing which Ella immediately vetoed in horror. 'You can't use that thing! What have you been doing with it?'

Bets looked innocent. 'I might have used it to clean out a leaky gutter.'

Ella didn't bother responding to that. 'And you need proper masking tape, not Sellotape.' She put her hands on her hips and gave Bets a mock glare. 'You're hopeless.'

'Can't we just paint carefully around the edges?'

'No, we're going to do this properly. You'll thank me later.'

'I think I preferred you before. You've turned into a bully overnight.'

'I like to do things properly.' And she really wanted to do a good job for Bets. 'Lucky for you I went to B&Q and I have proper nice new paintbrushes and I dug out Magda's roller and paint trays. Come on, get this overall on. We've got work to do.'

Bets dashed off to change, leaving Ella to plan where they'd start. It was a good-sized kitchen with one wall of cabinets in cream wood which she'd describe as 'modern cottage'. The run of units was intersected in the middle with a range-style cooker and opposite was a long wooden island in the centre of which was a ceramic sink. Ella knew from a brief module on design at college that this was a particularly well-designed kitchen. She guessed that a fridge would be situated as part of the perfect kitchen triangle of sink, cooker and fridge.

Luckily the wall with the cabinets and cooker was tiled, so had escaped the hideous colour. There were really only two walls that had been painted – unfortunately one of them ran the whole length of the room and then beyond into a little corridor.

'Ta-dah.' Bets jumped into the room, hands whipping through the air in a series of karate poses like a little white ninja, making Ella laugh.

She did a quick twirl. 'I feel like we're in a girl band or something. We need music. What do you fancy?'

'Anything?' Ella's mind was on where she'd start with the masking tape along the skirting. 'I think we'll do this big wall first.'

Bets was busy scrolling through her iPhone. 'Here you go. Painting music. I've made a playlist.' She plugged the phone into a docking station as Ella poured paint into the tray.

The duck-egg blue colour was going to look lovely in here and co-ordinate beautifully with the cupboards.

'Here you go,' Ella handed the roller to Bets.

'Great,' she took it enthusiastically and pressed the play button. 'I'll be Beyoncé, you can be Rihanna next.' The opening bars of 'Crazy in Love' filled the room at top volume. With rolling hips, Bets pranced towards the wall holding the roller up to her face and began to sing along, before flattening herself against the wall writhing suggestively. Ella burst out laughing.

Bets whipped round. 'Uh oh uh oh,' she sang, the roller zig-zagging up and down the wall in time to the music. Her bottom stuck out, waggling with great enthusiasm, as she circled her hips. 'You're mad,' said Ella shaking her head but unable to stop her shoulders shimmying. The pumping beat had her feet tapping and she snatched up her paintbrush and danced over to the wall. 'Da de de da, da da,' they both sang. Bets' moves grew even more outrageous and silly and before long Ella matched her, swivelling her hips, shaking her shoulders.

As the music built to a crescendo they danced along together, each trying to outdo the other and painted along, every now and then, the paintbrush and roller doubling as a microphone to join in the chorus.

Beyoncé gave way to Rihanna's 'Umbrella' which led to Bets marching around waving the roller in the air for a little while, before she loaded it up again with paint, then managing to get a big blob of paint on her nose, which she brushed off casually with a laugh. Ella's face actually ached from smiling and laughing so much.

Gradually things calmed down as Bets' playlist led on to Lady Gaga, Katy Perry, Taylor Swift and a couple of catchy dance numbers that Ella had never heard of.

By eleven-thirty, they'd worked steadily and completed a whole wall.

'Oh my, it's looking so much better already. Why did I live with cat-sick for so long?'

'Because you're an idiot,' teased Ella, from the crouched position where she'd bent to paint the line around the skirting board. They'd agreed that she did the fiddly bits around the skirting boards and ceilings because she had a steadier hand and as Bets freely admitted, she was far too slapdash for that sort of job.

'I need a cup of tea,' said Ella, pleased that she'd reached the last part of the edge of the wall she was doing and was able to stand upright. The ache in her back reminded her she wasn't used to working like this.

'I have to admit, boss lady, you know what you're doing. I would have slapped a coat of paint straight on. None of this washing the walls down first.'

As they drank huge earthenware mugs of tea, Ella noticed the fine lines around Bets' mouth. She looked tired and a little drawn as she bustled around behind the island counter.

'Thanks for helping me. Living here must be very different to what you're used to. Your friend was very elegant.' Bets touched her auburn curls self-consciously and stood awkwardly, shifting from one foot to the other. 'And grown-up and self-possessed. I bet all the girls on Jack's course are like that.'

The uncertainty on her face surprised and upset Ella. A stab of guilt hit her as she contrasted Bets' easy acceptance of Britta's affectations. Bets had a far more generous nature.

Giving in to a sudden whim, Ella crossed to her and gave her a quick hug. 'No one on the planet is like Britta.' Ella sighed and shook her head. 'And do you know what? She's not much of a friend, whereas you have been a very good friend to me from day one without ever asking for anything in return. Thank you.'

'Oh, God, Ella. Please don't be nice to me today.' Her face crumpled and Ella saw the madcap dancing and earlier energy for what it was.

'I'm so mad and so upset with Jack right now.' Bets clenched her fists. 'I just want to cry and then punch him. We've been together for so long. I can cope with him being away most of the time. I just get on with it. But this is the second time he's cancelled. I'm worried he's gone off me. Met lots of girls who are much more interesting. Who've done more? Been to places? Cleverer than me.'

'Don't be silly,' said Ella, hoping that she sounded reassuring. What did she know? She had no idea what Jack was like. For all she knew, he could have umpteen girlfriends down in Bristol. 'He's probably just busy with exams and things. I guess it must be pretty intensive training to be a vet.'

Bets gave a sad little shrug. 'I guess.'

Ella wanted to put the sparkle back into Bets.

'Right, come on. Ready for round two? I fancy something a bit heavier, have you got any Muse? We need a big thumping base.'

'What a difference already,' said Devon chugging down a beer and leaning against the island. He'd arrived after all the work had been done although to be fair, he'd had both dogs all day to keep them out of the way. They were now charging around the garden like a pair of dervishes.

'Do you take commissions, Ella? I could do with some advice for next door. Looks like I'm going to be here for quite some time.'

'Next door?'

'Yes, Dad did up the barns a few years ago. Turned them into flats and cottages as holiday lets and for Jack and I to live in if we ever came home. There are five in all. Bets lucked out and got the smallest.'

'I only need the smallest. I'm here on my own most of the time.' Her face fell. 'Although I couldn't afford to live anywhere half as nice as this and not on my own. Better hope Jack doesn't dump me.'

'Hey! Don't be silly. That's not going to happen.' Devon gave her a brotherly nudge. 'Dad wouldn't hear of it. Where else would he get the best veterinary nurse this side of the universe?'

Ella winced. He'd rather missed the point. She and Bets exchanged a glance which clearly said, *men!*

That odd look was back on Bets' face. 'So, it's Saturday night. As we're all a bunch of Saturday night losers, anyone fancy a takeaway and a Trivial Pursuit marathon?'

'Sounds perfect,' commented Devon, tipping back his bottle and swallowing the last of his beer. 'Count me in.'

Ella considered her options. Being alone in the cottage or here. 'Sounds good to me too.'

'Tell you what.' Bets beamed at them both. 'You two take the dogs for a walk. And I'll nip into Tring and pick up a takeaway. What do you fancy? Chinese? Pizza? Curry?'

'Curry!' Devon and Ella spoke in unison with equal vehemence as if there was no other choice. Ella caught his eye and they shared a smile.

'OK. Message received and understood,' teased Bets. 'I've got a menu somewhere.'

They chose their food and then Ella left, heading down the road with Tess to change into some sensible shoes and a warmer coat. Ella couldn't help feeling that Bets had engineered things, somewhat.

Predictably Tess was beside herself, twisting in and out of Ella's legs. 'Just let me change, you dumb dog. And I promise, we'll go straight out.' As she glanced in the mirror in the hallway she winced. There was just time to wipe away the spots of paint which had congregated in an acne rush across the top of her cheeks, run a brush through her hair, which had become flattened unbecomingly to her skull by her scarf, and maybe pop a quick slick of lipstick on. Oh God, had Devon really seen her like this? He was used to Marina and despite what he'd told her, she'd seen the woman on TV. The woman was the patron saint of animal care and bloody gorgeous to boot.

Perhaps she'd brush on the barest touch of mascara. Nothing to do with Devon. She pulled a face at herself, noting the nothingness of her hairstyle. It reminded her she hadn't had a haircut in weeks and that she usually never left the house without make-up. There was nothing wrong with wanting to look nice for herself. Nothing at all, she told herself firmly as she added a quick touch of discreet eyeliner to her eyelids and toyed with her blusher brush. A tad of colour wouldn't do any harm. She examined the results in the mirror. Her heart sank. What was she thinking? She was going on a dog walk, for God's sake.

The doorbell rang. She frowned at herself. It was too bloody late now. With a last look in the mirror, she tossed her head and marched down the stairs. Devon probably wouldn't even notice and if he did, so what. It certainly wasn't for his benefit.

Grabbing Tess's lead, she opened the front door. Tess immediately came padding through. The dog had bat ears or extra sensory perception when Ella so much as touched the lead.

'Hi, be with you in a sec.' She pulled on her wellies and coat, and grabbed a scarf. 'Right, all set.'

She switched on the porch light to guide her home later.

'You look nice,' said Devon.

Ella blushed. 'Saturday night. Thought I'd make an effort for a change.'

Devon nodded and thankfully didn't say anything else about it. 'Which way shall we go. Quick circuit of the reservoir? Bets said she'd order the takeaway and go pick it up at seven, so we've got plenty of time.'

'Don't mind.' Ella lifted her shoulders. 'Reservoir sounds good ... as long as the fishermen have all gone.'

'Don't worry, I'll protect you.' He drew himself up tall, pretending to draw a sword. It struck her that he seemed lighter and less unhappy.

'How was the painting today?'

'Got loads done.'

'What? In between the two of you strutting your stuff?'

Ella closed her eyes. 'You saw us?'

'Might have had a sneaky peek through the window on my way out.'

'Please tell me you didn't.'

'Oh, I did.' His mouth twisted in a teasing smile. 'You both looked like you were having a great time. Was she OK?'

Ella exchanged a sad smile with him. 'She's really unhappy, isn't she?'

'Yeah, but very good at putting on a brave face. The happier and more exuberant she is, the more she's trying to hide.'

'I thought as much. Her and Jack, they're very young, I guess.'

'Yup. Too young, although for all that, I always thought they fit well. I believed they might make it through, but what do I know. I thought I'd got it all sussed and the happy-ever-after in sight.' The bleak look was back on his face.

'Did it not go well at the bank today?'

'How did you guess?'

'Because if it had you would have said something and the fact that you haven't is probably to do with Bets being unhappy and not wanting to upset her any more.'

'The bank basically told me to get stuffed. I've got no collateral. I can't wait to tell Marina that one. Another ball-busting trip to London for me this week.'

'But what about all the extra work you've been doing?'

'As the bank manager pointed out, what if I got kicked in the leg by a bull and couldn't work for three months? How would the bank get their money then?'

'Seems rather short sighted of them.'

'It's all about risk. And I'm a poor risk.'

'Could anyone else lend you the money?' She thought of the holiday cottages – perhaps Geoffrey had some spare cash.

'I can't ask Dad. He's already helping me out by letting me live rent-free in the barn and run the practice for him. Usually you have to buy into a practice. I'm not even sure what he's living on at the moment.' He plunged his hands into his hair and looked up at the night sky. 'Oh God, it's all such a mess. Marina's still making noises about us getting back together again.'

'Oh.' Ella didn't know what to say. Should she be encouraging? She had no idea how he felt about Marina. Did he still love her? How could he not – she looked stunning, super-organised, efficient, successful, perfect girlfriend material. He hadn't given much away about her.

'I know part of it is because she's realised how much she relied on me for help with diagnosis. She's had a couple of complaints apparently from viewers about duff information. She never was much of an academic. Scraped through her degree. Not that she'd ever admit that to anyone. And spending so much time filming, she's not kept up with new research the way she should.'

'So do you think you might go back to her?' Ella asked tentatively.

'Who knows?' He shoved his hands in his pockets. 'Financially, it would make life easier if I did go back. And I could practise the area of medicine I really want to get into.'

Poor Devon, he sounded as confused as she was. It made her feel guilty. She needed to speak to Patrick, not keep him hanging on. Speaking freely to Devon the other day had made her realise she couldn't ever go back. Aside from not wanting the same as her ultimately, he hadn't done anything wrong. It wasn't as if they'd ever talked about family or marriage. They'd each made their own assumptions.

They continued their walk as daylight slipped into dusk. It gave the reservoir an ethereal feel, mist floating over the water, ducks hugging the edge.

'I've started painting again.' Ella didn't know where the words came from or why she thought Devon would be interested but they burst out of her as she watched the wind tossing the water up into a crossfire of ripples.

'What, different from the mice?' asked Devon without missing a beat.

'Very different. Landscapes. Watercolours even. I've never

done them before. They never appealed. I think they might qualify as real art.'

'Glad to hear it.'

'Not that they'd get any critical acclaim or anything but I'm doing them because I can't not.'

'Would you believe me if I said that's why I practise veterinary science? I can't not do it any more. I think that's why it was easy to leave Marina. I hated what I was doing. Clipping guinea pig toenails. Trying to persuade owners of overweight pugs to put them on diets. Whereas, even at four in the morning,' he shot her a mischievous look, 'I don't mind getting out of bed to help deliver a breeched foal. I never ever thought of doing anything else and I loved my job until moving to Islington. London was where it all went wrong.'

'But you're getting back on your feet now.'

'I would be if I could just clear this debt. Looks like I'll be doing locum work on call for quite some time, which I don't mind but it's just knackering and then I worry I might make a mistake through sheer tiredness. I nearly totalled the car last week coming back from stitching a sheep back together in Eaton Bray.'

'That's not good, Devon.'

'What is it about you? I spill all my secrets.'

'Maybe I'm a secret agent in disguise,' suggested Ella, with a quick light-hearted grin.

'You're certainly a champion painter. I can't believe how much better Bets' kitchen looks.'

'Hmm, and I can't believe that you didn't show up until beer o'clock,' teased Ella.

'Ah, I have a good excuse, Buster the knicker-stealing dog. Unfortunately he ate them.'

'Seriously?' Ella tilted her head, checking his expression. She had a feeling he was having her on.

'Yup.'

'Eeuw. What do you do about that?'

'Emergency op to retrieve them. If it weren't for my financial situation I'd be investing in keyhole surgery equipment and using cameras. Something like that can be retrieved, the same way they went in. Although they don't come out in the same state they went in.'

Ella shuddered. 'I dread to think. Do you get that sort of thing a lot?' She'd never really considered the sort of things he dealt with on a daily basis.

'On a reasonably regular basis.'

'How much does one of those cameras cost?'

'Tens of thousands of pounds and there's the training, although I had started that.' A dark expression doused the enthusiasm on his face. 'I started the training when ... well, you know I told you the other day about the weasel. The course finished early that day, the lecturer wasn't well ... cliché of clichés I came home earlier than expected to find Madam and the weasel giving our bed a through road test.' He screwed up his face. 'For a little guy he certainly had some stamina.

'I did carry on the training but then it quickly became apparent that at the moment I can't afford it or the equipment, but one day. It can make such a difference ... ' he trailed off. 'Sorry, I'm getting evangelical.'

'No, it's interesting. So how does it make a difference?'

'Well it's like keyhole surgery for humans. Instead of an

incision and cutting through layers of tissue, which has to be stitched up afterwards and takes days or weeks to recover, this is one small hole. You try explaining to a dog that they can't move or pull at the stitches. This makes things much easier for them.'

When they returned and towelled off the two dogs, they found Bets waiting for them in the newly painted kitchen and the air full of the scent of spices.

'That smells good,' groaned Devon in appreciation.

'Bhajis. Chicken tikka.' Bets rummaged in the brown paper bag, pulling little plastic tubs out with the aplomb of a magician pulling rabbits from a hat. 'Bombay potato. Sag aloo. Chicken balti. Ella, would you mind grabbing some plates from that cupboard next to the cooker? Devon, you're on drinks. Beer and wine in the fridge.'

Ella sank gratefully into the sofa with a loaded plate on her knees. The only sound in the room was the chink of forks on the plates and the odd moan of satisfied greed.

'This is delicious,' she said, finishing off the last mouthful, her stomach heavy and full. The sofa was so comfortable she could have happily curled up and snoozed right there. She couldn't remember an evening like it since she'd left college. Devon and Bets were easy, undemanding company. They chatted idly about the village, the dogs, the best walks and the forthcoming village fete.

Bets wasn't going to let go of her idea of playing Trivial Pursuit. Ella caught Devon's eye as she busied herself setting up the board. It felt like they were indulgent parents giving in to a child that need humouring.

'Right, who's the oldest between you two?'

'Bets, you're the youngest, you can go first and then we can go round clockwise. I'm not going to embarrass a lady by asking her age. It's just not what a gentleman does.'

Bets snorted rudely. 'Gentleman! Huh!' But she threw the dice pretty promptly before any further argument. 'Five. I'll go for yellow. That's History, isn't it?'

'How many old pennies were there in a shilling?' Devon read the card.

'What?' Bets groaned. 'That's impossible.'

'Dad would know it.' Devon offered.

'Thanks, that's no help.'

'Make a guess,' suggested Ella, who had no idea. 'Think of old weights and measures. They were all funny amounts.'

'You're not supposed to give her clues.' Devon pulled a face at her.

'Twelve,' said Bets.

Devon glared at Ella. 'See.'

'How was that a clue? I was trying to get Bets to think laterally.'

'It was a clue because there are twelve inches in a foot,' crowed Bets, wriggling in her seat with a smug shoulder shimmy.

'Oops,' said Ella, shooting Devon a mischievous grin. 'But she could have gone for the number of ounces in a pound.'

'I would if I knew.'

They carried on playing and when Ella and Devon were level, with almost a full pie of pieces each, Ella felt her head start to droop. Thankfully the game was nearly over.

Bets threw again and landed on an orange square. 'Blast.

I'm rubbish at sport. Jack normally answers these ones.' Her track record this evening suggested she wasn't much better at history, science, art and literature or geography.

Devon read the card. 'Yeah, I think you might need to phone a friend on this one. Who was the first simultaneous holder of the Masters, Open, US Open and PGA titles?'

'What?' She stuck her chin out and scrunched up her face, looking like a recalcitrant toddler.

'I'm going to have to hurry you for an answer.'

'I have no idea. Andre Agassi.'

'No! That's tennis, you numpty. The Masters is golf.'

'Well, how was I supposed to know that?'

Devon shook his head and threw the dice. 'Science, green.'

Bets pulled out a card. 'I don't flipping believe it. What items of cricket equipment share their name with mammals that fly? Well, that's a tricky one.'

'Bat?' Devon didn't even try to hide his glee.

'I think you should have another one because that was too easy.' Bets grumbled.

He threw again this time, landing on a brown one. 'Art and Lit. I hate these. Will you be my phone a friend?' he asked Ella.

She looked pointedly at her piece and his. 'I don't think so.'

'Which artist had a blue period?'

'What, was he depressed?' asked Devon.

'There were plenty of those,' quipped Ella.

'I bet you know this one, don't you?'

'I could hazard a guess,' hedged Ella with a smug grin.

'Do you know, you two ought to go on a quiz team together,'

Bets suddenly said. 'You'd be brilliant. There's that one at the Old Boot in Tring. Ella could do the brown, pink and yellow and you could the blue, green and orange.'

'And I can do the brown, too,' said Devon with a sudden triumphant grin. 'Picasso.'

'Oh bugger, he's right.'

Devon threw the dice again.

'Blue. What river shares its name with a Teletubby?'

'That's not a real question,' howled Devon, trying to snatch the card from Bets.

'Yes, it is.'

'Oh God, I don't know their names. Handbag one, smiley one, short fat red one and the other one.'

'I'll have to hurry you.'

Devon glared. 'Orinoco.'

'No, that's a Womble.'

Ella threw the dice quickly. 'Art and Lit, brown please.'

Bets groaned again. 'What aged while Dorian Gray stayed young?'

Ella laughed. 'A portrait in the attic.'

'Ah, not quite correct. It says *his* portrait.' She held the card up with a teasing smirk on her face. 'So not any old portrait. I'm not sure I can give you this one.'

Ella raised an eyebrow. 'You're going to play dirty?'

'Hell, yeah.' Bets grinned.

'Bring it on,' replied Ella.

'Oh Lord, spare me, are you two going to get all competitive over the last piece of pie?'

'Of course,' Ella winked at Bets. 'To the death.'

'As you almost got that one right, you can throw again,' said

Bets magnanimously, with a regal nod which was spoilt by the sudden dimples that appeared in her cheek.

'Pink,' said Ella as she counted out three places. 'What subject's that?'

'Entertainment,' said Devon.

'Which rock 'n' roller introduced the duck walk?' asked Bets immediately flipping the card over to check the answer. 'Hmm, never knew that.'

Ella knew that tactic. Bets was trying to put her off. She had no idea but she wasn't going down without a fight. 'Duckbill Hailey.'

Bets sniggered.

'Chick Berry,' suggested Devon.

'Quacky Wilson,' Ella added.

'Bo Paddley.'

By this time they were all laughing so hard, the game was abandoned.

As Ella walked back to the house, Tess padding beside her, she smiled before wincing. She'd laughed so much today she'd pulled something in her side but she was still smiling now. She couldn't remember when she had so much fun and she'd been to some much more supposedly fun, sophisticated events in her time. She also had a sneaking suspicion Bets was attempting a bit of matchmaking.

Chapter Twenty

'Sorry I'm late. Guinea pig emergency. I've left Devon handling it on his own.' Bets giggled as they rushed the down the road to the Village Hall, Ella tripping along in her sparkly red shoes. 'He wasn't impressed. I'm going to have to buy him a pint later to make it up to him.'

Ella shook her head. 'What the hell constitutes a guinea pig emergency?'

'Let's just say, for a little fella, he produced a lot of liquid from one end. Believe me, Devon didn't look very happy.'

'I'm so glad I don't do your job.' Ella shuddered as she hauled open one of the glass double doors to the hall. 'Mopping up animal poo sounds hideous.'

Bets just grinned as she shot forward, following the sound of a Latin American rhythm pumping.

'Ah, ladies. Don't be shy. There's plenty of room here on the front row.' The loud bellow was completely at odds from the tiny woman prowling like a territorial cat in front of the stage. Up on the raised platform behind her sat a boom box, pulsating with music, which was almost as big as her, even though the hair piled on top of her head in some astonishingly over the top do with tendrils tumbling like an errant waterfall added a good few inches to her diminutive height.

Audrey gave them a cheerful wave from the middle row, while a woman with fluffy white-blonde hair teased upwards like albino candyfloss cleared a space for them. 'Here you go,' she whispered. 'You youngsters can show me what to do. I can copy you.' She took a step back.

'Audrey bully you into this too?' asked Bets in a loud whisper.

'No, love. It's just the teacher is a bit of blur. Can't see a thing past the end of my nose.' She gave an impish grin. 'Makes driving very tricky these days.'

Ella turned to Bets, her eyes widened. What the hell had she got herself into? Bets shrugged.

'Right, ladies,' boomed the teacher. 'For our latecomers, a quick recap. Watch me. We're going to take a step forward, then one back and two.'

She demonstrated with a fluidity that brought recognition. The drinks in the Latin American bar three streets away from Ella's college digs had been the cheapest for miles. She'd spent a lot of time there as a student.

Her hips wanted to respond to the sinuous siren call of the familiar beat. She knew the steps and recognised the layered rhythms of the music, the drums, the keyboards and more percussion. One two, one two three, one two, one two three. It was all there but something held her back, perhaps the awareness of all those eyes on her back.

'Now, ladies. With me. We'll just mark the steps very slowly without the music and then when you've got them we'll try it again with the music.'

Ella focused hard on the teacher's feet, tentatively marking out a few steps with small conservative moves, her hips stiff and unyielding. Next to her a beady eyed OAP with a definite tinge of lilac to her helmet of coiffured curls didn't seem the least bit self-conscious. Doris, that was her name. She lived next door to George. Mind you, anyone wearing a silver sequinned waistcoat over a white shirt over the top of a bright yellow chiffon layered skirt probably didn't care what they looked like. Ella stared with fascination at the skirt.

The woman caught her and nodded. 'Like it?' She did a twirl. 'I thought I'd get in touch with my inner *Strictly*.'

Ella nodded and smiled, not daring to admit she'd only seen the programme a couple of times.

'I'm Doris, by the way, and I live next door but one to you.'

'I know.' Ella nodded, being polite.

'You're very quiet.' The older woman looked disappointed. 'I was hoping for a bit of loud music, the odd wild party and lots of handsome young men with beards visiting from London.'

The significance of facial hair was a puzzler but Ella couldn't help smiling. 'Not yet, but there's still time.'

'Thank God for that. I wouldn't want to die before I got to try cocaine.'

Ella snorted in an attempt not to laugh out loud. 'I'll see what I can do,' she said, unable to hide her smile.

'Here we go, ladies.' With great gusto, the teacher pressed the button on top of her ancient CD player and music blasted out with tinny reverberation.

Like a pocket rocket, Doris was off. Despite her advanced years, she knew how to move.

Ella followed, her steps a little wooden. It would have been a lot easier if she wasn't on the front row and all those other women weren't behind her able to see her every move. She wished she hadn't given in to vanity and put on the shoes; it made it look as if she knew what she was doing.

Doris certainly didn't seem to care as with a joyful chortle she began to sing, 'Ay, ay, carumba', her hips moving with a snake-like fluidity that belied her age and sent the lemon chiffon whipping through the air. Ella had no idea whether it was a salsa song or not and she suspected that neither did Doris.

'Come on. You.' Doris poked her in the ribs. Hard. Bony fingers arcing with precision to the tender spot right between the ribs.

'Come on, artist girl. Show us what you're made of. Those shoes deserve a proper outing.' With a shimmy of bony shoulders, sending the sequins twinkling, Doris danced round her.

'Nice moves, but come on, loosen up those hips, now. Stiff as a board, you are.' She placed bony fingers on Ella's hips, twisting them this way and that.

She smelt of freesias and up close Ella could see the powder dusting her lines. Despite the whites of her eyes being dull and underpinned by bags with a net of lavender-veined lines, a devilish twinkle lit them. 'Lord, we used to have so much fun doing this. You wouldn't believe what we got up to. You young people think you invented sex and being naughty, but I can tell you a thing or two.'

It wasn't hard to imagine Doris up to no good. The pixie face, over-active eyebrows and deeply furrowed laughter lines suggested a life well-lived. The older woman threw back her head, shimmied her shoulders and danced with delicious joy.

Ella gave a polite smile, feeling her muscles freezing. She

put her head down and focused on her steps, feeling her feet bed into the heels. One, two, one two three. Inside her stomach churned. She knew how to do this but it was so hard in front of everyone. They'd think she was ... What would they think?

Ella sneaked a look around the room. No one was watching her. On her other side, Bets laughed as she fluffed her steps, copying the woman next to her. 'Lordy, I am rubbish at this,' she said as she stepped back onto Audrey's toes. Audrey wasn't bad at all, dancing with neat little steps, her arms bent and moving in time to the music. What struck Ella was the huge beam on her face.

Next to Ella, Doris was having a whale of a time, dancing up to other people so that they could mirror her steps.

'Come on. Give me a shimmy.' The chiffon skirts brushed Ella's jeans. Watching the waves of sunshine fabric lapping at the dark denim, an image of a painting she'd seen at an exhibition last year popped into her head. Sonia Delaunay's work. Dancers in a bar, absorbed in their world. Ella drifted for a second, remembering the pictures.

'That's more like it.' Doris whirled past her, catching one of her hands, jerking her forward. The momentum made her stumble and then like magic everything clicked into place. Somehow the music had seeped in note by note, commanding her muscles and with almost a sigh of relief her limbs relaxed, sinking into the rhythm. The bands of tension lacing her shoulders fell away and even breathing suddenly seemed easier.

With a grin, she added a shimmy of her shoulders in time with Doris. It all came back, those nights in the dimly lit bar of Havana Straights, the hip action, rolling them with ease, from left to right, the steps second nature. Closing her eyes, she let the music flood through. A sense of joy burst bright, her body lighter. Her feet knew what to do on their own, she didn't even need to think about it. How could she have forgotten this? This sense of ease with herself. It didn't matter what anyone else in the room thought. Whether she was a good or a bad dancer. Who cared?

'You go, girl,' yelled Doris, with a few wild turns before taking Ella's left hand in her right and placing a loose hand on her hip. 'Come on, you can be the man.'

In perfect synchronisation, they danced together, forward and back.

'Ooh, it's just like *Dirty Dancing*,' said Doris, immediately throwing in a few showy turns. 'Except I'm no one's Baby,' she added with a wink before letting go of Ella's hand and whirling off to dance with Bets.

With a smile, her hips still rolling, Ella watched Doris valiantly try to teach Bets the moves in time to the music. Bets still hadn't quite got the rhythm, not that it seemed to faze her, and she grinned as she pointed at Ella's hips. 'Nice moves.'

'Thanks.'

'It's like the darts all over again. I suppose you're going to tell me that you lived next door to a salsa bar.'

Ella grinned. 'Down the road. Havana Straights.'

Bets rolled her eyes good-naturedly.

Her feet tingled and her hips ached but it was worth it for the high she felt. Ella couldn't remember the last time she'd had so much fun.

'Bye, Doris.'

'Bye, and don't you forget. I want a party invitation.'

'I won't.' Ella was conscious of Bets beside her jumping about in agitation.

'Come on, we need to go.' Dragging Ella by the arm, she hurried her to the exit. 'Damn.' Bets muttered under her breath. 'Whatever you do, don't stop.'

'Thanks, Audrey, that was brilliant fun.' Bets almost threw her fiver at the older woman, waiting at the door with an old margarine tub in her hand.

'Yes, thank you,' added Ella placing her money more carefully into the container.

Audrey stepped in front of her, making direct eye contact. Next to Ella, Bets let out a low groan.

'I'm so glad you could both make it. Always good to have some younger blood at these things.' She shot an amused look at Doris's retreating figure. 'I don't suppose either of you are first aid trained. I really must talk to the Village Hall Committee about perhaps fundraising for a defibrillator. Which reminds me,' she flashed a charming, shark-going-in-for-the-kill smile at Ella, 'I know you've agreed to do our little talk at the WI and Bets says you've agreed to donate a picture for the hall roof fund raiser but I wondered if you'd give us a pair.' With an encouraging smile she carried on, completely oblivious to Bets trying to sidle away. Ella nodded but didn't manage to get a word in before Audrey was off again.

'And I shall see you both at the Spring Fayre. My gosh, we're going to miss your godmother this year. We're going to need something really spectacular decoration-wise for the Chiltern Bake Off, but that's a month away, so we'll worry about that after the Fayre.' Audrey gave a plaintive sigh. 'No one bakes cakes quite like Magda. I daresay the cake stall will manage.'

She whipped out her notebook. 'Now, Bets, you said you'd manage the dog agility competition, so I've left you to do that.' She turned to Ella and with a shrewd assessing look gave her up a quick up and down. 'Hmm, I think it will have to be the tombola stall for you. Shall I put you down for the ten till twelve slot?'

Ella looked helplessly at Bets.

'Excellent. Now all we need is good weather on the day.' With a bird-like tilt of her head, Audrey spotted a new victim. 'Ah, Judith. Glad I caught you. Now with Magda away . . .'

Devon watched the two women as they approached the table he'd snagged in the pub, Bets throwing back her head and laughing and Ella's grave face softening before they both burst into giggles. Thinking back to the woebegone creature he'd first seen up in the woods, the transformation on Ella's face was nothing short of a miracle. With her flushed cheeks and glittering eyes, she looked like a different person.

'I take it salsa was a hit.'

'So much fun,' enthused Ella, demonstrating with a few quick steps, still wearing her red shoes. 'I loved it.'

Bets dropped her bottle on the table in front of him. 'Old snake hips. What a laugh. You've got to hand it to her, Audrey gets some good things organised, although I could do without the blinking dog agility thing.'

'Hmm,' said Devon dubiously. 'I'm doing my best to keep my head down, but I think she's starting to ramp up her campaign. I've tried to lay it on thick about how busy I am.'

'What does dog agility entail?' asked Ella, taking a long slug of beer. Devon watched the smooth column of her neck as she chugged straight from the bottle with evident enjoyment. It was as if someone had a lit a candle inside her; she glowed.

Ella turned to Bets. 'I've got visions of aerobics for dogs. Seriously?'

'No, I build a course of jumps and tunnels and gates. The dogs have to go through the course. Except they often get a bit excited by the crowd and other dogs, so don't behave, run off, go the wrong way around the course. It would be hilarious, except I'm supposed to keep some sort of score, and lots of the kids enter and then I get irate parents challenging the result. Tiger moms.'

'I think I might have got off lightly. Apparently I'm doing the tombola.'

'Lucky you,' said Bets. 'I'd love to do the tombola. Dead easy. And what's this about a talk to the WI?'

Ella suddenly frowned. 'I was hoping to get out of that, and to be honest I'd forgotten. She collared me in the hospital when I was visiting George.' An expression of sheer panic suddenly blossomed in her eyes. 'How does she do that?'

'It's called the Audrey Factor,' said Devon fondly. 'She's an irresistible force of nature that you just don't mess with. And I should know, I've had to put up with it all my life.'

Bets shot an apologetic glance his way before saying, 'With Audrey there's no getting out of anything, you're committed now.'

'That's what I was afraid of. What the hell am I going to talk about for an hour? I've got nothing to say.'

'Don't be ridiculous,' Devon chipped in. 'Of course you

have. How did you get started? How do you come up with the ideas? You can talk about the flamenco pictures.' He winked, reminding her of how he'd caught her dancing.

She rolled her eyes at him.

'You can talk about how you work? You know draw, dance, draw.'

Ignoring his teasing, she worried at a loose thread at the bottom of her shirt. 'I'm not sure that it's going to be terribly interesting.'

'Rubbish. If you talk with enthusiasm and passion, you can make anything interesting.'

'But standing there talking is a bit dull.'

'You could give them a demonstration. Do a dance.'

Bets raised an intrigued eyebrow. 'What's with the dancing?'

'It's a long story,' said Ella glaring at him, although there was a twinkle in her eye. 'Will you shut up with the dancing. You caught me once. I don't normally work like that.'

'You should. It looked like fun.' He sobered. 'Seriously. You drew that sketch in the pub pretty quickly, as I recall. Make it interactive.'

Ella paused. That might be fun.

'I've got an idea!' She grabbed a beer mat and fished a pen out of her bag. 'Think of a hat.'

'What?' Devon and Bets looked at each other, puzzled.

'A hat.'

'Cowboy hat,' said Bets.

'Perfect.' With quick deft strokes, she sketched Cuthbert wearing one looped around his neck.

'Wow, that's amazing. You've even captured the John Wayne bow-legged look.'

Ella beamed. 'That's what I'll do. I'll get the audience to suggest different hats. And it will give me plenty of material for the future. And I could display some of my pictures – I've got loads in storage. And seven of them are already framed. I'll need to get a couple more done, so that I can do a bit of a display. I can probably buy a few nice frames with mounts, although time's a bit tight.'

'Bets and I could pitch in to help. If you just bought a job lot of frames in IKEA, they wouldn't be expensive.'

'That's a brilliant idea. The original illustrations can be cut down easily to fit as they're all on A4 cartridge paper.' Ella frowned. 'Although I'm not sure how I'll get them out here. I don't fancy taking Magda's car into London and I can't carry them on the train.'

'That's easy,' said Devon. 'I'm going into London on Tuesday. You'd get them all in the Volvo. Where's your storage?'

'It's just off the North Circular in London.'

'Perfect. I can drive you there and park the car and then get a Tube into central London. I'm going to see a vet friend of mine. You can come and meet him. Nice chap. We could grab some lunch together.'

'Thanks. That would be great.'

'OK. We'll need to leave earlyish. I expect we could persuade Bets to have both dogs for the day.' He flashed Bets a smile, knowing it was a rare day she turned down a chance for a dog fix. 'Shall I pick you up about eight? Then we'll miss the worst of the traffic in town.'

Chapter Twenty-One

Ella punched in the pin code to the storage room, flinching slightly at the brightness of the well-lit corridor.

'I've never been in one of these places before,' said Devon looking around at the wide corridor stretching beyond them. 'It's huge.'

'They store all sorts of things here. The first time I came, there was a guy loading in a full-size grizzly bear.'

'You're kidding?' Devon looked alarmed and turned to look at the brightly coloured doors lining the corridor.

'It was stuffed.' Ella giggled at the horrified expression on his face. 'He worked for some museum and they'd had a flood and they needed emergency storage.'

The pin pad beeped and Ella pulled open the door. Fluorescent light flooded the room, stark on the almost empty room.

Ella's heart thudded painfully as she took a disbelieving step into the room. Where was everything? There were a few tatty boxes, a couple of old sculptures she done at art college and two large abstracts propped against the wall.

For a horrible moment she wanted to cry. Surely Patrick hadn't thrown everything away. He wouldn't have, would he?

Although she hadn't worried about her drawings, now that they weren't here, nausea swamped her. Grief reared up so sharply, it took her breath away. Her creations. The history of Cuthbert and his siblings.

Devon didn't say a word. He didn't need to. The facts were glaringly obvious.

'They're gone,' she stuttered turning in a slow circle as if items might miraculously materialise à la Harry Potter. 'There's nothing here.'

'I can see that,' said Devon drily.

'I don't understand. It was all there.' She pointed to the wall on the right. 'Stacked up against that wall. The framed prints and a stack of portfolio holders. Just there.' She walked to the spot.

'Does anyone else have access?' asked Devon.

'Only Patrick. But what would he want with them?'

Devon looked searchingly at her. 'I've no idea. Emotional attachment. He's missing you, he needed them like a security blanket.'

Ella gave a mirthless laugh. 'You don't know Patrick.' They were too much of a reminder of her failure to fulfil the artistic promise that had first attracted him to her. 'They're the last thing he'd have emotional attachment to. He thinks I waste too much energy and time on them at the expense of my creativity.'

Devon frowned.

Where were they? The sudden stomach clench of panic didn't make sense. She'd not really looked at them in years, certainly never missed them, but now acute fear filled her. What if they'd gone for good?

'I'm sure there's a simple explanation,' she announced a little more confidently than she felt.

'Yes.' Devon nodded. 'So what do you want to do?'

Ella looked at her watch. 'What time are you meeting your friend?'

'At twelve-thirty. We're meeting for a pint and then we've got a table booked for one-thirty.'

Ella made a sudden decision. 'Would you mind if I joined you at the restaurant? I can be there by half one and then you can catch up with him properly on your own.'

'No, that would be fine. We're only meeting in Carluccio's in Garrick Street.'

Ella bit her lip and smoothed clammy palms down her jeans. 'I think I might go to the gallery. See Patrick.'

Devon raised one eyebrow. 'Sure you want to do that?'

'No, I'm not sure at all. I've been avoiding it.' It was time to face Patrick. Even though her head was telling her it was time to have a talk about going their separate ways, her heart worried that when she saw his familiar face, the slim angular body, she might change her mind. She'd be giving up so much. A life built together over the years.

'Are you going to be OK?' Devon asked, his eyes shadowed with concern. 'Do you want me to come with you?'

She swallowed and tried to school her face into a blank mask. His obvious anxiety on her behalf touched her. She wanted to clutch at the firm hand on her arm. His eyes held hers, his gaze strong and steady as if he could see all the confusion and hurt raging inside her, offering reassurance.

That calm, solid demeanour he wore like a second skin gave her a tiny bit of comfort. Inside, her stomach churned at the thought of walking into the gallery and seeing Patrick. Taking Devon along would be like putting on a suit of armour. It would also be incredibly cowardly and unfair to Devon. He had enough problems of his own.

'No, you go on and see your friend. I'll meet you there. I shouldn't be long.'

'Can I help you?'

Ella couldn't help staring at the rather magnificent cleavage on display. It was rather hard to miss. In a royal blue dress cut to emphasise her assets, the woman in front of her reminded Ella of Snow White with her glossy black hair and dark red lips. For a moment, Ella wondered if the colour of the dress had been chosen deliberately to evoke just that image. She thought the red Alice band might be overdoing it a bit, or was that her being bitchy.

'Hi. I'm looking for Patrick. Is he in?'

'Patrick?' Snow White asked, looking coy and startled.

Ella sighed inwardly. She didn't need any one-upmanship today. 'Yes, Patrick Clarkson. The owner.'

'I'm sorry.' The girl's saccharine sweet smile made Ella want to throttle her. No, she wasn't. She wasn't the least bit sorry. She was about as far from sorry as humanly possible. 'No, I'm afraid he isn't.'

Ella gritted her teeth and tried to smile politely. It wasn't like her to take an instant dislike to someone.

'Do you know when he might be back?'

It was unusual for him not to be here and she felt quite

aggrieved that she'd screwed up all her courage to saunter so casually into the gallery and find he wasn't here.

'I'm sorry.' The sickly factor of the smile had dimmed. Even less sorry than before. 'He's at a meeting. I've no idea when he'll be back. Would you like to make an appointment?'

'No,' said Ella.

'Can I take a name?'

'I'll just take a look round.' After all, it was an art gallery.

Snow White pursed her lips and pointedly went back to whatever she was doing behind the high gloss wall of the reception desk.

Ella invested a huge of amount of time and energy helping Patrick set this place up but as she went into the main room, she realised it had undergone quite a makeover in the last few weeks. It was odd that Patrick hadn't mentioned any plans to make changes.

New windows and skylights had made the place much brighter and the slate black floor made a vast improvement on the previous white painted wooden floor boards which had needed touching up every couple of weeks to keep them looking the part. She scowled down at the new stone – she'd invested a lot of hours in that damn floor, it seemed an insult for Patrick to have finally replaced it without even telling her, but that's what life would be like going forward. The knowledge came with an unwelcome pang.

It looked as if things were finally going well. The gallery had been open for ten years now and the first couple of years had been real touch and go as to whether it could be sustained. Patrick had felt that sense of insecurity keenly. Always on the look-out for the next big artist that would make his and the gallery's name. Ella winced. She was supposed to be the draw when they first got together but several miserable shows later followed by poisonous reviews had killed her confidence stone dead and the more Patrick wanted her to be able to paint, the less she was able to deliver.

She turned to study the first picture on the wall to her left, her vision blurring with sudden tears. Coming here brought home what she stood to lose. Investment in ten years of life. She'd leave with nothing. She didn't even have a job any more.

Blinking hard, she stared at the image painted on a large jagged edged sheet of Perspex. Black and white with electric blue spots colonising one corner. The blurb beneath talked at length about the connection between man and technology. She took a step nearer, focusing on the blue spots. Nope, she didn't get it at all. Nothing new there, then.

Her boots clunked on the hard floor as she rounded a corner, passing a couple more pictures that failed to speak to her. No wonder she couldn't paint proper pictures. She didn't have a clue any more. This was cutting-edge stuff. Patrick had an eye for the avant-garde. Actually, she thought as she took a step back and studied the nearest picture, it was utter bollocks. With a smile, she turned her back on it.

Voices were coming from behind her and she could see a few other people looking at the pictures which were in the series of smaller rooms leading off this room It was odd, normally people adopted hushed tones in the gallery, which she never really understood, but these people were talking normally.

She walked towards the voices. In the first room there were several groups of people. The most she'd ever seen in here.

Most of these pictures had red spots on them, denoting they'd been sold. At least she thought they were red spots, although it might just have been her seeing red. Rage surged hot and fast. Ranged along the walls, admittedly displayed to beautiful advantage, were six illustrations of Cuthbert. Cuthbert in a shower cap. Cuthbert running up a curtain in a jester's hat and Cuthbert dusted in flour with a chef's hat. Her eyes narrowed and in quick angry strides she crossed to one particular illustration. She stood in front of it, her hands clenched to her sides with shoulders so taut they were in danger of removing her ears.

She studied the lines of the Cavalier's hat, the brilliant purple plume inked so painstakingly ... only two weeks ago. White heat burst and spiralled through her. That particular image hadn't even gone to the publishers yet. Was this the reason for Britta's unexpected visit? Or had taking this picture been a spur of the moment thing? Without stopping to think, she lifted it from the wall with both hands and held it in front of her. Cuthbert's cheeky face stared back as if in encouragement.

Next to her a middle-aged woman gasped.

'I don't think ... '

Ella wheeled around and shot her an incendiary glance which had the woman taking a wide-eyed step back.

She tucked the picture under one arm, wheeled around and marched through the gathered crowd, all of whom stepped out of her grim determined path.

'Excuse me, you can't do that,' called a surprised voice. 'If you want to buy the picture, you need to let Sandra at the desk know. You can't just go round removing them from the wall.'

The young man came right up to Ella and put out his arms, but she shook him off, avoiding his touch. Another new member of staff. Ella didn't recognise him. Where were all the usual staff?

'It's OK,' she snarled and he took a nervous step sideways, letting her go.

Snow White at the desk plastered a customer-friendly smile on her face, now that she thought she was about to make a sale. 'Can I help you with that?' She put out her hands to take the picture.

Ella reared back, noting with satisfaction the sudden alarm that flared in her eyes.

'No!' She hugged the wooden frame closer. 'Tell Patrick that Ella was here.'

'Madam, you can't just take the picture.' She jumped up and ran around the desk attempting to bar the way to the door. 'I'll ... I'll call the police.'

'You do that.' Ella raised one eyebrow daring her to. 'But before you do ...' She turned the painting, still holding it tightly in both hands. 'See that, Ella Rigden.' She indicated her name on the white mounting around the picture. 'That's me. *My* painting. Go ahead, you call the police.'

'It might be your painting but ... you've got a contract. You can't just come and get them. There's procedures. Paperwork.' Her head bobbed like an agitated chicken and for a moment Ella almost let guilt get the better of her. 'How do I know you are her? And even if you are, you can't just take it.'

She shrugged her shoulders. 'I can if it was stolen from me.'

Inside, another Ella recoiled in horror and shouted at the

top of its voice. *What are you doing? You never do things like this.*

'Carl,' the girl shrieked. 'Do something.'

The young man came racing over.

Still furious, Ella pushed him away hard and as he hit the ground, she heard the loud peel of an alarm. Snow White looked triumphant.

Ella stopped for a moment, feeling the fierce shriek of the alarm vibrating through her. Damn, it was connected to the police station. Horrified, she stared at the girl behind the counter and she froze, her fingers cramping on the edge of the frame.

With a sudden decisive intake of breath, she spun round, pushed hard at the door with her shoulder and legged it down the street as fast as she could.

Chapter Twenty-Two

'It's a really generous offer, James, and I appreciate it.' Devon stopped and fiddled with the knife in front of him. Carluccio's resonated with the noise and vigour of a busy lunchtime crowd. Too reminiscent of life with Marina. Loud, busy with people jockeying for attention. Having his own practice again – what he wouldn't give for that, but there was no way he could accept the offer. Not while he still had debt up to his eyeballs.

'I can tell by that stubborn set on your chiselled manly chin, that you're not even going to consider it.' James grimaced. 'Why the hell not? We're mates. Let me help.'

Devon sighed, sourness churning in his stomach. He could stall. Give James a million excuses and he knew that he'd see through every one of them. The knife slipped through his fingers, falling onto the floor with a metallic clang. Like a bell ringing time.

He looked up. Even though James was his oldest friend, he found it hard to tell him the truth. This was his mess and he was going to work it out. He didn't want anyone's help. No one needed to jump to his rescue.

'I'm not taking your money. I'm OK.'

'Man.' James shook his head in frustrated disgust. 'Stop being so damned proud.'

It wasn't a question of pride. Devon wanted his self-respect back.

'James. I'm going to fix this and in a while,' a hell of a long while, 'I can think about setting up my own practice again.'

'But why don't you just take over your dad's place?'

'Because the village wants Dad back. And Dad needs to get back to work. There's nothing wrong with him now. I know what he's up to. He's helping me out and I don't want him to. I can stand on my own two feet.'

'And what about Marina. It's definitely over? I never thought you two guys...' James's voice trailed off.

Devon shrugged. 'These things happen.' There was no way he was going to admit to James that he'd caught Marina in bed with another man. That had been the final car crash act on their relationship but like a juggernaut without brakes it had been slowly careering to an end and he'd done nothing to stop it.

Devon rocked his head back, trying to ease the stiffness in his shoulders.

'Can't you expand your dad's practice, make it more profitable? Come on, you said it was in desperate need of modernisation. I thought you said that you should be selling nutritional pet foods. There's always a good margin in those.'

'I'm not staying there.' Devon grimaced. 'I'm Mr Unpopular. I've got to overturn a generation's way of doing things. People don't like change.' His attempts to educate pet owners, mainly around diet, were dismissed with, 'Old

Mr Ashcroft never said that'. The minute he tried to insist a bill was paid on time, they went running to Dad, complaining about him being hard or difficult. In an attempt to balance his life and allow him to do more locum work on call, he'd had to be stricter about opening hours but people still expected him to run an open-all-hours regimen.

'Rome wasn't built in a day and all that. They'll come round. It just takes time.'

'I've got plenty of that, I'm just not sure I've got the energy to stick at it.'

'And the bank won't relent.'

'No.' Devon straightened. 'And listen to me. This is boring. How's married life?'

James's face lit up. With a slight touch of envy, Devon leaned back in his chair as James chatted happily about his new bride, their new home and their plans for the future.

By the time the waitress delivered their starters, he felt fidgety and cross about nothing in particular. It would have been nice for Ella to at least have contacted him to let him know she'd decided not to join them for lunch. He guessed her mind was elsewhere.

'If looks could kill, you'd be up on a serial murder charge,' observed James, one eyebrow lifting in amusement. 'Going to tell me about it?'

'Nothing to tell. Just pissed off that Ella hasn't got the manners to let me know where she is.' He took a mouthful of the bruschetta he'd ordered.

'Maybe she and the boyfriend are making up.' James winked.

Devon's appetite vanished as a dull pain clamped around his heart.

Should he phone her? Better not, she might be deep in discussion with Patrick. They might even be mid make-up sex. His heart flipped over. God forbid, he really hoped not.

Devon shot James a dirty glare as he crunched through ciabatta and piquant tomatoes.

'So who is this Ella chick? I've not heard you mention her before.'

'No one.'

'No one?' James's brow furrowed into disbelieving lines. 'And I'm Brad Pitt. Come on. I'm beginning to think that phone is surgically attached.'

'She's just a friend.'

'Yeah, and I've heard about those types of friends.'

'She's living in the village. It's a small place, you run into people a lot. She's a friend of Jack's girlfriend, Bets. We walk the dogs sometimes.'

'So what's she like?'

Devon shrugged. 'Not my type, really. Touchy. Reserved. Artist. Bit buttoned up.' Except when she was dancing around Bets' flat in white overalls or cheating at Trivial Pursuit. 'Good at darts.' He smiled. 'She draws. Cuthbert Mouse. Clever, funny pictures. Quirky sense of humour.'

'I meant what does she look like? Is she a babe like Marina?'

'No! Not at all.' Marina dressed in smart shift dresses and heels and always looked immaculate with lots of make-up. Ella didn't seem to do make-up or if she did, he'd never noticed it. 'Blonde hair.' Soft and sweet-scented. 'Slimmish.'

Soft curves when he'd held her. 'Gentle.' He thought of her talking to George while they waited for the ambulance as he took another mouthful of his starter. 'Although she can be a bit spiky.'

'Sounds as if you like her.' James grinned, lifting his lager glass in ironic toast. 'She also sounds a hell of a lot nicer than Marina.'

Devon stared at his friend.

'Come on, Devon. I admire the fact you don't badmouth her but seriously ... she was one high-maintenance babe. And my wife ... can't stand her. Sorry, mate.' James suddenly looked horrified. 'Oh shit, don't tell Clara I said a word. She said I wasn't to tell you. In case you ever get back together.'

'You're safe. I doubt we'll be getting back together. I was tempted at first but ... '

'You fancy this new chick.'

'James!'

'I can see the signs.'

'She's just a friend.' Unfortunately, the more he said it, the more he questioned it.

Right on cue, his phone vibrated on the table. Finally, Ella calling. He snatched his mobile up to hear her unleash a torrent of agitated words. Listening and nodding, ignoring the avid curiosity on James's face, it took almost a minute before he could get a word in edgeways.

'I'll be right there.'

Chapter Twenty-Three

Devon took the steps of the police station two at a time. He'd crossed town in record speed, abandoning James in the restaurant. How did someone like Ella get arrested?

And there she was huddled into a seat, clutching a framed picture to her chest as if her life depended on it, with a mutinous expression on her face, looking ready to punch anyone who came too close. As he came through the double doors, she jumped to her feet.

'Devon. Oh, thank you.' She crossed the floor, bumping into plastic chairs, completely ignoring the bumps and bangs to her legs in her haste. 'Did you bring your car with you?'

'Yes.'

'Good.' She grabbed his arm, in an uncharacteristic show of bossiness, and shepherded him back the way he'd just come, so he had to walk backwards. 'Let's get out of here.' She shuddered.

Devon looked back uncertainly at the uniformed desk sergeant, who was half-heartedly keeping an eye on proceedings in between looking at a computer screen on his desk. 'Are you free to go? I thought you'd been arrested.'

She gave a contemptuous pout, which shouldn't have amused him but it did. Grumpy primadonna was a side to Ella he'd not seen before. 'I was. And then they realised,' she raised her voice, shouting the last few words and shooting a pointed look at the officer, *'they'd got it wrong.'*

All heads turned their way. 'Right.' Probably best to get her out of there quickly before they decided to arrest her again for disturbing the peace. Her body language suggested she was spoiling for a fight.

'So are you going to tell me what the hell has happened?'

'As soon as we get out of here.' She pushed him again, clearly keen to get away.

'So what happened? Did you see him at the gallery?'

'No, I flipping didn't. He wasn't there. But this was.' She held out the painting of Cuthbert in a black hat with a fancy purple feather. It looked familiar and he realised he'd seen it on her drawing board not that long ago.

'Nice price tag,' he said, squinting at the white label in the corner of the picture.

With a frown she spun the painting around to take a better look. 'How much! I don't believe it. I'm going to kill him. I am absolutely going to kill him.' She bounced on the balls of her feet, with the pent-up angry energy of a lightweight boxer pumped for action.

'So what happened?'

He'd never seen her like this. Energy fairly buzzed from her as she fizzed with manic agitation, emotion spilling out with tangible movement. What had happened to reserved, restrained Ella who even when pouring her heart out, kept a tight rein on her emotions?

'I went to the gallery. Patrick wasn't there.' Her voice vibrated with suppressed fury. 'I would have probably walked out but the new manageress, who didn't know me, was so snotty.' She pulled a disgusted face. 'Seriously snotty. She made a song and dance about not knowing where Patrick was. Cowbag had no intention of telling me when Patrick would be back. I didn't want to look stupid and there was no way I was going to give her the satisfaction of walking out, so I stayed to have a look round.' She screwed her face up in an expression which might have been comical if she hadn't been so cross. 'Not because I particularly wanted to but just because I could. I should have realised something was up.'

She looked at him as if he was supposed to say something but he wasn't falling into that trap, not with her in this manic, agitated mood.

'There were more people there than usual. And Patrick doesn't run that sort of gallery. Empty is more his style. Dead is normal operating procedure. He wouldn't want the masses in there anyway. I thought it was intriguing. So I went into the other room to see what they were all looking at.' She paused and he felt her shoulders rise in tension before she burst out, 'Only an exhibition of *my* flipping pictures.' She clutched it tighter to her chest, her elbows winging out like an indignant penguin.

Devon didn't quite follow. 'I thought having an exhibition was a good thing.'

From the icy glare she gave him, it didn't take Einstein to surmise he'd said something exceptionally stupid.

'It is if the pictures haven't been *stolen*,' she spat the word, 'from you.' She stopped in the street and turned to face him, her face full of irate indignation. 'Patrick took them. From the lock-up. All my mice pictures. They were mine. He stole them. After all he said.' Her eyes widened with every sentence.

Her mouth opened and shut for a couple of seconds, her cheeks reddening. 'I didn't know anything about it. I can't believe ... I just ... how dare he?'

'Ah.' Devon floundered for a minute. In the face of her anger, it would be as easy to say the wrong thing as it was to take a wrong step in a minefield.

'Not just that.' Her eyes widened, flashing with fury. 'This,' she stabbed at the image of Cuthbert with venom, 'is a new one.' With clenched teeth, she made a noise pretty close to a growl. 'It wasn't in the lock-up. No! Not even my publisher has seen it.'

It took a minute for Devon to work out what the implications of that were.

'So how did he get hold of it?' he asked cautiously, still aware of his precarious position.

'As to the exact process, your guess is as good as mine, but it wasn't legit. He's never been to the cottage. So who has?' Her eyes burned with a sheen, suggesting she was close to tears. 'He must have phoned a friend. A mutual friend. Britta.' She slowed down and he could see the weariness settle heavy on her shoulders as her posture sagged. Betrayal did that to you.

'I'm sorry. That's shit.'

'I think that's what tipped me over. I don't care that he's

selling the pictures. It's that he's such a hypocrite. And that she came and pretended to be my friend. I lost it. Just took it off the wall and walked out with it.'

'Ah,' he could picture it, the sense of injustice powering her, 'and that's when you were arrested.'

Ella's face fell with chagrin. 'Yeah. It never occurred to me that they'd set the alarm off. I didn't really think that far ahead. I don't know what I thought they'd do. Or what I'd do. I didn't think at all, just acted.'

She suddenly looked so woebegone as she stared down at the picture, holding it out at arm's length. He stopped and they looked at it together. He smiled – it was Cuthbert at his finest. The mouse had an imperious look on his face as he posed paw on furry hip, the feather of his hat tickling him under the chin. Devon slid an arm along her shoulder and pulled her closer to him.

'You're very talented. This is brilliant.'

'It's not brilliant.' She wrinkled her nose and then her mouth softened. 'Although, I like it.' Her mouth curved into a smile. 'Yeah, I really like it.'

'You should. It's clever. Witty. Warm. You can almost imagine what Cuthbert is thinking.'

She shot him a quick grin. 'I know what he's thinking.'

'I'm the bee's knees and isn't this just the best hat you've ever seen?' said Devon. 'But you love me despite my vanity.'

He felt Ella's shoulders lift and she turned her head towards him, delight showing on her face. 'Ten out of ten, Mr Vet.'

'And I'd say achieving that takes real talent and a certain skill.'

'Thank you. That means a lot. I'd not really seen it like that before. Too wrapped up in worrying about the pictures not being meaningful.'

'I'd say that's in the eye of beholder and you. Cuthbert looks like he means to get up to plenty of mischief.'

Ella nodded. 'He does that all right.'

Devon was pleased to see he'd put a smile back on her face – she had to be feeling pretty crappy at the moment. Being let down by people you loved and trusted ranked up there as being officially shit.

'So, now that you're a master art thief... Were you charged? What happens next?' He slowed down; the car was in sight now.

'They arrested me. Took all my stuff away, so I couldn't even phone you. I had to wait for a duty solicitor except there wasn't anyone.' Her mouth trembled and he could tell she was getting upset again. Of course she was, it had to have been quite a traumatic experience.

'Hey, it's OK. You're out now. So what did the solicitor say?' He gave her another squeeze and she responded by nudging up to his body which wasn't that easy when she was still hanging onto the picture.

'It didn't get that far. The custody sergeant came in and told me they'd received fresh information and I was free to go.'

'Ella!'

'Oh shit.' The colour leached from her face. 'It's Patrick. I do not want to talk to him.'

'Ella, wait!' The shouted cry came from down the street.

Although taller than Devon had expected, Patrick looked

exactly as he'd thought he would. Seriously, outside of films and Sunday supplements, who wore a wanky, cream-coloured linen suit? They were in downtown East London, not the bloody Tropics.

It was a personal prejudice, Devon knew that, but seriously, this man had a hairstyle. Shaved at the back, long at the front. Real men did not have hairstyles, at least not in his book.

Ella prodded Devon in the back, as if to hurry him along.

'I don't think you've got much choice. He's clearly seen you.' As soon as he added, 'And it's better to get it over with,' he regretted it when she shot him a very dirty look. She slipped from underneath his arm and turned to face the man striding down the street towards them.

'Ella, my God, are you all right? I am so sorry. I nearly fired Sandra for having you arrested. A complete overreaction.' He put both hands out in a dramatic grasp of her upper arms.

To Devon, the gesture looked staged and phony. Worse still, he could see from Ella's sudden stiffness that it made her acutely uncomfortable. She'd shut her mouth tight, the lips pressed in a firm line as if to stop the pain escaping. He saw the previous sparks of ire in her eyes snap out with heart-breaking finality, to be replaced with unutterable sadness.

'Ella. This has all been a terrible mistake. It's so good to see you. Talk to me. I've missed you so much.' Patrick lifted a hand and stroked her cheek, his eyes gazing at her adoringly. 'I phoned the police station as soon as I'd heard what had happened.'

What a prat. Devon looked hurriedly at Ella's face. Surely she wasn't taken in by this?

*

When Ella looked at Patrick's face just inches from hers, his eyes channelling earnest entreaty, she wrenched herself out of his reach and instinctively moved closer to Devon.

Although Patrick had a few inches in height over Devon, he was definitely smaller in stature. Next to Devon's broad shoulders and muscled forearms, his frame looked flimsy and lightweight, rather like his character. The piercing revelation rocked home, shocking her. She stared at him as if seeing him for the first time.

'Patrick,' she managed in a breathless gasp.

'What idiots for arresting you! Talk about going overboard. I'm really sorry you had to go through that.'

She stared at him, taking in the familiar pale skin lightly dusted with the heavy freckles of an almost redhead, focusing on the cluster of them just beneath his cheekbone which she'd always thought, but never told him, looked like a Scottie dog. It took a while for her to muster the words and when they came out, in a sudden hot rush, they didn't sound like her at all.

'I don't care about being arrested. You think *that's* what's upset me?'

'Hey, Ella.' He held up his hands in a gesture of surrender. It looked patronising. 'Calm down.' He looked around anxiously.

Her fists clenched. Calm, she'd give him calm.

'There's no need to make a scene. We can talk about this. Why don't you come back to the gallery, with your ... ?' The dismissive look he gave Devon infuriated her.

It was one thing Patrick being an arse to her, but she was buggered if she'd allow him to be rude to Devon. Not when

Devon had dropped everything and come rushing to her rescue.

A sensation of warmth flooded through her and she looked at Devon. Completely at ease, he gave Patrick a pleasant smile and like the perfect gentleman he was, he smoothly took charge, and ignoring the undercurrents of emotion swirling, with diplomatic ease immediately extended a hand. 'Devon.'

Pride filled her at the way in which he dismissed Patrick's attempt at oneupmanship, making Patrick look like a small puppy nipping around the heels of an elder statesman.

Patrick had no choice but to extend his own hand and shake Devon's, even though the look of distaste accompanying the gesture suggested he'd rather handle a cobra.

'Ella, we need to talk. I can explain. I can explain everything. I should have told you but I wanted to make sure it went well first.' He put his hands out in urgent appeal. 'The exhibition was a bit of an experiment. I thought you'd be pleased but I ... I didn't want to tell you in case it wasn't a success. And it has been. Fabulous.'

'Bollocks.' Her rage erupted, making both Patrick and Devon start. Good! 'You're a liar. A cheat. Admit it, You've been selling them.' She pointed to the price tag on the picture. Suddenly Bets' comments all those weeks ago made sense. Patrick had been selling her pictures for years. 'That price wasn't plucked out of thin air. If my commercial work was as mediocre as you've always claimed, then you wouldn't be pitching the price at the same level as everything else in your precious gallery. You've must have had some idea of a market value.'

Patrick's patrician face grew haughtier. 'Ella, calm down. You're making a show of yourself.'

'I don't care, you two-faced, hypocritical, cheating, lying, bastard toad.' As the anger spilled out she became more incoherent but she couldn't stop herself. 'How long have you been selling my pictures?'

'Not long.' Patrick's attempt at sincerity did him no favours. She didn't believe a word he said.

'*How long?*'

'A year? Maybe two.'

'And the pictures in the gallery and in the lock-up, is that all that's left?'

Shame-faced, he nodded.

Gone. They'd all gone. All that work.

What started as a slow simmer in the police station, like a smoking volcano, exploded into a full eruption which she couldn't put the lid back on. Her face turned red and her palms itched. With her feet planted firmly on the pavement, pugnacious and aggressive, she didn't care what she looked like or what anyone thought.

'Ella, you need to calm down. You're being far too emotional about this.'

She froze. *Far too emotional about this.* The words seeped in like poison, reaching into her heart, an echo of the exact words she'd heard once before. Every nerve ending in her body stood to attention as rage, despair, desolation and fury fused in one coordinated flare of white hot painful combustion. She couldn't be calm. She couldn't even put words together. They'd come out in a crazy-woman stream of consciousness uncontrolled rant. So, raising the picture with both hands, she brought it down as hard as she could on top of Patrick's head.

'Fuck.' Devon breathed as Patrick crumpled to the pavement.

She watched dispassionately as the man she'd once loved with all her heart rubbed his head, looking unaccountably aggrieved. 'Ow,' he wailed.

Devon took the picture from her and turned to the crumpled figure on the floor.

'Ella's solicitor will be in touch.' He tugged at her hand and pushing through the crowd of people who had materialised, led her to his car, saying, 'Show's over, people. Nothing to see here.'

Chapter Twenty-Four

'I can't believe I did that,' said Ella for the third time, as Devon manoeuvred the car out of the narrow side street.

'Neither could Patrick,' replied Devon and even though his face was in profile as he concentrated on the stop–start bumper to bumper traffic, she could tell from the odd contortions his chin went through that he was trying to hide his amusement.

'It's not funny. In the space of one day, I've become a felon and committed two serious crimes, stealing and assault. I've never even been in a police station before.'

'That makes two of us,' said Devon.

Ella rested her chin on her knees, her head felt too heavy to hold up any longer. Who knew that high drama could be so draining? 'This has to be the worst day of my life. I was arrested in front of a whole gallery of people and minutes from being put in a cell!'

'I did wonder, when I got there, whether I should have brought legal back-up with me.'

'Oh no, they supply that. Duty solicitor.' Ella felt positively knowledgeable and not in a good way. 'They'd called one.' She picked at the fabric stretched taut over her knees. 'What must you think of me? I've never done anything like that before.'

'Done what? Stealing a painting or assaulting someone?' He shot her a cheerful look. 'I think you've gone up in my estimation. A woman who's prepared to take charge.' His hands drummed on the steering wheel as the car inched forward in the grindingly slow traffic.

'Has he really taken all your pictures?'

'Yup. There are still a few at the gallery, although marked as sold. I'm not sure where I stand on those.' A flicker of sadness ran through her. She should be so proud of all those red stickers denoting the work had been sold. Patrick had denied her that pleasure.

'So has he been pocketing the money?' Devon's attempt at diplomacy rather than accusing Patrick outright of being a thief made her like him all the more.

'Pocketing is one way of putting it. As I haven't seen any money and I doubt he ever had any intention of passing it my way, I'd say he's been stealing it,' she said with a bitter edge to her voice. 'As this is all that's left of my work, I'd guess he's been selling my pictures for years.'

That huge tax statement now rang alarm bells. 'I don't know what else he's been up to either but it's not looking good. He's managed all my business interests for years. I don't know where to start trying to untangle it all. He deals with my publisher, the merchandising stuff and my artwork. I loved your parting shot about my solicitor being in touch, as if you knew I'd got one, which I incidentally haven't but I'm thinking I need one. Do you know anyone?'

Devon let out a long unhappy sigh. 'Unfortunately I do. An old university friend. I'll contact him and see if he'll do a bog-off deal, buy one get one free.'

Devon's stomach let out an almighty rumble as his car pulled onto the drive outside Bets' house, the wheels scrunching on gravel. He killed the engine and switched the lights off. Ella welcomed the quiet as she opened her door and stepped out. After a day in London, it seemed incredibly peaceful. For a minute she listened to the heavy silence of the country evening, which when you really took notice, wasn't so quiet after all. Wind rustled the hedgerow, teasing the leaves and branches; she could hear the distant cry of a bird in the sky as it wheeled away to the far distant horizon and, closer to home, the steady baa of sheep was coming from the next field.

She heard Devon's stomach grumble again.

'You sound like Tess. She's always hungry.'

'Except that I'm not a dustbin on four legs,' said Devon as he waited for her to walk around the car before they went towards the house. Ella liked the unconscious, old-fashioned gesture. 'I just didn't eat today.'

'Oh no. What happened to lunch? You were meeting your friend.'

'A damsel in distress called just after I'd taken my third bite of a very nice bruschetta.'

She looked at him appalled. 'You didn't just abandon your lunch, did you?' Of course he had. How else could he have got there so quickly?

He nodded.

She took his arm and squeezed it. 'Oh no, I'm so sorry.' She looked at her watch: it was now half past five. 'I didn't realise. You really didn't have to do that.' Although she was grateful he had. She'd never been more pleased to see anyone in her life than when his tall figure marched through the door into the police station, like the cavalry arriving. Once he was there, everything had suddenly seemed so much better.

'I don't know what I'd have done without you.' And she didn't. His arrival had changed everything.

He shrugged.

'No, seriously.' She put a hand on his arm. 'I know it was all sorted when you arrived but it was just such a relief that ...' Oh God, it was going to sound really cheesy, 'that I knew I could phone you and you'd be ... there. Thank you.'

'No problem. Glad I could help.' His calm, stoic response made her smile. Typical Devon, rescuing people was all in a day's work to him, but she really wanted him to know how grateful she was. She wanted to do something nice for him. Except she couldn't think what. He was so self-possessed and sorted.

'Do you think Bets is in? The house looks very quiet.'

Devon pulled out his phone and with his thumb swiped the screen. 'Ah, text from Bets. She's gone out. Left the dogs with Dad. Mum will be out. One of her meetings.' He ran a hand through his messy hair and turned in the opposite direction to the three-storey brick built farmhouse. With its large red central glossy door and an arched fanlight above, the regency-style house had a grandeur and elegance that suggested this had once been a very well-to-do farm.

'Come on, come meet the old codger and let's retrieve our hounds.'

Devon let himself in the front door, yelling as he went. 'Hi, Dad.'

'In here. Your mother's out.'

Both dogs were sprawled across rugs on the floor, looking completely comfortable and at home. Dexter opened one eye as if to acknowledge Devon before quickly closing it. Tess, more sluggish and reluctant, lurched to her feet and staggered towards Ella, promptly collapsing at her feet with a silly grin on her face.

'What have you done to them?' asked Devon, laughter in his voice as he crossed the room to shake his dad's hand and give him a man-clap to the back. 'Or is that a stupid question?'

'Bets took them out at lunchtime and I took them out at teatime.' He smiled at Ella.

'Sorry, Dad. This is Ella.'

'Hello,' said Ella. 'Thanks for looking after Tess. It was very kind of you.'

'No worries. I enjoyed taking them out, although they're both knackered,' said Geoffrey unfurling his spider limbs from the sofa and reaching forward to shake her hand. 'Nice to meet you. Ella, was it? Is that short for something? Cinderella?' He laughed gently at his own joke.

'No. Just Ella.'

'Excellent, Just Ella. Welcome and welcome to your rather charming dog who has been on her absolute best behaviour,' he paused, 'except for a slight dairy incident.' He gave a positive smile. 'But at least her coat will be lovely and shiny.'

'Oh no! Not again. She didn't eat your butter, did she? Tess! You are naughty.'

Tess lowered her head, eyes looking up from under lashes.

'Fraid so. My fault. I should know better. You know what Labs are like.'

In unison the three of them chorused, 'they eat anything.'

'I'm so sorry.'

'Don't worry, my dear. Dogs will be dogs. My fault entirely. Do take a seat. Would you like a sherry? Or a G&T?'

Ella looked at the tall, spare figure who'd already crossed to a highly polished sideboard where there was a tray holding a decanter and odds and sods of antique silver.

Devon shot her an apologetic look. 'I think Ella wants to get home, Dad. It's been a long day.'

If there hadn't been a mirror on the other side of the room, Ella would have missed the naked sadness on the older man's face, and the lonely longing look he gave Devon.

It made her own heart ache. Stopping for a drink was the very least she could do, especially after all Devon had done for her today.

'I'd love one. It has been quite a day.' Geoffrey's stooped shoulders relaxed and Ella knew she'd done the right thing despite Devon's perplexed frown. 'You probably won't want me associating with your son once you find out the crime spree I've been on today.'

'You've intrigued me.' He poured the drinks and escorted Ella to the sofa. 'Now tell me all about today. Bets said you'd gone up to London to get some paintings for Aud's talk at the WI. Did you get everything you needed?'

Ella sank into the feather cushions of the faded raspberry velvet sofa and took a slug of her drink, Tess's head already pressed against her legs as if the dog was worried Ella might abandon her again. Despite there being several comfortable seats around the room, Devon chose to flop down next to her.

'It was a bit of an abortive trip, unfortunately.' Ella bit her lip as she thought about the events of the day. Her lips twitched. Devon caught her eye and winked.

Geoffrey lifted an eyebrow in amused patience.

'I stole a painting.' She swallowed, valiantly holding back the laughter that threatened to bubble over. 'Then I was arrested.' A snigger slipped through. 'Then I was released and I hit my ex-boyfriend over the head with the painting, which, I might add in my defence, he had stolen from me.'

Beside her she could feel Devon's body shaking with laughter. It was no good, the images in her head replayed themselves and she couldn't help but see the funny side of events.

'My, that sounds like quite an adventure,' said Geoffrey, a teasing light glinting in his eyes. Ella recognised the expression – she'd seen it on Devon's face.

'It was hilarious,' chipped in Devon. 'Don't mess with Ella. She really clouted him one with the painting.'

'I was just so mad at him.' She turned to Geoffrey. 'I don't normally do things like that.' Quickly she explained the full story.

'Good for you, dear. It sounds as if he probably deserved it.'

Ella pulled a face as she sank back into the sofa and took a sip of her drink. The generous measure of gin almost took her head off but after the day she'd had, it was rather welcome. Absently she reached down to rub Tess's head and reassure her that she was there.

'And you, Devon. How was James?'

'Good, he's very happy. Enjoying married life.'

'And did he make you an offer?' Geoffrey's voice, although bland, held a note of expectation.

'Yes, but I'm not interested.' Devon's tone was clipped and Ella wondered at the undertone.

'I don't mind, you know.'

'Don't mind what?' Devon scowled and took great interest in Dexter's jaws.

'I don't mind if you decide you want to go off and do your own thing. Go and work in another practice.'

'I don't want to go and work in James's practice. It's another City practice. I've realised recently I want to work with large animals.'

Devon's dad didn't look convinced and Ella could tell that there was some hidden tension between them.

'So where did you take Tess and Dex this afternoon? They both look shattered.'

'Just around the reservoir.' Geoffrey gave her a candid stare.

Devon smiled, the quirky twisted smile that made Ella's heart pick up a pace. 'At what speed?'

The older man responded to his grin. 'Set a cracking pace. I'm definitely on the mend.'

'Great, Dad. You might be well on the road to recovery but what if you'd given Ella's dog a heart attack?'

Geoffrey looked a tad nonplussed, as if the thought had

never occurred to him. Devon shook his head. 'Sorry, Ella, my dad's warped sense of humour. He likes to run, so he took the dogs with him.'

Ella looked down at Tess, who she had to say was looking a lot slimmer than she had a couple of weeks ago. 'I guess she'd have voted with her feet if she wasn't happy. She's a lot fitter than when I got her.'

'Rescue?' asked Geoffrey.

'What?' Ella looked up. Was this some secret dog code?

'Is your dog a rescue dog?'

'No, I think she's just a normal regular sort of dog. A Labrador.'

Devon sniggered and Ella looked up.

'What?'

'Dad meant, did you get her from a rescue shelter?'

'Oh? No, I didn't. She came with the house. She's Magda's dog.'

Geoffrey let out a riotous shout of laughter.

'What?' Ella couldn't understand what he found so funny.

Geoffrey carried on laughing, his eyes shining with tears. 'Magda!' He sniggered some more. 'A dog.' He burst into peals of laughter.

Ella felt the familiar sensation of being the odd one out and the last to know anything, but where once she would have retreated into herself, she nudged Devon.

'Spill. What's the joke?'

Geoffrey immediately stopped laughing, as Devon shook his head, equally bemused.

'Ella, I do apologise. Tess is a lovely dog. However, Magda didn't do dogs. She refused to have anything to do with them.

Said she'd been bitten as a child and wanted to keep out of their way.'

Ella frowned. 'Then whose dog is she?'

That didn't make sense. She thought back, going over the scene of her arrival in her head. Now that she thought about it with a bit of distance, her parents never actually said that Tess was Magda's dog, just that she needed to look after it while Magda was away.

'I assumed she was Magda's, too,' said Devon. 'Now some of Bets' comments make sense.'

'I must have misunderstood,' she said, remembering her parents' sheepish looks. She gave a sudden grin. 'I think my parents have got a bit of explaining to do.'

Geoffrey shook his head. 'I'm starting to feel quite sorry for them. There's a definite look of mischief on your face, my dear.'

'After all I've been through with this damn dog,' she paused. She stroked Tess's ears. 'You're lovely now, but you've had your moments.'

'Haven't we all,' chipped in Devon with a wry twist to his mouth. 'Thank God she's not howling the place down. It's nice getting some sleep.'

Geoffrey did a discreet double-take.

Ella laughed. 'When I first arrived, Tess cried all night. I thought she was ill, so I phoned Devon. He wasn't very impressed.'

Geoffrey frowned.

Devon poked her in the ribs. 'Er, you haven't mentioned what time you called. Four o'clock, wasn't it?'

Geoffrey laughed. 'I don't miss those calls. In fact, I'm

rather enjoying my semi-retirement.' He looked thoughtful for a minute as if weighing up his next words carefully. It gave Ella the impression that her presence created a handy shield. 'I'm thinking of training to do the London Marathon next year.'

'Good for you, Dad. I think that's absolutely brilliant.'

'Yes.' Geoffrey paused. 'Putting in the mileage is going to take a lot of time. A lot of time. Hour and hours. But I'm serious about this. I'm not aiming for any records. Not at my age.'

Next to her, Ella felt Devon tense, his legs uncrossing as he planted them firmly on the floor. There was a definite subtext she wasn't party to here. Devon didn't say anything, his mouth firmed in an implacable line.

'Let's talk about this later, Dad.' His low voice sounded taut with tension. 'It's been a long day. Ella, shall I walk you home?'

The grim expression on his face suggested it would be best not to argue with him.

As he ushered her out of the front door, a figure came bustling up the path.

'Ah, Devon. How was your day in London? How was James?'

At the sight of Audrey, Ella fought a cowardly urge to duck behind Devon. She really was in tune with the local gossip. She seemed to know rather a lot about Devon's movements.

'And I've missed you tonight. Honestly, I think I see less of you now than when you lived in London.' Audrey shook her head with an affectionate smile and then patted Dexter's head. 'I do get to see a lot of this lovely boy, though. I hope your father's cleaned up all the muddy paw prints from the laundry room.'

'If he knows what's good for him.' Devon's teeth flashed white in the dark, lit by the lamp above the door. 'And I've seen you plenty. You had me rebuilding the Splat the Rat this week.'

'Yes, and you've done a great job. It really was looking a bit sad. I just hope Doris comes up trumps with a new rat. I'm glad I've seen you. Both of you actually because I need you to take all the bottles over to Ella's for the tombola box.' Audrey turned to Ella. 'Hello, dear. When would be a good time for me to drop everything round? I've got raffle tickets for you. Sellotape. All the bottles. So all you need to do is stick all the tickets on the bottles. Nice and easy. Are you around on Thursday?'

Ella nodded, struck dumb by the sudden realisation that Audrey was Devon's mother.

'Right you are. I'll see you then. About ten o'clock?'

Ella nodded again.

'Toodle pip.' She kissed Devon on the cheek and disappeared through the front door, calling, 'Geoffrey, Geoffrey! I'm home.'

'Audrey's your mother?' Ella blushed. 'I didn't mean to be . . .'

Devon smiled. 'Don't worry, I know what my mother's like.'

They walked along the lane towards the green.

'Now you know why I live on the other side of the courtyard. As it is I get roped into most things, but this year I managed to get out of being Santa, the Easter Bunny and

Captain America and I'm only judging one dog competition at the Spring Fayre.'

'It seems impossible to avoid being roped in around here,' Ella observed as they turned left to cross the green. 'And I thought I'd be bored.'

'And I thought once Dad was back on his feet I could leave.' Devon frowned and sighed heavily. 'He's muttering about retirement, but it's only because he thinks he's helping me out.'

Ella nudged him. 'It's not that bad here, is it?' She laughed. 'And I never thought I'd say that.'

'It's not bad here at all. But I'm a grown-up. I don't need my dad giving up his livelihood for me.' His mouth curved with a derisive twist.

The gate squeaked and Ella glanced over at George's house as they walked up the flagstone path, pleased to see that the lights were on.

'George is back.' She craned her neck to see if there were any sign of him through the windows. 'He said they were discharging him this week.' She ought to pop around and check he was OK and had everything he needed. 'I know just what he needs,' she added with a broad smile.

'What's that, then?' asked Devon, his blue eyes dancing with amusement.

'One of my special cappuccinos with chocolate sprinkles. I'm going to make a stencil so I can put a G on the top in chocolate.'

'I'm sure he'd appreciate that, although I suspect he just likes the company of a gorgeous young woman now and then.'

Ella's step faltered and she shot him a look, just in time

to see a deliberately bland expression slip into place. A little glow lit up in her chest as Devon suddenly found the front door incredibly interesting.

He waited for her to open the door and Tess darted inside. Turning to face him, Ella put her hands in her pockets and stood on the doorstep, shifting her weight from foot to foot, looking at the neckline of his cherry-red wool sweater. 'Thanks for today.' She took her hands out of her pockets, feeling them hang limply at her sides. 'For rescuing me.' She rubbed the seams of her jeans. 'Again.' She managed to raise her eyeline to look at his face, feeling a funny swirling sensation in her stomach.

'No problem,' he said gravely, making no move to leave. The expression of gentle amusement and warmth in his eyes as he gazed down at her stopped her heart. Without thinking, she bobbed up to brush her lips along his jawline. 'You were brilliant today.'

He caught her chin in his hand with a featherlight touch, which sent tingles racing across her skin.

Their eyes held each other's. Ella's breath hitched. The moment shimmered between them. He lowered his head. Her heart somersaulted.

And Tess nudged her in the back of her knees, pitching her forward to headbutt Devon right on the nose.

'Oh no, I'm sorry! Are you OK?'

With a rueful smile, Devon rubbed his nose and said with a muffled voice, 'Yes, dime fine.' Or something like that. 'Died bedder go.'

'Yes, well ... er, thanks again.'

He turned to leave, and stopped.

'Erm, would you ...'

Just as she said. 'Would you like ...?'

'Ladies first.'

'Well ... you've been ... so ... I just wondered if you'd like to come here for a meal. To say thank you. For today. Make up for your bruschetta. Nothing special. I'm not a great cook. Well, not any kind of cook at all but ...'

'That would be great.'

'Oh.' The air whooshed out of her lungs in relief. Which was a bit crazy because she was only asking him for dinner. To say thank you. That was all.

'Right. Monday night?'

'Sounds perfect. See you then.'

She managed to keep a straight face as she watched him walk down the path; it was only when she closed the door and leaned against it that a silly smile decided to take over her entire face.

Tess gave a little yip and a bounce.

'It's just dinner, Tess. Don't go getting any ideas.'

Chapter Twenty-Five

As her parents' house was just off the main road, she opened up the boot and let Tess jump straight out. 'Come on, girl, let's see what the oldies have to say for themselves.'

Her father opened the door so promptly, it was as if he'd been hiding behind it in wait and the delicious smell of roast beef filled the air. Her favourite. She hoped her mother had done Yorkshire puddings as well.

'Tess, look at you.' He beamed at Ella. 'Gosh, she's looking good. Lovely glossy coat.'

'Really? Since when did you become an expert on dog care?' she asked, her eyes dancing with pleasure at the sight of her slightly stooped father.

'You pick these things up,' he grinned back, his eyes surrounded by laughter lines. 'And if you . . .'

'. . . say things with enough conviction, people will believe you.' She finished for him. He was a great one for making things up rather than admitting he didn't actually know the answer.

'How are you, love? I must say,' he said enfolding her in a hug, one of his familiar lambswool sweaters tickling her nose, 'you are looking very well.' He led the way down the hall to the big kitchen diner which took up the whole of the back of the house.

'Don't you start, Dad. The way Mum carries on you'd think I was at death's door when I came back a few weeks ago.' Although to be honest compared to how she felt then, she now felt a million times better. Maybe her soul had been in terminal decline.

'Tea, dear?'

'Yes, please.'

He nodded as Ella settled at the breakfast bar of the big open plan kitchen and watched him potter around the kitchen intermittently stopping to pet Tess, who like an animated hoover was busy chasing crumbs around the floor and sniffing every nook and cranny.

'Where's Mum?' Ella asked.

'She's just popped next door to see Marion. She'll be back in a minute.'

'I wanted to know if I could borrow the framed Cuthbert pictures you've got on the stairs.' She'd given all the illustrations from her very first book to her parents. 'I'm giving a talk to the WI.'

'Of course, love, but make sure you bring them all back. You're mother's very proud of them.' He winked. 'And I think they're pretty good, too.'

Once the tea was made, he came to sit down next to her at the long walnut wood bench in the centre of the kitchen and Tess, having made a thorough exploration of the room, decided that her work was done and flopped at Ella's feet.

'So how's village life?'

'Better than I thought it would be.' And completely

different. How on earth had she thought she could hide herself away and keep herself to herself? 'I've got to know a few people. Even have a bit of a social life. It's been easier to get to know people than I thought it would be.'

'Oh, that's having a dog for you. Ah, Shirley.'

Ella's mother returned and hurried over to kiss her cheek. 'Ella, darling, sorry I wasn't here. You look wonderful. Yes, Howard, I'd love a cup of tea.'

With long suffering grace, Ella's dad stood up to make tea and her mother promptly appropriated the high wooden stool he'd just vacated. 'I'll make you one, then,' he said, with a teasing wink.

Ella watched them. Married for thirty years, they still held hands when they went out for walks, teased each other about who was the best cook and laughed a lot. A good team. An image of Devon bending over George came into her head. Holding her hand at the top of the Beacon. Standing over her drawing board admiring her mice.

There was a lot to be said for teamwork.

And there was no doubt that her mother and father had been in cahoots. Ella sat up straighter, she was going to enjoy this.

'So, Mum, how long has Magda had Tess. Since she was a puppy?'

Her parents answered simultaneously, her dad saying, 'Yes. From a litter in Leighton Buzzard,' while her mother said, 'No, she was from Chiltern Dogs, the rescue people.'

Her mother's cheeks turned fiery red. 'Maybe I got that wrong. I didn't really pay attention. How is living in the cottage? Is it warm enough for you?' she asked.

'It's fine. I've had a couple of fires in the evening. Tess is a real hearth dog, she loves to lie on the rug right in front of the tiles. Of course she's chewed it quite a lot but then I'm sure she did that before, so Magda is used to it. And the furniture.' Ella was on a roll now. 'The kitchen table is a bit of a mess, especially the leg by the French doors. That one seems to be her particular favourite.'

Her mother paled under her make-up. 'That's not good,' she said faintly, with an imploring look at her husband.

'She's also scratched some of the wallpaper off the wall in the downstairs toilet. Bit naughty, especially as Magda spent a fortune on it.'

'Did she?' Her father swallowed hard.

'Yes. It's lovely. Osborne and Little. It took her ages to track it down. It was over a hundred pounds a roll. You all right, Mum?' Ella asked, as her mother spluttered, turning slightly pink in the face.

It was hard to keep her own face straight and she very nearly relented, but seriously, who dumped a dog on their daughter? They deserved a bit of payback for those early few sleepless nights with Tess howling the place down, for the awful morning when she'd been terrorised by the local fisherman and for bingate. They should try cleaning up a pot of coleslaw spread across every corner of a kitchen.

Her mother's hands flapped at Dad, in a desperate say-something signal while his face contorted through a variety of ill at ease expressions.

'The thing is, darling ...' her mother started desperately looking towards her father for back-up. 'Howard ...'

'Don't look at me, it wasn't my idea,' he said, holding up his arms in a gesture absolving all responsibility.

'Well, you were the one that suggested we gave Tess to Ella,' her mother pointed out almost apologetically.

'Yes, but I wasn't being serious. And you were the one that offered to have the dog in the first place.' Dad's eyes twinkled. 'And you said you were sure Magda wouldn't mind.'

Her mother dropped her head. 'Well, poor Mrs Bosworth couldn't afford kennels and it's just as well we did take Tess in, I had no idea she was going to be in hospital for so long or that it was going to take all this time for her to recuperate. And I'm sorry she's been so much bother. I . . .' she shrugged helplessly, 'didn't realise she'd cause so many problems.'

'Yes. Well.' Ella gave her mother a stern look as she tried to bite back another smile. 'It's not been easy.'

'Really. Now I feel bad, but Mrs Bosworth really needed the help.'

Guilt pricked at Ella. So typical of Mum. She was absolutely incapable of not offering to help someone in need. She and Dad had often joked that they should tape her mother's hands to her side to stop her agreeing to volunteer for things so often.

'So,' Ella hid her amusement and put on her crown prosecution cross-examination face. 'You're telling me that this dog doesn't belong to Magda at all.'

'No, dear.' Her mother straightened, which made Ella smile. Now she had fessed up, she was going to take it on the chin. 'She belongs to Mrs Bosworth.'

'Mrs Bosworth? And why do I have Mrs Bosworth's dog?'

Her dad stepped in, putting his arm around his wife's shoulder. 'We were worried about you. We didn't like the idea of you living there on your own.'

'I've lived in some pretty dodgy parts of London over the years.'

'We were more worried about you being ... lonely. You weren't ... your usual self.'

Both her parents looked distinctly uncomfortable but her father tucked his arm around his wife.

A fist closed around Ella's heart and she swallowed. Ducking down to hide the tears, she stroked Tess's head again. They were right. She hadn't been herself.

She slipped off the stool and went to hug them both. Despite her doing her absolute best to shut them out and keep them at a distance while she grieved, they'd known her well enough to know the depth of her misery but respected her enough to leave her be. Tess had been their compromise.

'Thank you,' she whispered as their arms linked around her and an overwhelming sense of love and security filled her heart. As they stood there, she felt Tess wriggle in beside her legs as if to say *don't forget about me, I'm one of the family too*. They all looked down and laughed at Tess staring with those beseeching amber eyes up at them.

The roast beef was every bit as good as it smelled and as Ella pushed her chair out from the table to slump in satiated happiness, her mother jumped up and insisted she stay and talk to her father while she made coffee.

'In fact, why don't you two go and sit in the comfy seats in the lounge and I'll bring it through.'

Ella and her father settled amicably into the big squashy sofas in the L-shaped lounge.

'So, what's this tax letter you said you'd had?' he asked.

'I nearly forgot. I brought it with me. I've no idea what it's for. Patrick's always looked after that sort of thing.'

His mouth pinched in disapproval. 'You shouldn't leave your tax affairs to anyone but your accountant.'

'I don't have an accountant. I didn't think I needed one, it's not as if I earn anything. The shop paid me and I got a payslip with my tax showing on it.' She delved into the handbag at her side, trying to find the letter.

'Yes, but what about your Cuthbert Mouse earnings. That's separate so you need to declare it.'

'Like I said, Patrick took care of all that.' She pulled the letter out, crumpled from being stuffed into the side pocket. 'He's used to that sort of thing, so he's always done the business side of things with my publisher.' She'd have to speak to her publisher and explain that arrangement had changed. It was time to start extricating her life from Patrick's and find out how much money he owed her from the sales of her pictures. And then there were the merchandise deals and what about the royalties from her books? Had he been honest about those in the past?

She smoothed the letter out and pushed it over to her father.

His forehead immediately crumpled with consternation. 'Ella, this is a tax demand and your statement on account.'

'All I know is it's a lot of money. Seven thousand pounds. Do I have to pay it?'

'Yes, you do,' he said emphatically. 'This is based on whatever was submitted on your tax return.'

Shit, she didn't regret hitting Patrick over the head with

the picture. It looked as if he owed her far more than she'd first thought. First thing tomorrow she was going to get on the phone and speak to her publisher. Perhaps she should ask Devon for the details of that solicitor too.

'Here we go. Coffee. And some nice chocolate.' Ella's mother put the tray down on the coffee table and busied herself arranging coasters on the polished table before pouring out heavily scented rich dark filter coffee from a huge cafetière.

Her father picked up a section of the Sunday paper and started reading. Ella and her mother chatted, catching up. It had been a while since Ella felt so completely relaxed.

'So do you know what you will do when Magda comes back?' asked her mother – destroying, in one fell swoop, any sense of peace. Ella paused, taking her time and a long thoughtful sip of coffee.

'I don't know yet.'

'Do you think you'll go back to London?'

The million-dollar question. And now Ella didn't know the answer. A few weeks ago she wouldn't have even had to think about it.

She hoped her non-committal shrug would deter any more questions.

'Magda's not back for ages. I've got plenty of time to think about what I'm going to do.'

'Well, I must say, you look a lot better. Eating properly, no doubt. Would you like to take some beef back with you? For sandwiches. Be lovely cold with some horseradish. Or mustard. I've got both in the cupboard from the WI Food Fayre last week. I'll get you some.'

Ella watched her mother bustle away out to the kitchen. Her dad's eyes had drooped shut and the paper lowered. She smiled as he dozed.

They both started when her mother gave an outraged shriek.

'No! Bad dog.'

Rising rapidly to her feet, Ella tossed a quick glance at her father as she followed her mother's voice.

'What's wrong?' her father asked.

'Dratted animal.' Ella's mother stood glowering, hands on her hips, by an empty chopping board. 'That dog has eaten the rest of the beef.'

'Are you sure?' asked her father, his brow wrinkling in disbelieving confusion.

Ella sighed and looked over at Tess who had slunk over to the bi-fold doors leading out into the garden, pressing up against the glass in a misguided attempt to blend into the background. It didn't work. Her hangdog expression shouted her guilt.

'Mum, I'm really sorry.' And then because she still owed them for dumping Tess on her, she couldn't resist winding them up a bit more. 'She's a nightmare. You can't turn your back on her for a moment. She eats anything and everything. You can't leave a thing out.'

Ella was pleased to see that her mother looked suitably chagrined, although she did feel a bit guilty maligning Tess quite so much. The poor dog's tail had drooped and her head dipped. Definitely the picture of shame.

Chapter Twenty-Six

When Tess's excited scuffle announced Devon's arrival before he could knock at the door, Ella's pulse began to misbehave in the most ridiculous way.

He's just coming for a meal, she told herself sternly as she walked slowly and calmly back down the stairs to the front door. Tess was already there, chief ambassador for the official welcoming committee. Her tail was wagging with delight.

It was odd how even through a solid door the dog could tell friend from foe. How did she do that?

Ella opened the door, amused to find that her hand shook as she lifted the latch.

She found two crates of bottles on the doorstep and Devon coming down the path towards her with a final crate.

'This is the last one.'

Her eyes widened. 'Tombola?'

'Oh, yes. Mum insisted I brought it over.'

With a broad grin, she took one of the crates from him, almost buckling at the weight. 'Crikey, I didn't know there were this many people in the village to donate so much stuff.'

Devon gave a wry grin. 'Looking at some of the dodgier bottles, I think they're recycled back into the tombola every year. This one,' he inclined his head towards a bottle of red wine lodged on the top of the box he carried, 'is for you, but if you wanted a different colour, we can always swap it.'

Ella shook her head. 'Best stick with this, I think.' She gave the bottles in the box a grimace. 'I think we'd rather know what we're dealing with and more importantly it will go perfectly with dinner.'

'Something smells good.'

'There's enough of it.' Ella gave him a dubious look. 'You might be taking a food parcel or three home with you.'

Devon raised his eyebrows in question.

'I've made bolognese sauce.' She winced. 'Quite a bit. A huge vat.' It was no good. The laughter bubbled out. 'Small weights and measures issue at the butchers.'

'I'm intrigued. What on earth constitutes a weights and measures issue?'

With a sheepish frown, she asked, 'Have you any idea how much meat there is in two and half kilograms?'

'Yup.' His voice rang with confidence, making Ella scrunch up her nose. He would. Of course he did. 'It's two thousand five hundred grams.'

'Smart.' She smiled and rolled her eyes. 'It's also an awful lot of raw mince. More than I've ever seen in my life. By the time I saw the butcher weighing out enough to feed ten armies, and he'd asked me three times if I was sure I wanted that much, I couldn't admit I'd made a mistake.' She was going to be living on spaghetti bolognese and lasagne for the next six months.

'Good job, I love spag bol.' Devon's cheerful wink made her smile.

'I didn't say it was any good.'

'It's got to be better than my cooking or my mother's.'

'What, Audrey?'

'She's the only mother I've got.'

'Audrey can't *cook*? But she's president of the WI. I thought cooking was mandatory.'

'That's why. She's so busy she never has time to do it properly. The problem is she'll start something and then become sidetracked, so recipes never quite work or they're burnt or overcooked.'

Ella stifled a giggle, still not able to believe it. 'Well, don't get too excited.'

Although with the amount of tomatoes, onions, red wine and herbs that had gone into it, it ought to be bloody brilliant.

'To be honest, at this point my stomach doesn't care. Is it all right if I bring Dexter in with me? He's in the car.'

As she said the words, 'Of course,' Ella marvelled at how much things had changed. Who'd have thought two months ago she'd be calmly inviting a second dog into her home? Let alone be living with one. And there was Tess's excited bark. 'It's yes from me and a yes from Tess.'

Dexter burst through the door despite Devon's restraining hand on his collar and even though he'd met Tess a million times before immediately homed in on her back end. Ella had to plant her feet firmly, so she didn't get knocked over by Tess and Dexter's excited tails sideswiping her with every manic circuit of her legs.

'Dex, behave!' said Devon, hauling on the exuberant dog's collar. 'Sit. Where are your manners? Leave Tess alone.'

The dog promptly sat. Plonking his full weight on Ella's feet, panting up at her with adoration. Tess bounced up and down in excitement.

She gave his ears a quick ruffle and Tess immediately stuck her nose in, pushing at her hand in good-natured jealousy.

'Don't worry, I still love you.' Ella shook her head and carried on stroking Dexter's head. 'But you, Dex,' she complained, nudging him with her thigh and shuffling her feet out, 'are heavy.'

'Sorry,' Devon grinned. 'He just wants to be friends.'

'I can see that, but my toes aren't convinced.' Ella wiggled her feet. 'Come on through.'

Devon handed over the bottle of red wine and she promptly handed it back to him.

'Actually, would you mind doing the honours? I need to put the pasta on. Corkscrew in the drawer by the bread bin.'

There was a loud clang as Devon, dodging the two dogs, tripped over Tess's bowl in the middle of the kitchen floor.

Ella leaned down and scooped it up, taking it over to the far side of the kitchen where Tess's bed and water bowl sat and opened the French doors to let the two mad dogs out. 'Sorry, Tess is incapable of eating without chasing the bowl around the room.'

She crossed the room and opened the cupboard to pull out two wine glasses, horribly aware that her hands were shaking a little. 'Honestly, she attacks her food as if it were her last meal ever. It's a wonder she doesn't go through the French doors. In fact, she eats so quickly, I think she just inhales the biscuits. She can't possibly taste them. Although they look and smell so disgusting, you can hardly blame her.'

Devon raised an eyebrow at her sudden flow of words but calmly poured two rich ruby red glasses of wine and handed her one.

'Thank you.' Ella took a sip, while still on the move. 'Sorry, you must be starving. I haven't even got the water on to boil. Do sit down or would you rather go into the lounge and I can call you when it's ready.' *Shut up*, she told herself. *Stop talking.* Clamping her mouth shut, she busied herself putting the kettle on and trying to get into the pack of spaghetti. Since when had they put childproof packaging on pasta?

He leant back against the counter, watching her, and sipped at his wine.

'You know you can get special slow dog bowls to stop them guzzling their food down.'

'Really?' Her fingers still wouldn't work properly.

'Yes. Just look them up on the internet. They work quite well.' He put his glass down and gently removed the cellophane packet from her hand. 'Here, let me.'

'Thanks.' She almost snatched the pasta from him when he was done. 'I'm so going to get one for Tess.'

'What sort of food do you give her?'

'Vile horrible smelly biscuits.' She nodded to the wooden pantry door. 'They're in there. You'll smell them as soon as you open the door.'

'Mind if I have a look?'

'Be my guest.' Him standing watching her was so unnerving.

The kettle had boiled and she filled a saucepan with the

boiling water. As she took the bolognese sauce out of the fridge, she heard rustling from inside the cupboard. Devon was clearly taking this seriously. At last he came out, a non-committal look on his face which clearly suggested he had a view but was trying to be diplomatic about it.

'What?' she asked a touch defensively.

'Nothing.' His face took on a guileless expression which didn't fool her one bit.

'What? And don't give me nothing. You've got that look on your face.'

'What look.'

'The "I'm trying not to be patronising here but..."'

'That's a look?'

'Yes, that's a look. One that know-it-all vets use on unsuspecting completely-new-at-this-dog-owning-lark people.' She put her hands on her hips to emphasise her point.

'Sorry.' His apologetic grimace made her feel slightly better. 'There's nothing wrong with it, but you could do better. It's quite a cheap brand and nutritionally OK but they're using the cheapest ingredients, so the quality's not that great. It's fine, don't get me wrong—'

'But...'

'Tess would probably be better off with a dog food designed for bigger dogs.'

One more thing to feel guilty about, except this time it wasn't her fault. 'To be honest, I just carried on buying what she was already having.' Who'd have realised that talking dog food could be so usefully distracting?

Ella looked out at Tess, who was still cavorting in the garden with Dexter. She looked much slimmer than she had a couple of weeks ago. 'I guess she'd have voted with her feet if she wasn't happy. She's a lot fitter than when I got her.'

'You've done wonders with her. The difference is quite incredible. Now, she's glossy, bouncy and the picture of health.' His gaze rested on her face, the expression on his face gentling.

Butterflies took flight, racing upwards, a fluttering sensation in her chest as he tilted his head to one side, his mouth twisting with suppressed amusement and that damned dimple appeared in his cheek.

Ella found it impossible to turn away, even though she had no idea where to look. Devon stepped forward, closing the gap between them, allowing a smile to curve his lips.

'I wasn't very nice to you that day. I'm sorry. I shouldn't have said what I did.' The searing appraisal he gave her made her breath catch. 'You've changed, too. You look...'

'Glossy? Bouncy? The picture of health?' Ella couldn't help filling in the words. Why couldn't she just shut up?

'All of those but... something else.' He studied her face. The careful scrutiny, like a caress, making her heart leap in response. 'Different. Content. Happy.' His hand lifted and where his eyes had tracked, with each word he traced along her jawline.

She swallowed. Oh boy. Her heart bumped. Warmth bloomed in her chest.

'You look like you.'

'Me?' She whispered, her breath catching in her throat.

'Yes.' He frowned, his eyes narrowing like he was working to solve an intriguing puzzle. 'When you first came,' his finger traced her forehead as if soothing away lines, 'you were hidden. It was as if the real person was just peeking out now and then. Like a voice that's grown croaky and rusty with disuse. It was like you'd forgotten how to be you.'

Her eyes widened. How could she be insulted when he peeled the layers back so beautifully to lay bare the truth?

'This last few weeks, it's like a butterfly emerging from a chrysalis.' With a sudden gear change, his eyes twinkled. 'Actually, that's not true at all, the other day with Patrick it was more like Muhammad Ali leaping out to sting like a bee.' He leaned forward, putting his hands on her waist, and closing the gap between them.

Staring up at him, unable to break the gaze between them, she held her breath as he placed a gentle kiss on her lips. 'You were quite something, Miss Rigden.'

Her heart fizzed and her nerve endings went on high alert, her answering smile uncontrollable as she saw the appreciative glint in his eye.

'I shouldn't condone violence, but I was so proud of you when you nailed him with that picture.'

With a shy smile, she looped her arms around his neck and kissed him back. 'Me too.'

Kissing Devon felt new and strange but oh so right. It had been so long since she'd kissed anyone other than Patrick. If she'd had time to think about it she'd have worried about it but there was no chance to. They fitted. He was just the right height, his lips exerted just the right amount of pressure and he took his time in a long, slow, lazy exploration of her mouth as if he had all the time in the world and wasn't going to be hurried on any account. He was thorough, very thorough and she sank into the kiss. Just feeling. Enjoying the sensations. Heavenly kisses. The warmth of lips on hers. Strong hands gentle at her waist. That extraordinarily beguiling sensation of being the absolute centre of someone's focus. The kiss built in intensity but with no pressure, no sensation of being in a mad race of having a place to go. It was a meandering journey with no sense of having a destination. Of needing to be anywhere, to have to get anywhere. Ella wondered if it were possible for a kiss to last for ever.

With her eyes closed she took in a breath and stiffened at exactly the same moment as Devon. They pulled apart.

'Ugh! What's that smell?' Ella realised Tess had padded back into the kitchen and stood gazing up at her and Devon, her head cocked to one side with a this-is-new tilt.

'Oh, Tess!' Devon screwed up his face, turning his head away. 'Out. Go on.' He pointed firmly at the dog who lowered her head. 'Now. Outside.'

'Pooh! What is that?' asked Ella, the horrible stink now really taking a hold and making her feel quite sick.

'Poo! Quite literally. It's fox poo.'

'Seriously? It's vile.' They caught each other's eye and Ella broke first. She started to laugh. 'Talk about a mood killer.'

'I don't suppose you have any dog shampoo?.' He looked forlornly at the boiling pot of pasta.

She shook her head.

With a heavy sigh, he gave a brief kiss on her cheek. 'I'll go now and get some from the surgery. Be back in two minutes.'

After dinner, which wasn't as romantic as it might have been, thanks to the two plaintive faces pressed up against the window, the shampooing commenced. Ella perked up when Devon filled up a bowl of warm water and stripped off his jumper to reveal a lean muscled chest in a navy T-shirt. Perhaps dog shampooing wouldn't be so bad after all.

Thankfully only Tess had availed herself of the fox poo. Devon showed Ella how to rub the shampoo into the dog's coat.

It was a messy business and by the end of it they were both soaked through.

When they came back into the kitchen leaving Tess outside to dry off, along with Dexter, Devon unselfconsciously stripped off his soaked T-shirt.

'I'll nip upstairs and change,' said Ella, hoping she'd hidden her quick intake of breath. That was one nice body. 'Do you want me to see if I can find something that might fit you?'

'No, it's fine. I'll put my jumper back on.'

'Are you sure?' asked Ella.

He grinned with a sudden gleam in his eyes. 'Want me to leave it off?'

She swallowed and fled up the stairs.

When she came back down, Devon had taken their wine into the lounge and lit a fire. Grateful that he had put his jumper back on – she wouldn't have known where to look – she stood with a touch of self-consciousness until he reached up and pulled her down to sit next to him on the sofa.

'Well, that was fun,' he teased.

'Hmm. I'm not sure that was what you were expecting when I invited you for a meal.'

'I'm not complaining.' He slid an arm around her, drawing her closer. 'Now where were we before your pesky dog interrupted us?'

She turned to face him. His face was so close she could see the tiny pricks of stubble starting to break through his skin and his eyes were still and watchful.

'You OK?' he asked, his voice gentle with a suggestion of hoarseness.

'I am now.'

He lifted one hand to cup her face. The crackle of the fire suddenly seemed loud and her heart pounded so hard she thought it might burst through her chest. With a tiny exhale, an almost sigh, she opened her lips, unable to take her eyes from his.

Tracing a sure path, his hand slipped along her jaw and cupped her neck as he pulled her towards him. Their mouths met on a shared sigh.

Kissing Devon was like sliding slowly and languorously into the enveloping warmth of a hot scented bath, heating every bit of her, making her body pliable with longing. She wrapped her arms around him, her hand sliding into the hair at his nape, pressing her body up to his. He explored her mouth with thorough gentleness, his hand sliding through her hair while his other hand supported her back. The tender trace of his lips was intoxicating and addictive. The sense of wanting to gather him close and not let go almost overwhelmed her.

Together they settled into a more comfortable position and at last drew apart. Ella's breath seemed to have stalled somewhere in her chest and her blood sizzled as she gazed into his face. A flush seared her cheekbones, all her nerve endings tingling and dancing in delight.

'Wow.' She didn't know what else to say. Giddy elation whirled through her system as the enormity of the kiss sank in. Different to any other, it felt grown-up and precious. One that went somewhere and could lead to more. As she looked at Devon, certainty settled in her heart with horrible intrusion. She could love this man.

And that was the last thing either of them needed.

He leaned forward to touch his forehead against hers in a silent heartfelt salute.

'Wow, indeed. That's quite a thank you-for-cleaning-my-dog kiss. Maybe I should give Tess a treat. I owe her.'

She eased back to make sure he could see her face, the moment weighted with sudden seriousness. 'It should be a thank-you-for-everything kiss. You were so kind up at the Beacon, talking really helped. It was the first time I'd been able to speak about it and it was like lancing a boil. I feel so much better. You really helped.'

'You didn't need saving.' Devon traced her lips with a single finger. 'Just waking up.'

Ella smiled. 'I can see you hacking through the forest to rescue Sleeping Beauty.'

'I'm no knight in shining armour. Marina certainly wouldn't agree.' He sobered for a second.

She put a hand over his.

He sighed and she could almost see him pushing the negative thoughts away. 'Where you're concerned, I just seem to be in the right place at the right time.' He paused and then added wickedly. 'Although with all the scrapes you get yourself into, it's not exactly difficult.' The arm he snaked around her waist to pull her into him robbed the words of any sting.

'I never used to... do such stupid things in London.' She shook her head. 'Life there was so much narrower. Funny, you always think that a city is where everything is going on, where it's all happening, but actually the scope is quite limited.'

'What do you mean?' Devon put his wine glass down, looking interested.

'You stay within your confines. The world you construct and you're so used to it, that it creates its own boundaries. You restrict yourself.

'I got so used to the galleries we went to. The art we saw. The people I mixed with. I forgot there was a much broader spectrum out there. Another way of seeing or doing things. I was so bound by habit. I stopped questioning anything for myself.

'You asked me "what is art?" I looked it up. There are loads and loads of definitions. Some dead simple, some so pretentious and laborious. For me it has to be simple. Thomas Merton expressed it beautifully, "Art enables us to find ourselves and lose ourselves at the same time."'

Devon nodded. 'I like that. Do you think you've found yourself?' The direct question hovered between them, suddenly full of import. To her, anyway; his face gave nothing away.

Her heart hitched. 'I'm certainly on the way.'

He tilted his head, listening, encouraging her to go on. She loved that about him. He knew when not to talk.

'When I came here ... well, you know what it was like. This was a prison sentence. I was miserable, so I came here not expecting anything. Just to ride out my misery.'

Devon nodded and looked down at his hands. She waited until he lifted his head again, meeting his eyes with her steady gaze.

'To hide away and hope that all the problems would vanish while I wasn't looking directly at them.' She gave a half-laugh. 'Life doesn't work like that, does it?'

Devon's lips twisted. 'Sadly not. It's easier to hide. Easier to bury your head. Distract yourself. But it doesn't solve the problem.'

Distraction was his tool. Running away was hers. They were both as bad as one another.

'Yeah.' With a sigh she picked up her wine glass to take a sip, before adding sadly, 'But at some point, you have to face it and sort everything out.'

'This,' he touched her lips, a sad smile playing at his mouth, 'is probably muddying the waters.' He paused before adding, 'For both of us.'

His words caused a funny hollowness in her chest.

'So what's happening with Marina?' Despite the bluntness of her question Devon didn't seem to mind. She studied his face in relief as he watched the flames of the fire.

'Same as ever. I get daily emails from her asking what the progress is. Putting the pressure on. At first I wasn't quite sure what she expects me to do. I can't magic the money up from thin air. Then I realised she's decided she wants me back and this is her means to do it. The only way to make my debt disappear is to go back.'

'And you don't want to.'

His face closed down, a stern expression telling her all she needed to know. 'Absolutely not. I considered it. Would have been easier. To go back to the status quo but once you realise something's broken, it's really hard, if not impossible, to fix.' He sighed. 'Now that I'm here and away from the day to day life, I know I couldn't go back. I wasn't happy but I didn't know it at the time.' He touched her face. 'Does that sound familiar?'

With a lightness of heart, Ella nodded. 'Yes. I wasn't unhappy but I wasn't as happy as I could be. Coming here wasn't what I wanted at all.'

'Me neither. I'll stay for now but it is temporary.' With a candid look, he straightened. 'Sorry. This ... ' he spread his hands out. 'I shouldn't have ... kissed you.'

'Devon, it's fine. I'd rather you were honest. This, staying in the village, is a stopgap, for me as much as you. I've no idea what I'm going to do. I said I'd stay for six months.'

'I ... like you, a lot.' He pulled a face. 'That sounds pathetic. What I'm trying to say is, I want to spend time with you but there's no ... sounds callous, happy ever after, but at the same time, if I said it's just casual, that sounds shallow and empty and I can't do that either.'

Ella laid a finger on his lips. 'I thought women overthought things. Why don't we just enjoy each other's company, while we figure out our own lives? I don't expect anything from you.' She trailed her finger down his chin and laid her hand on his chest. 'Well, perhaps the odd thing.'

'Dessert maybe.'

His pulse leapt at the husky tone in her voice.

'Dessert, I can handle.'

Yup, he could definitely handle that. So why did her previous words, agreeing with him, dammit, cause a twinge of regret that twisted in his gut? Having a bloody protective streak a mile wide had a lot to answer for. He had a feeling the type of things she expected from a man were the sort of things he could give without too much effort if his circumstances were different.

Her fingers had found their way to bare flesh, so he leaned back, pulling her with him, as they skimmed just above the waistband of his jeans.

'Who are you calling odd?' he asked, feathering a kiss at the side of her lips. 'I might have to prove there's nothing odd about me.'

'I might just have to let you.'

Dimly he heard the crackle of the fire in the background as he settled into her, their kisses deepening as daylight slipped away outside.

Chapter Twenty-Seven

'You look a bit flushed, dear.' Audrey greeted her at the door of the village hall. 'Don't worry, we've got everything under control.'

Ella wondered what she'd say if she knew what had put the colour on her cheeks and the warm tingle coursing through her bloodstream. Devon had stopped by as she was loading her pictures into the car and offered to take Tess for her for the afternoon and then they'd got a little distracted. Boy, was he a good kisser.

He was the one who'd convinced her to bring along her three new watercolours when he'd spotted them in her studio. She'd been dithering about whether to bring them along. Part of her didn't want to share them with anyone yet. They were still too private. They were hers. Raw. Untried. She tilted her head to one side. How could she be objective about them? She had no idea if they were any good or not, couldn't even say they were her best work. All she knew was that for the first time ever, she'd manage to faithfully reproduce the image in her head with such crispness and clarity it made her heart sing. The greens were exactly the right greens, the shadows had a depth to them she imagined losing herself in and the mist rising had a magical opalescence to it.

Before she could speak, Audrey's team of helpers, primed to unload the pictures from the car, were soon carrying the pictures inside, ably directed by Audrey who coordinated her team with a voice as loud as a foghorn, dictating exactly where each one should go.

Within fifteen minutes the room had been laid out, a couple of easels at the front displayed the Cuthbert pictures she'd borrowed from her parents and then a makeshift gallery around the back of the room to the right of the refreshment table, displayed some of her recent sketches and pictures which Bets had helped her to hastily mount and put into cheap IKEA frames.

Ella scarcely had a chance to draw breath before the room began filling with a range of ladies of various shapes and sizes, all talking like vivacious parrots.

She stood at the front of the room, twisting her cold hands together. The words she'd rehearsed in her head were harder to recall now she was faced with an audience. Why had she agreed to do this? Luckily it seemed that everyone in the room had been in solitary confinement for the last six months – the nearest group of ladies fell upon each other with cries of delight and barely drew breath as they talked non-stop, completely ignoring her.

Audrey glided to the front to stand beside Ella. 'Don't worry, they'll shut up in a minute,' she whispered and sure enough the talk died away, which was actually far worse because one by one every head turned with intense, focused interest to survey Ella. If it weren't for the fact that her feet were frozen to the floor, she might have made a run for it.

'Ladies.' Audrey signalled to the corner where Ella realised there was a woman seated at the piano. Everyone stood up. Ella shifted and looked behind her.

With more enthusiasm than skill, the woman began to play. Ella was no musician but she could tell that a few of the notes were off. At least she recognised the tune.

There was a lot to be said for starting things off with a rousing version of 'Jerusalem'. It certainly engendered a positive atmosphere and as the last note died away, Ella's confidence returned. She could do this.

'Ladies, today I have the very great pleasure of introducing local artist Ella Rigden. Many of you may know her work from the popular Cuthbert Mouse series of children's books, but she is also an accomplished artist, a winner of the prestigious Gerber Stein prize, shortlisted for the Ashurst Emerging Artist Prize and according to my sources, hard at work for an exciting new exhibition.'

Audrey had done her homework, although sadly most of it belonged to ancient history. Ella hadn't been shortlisted for anything for a very long time, and she definitely wasn't going to have an exhibition anywhere soon.

Everyone was looking at her expectantly. With a measured breath she scanned the audience and forced herself to smile.

'Good afternoon and thank you for coming.' Lots of heads bobbed up and Ella let out a breath. She held up one of her pictures and as she raised it up to show the audience, it brought back a vision of bringing the same picture down on Patrick's head.

'Do any of you recognise this little fella?' she asked, beaming at the audience.

Heads nodded and bobbed in assent and she was off, up and running.

Once she started, there was no time to feel self-conscious or nervous. It was as easy as Devon had suggested. All she had to do was talk about things that she knew about and show the passion she had for her characters. That thought brought her up short and she almost laughed out loud in delight as it hit her that in recent weeks she'd fallen in love all over again with her characters.

'For example, when I draw Cuthbert, I have a hat in mind for him. As a consummate show-off, he invariably adopts the characteristics of the type of person who would wear that type of hat.' She showed them the picture of Cuthbert in his feathered Cavalier's hat and his courtly bows and buckled shoes, pointing out the details to the appreciative audience. As she talked, Ella began to enjoy herself more and more. The WI membership was considerably younger than Ella had expected – some admittedly were pensioners but even they were of the youthful, enquiring, still full of beans persuasion. The audience asked lively and interesting questions and were incredibly complimentary about her mice.

In the second half of her talk, Ella introduced some audience participation.

'You know each of the mice have their own character and,' she gave the audience a conspiratorial smile, 'I know I shouldn't have favourites but I think Cuthbert might just have sneaked into first place.' The audience, as one smiled and nodded. With deft strokes, she started to sketch an outline of Cuthbert. She'd been worried about stretching her talk out and this was the crunch point. She'd asked Audrey to prime her audience in advance and hoped that at least some of them had responded.

'But today I'd like a bit of inspiration from you. I did ask Audrey if you'd bring along a few props. So did anyone bring along a hat?'

She need not have worried. The minute Ella launched this line, it was an instant success. The audience needed no further prompting and suddenly all the ladies sprouted headgear of all shapes and sizes. Huge floral wedding hats, saucy, sexy fascinators, a 1920s flapper girl hat, a full Indian feathered headdress, felt hats, tweed hats, deerstalkers.

'Blimey, I've got enough inspiration here to keep me going for months.'

The Indian headdress on top of a lady of vast girth took the prize, and Ella could imagine Cuthbert halfway up the curtains with the feather headdress trailing around his tail behind him. Her mind took off. Quickly she sketched him, pencilling in the elaborate feather headdress, his tail coiled around one of the smaller feathers on the very end of the headband. As she made the deft strokes on paper, demonstrating to the audience how she worked, she gave a running commentary of her thought processes.

'So, with this, I'd think the headdress might lose a feather that one of the younger mice might play with. A feather might tickle Catherine, his sister, and make her cross, or giggle, or she might pluck it from him to do some dusting.'

Before long she had quite a rapport going with the audience and it was Audrey that had to interrupt with a reminder that tea and cake would be served and that the audience could ask her any questions then.

Bringing the talk to a close, Ella was surprised by the enthusiastic three cheers from Audrey and the rapturous clapping.

As tea and an amazing range of cake was served, she was besieged with questions.

'So how much would one of these cost?' asked one lady, with an earnest piercing stare, as she balanced a huge slab of coffee cake in one hand, her handbag looped over her elbow and an elegant walking stick in the other hand, nodding towards one of Ella's parents' pictures. Ella stared at her hair, fascinated by the pearl-pink rinse which was lifted at the ends with a touch of purple.

'Unfortunately these aren't for sale, they belong to my parents. I gave them to my mother when I was first published.' Ella explained. 'And the others haven't been published yet, so I can't release them.'

'Bet they're worth a bit now,' she grinned.

Ella nodded, hiding the nausea brought on by the question. Patrick had slapped quite a price tag on the ones he'd had in the gallery.

Another woman joined her. 'I love your landscape. Are you selling it?'

Ella pulled a face. 'To be honest it's quite new, I've not even thought about it.'

'You ought to, they'd be jolly popular round here. Wouldn't they, Margery?'

She called over to a rather severe-looking woman who was studying the reservoir picture. The woman raised her head and looked over with piercing blue eyes and immaculately coiffured hair, there was no other word for it. She looked as if she'd just stepped out of the tea lounge in the Savoy rather than come to a village hall in Hertfordshire.

Without responding she carried on studying the picture, her eyes fixed on it with an unnerving intensity. Admittedly it wouldn't be to everyone's taste, not your typical landscapes and to a traditional eye, the trees were probably a bit abstract. Trying to steel herself not to care when this slightly scary woman denounced it as too modern, Ella turned back to the first lady who'd changed the subject and began talking about a friend of hers who wrote children's books.

A tap on the shoulder made her turn and she found Margery standing there, the blue eyes intent and thoughtful.

'I run a gallery in Missenden. Have you got any more of these?' She pressed a card into Ella's hand. 'Come and see me,' she paused and gave the nearest mouse picture a rueful look,

'The mouse ones, well executed,' her face softened and with a distinctly naughty twinkle she added, 'but not my thing. I leave the cute stuff to the old dears.'

Ella raised a brow and grinned with her. She was easily the same age as most of the other women in the room, although something indefinable set her apart.

'And let me know when your exhibition is.' Ella turned the smooth matt card over in her palm, dying to look at it but it seemed rude to pick it up and peer at it. No doubt she ran one of those lovely little home interiors type shops where you could buy candles and tea towels and calendars.

'Margery, you're not monopolising our guest, are you,' Audrey bustled up to join them.

'Wouldn't dream of it.' She looked down her nose so pointedly that Ella realised she was sending herself up. 'You surpassed yourself this time.'

Audrey rolled her eyes with good humour. 'I admitted the lady poultry expert was a bit dull.'

'Dull!' Margery gave a very unladylike snigger.

Audrey huffed in exasperation, 'But there are lots of the ladies who are thinking of getting chickens.'

'Thankfully they were bored into submission and the village won't be overrun with chickens. Saves us being inundated with eggs at every meeting. We have enough baking competitions as it is.'

She walked off, leaving Audrey pursing her pink-lipsticked mouth. 'Honestly, I admit we do get some duffers sometimes but she should try booking speakers. You were brilliant, and if Margery Duffle was impressed then you were good. She runs a very smart gallery in Missenden.'

'Duffle, did you say?' Ella's pulse raced.

'Yes,' said Audrey with a complacent beam at her. 'She's very well known, I believe.'

'Just a bit,' said Ella faintly as blood rushed to her head. 'Oh God, I'd never have brought those if I'd known.'

Chapter Twenty-Eight

'Margery Duffle. Margery Duffle.' Ella kept repeating the name as she danced around her studio. Margery Duffle liked her picture.

A demanding knock at the door stopped her excited moves but her heart started skipping. Devon, bringing Tess back. He'd been out with her for ages. She tripped quickly down the stairs to open the door. He deserved a medal and dinner and maybe dessert this time. Memories of the sofa made her smile as she ran the last few steps to the door and threw it open.

'Patrick!'

She stopped dead, holding the door in one hand, instinct shouting at her to slam it in his face.

'Ella.' He pushed a foot in the door. 'We need to talk.'

Framed in the door in a waxed jacket and corduroy trousers, holding out a Fortnum & Mason bag, he looked just like Patrick. Not a monster. Although the country attire amused her. Typical.

Oh shit! He was probably right. She'd been running from this since the day she got on the train to Tring.

'You'd better come in,' she said in a low voice, as sadness pierced her. This wasn't going to end well for either of them.

Time to be honest with him and herself, if he gave her the chance to get a word in edgeways. From the determined look on his face, he had it all worked out. Like the last piece of a jigsaw slotting into place, she saw the familiar patterns of the way their arguments had panned out in the past. Patrick being utterly reasonable. Wearing her down with his appeals and entreaties.

'Ella, I've missed you. You're looking amazing.' He used the boyish charm that had worked so often in the past. Brown eyes big and soulful. Voice lowered in meaningful entreaty. What once seemed sexy and charming looked posed and artificial. And very different from the naturally masculine man she'd got used to in recent weeks.

'Really?' She'd made a bit of an effort for the WI but she hadn't had her hair cut in weeks.

'Yes,' his voice held a note of surprise as he examined her face. 'Yes. You look different. Maybe it's the hair. It's longer than usual.' He tilted his head and then, as if he'd worked out the answer to a difficult sum, relaxed. 'I see what it is. You've adopted the natural look. Bucolic charm. Roses in your cheeks.'

She raised an eyebrow. Her natural healthy glow came from daily walks in the sunshine which had also lightened her hair, while leaving it to dry naturally, instead of blow drying it into stylish submission, had given it a gentle curl.

It occurred to her that they were standing on the opposite sides of a chasm that couldn't be crossed except he wasn't even close to being aware of it. She couldn't raise the energy to be cross with him when all she felt was a bone-deep weariness.

She led him to the lounge, deliberately avoiding the kitchen.

'This is nice.' Patrick surveyed the cream sofas and the deep blue of the wallpaper on the accent wall. 'Very rustic but in keeping with the exterior. Not my taste but charming all the same. How are you coping living out here? It must be hard adapting?'

'Patrick. You didn't come to discuss interior design. Why don't you take a seat?'

'You're upset. I can tell.' He peeled off his coat. It still had the label inside.

She deliberately sat on the other side of the room but he followed and crouched down beside the arm of her chair, staring earnestly up into her eyes.

'I don't blame you.' His face softened. 'I'm an arse, but I need you. I love you.'

Guilt tinged with sorrow hit her. He probably did love her in his own way. She'd never given him any reason in the past to think that she'd wandered off the page they shared. Unfortunately, it had become glaringly obvious to her that they were not so much on different pages but reading completely different books in different languages.

'Ella, we need to get back on track. I admit I made a mistake going ahead with the show without telling you.'

'That was a mistake?' Did he think she was stupid? 'It looked pretty deliberate to me. I don't think you ever had any intention of telling me about the show. You were hoping that I might never find out about it.'

'Everyone makes mistakes. I can explain everything.'

'Really? The list of mistakes is pretty long. Have you got all day?'

'Ella,' Righteous confusion furrowed his brow. The sort that might belong to a hen who'd sat on an egg fully expectant of the arrival of a fluffy chick and instead was faced with a small snappy alligator. 'You're being unreasonable. Have decency and manners gone out the window? You could at least offer me a cup of coffee.'

Damn, how did he do that, wrong foot her and take the superior high ground?

'Would you like a coffee?'

'That would be civilised.'

She sighed and then sighed even more when he followed her into the kitchen.

Ignoring him, she concentrated on the familiar motion of making coffee. Cups. Kettle. Milk.

Patrick pulled out a chair at the kitchen table and in that stupid cowboy fashion turned it round and sat astride. She'd seen him do it a thousand times before, thinking it looked cool. Today she winced. For no reason she could possibly explain, she did not want him in her kitchen. 'I brought you your favourite Champagne Truffles. I was passing and thought you might like them.' He took the familiar box out of the bag and left it on the table.

Even though it was the largest box they did, he had seriously underestimated the size of the war with this peace offering.

'Er, Ella. Don't you have proper coffee?' he asked as she spooned instant granules into a mug and pulled a pint of milk out of the fridge. 'Or skinny milk?'

She glared at him.

'It's not a flipping coffee shop.' He didn't need to know that since George's return from hospital she took him a cappuccino every morning after she returned from her morning walk with Tess.

She took the two mugs and went back to the lounge. Patrick fitted in better here.

'So, you were going to explain everything to me.' She clutched her mug in front of her in two hands. 'Do we need an agenda?'

Patrick looked dubious.

'Item One. How come you were selling my pictures in the gallery?'

He had the grace to look ashamed. 'Ella, I needed the money. The gallery's not been doing that well recently. I needed the refurb to give it a bit more pulling power. And it would have been all right if you hadn't decided you wanted a break.' The disgruntled downturn of his lips signalled his bitterness. 'I'm having to cover all the bills on my own.' He settled back into the sofa with a mulish huff.

'So it's my fault?'

'I didn't say that. However, you didn't exactly give me time to make alternative arrangements. And with regard to the paintings, I was planning to give you the usual percentage of the sales. It's not as if you've lost out.'

'Except that I had no intention of selling those pictures.'

'Ella. What would you do with them? Keep them in storage for ever? They were collecting dust.'

'They were collecting dust because you've always said they held no artistic value and it would damage my artistic reputation if I were to, "peddle" them, I think that's the technical term you used.'

Patrick's jaw tightened.

She rounded on him. 'That's what upsets me the most. For years you've been putting my mice pictures down. And then when you need some money, all your artistic integrity flies out of the window. And do you know what? It's taken me a while to realise it, but I'm bloody proud of those pictures. They're honest. They give genuine pleasure to people. That's worth so much more. I'm gutted that you've sold so many of them, that was my work. A body of work but I do take comfort in the fact that the people who have paid your extortionate prices must really like them to have paid that money. I'm hoping that they get great pleasure from them.'

'I told you I made a mistake.' He held out a hand in entreaty. 'An honest mistake. I didn't realise that people would love them as much as they do. But that's what art is, completely subjective. If we all liked the same thing, we'd still be rolling in Old Masters.'

Ella's throat tightened. He didn't get it. Completely and utterly had no idea what she was getting at.

'What about the earnings from the books?'

Patrick blanched but rallied with an easy smile. 'What do you mean? They don't earn that much.'

'Don't lie to me, Patrick. I've just had a tax statement.'

'What do you mean? How? I manage your tax affairs.'

'I gave my address to Gavin in the art supplies shop for my P45.'

'Well, I can sort that out for you. Don't worry about it.'

'Don't worry? But I am. My dad says it's a statement on

account. How much they predict I will owe, based on previous earnings. Do you know how much it was for?'

Patrick studied the mirror above the fire with seeming nonchalance. 'They make mistakes all the time.'

'Patrick. It was for over seven thousand pounds. They don't make mistakes that big.'

He frowned. 'I'll have to look into it. Without my records I can't be—'

'Bullshit.' She lowered her voice, aware that she'd started to shout. 'I phoned the publisher. They emailed me royalty statements for the last year. I earn enough to live on but you never told me that. What happened to that money?'

'Well, it ... you've benefited. The gallery needed a cash injection. I knew you wouldn't mind. It was for us. We're a team.'

'So why not tell me?'

'Ella, you're getting this out of perspective. As if I was deliberately stealing from you. That's a terrible accusation.'

He pursed his mouth, his eyes softening. 'I know it's been tough for you recently. I didn't realise how tough. You're still a bit off balance. I spoke to Britta and she said you weren't yourself.' He nodded slowly. 'It's still the hormones, isn't it?'

Red hot fury raced through Ella and she jumped up. 'You ... you ... ' Incandescent, she couldn't find the words.

Patrick jerked back, sloshing a spattered stripe of coffee all down his cream flannel shirt and across the cream cushion of the sofa.

Ella pushed him out of the way and seized the cushion, her heart thudding furiously. If she focused on the cover, she wouldn't give in to the powerful temptation to punch him. The coffee would stain. It would ruin the sofa for ever. She had to get the cover off the cushion. She had to get the stain out.

She ran into the kitchen, tears fogging her eyes. *Bastard, bastard, bastard.*

The image of those bloodsoaked jeans filled her head as the pungent cleaning spray tainted the air and she paused as the pain of loss rolled over her, bringing wave after helpless wave of misery. She set to scrubbing at the stain on the cushion, rubbing at the unfocused edges of the dark brown stain which bled into the fabric. *Just get it clean. Just get it clean.* She kept telling herself the words, as she tried to shut out the explosion of thoughts and emotions jostling for space in her head.

Behind him the dogs explored the undergrowth in the garden as Devon strode up the path eager to hear how Ella had got on. She'd looked so nervous as she'd headed out.

He knocked on the door, watching the dogs as they pottered their way towards him. Tess no doubt would collapse in a heap. He had to admit Ella had done wonders with her. Nothing like the pitiful, overweight and sad-looking creature he'd seen all those weeks ago up in the woods. Now she looked bright-eyed and alert, her tail on warp speed most of the time which was a pretty good indicator that she was one happy dog. Rather like Ella these days.

His pulse quickened at the thought of her opening the door, the sparkle in her eyes and the roses blooming in her cheeks. Her smile came far more readily and she'd lost that stiff repel-the-borders-at-all-costs attitude. He smiled, not sure how Ella would react at being compared with a dog.

Probably quite well these days. She definitely found it much easier to laugh at herself. Quick anticipation raced through him as he heard the latch on the door. While out walking he'd decided that he'd take her out somewhere nice for a meal. There was that new place in Wendover, he'd heard good things about.

'El—' His voice died.

Patrick stood in front of him.

'Can I help you?' he asked with an arrogant tilt of his head, his long neck reminiscent of one of the swans on the reservoir spoiling for a fight.

Devon gave him a pleasant nod. 'Ella in?' Tess barrelled past him with her usual enthusiastic pleased-to-meet-you waggle of her back legs, circling and dancing around Patrick, coating his trousers in mud and black hair. It gave Devon some small satisfaction when Patrick reared back with horror, pushing and patting with equal panicked moves to get Tess away and brush off the dirt.

'Devon!' Ella came scurrying to the door, her eyes shining with what looked like tears. She gave him a tense smile. 'Thanks for looking after Tess.'

Patrick was still backing away from the dog.

Devon focused on her face – she looked haunted and sad. He hadn't seen that look in her eyes for a few weeks. He immediately stepped forward, wanting to take her into his arms. 'You OK?'

She gave a tiny nod, her mouth pursing. 'Patrick's just leaving.'

'Call me later.'

'Yes,' she smiled at him and his heart stuttered at the steady trust in her eyes.

Chapter Twenty-Nine

'New beau?' asked Patrick, shutting the door as if he had every right.

She glared at him, wanting to unpeel his fingers from the latch. It was her door.

'He's a very good friend.' She tilted her head, unable to block the rush at the memory of Devon's kisses. 'He's been very kind.'

'Kind. You're naïve. Men like that don't do kind.'

'Men like what?' Her hand dropped to Tess's silky head.

'Boorish, Neanderthal. Or is that what you're into these days?'

'I'm not into anything.' She was conscious of the weight of the dog leaning against her leg. 'Just because he's not dressed in a Savile Row suit doesn't mean that he's not civilised. He's a vet, so I'm guessing pretty highly qualified. He's been a good friend.'

'Really?' Patrick raised one of his sculpted eyebrows. Did he pluck them? Or wax them like he did his moustache. She wondered what Devon would say about that. He'd probably take a fairly dim view of Patrick's effete male grooming. Devon always smelt of outdoors, fresh, woodsy. His hair never looked brushed and was too long but he was strong and steady. An oak to Patrick's reedy willow that bent with the wind of fashion and whatever trend was on the up.

'Are you sleeping with him?'

'Patrick, you should go.' A tinge of heat pinked her skin. Tess licked her hand.

'But we haven't talked properly.' Panic flashed in his eyes. 'You're still ... you obviously need more time to ... you know ... get your equilibrium back. I can wait. I know we said six months but I ... I was desperate to see you. Too soon. I should have been more patient. It was much more of a shock to your system that I realised. Let's give ourselves some more time. Britta says you've started to do some exciting new stuff. Sounds cathartic.'

Ella felt the pain balling up in her chest. 'You can't bring yourself to say it, can you?'

'To say what?' Puzzlement deepened the frown lines across his forehead. 'What do you want me to say?' His mouth pursed. 'Don't you think you're being over-emotional?'

She stiffened and the last tiny hope he might ever understand blinked out.

'Get out.'

Patrick almost sprang back, wide-eyed with surprise. Tess jumped up and stood squarely between them.

'Calm down,' he said, his hands patting the air.

'Calm?' she bellowed, relishing the sensation of filled lungs and the release as she shouted, 'You want me to be CALM?'

Tess growled.

Ella took a step towards him. She probably looked like a mad woman, her eyes bulging, but she didn't give a toss.

'You can't bring yourself to say or acknowledge it, can you?' she asked, spite lacing her words. '*We lost a baby.*'

He looked at her, incomprehension written into every line on his face.

Her energy evaporated.

'Patrick, we're done. Get out.'

She'd lost any desire to explain. He didn't deserve to know.

'But—'

'Out!' She pointed to the door. He paused.

'Now!'

Tess padded out of the kitchen and followed her back into the lounge where she collapsed onto the armchair, staring into the empty fireplace. Patrick would never know what he'd lost. Never understand that she'd had a precious life growing inside her or the overwhelming sense of loss when she miscarried the baby. It wasn't *hormones* and *being overemotional* that made her wonder what the baby might have grown up to be like or whether the baby would have been a boy or a girl or what type of mother she would have been. All those things, she'd never know but one thing she did know. After months of uncertainty, it was relief to realise she and Patrick were over.

She burst into tears, letting these last few months of guilt, shame and worry come flowing out. Tess nudged at her and she put an arm around the dog, burying her head into the soft fur, giving way to full-scale sobs.

*

A loud groan from the kitchen roused her. She'd fallen asleep on the sofa, a trail of drool dampening her top. A second, longer, moan made her get up and investigate.

Tess lay on the floor, her head lifting and drooping. Next to her were the remnants of the beautiful Fortnum & Mason box. Truffle cases dotted like little brown flowers across the floor.

'Oh no, you didn't!'

Ella's eyes darted from truffle case to truffle case, joining up the dots.

Shit, she'd eaten the entire box. That was a lot of chocolates. And ... Bets had said they were poisonous for dogs.

Chapter Thirty

'Devon,' hissed Bets, grabbing him as he came out of an hour and a half's surgery having just spayed a very nervous greyhound called Matilda. He was dying to call Ella and find out if she was OK.

She waited until Angela, the other veterinary nurse who assisted him, was out of earshot before adding with wide-eyed indignation. 'Marina's here.'

'What? Here?' What on earth did she want?

'She arrived about ten minutes ago. She's up in your office. Flounced in as if she owned the place and said she was happy to wait.' Bets glared at him as if he were personally responsible for Marina's behaviour. 'And could I get her a coffee.' She ground her teeth.

'Right. Sorry about that.' Although, how was that his fault?

She rolled her eyes. 'Just so you know, I haven't made her one and I have no intention of doing so.'

Bets tossed her curls and with indignation steaming out of her ears, marched down the corridor to the holding area where they kept animals in cages pre and post op. He could hear her muttering to one of the tabby cats waiting to have a growth removed from its nose that afternoon.

Wearily he took the stairs two at a time.

'Devon, darling! Good news.'

Glossy and pristine as ever, she launched herself at him and kissed him on the cheek. 'Gosh, you look done in. Another late night?'

'Not particularly.' He pulled away from the clutch of her hands on his upper arms and crossed to sit at his desk. 'What are you doing here? I'm busy.'

Marina's mouth dropped open.

'Someone's a crosspatch today.'

'I've had a . . . busy afternoon. I need to get on. You should have phoned. I've got evening surgery and a cat waiting my attention.'

'So,' she shrugged and beamed at him, 'you just got yourself an assistant. I haven't done much surgery recently. It will be good to keep my hand in.'

'I don't need an assistant, I've got Bets.'

'Don't be ridiculous, Devon. You're just cutting your nose off to spite your face. She could be doing something else. No wonder you look so tired, being a big bad grumpy martyr.'

'What do you want, Marina?' He was fed up with playing her game.

'To show you how it could be. Us as a team, working together this time. I've got the TV company to agree to fund the equipment you wanted, the laparoscope, the ports, the cannulas and the training. We'll be able to broadcast the view as you operate, the producers think it will be a real ratings winner.'

'Is that my consolation prize?'

'Devon! Devon!' Bets came running up the stairs, her curls bouncing with agitation, a phone in her hand. 'It's Ella. She's frantic.'

'Ella! Are you OK?' His heart thumped. Had Patrick done something to her?

'Devon, it's Tess,' said Ella, her voice thin and reedy. 'She's eaten chocolate. A whole box. She's been really sick and now she's just lying here.' The words rattled out at speed, but he was already moving. He let out the pent-up breath. This he could deal with.

'OK, sweetheart. It's OK. Don't worry. First, do you know how much chocolate she's eaten and what kind?'

'Fortnum and Mason. A whole box, maybe 250 grams, I don't know,' her voice went up in a wail.

Shit, that was potentially a lot of chocolate.

'OK. Don't worry. Tess will be OK but we need to establish the type of chocolate. Can you find the packaging? I need to know what's in them.'

Even as she said quietly 'OK,' he began barking orders at Bets to grab a few essentials from the pharmacy.

'I'm on way. I'll be there in two ticks.' He clicked off the phone. 'Bets, we might have to wash out Tess's stomach. Get the charcoal out.'

Marina trotted after him down the stairs.

'I'm sure you could use an extra pair of hands.'

'Whatever.'

She hopped in the Volvo next to him and he drove the short distance to Ella's cottage. The door was ajar and he pushed it open, hearing Marina clicking on her heels up the front path. Ella sat on the kitchen floor, kneeling beside Tess. He dropped beside her, giving her cold hand a quick squeeze before turning his attention to the dog.

The place was a mess; Tess had already been very sick, which was a good sign, but she lay pathetically, her side heaving, making tiny pitiful moans. Her trusting eyes were focused on Ella.

'Hi, I'm Dr Marina Scott.' Marina waltzed in, holding her hand out to a frightened-looking Ella. He could quite happily have killed Marina for tagging along.

'Hi,' she replied faintly.

'You don't need to worry about a thing. Your dog is in really good hands.' She bent down next to him as he took the dog's pulse. Racing along at runaway train speed, it was faster than he would have liked. They needed to hurry and he wished that Marina would stop leaning against him like that.

'What's her pulse doing?' Marina asked.

Devon rolled his eyes. What the hell did she think it was doing? They weren't on frigging telly now.

'It's higher than I'd like.' He avoided looking at Ella. He didn't think he could keep the seriousness of the situation out of his eyes.

Marina rattled off some technical phrases but thankfully Ella seemed to be too focused on Tess's heaving flanks to take much in, which was just as well as Marina was spouting complete rubbish. Any idiot could see the dog's heart was beating too damn fast, you didn't need to dress it up as supraventricular tachycardia.

'Please help her, Devon.'

'We will,' said Marina, her eyes soulfully sympathetic as she patted Ella's hands. 'You need to let Devon do his job. He's a wonderful vet. Don't you worry. We'll have this young man back on his feet in no time.'

'She's a she,' whispered Ella as Devon suddenly barked impatiently, 'Marina, could you help? You lift Tess's back legs. We'll get her back to the surgery in the car.'

'Can I come?' asked Ella, looking fearful.

'You'll only be in the way,' said Marina before he could say a word. 'Leave it to the professionals to do their job.'

'You can come if you want,' Devon said firmly, 'but we need to get her over there now.' He and Marina manoeuvred the dog up and out towards the door while Ella hovered as if she couldn't bear to separate herself from the dog.

'Can I do anything?' she asked.

'Can you—' Devon started.

'—bring the chocolate box?' finished Marina, sending him a fond smile. 'We need to know the cocoa content and the exact ingredients.'

Although Ella's face was so pale and worried, he couldn't afford to take his focus from the dog.

As they arrived at the surgery, he pulled Tess gently from the car and carried her in his arms, feeling the early warning signs as her stomach rolled and heaved.

'Watch out,' he warned just in time as a stream of projectile vomit spattered the stone stairs, the walls, his trousers and shoes. Of course, not a drop touched the dairyman's coat he wore for just such eventualities. Marina, he noticed, had kept well out of the way.

'Eeuw,' she wrinkled her nose. 'I don't miss this emergency stuff.'

'Oh God, is she all right?' Ella called as she came racing over. She stared, horrified, at the greenish tinge down his trousers and he gave her a glimmer of a smile.

'That's a good sign,' he said. 'And unfortunately just the start. We need to—'

'—get as much of the chocolate out of her system as possible.' Marina's voice sounded almost triumphant.

He hurried inside and shouldered his way through the doors through to the main room.

Marina was busy pulling out equipment as if she knew her way around the surgery.

He slid the dog onto the table. Tess let out a lethargic moan, which had Ella wincing.

Marina steered Ella towards the door; he thought it was probably a good idea that Ella didn't see Tess in any more distress, although he was irritated by the way Marina had assumed charge in his surgery.

'Ella, you might be better outside in the waiting room,' said Marina. 'This isn't a pleasant or pretty procedure, but Devon and I have lots of experience. We need to make Tess vomit again, just to make sure we've got as much of the chocolate out of her system. Then we'll give her some charcoal to help absorb the theobromine, which is basically the poison in chocolate which dogs are unable to absorb.'

Bets had the syringe ready. Devon lifted Tess's jowls, to open her mouth. She didn't even resist.

'Come on,' said Marina, slipping her arm under Ella's elbow and virtually frogmarching her out of the room. He wondered at her motives – was she dodging the messy part or trying to prove to him she was the perfect support?

Ella paced up and down in the waiting room until Marina appeared.

'All being well, she should be OK.' Marina peeled off a pair of surgical gloves. 'We did what we needed to do. She's stabilised. Her heart rate has been lowered. And Devon and I are very happy with her. She could have died you know... but we've saved her. Although the next few hours will be crucial. She could still have a fatal heart attack.'

'God, I can't believe ... I never normally have chocolate in the house.'

'It's easily done. One small lapse. Don't worry, Devon and I have seen it many times before.' Marina patted her on the shoulder, looking absolutely immaculate. Her white coat didn't even have dog hair on it. How was that possible?

'Careless pet owners. It happens a lot.'

Ella felt sick. It hadn't even occurred to her that Tess would get into the chocolates. She hadn't thought. Marina was right, she was careless. Poor Tess.

'Oh God, I'm so sorry. Is she going to be all right?' Had she asked that already? She couldn't think straight.

'I'll be honest, it's touch and go at this point but don't worry, Devon's one of the best.' She gave Ella a cheerful if somewhat patronising smile. 'He's a brilliant vet. That's why I'm here. You might have seen me on television, celebrity vet to the stars. I've got a new slot starting which Devon's going to star in. *Inside Out*. He'll be doing pioneering laparoscopic surgery on screen, that's keyhole surgery. It's going to make great TV and he does look good on camera,' she sighed, looking lovelorn. 'He's got it all and doesn't even realise it. Bit of a heartthrob, isn't he?'

Ella stared at the satisfied smile on Marina's face.

'We make a great team. He's so excited about the technique. We've invested in all the equipment, no mean feat, it costs thousands but it's worth it to get Devon on board.' Marina clasped her hands together. 'We've scheduled the first couple of operations already.'

'Oh. I didn't think ... ' Ella paused. 'I mean, is Devon going back to London, then?'

Marina looked a little disgruntled and gave Ella a narrow-eyed appraisal.

'Well, of course he is. I guess in a village everyone knows his business.' She hiked up the wattage on her smile. 'But Devon and I make a great team. His dad's on the mend. There's no reason for him to be out here any more and he's desperate to get cracking with the new kit.' Then her face softened, and she put out a hand to touch Ella's arm. 'He's a good man. I didn't ... ' her voice hitched with a slight indrawn sob, 'I made a terrible mistake. You probably know we've had our issues.'

Ella swallowed. She didn't want to hear this. Marina couldn't be human or nice or heartbroken.

'Do you know, I'd do anything, anything to undo what I did. Devon's so proud.'

Yeah, Ella knew that. It ought to be his bloody middle name.

'But I think in time, he will forgive me. It's going to take a lot on my part to show him that he can trust me again. But do you know what, he's worth it.' Her eyes blazed with determination. 'I love that man. I'm not going to let him down again.'

Inside her chest, Ella's heart clenched. Watching Marina and Devon working seamlessly together to save Tess had been a real eye-opener. Marina had seemed to pre-empt each of Devon's requests. Whereas Tess could have died because of Ella's carelessness. Devon must think she was a complete idiot, she'd messed up with Tess so many times.

She didn't belong here, but after seeing Patrick she felt even more at sea. What was she going to do when her six months were up? And what would she do if Tess died? She felt sick at the thought.

Chapter Thirty-One

She stumped across the green, wanting to feel the thump, thump of Tess's tail against her leg and to have to slow her pace when Tess sniffed at every gatepost along the path.

Without Tess's bustle and fuss, the cottage seemed hauntingly silent, except when Ella listened she could hear the creaks, taps and ticks of the house, the hot water pipes from the boiler in the kitchen expanding, the broken latch on the bathroom window lifting and rubbing in the early evening breeze and the familiar click of the wood of the bedroom door as it cooled down after a day in the sunshine.

She wandered into the kitchen, did a circuit but was too listless to tackle the small pile of washing-up. The empty coffee cups she and Patrick had used earlier sat on the side along with a breadboard full of crumbs. Breakfast seemed a lifetime ago. The nerves of public appearance long forgotten. With a shake of her head, she paused before walking back into the hall.

She couldn't face going up to the studio, there was no way she could even think about doing any work.

Drawn to the door, she unlatched it, slipped out into the garden and went to sit down on the stone bench, her ears pricked ready for the sound of her mobile. Summer was just around the corner. She could paint the reservoir in summer under brilliant blue sky with sunlight as streaks of gold on the water. *Please God, let Tess be all right.* It was impossible to imagine making her way along the footpaths at the edge of the water without Tess crossing and doubling back in front of her. Her tail just visible waving through the undergrowth. Or Devon accompanying them. Which was stupid, because like he'd said, this was temporary. Always had been. It shouldn't matter that Marina was back on the scene or that he might go back to her. He was never staying anyway. But it did.

Ella swallowed and focused on the petals of the blousy lilacs as the light breeze caught them, ruffling the edges. She lifted her feet onto the bench and clutched her knees to her chest.

What a day. Funny, why was it the things you didn't know you wanted that made the strongest impression? The baby. Tess. Devon.

Thinking about the baby brought with it that deep-rooted pull tugging low in her belly but it was less insistent. The sense of loss was still there but not so overwhelming. It didn't blanket her thoughts in grey any more.

Tess couldn't die. Devon wouldn't let her. With bone-deep certainty, she knew he would save her. He just would.

Devon. Friend. Rescuer. Always there when she needed him, even when she didn't know she needed him. His image came easily; she could almost smell the outdoor woodsy scent she associated with him, the slow serious smile and that unruly hair lifting in the wind, flipping over his face up on Ivinghoe Beacon. That steady, sexy masculinity that made all her hormones sit up to attention whenever he was in the vicinity. Her skin prickled at the memory of his kisses.

Where Tess was concerned, he wouldn't let her down. Where her heart was concerned, she wasn't so sure.

Magda's lavender bags had no effect that night and despite the relief of Bets' text to say that Tess was stable and snoring gently, Ella didn't get much sleep. Leaving Tess behind had been as hard as seeing Marina laying her perfectly manicured hands on Devon's sleeve and cooing up at him.

After fitful sleep, she got up early, checking her phone for any more news.

Nothing. She went up to the studio but couldn't bring herself to pick up her brushes. She checked her phone. Still nothing.

She returned to the kitchen. Cleaned the sink. Wiped down the cupboards, removing a pawprint from one of the doors. Checked her phone again. Exasperated with herself, she pulled out the broom to sweep the floor. As she rounded up the dark dog hair, it only reinforced the emptiness of the house. Eventually, after several aimless circuits of the cottage, she gravitated to her favourite spot in the garden for her morning cup of tea. Looking up at the sky, she took a deep breath. This was crazy, but she needed all the help she could get. She pulled the blue envelope which she'd snatched from the pinboard from her pocket and quietly spoke the words, glancing about to make sure no one was about.

Under Spring's awakening gaze
Breathe Earth's bountiful fragrances
Enjoy slow lengthening days
Find peace among the blossom
the warmth of deepening rays
breathing life back
Pay homage to nature's beauty
and circle the blooms daily
And take peace as yours
Blessed be

As the wind whispered through the plants, did she feel a sense of ease settle upon her? Or was it her imagination? What had she expected, some sort of pumpkin-changing, mice-into-footmen, glass-slipper magic?

'Yoohoo.'

She started.

'Ella. There you are. Is everything all right?' Doris's head popped up over George's fence. 'I saw Devon taking your dog away with his lady friend. And I saw your gentleman friend.' Coy curiosity filled her faded blue eyes.

'Hello, Doris.'

The older woman swayed a bit and then disappeared before popping back up again like a determined jack-in-the-box.

'Sorry, love. Damn wheelbarrow moved. So what's wrong with the dog?'

'Tess has had a bit of a ... ' Ella found she was able to say it without bursting into tears, ' ... mishap. She ate chocolate.' To her relief, she felt a lot calmer. 'Did you know it's poisonous to dogs?'

'Well I never. Oh, you poor love. Don't you worry. Devon's a good vet. Might not have the kennel-side manner but he's good. She'll be fine.'

'I had to leave her behind.' Ella hadn't wanted to do that. Bets said that someone would be checking on her at regular intervals. How often was that? It seemed heartless. Tess might just be a dog but she'd be lonely.

'You come right over. I promise you Tess will be as right as rain. I feel it in my bones. I'll make you a nice cup of tea. Come on. You can't mope there by yourself. I've got some lemon cake. And if you're really good. I'll show you some photos from my dancing days.' She waggled her eyebrows with great gusto.

A refusal was at the ready, tipping her tongue – she'd rather be on her own – but something, possibly Doris's hopeful expression, made her say, 'Thank you,' and swallowing and dredging up a reluctant smile, she added, 'That's an offer I can't turn down.'

'I'll have you know my lemon drizzle cake brings folks over from Long Marston when the Spring Fayre's on.'

'I meant the photos.'

'I was a Tiller Girl, you know.' Doris drew herself up with pride.

'Were you?' Ella asked politely, not having a clue what that was. Probably nothing to do with farming; her only frame of reference to the word came from some song: 'we till the soil.'

'See there. That's the London Palladium. On the bill, we were, on *Sunday Night at the London Palladium*. Appeared on ITV.'

'Wow, these pictures are amazing,' exclaimed Ella as she studied the black and white shots of a long line of girls in identical costumes, their legs kicking in perfect unison. She was glad to focus on the pictures as the lounge contained a rather distracting Aladdin's cave of stuff. Who'd have thought that Doris would have such a large television screen or a state of the art Bose sound system?

'Some famous photographer came in and took those.' She turned the pages of the album. 'That's us on Broadway. And at the Folies Bergère in Paris.' With a perfectly painted fingernail she tapped one of the pictures. 'That was us on the Eiffel Tower. Lord, we had so much fun.'

'Gosh, Doris. I had no idea. You were quite famous in your day.'

'Had a lovely time, I did. Of course I'm not nearly as famous as Alice Benthall, the WI treasurer.'

'Did I meet her yesterday?' The talk seemed a lifetime ago and with a sudden thrill, Ella remembered Margery Duffle.

'Yes, you would have done. Pink rinse, with a tinge of purple.'

'Oh, yes. I remember her.'

'Hair like that, you're not going to forget her,' observed Doris with a cheerful grin that robbed the words of any malice. 'She, Alice, was a world-famous cellist. Contemporary of that Jacqueline du Pray woman. Soloist with the New York Philharmonic.'

With a guilty start Ella realised how much she'd underestimated the people in the village. Although the fact that they were famous or successful once didn't take away from the way they'd all welcomed her and been kind to her.

A ping announced a text. Doris's eyes sharpened and Ella eagerly pulled her phone out of her pocket.

> Tess fine. Sleeping it off. You can pick her up this afternoon.

'Phew.' Ella sagged, suddenly aware of the weight of her fears. 'She's going to be all right.'

'Of course she is, dear.' Doris waved a serene hand. 'I think this calls for sherry.'

Before Ella could answer, she jumped up a bit too quickly and then winced. 'Oops.' She rubbed at her knees. 'Still paying for all that dancing the other day. Bit stiff.'

'Let me. In the kitchen?'

'Yes,' Doris sank thankfully back into her high-backed arm chair. 'Always keep my Tio Pepe in the fridge.'

Like the living room, Doris's kitchen was full of very expensive gadgets: a cranberry-coloured Kitchen Aid, a rather grand Rangemaster oven, two sets of Le Creuset saucepans, one red and one blue, hanging from shelves on the wall and a pink Smeg fridge in the corner.

You could barely see the front of the fridge for the little magnets pinning all sorts of notes and reminders. As Ella grasped the bottle of sherry and went to close the door, she noticed a familiar sheet of navy blue paper and the slash of silver writing.

Doris appeared at the door. Ella averted her eyes quickly.

'Glasses are in that cupboard.' She pointed.

'Oh my word.' The cupboard was full of fine crystal glasses in every shape and size.

'I do a lot of competitions. Win a lot.' Doris grinned. 'All down to Magda, of course.'

'Magda?'

'Oh, yes, she's got the magic touch. Ever since she discovered she was related to a witch, she's been dabbling with a few spells here and there.'

'Spells?' Ella raised a sceptical eyebrow.

'Mmm – that's what I thought, but ever since she gave me a little poem to say before I send off my entries, I've had the devil's own luck. Won all sorts, I have. Although I'm still not sure what I'm going to do with the Mini Cooper. Never had a driving licence in my life.'

Ella smiled, thinking of the sense of serenity she'd felt after reciting Magda's blessing. 'I think you might be right.'

Maybe Magda did have a touch of magic after all.

Chapter Thirty-Two

At Ella's feet, Tess yawned and stretched.

'I think it's time we got some fresh air, don't you?' said Ella.

They were only allowed to take very short walks. Tess needed to rest, as her heart had had rather a thorough workout.

'Come on, then,' said Ella. She'd taken to walking Tess around the rec twice each day but she missed the routine of their long walks and the good couple of hours' exercise they normally took each morning. On the plus side, she'd invested the extra time in painting and her work had suddenly seemed to flow. It was almost as if saying goodbye to Patrick once and for all had loosened something inside her. Now her painting was for herself and she could enjoy it – indulge in the colours, the light and shade and the sheer joy of creating without worrying about anyone judging her work.

Tess rolled to her feet as if she understood what Ella had said. 'It'll do us both good to get out. And why am I even asking you? You're not going to answer me.' Tess looked keen, though.

As they left the cottage, Ella picked up her pace. Today was not the sort of day for hanging around. A fine drizzle filled the air, the sort that gave off the type of dampness which seeped through the gaps and cracks of your clothes. No one else had been stupid enough to venture out and Ella and Tess completed a solitary circuit of the park. The swings swung disconsolately, empty and lonely, the benches were bare of the usual toddlers and mothers and the playing field was empty of any playmates for Tess. Ella had to plod along rather than being able to stride quickly to get rid of the restless energy that seemed to have built up and was now ready to burst.

On a sudden whim as they were heading home, she diverted to the village shop.

As she piled her stash of a dozen eggs, self-raising flour, baking powder, caster sugar and two boxes of icing sugar, the man running the shop looked on gloomily.

'Baking?' He shook his head. 'You can always tell when the Spring Fayre's coming up. Everyone starts baking.'

'Isn't that good for business?' Ella asked, intrigued by his depressed demeanour.

He released a long-suffering sigh that seemed to go on for ever. Ella wanted to giggle but managed to hold it in.

'My wife – I'm Peter Reynolds, by the way – has been baking for three straight days. Frozen pizza for dinner every night.' He shook his head with a mournful expression, unconsciously rubbing at his belly contained by a burgundy sweater. He looked like a rather juicy berry. 'And then I can't get any bugger to work in the shop because they're all too busy baking, or putting up tents or making new drainpipes for Splat the Rat. Then of course we're run off our feet on Saturday because loads of people come to the fayre and they suddenly remember they've forgotten to buy any milk or Saturday papers, so I'm stuck here. All the cakes that don't sell on the cake stall wind up here. I spend the next week trying to persuade people to buy them. Thing is, by then everyone is caked out, they've had enough bleedin' sugar. I tell you, I'll be glad when it's all over and everything goes back to normal. Which reminds me, I don't think I've got you down on the rota...?'

And there was Devon, head down, not looking where he was going, coming straight towards her, his long stride eating up the narrow pavement.

There was no way she could avoid him. Not dressed for the damp morning, his habitual dark blue Guernsey sweater was dusted with fine drops of water and the curls of his hair had tightened in the light rain. Every one of her nerve endings seemed to dance at the sight of him. She took a measured breath and tried to muster up a casual smile. It sounded as if Marina had made him an offer he couldn't refuse. Ella knew how much the idea of the new style of surgery meant to him. Now that she'd rediscovered her passion for painting, she could understand him taking this chance.

He looked up and smiled, his frown lifting. 'Ella.'

He sounded pleased to see her, which hurt more than she'd thought it would. How could she hope to compete with Marina? 'Hi, how are you?' she asked inanely, suddenly tongue-tied. When she'd picked Tess up he'd been busy with another patient, so they'd barely spoken.

'Fine. Busy. That bloody dog Buster has eaten another pair of tights. Emergency surgery plus my planned list.' His mouth crumpled in frustration. 'You'd think his owners might have learned their lesson by now.'

Instinctively Ella put her hand down on Tess's head. She'd certainly learned hers. 'How're you doing, young lady?' He bent down to stroke her head and she nuzzled up to him. 'She had a close call, but she's looking a lot better.'

Ella felt a pang as she watched him fondle the dog's ears. How could you be jealous of a dog, for goodness' sake?

'I've been taking it easy with her. Gentle exercise, like you said.' She gave him a terse smile, aware that she'd failed poor Tess badly and that she needed to keep her distance. Desperate to get away, she looked at her watch.

'Gosh, I need to get back. Nice to see you.' With a quick nod, she tugged at Tess's lead and started to walk away, pinching her lips tightly together.

He took a step back, surprise registering on his face before he frowned. 'Right. OK.'

She walked off, resisting the urge to look back over her shoulder, horribly aware of the regret pinching at her heart. It shouldn't matter to her if Devon and Marina did get back together, but it did.

Magda had an extensive collection of recipe books, which hitherto Ella hadn't taken that much notice of. Now, in the kitchen, she perused the shelf. What she really wanted was a book entitled *The Complete Beginner's Guide to Baking a Perfect Cake and How to Stop Thinking About a Certain Yummy Vet.* There were quite a few notebooks which bulged with recipes torn out from newspapers and magazines, but everything looked quite advanced.

Then she remembered the blue box and the sheaf of papers in there. Sure enough, in Magda's elegant script was a recipe. *Perfect Victoria Sponge*. Beside the recipe, which had originally been copied out in blue biro, there were additional handy hints in red. *Watch the baking powder. Slightly less sugar.* None of which was terribly helpful to Ella. But the basic recipe of butter, eggs, sugar and flour looked familiar enough.

Determined not to give Devon another thought she began to measure out her ingredients, beating butter with sugar, sifting flour and beating eggs. The recipe called for a something-spoon of baking powder; a grease spot on the type had obscured the first part of the word. She made a quick guesstimate and put in the baking powder into the flour just as she was interrupted by a muffled banging at the window.

'Hello there.' Audrey waved her head, bashing at the glass with her elbow, her arms full of something.

With a regretful look at the bowl of cake mix, Ella dusted her hands down her jeans and went to let the other woman in.

'Hello, dear.' She shouldered her way in as Ella stepped aside, and moved straight through to the kitchen. 'Oooh! Baking. Super. Another cake for the cake competition. I bet you've got Magda's lightness of touch with a sponge. All right to put this here?' she asked, putting a large red and blue hexagonal-shaped barrelled box on the table.

Ella nodded. Where did Audrey get her seemingly inexhaustible supply of energy? She looked at the cake mix. She'd followed Magda's recipe, so maybe this sponge would be as light and fluffy as the increasing expectation.

Audrey rubbed her back and groaned. 'I forget every year how heavy this thing is. Right, tickets are in the car. I brought you Sellotape and plenty of raffle tickets because I wasn't sure what you'd have. I've got two more boxes of bottles for labelling up – Devon will bring some more later.'

'More?' said Ella faintly as Audrey bustled back out of the house. She already had the first three crates he'd brought previously. Following Audrey to the kerbside, she arrived just in time to take a clinking box from the older woman.

'Here you go. Mainly spirits in there. The scouts collected that lot. WI donations will all be sherry and Campari.'

Ella, almost buckling under the weight, carried the box inside.

'Right, that's that lot. Devon will bring the rest over tomorrow, he's too busy today. Poor boy, he's so good. Up half the night again last night and on call again tonight. I do worry about him. For the last couple of days he's been in a foul mood. Even Bets is about to throw in the towel and that takes a lot. I blame that bloody woman, Marina. I could strangle her. He's stuck between a rock and hard place. Working all hours God sends.' Audrey paused, her face suddenly sombre. 'He's so bloody proud. He won't take any money from us.' Ella saw the worry lining her face, quite at odds with Audrey's normal confident serenity. 'Doesn't eat properly. And still willing to help.'

Ella paused, her heart almost stopping. 'I thought … Marina. She said they were going to work together again.'

'Did she? News to me. Not that he tells me much.'

'She still cares about him,' offered Ella tentatively. And could offer him what he wanted. That counted for a lot, didn't it?

'Ha, all she cares about is herself,' said Audrey with a toss of her head. 'But I can't tell him that, can I? If it weren't for that bloody debt, I'm sure he'd just tell her to sling her hook. I couldn't believe she turned up the other day, all sweetness and light.' She poked at the bottles on the table and held up a tall thin bottle containing a startling cerise-coloured liquid. 'I do wonder where people get these things from.'

With a sigh, she put it back. 'Bets says she's up to something. Made him some offer. Whatever it is, isn't making him happy. He's been grumpy since he came back, but he seems much worse suddenly. He's always been difficult to read. Unlike his brother, Jack. All charm and smiles.' She shook her head, her face lighting up with a fond smile. 'But like an eel. Slithers off the minute there's work to be done, but with more charm in his little finger than you can shake a stick at. Bets is far too good for him.' Ella was less and less liking the sound of Jack. Bets had definitely lost a touch of her bounce in recent weeks. Jack sounded totally selfish to her, not that she could say that to his mother.

'I find it's best if you stick to the noughts and fives,' advised Audrey with one of her lightning changes of tack, 'then people know they've won something straight away. And arrange everything in number order, otherwise it's a nightmare trying to find the right bottles.'

Ella nodded. She hadn't realised she'd have to do this bit when she was volunteered.

'So I have to stick raffle tickets on every bottle?'

'That's right, dear. One on the bottle and the other ticket in the barrel.'

Ella looked at the collection of bottles on the table. She was going to have her work cut out. Before she could wonder out loud how long it might take her, Audrey had bobbed up and was off with a cheery wave. 'Cakes need to be delivered to the tent by eight-thirty, so that the judges can start their deliberations first thing. Stalls open at ten prompt. You're on till twelve and then someone will take over. Think that's everything. Look at the time. I still need to get to the hairdressers, pick up the new rat and make sure that Peter's got the trestle tables out of the village hall. It's all go. Happy baking.'

Watching Audrey's retreating figure, Ella sighed, reeling slightly. It was as if a tornado had just swept through.

She exchanged a look with Tess, who shook her head, kneaded her blanket with her paws, walked around three times and then with a mournful sigh, dropped into the bed, turning her back on Ella. 'I'm on my own, then,' said Ella.

She started combining the cake ingredients she'd previously measured out and then couldn't remember how much baking powder she'd put in, so added a tiny bit extra to the flour just in case. She had no idea that baking could be so therapeutic, although her arm was killing her and her mind kept straying to Devon. Whether he went back to Marina or not, she still wanted to explain about Patrick. She didn't want him to assume that she'd forgiven Patrick.

Audrey had looked so worried about him. It didn't seem right he owed so much money, not with the way property prices were in London. Something nagged at her, like a missing piece of puzzle.

Now the cake was in the oven, she wondered how she was going to decorate it.

She'd seen the odd episode of *Bake Off*. That nagging buzz at the back of her head surged forward again. Filmed in a tent in the grounds of some gorgeous house. Did they pay the house-owners to rent the grounds?

She needed to focus on the task at hand. Baking. Presentation. Making it look as good on the outside as on the inside. Not that she was particularly confident about the inside. But the outside, she could definitely do something about.

As she tidied the kitchen, wiping up the flour, washing the mixing bowl, under the watchful eye of Tess, she flitted from one idea to another. She could cut the cake into an intricate shape and ice it. Trim one edge into a straight line and tip the cake on its side so that the flat front faced forwards. That would be different, but then what would she put on the front? There were so many possibilities. Tess yawned with a loud groan.

'What do you think Tess? Fancy shape? Fancy icing? Or am I overthinking it?'

Tess stood up slowly, shook herself and came to stand in front of Ella, her amber eyes blinking up at her with a serious expression as if she were carefully considering the options. With a sudden gurgle of laughter, Ella crouched down to give the dog a hug. 'You don't care, do you?' Under her arms, Tess wriggled to get closer, almost knocking Ella off her feet. A surge of love bloomed in Ella's chest.

'Daft dog,' she whispered, feeling the prickle of tears in her eyes. There was nothing quite like this quiet, unconditional companionship. It was a shame friendship with people couldn't be like this. Although, Ella smiled to herself, it was rather convenient when one half of a pair couldn't talk back. She sighed and looked at her watch. While the cake was baking she just had time to make a phone call. The idea that had been nagging at her had bubbled away for the last hour.

'Britta, it's Ella.' She held the phone in one hand, the other stroking Tess's silky ears. The crazy dog had snuggled in so close, her head nestled on Ella's thigh and her breath was leaving damp patches on Ella's jeans.

'Ella, babes. How you doing? You and Patrick sorted things out yet?'

Ella refused to even discuss that yet. This call was going to be difficult and she would rather have avoided it but she needed to check something.

'Yes, we have.'

'Thank God for that. So when are you coming back to London?'

Ella chickened out. 'Britta, remember when you and Bryce did that video installation.'

'Lord, yes. What a palaver.'

'How much did you have to pay for the studio?'

'Daylight robbery. Only £900 a day.'

'And what did that include?'

'Ella, babes. What are you planning? Should I be getting excited? Is this a new direction?'

Ella wanted to groan out loud. Instead she looked down at Tess and rolled her eyes. The dog lifted her head and nuzzled in closer if that were possible, almost sitting on Ella. A definite show of support on the canine front.

'Yeah,' she lied quickly. It was probably easier. 'So what did that pay for?'

'Lights and electricity. That's it. Then we had to pay extra for the cameraman, the sound man, all the kit. Cameras. Mics. And then we went over one day. By an hour. Had to pay a surcharge of £250.'

Filming was an expensive business. Even more than Ella would have guessed.

'And is that standard?'

'No, that was cheap. Depends on the size of the studio you hire. How specialist is it? Depends whether you want sound and cameras. Whether you want to use their editing suite. Their editors. Licence to print money. Although you can get some great grants for video work. What are you thinking of doing? Have you told Patrick? Is it a solo project?'

Ella winced at Britta's flurry of enthusiastic questions. 'There's no project. I went to the gallery.' She sounded accusatory but Britta missed it.

'What, in London? Why didn't you call me? We could have met up for coffee.'

Ella swallowed. Her next words would be the equivalent of lighting a match and watching everything go up in flames but she couldn't pretend everything was all right. Her hand stilled on Tess's ear and the dog nudged her hand, giving it a swift lick. For a moment, she let the silence hang between them before saying, 'You knew.' The bald words dropped like stones down a well. One by one, impossible to take back.

'Knew what?' Britta's tone changed, her voice immediately guarded. Ella didn't have the energy to play games.

'That Patrick was selling my pictures. You took it, didn't you. Cuthbert in his Cavalier hat.'

Typical Britta; she didn't miss a beat or try to excuse what she'd done. 'He said he missed you and wanted a souvenir.' Ella could imagine Britta's insouciant, elegant shrug of her bony shoulders. Maybe she hadn't known what Patrick was doing. Difficult to believe, although she desperately wanted to.

Britta's next words robbed her of that hope.

'He wanted to know what you were doing. He said he wouldn't sell that one.'

'*That* one.' Ella swallowed, the hard knot pressing into her throat. Damn. She'd really wanted Britta to be innocent. To be as in the dark as she'd been. But the throwaway line confirmed that Britta knew full well that Patrick was selling Ella's pictures.

'Why didn't you tell me?'

'Tell you what? Does it matter that he sold them? I mean, no disrespect, but you're selling the images anyway? What's the difference? People buy them all the time in the books. Babes, you are very good at drawing. You're good at everything, sculpting, modelling, painting. You've got it. Technically those pictures are brilliant.'

'Shame you never said that before,' snapped Ella.

'Are you mad at me?' Britta's voice held a hint of amazed disbelief.

'Too flipping right, I'm mad. I'm furious.'

'Oh.'

That was all she had to say. Just 'Oh'. That was it?

'I have to go, Britta.' She hastily ended the call. She just didn't have the energy to explain to Britta how much it mattered or, more satisfyingly, any desire to do so.

Tess put a paw on Ella's hip and her head nudged at Ella's chin. The shift in weight made it hard for Ella to keep her balance. Tess's head nudged her again. Silly dog. Managing to regain her balance, she ruffled Tess's ears. 'You agree with me, don't you?' Tess's steady gaze immediately lifted her spirits. Britta had let her down. She'd told her how she felt and it was done.

'Oh, dear,' said Ella as she pulled the cake tins out of the oven when the timer went off. The last time she'd peered through the glass in the oven, the two sponges had risen rather well – in fact spectacularly well, like a pair of volcanoes. Since then they'd sunk and now each featured a definite dip in the top.

'Hmm, if I cut the tops off and cover everything with icing, they could be ok. What do you think, Tess?'

Tess's tongue was hanging out.

'Stupid question. You'd eat both in one gulp, wouldn't you?'

As the cakes cooled, she turned her thoughts back to Devon. She really wanted to do something for him for a change. With a sudden burst of energy, she sat down at the kitchen table and opened up a spreadsheet. She needed some more information. Thank God for the internet and Google. She scrolled through several websites, checking her facts. *Making Pets Well With Marina* was produced by a company called Vet Magic Productions. With a little more digging, lo and behold, it turned out that Marina part-owned the film production company. That made things really murky. Ella picked up the phone again. Why was she doing this? Some forlorn hope of rescuing Devon from Marina? Making sure that he had a choice? She didn't want him to be in the dark the same way that she had been for all this time.

By the end of the afternoon, after several calls including one to Bets to find out how long Devon and Marina had lived in the house and one to the registered offices of VM Productions, Ella had struck gold with a very chatty receptionist who'd been only too happy to tell her how long the programme had been running and the history of the show. It turned out that the first two series of the programme – which was now in its tenth series – had been filmed in a studio before they'd moved to the current location. And more recently they were doing the regular segment on the news magazine show on ITV.

With all the information she had, Ella set up a spreadsheet, typing in estimated figures. She was guessing, but even on the conservative side with the time period and number of series she created a compelling set of figures. In the last three years, eight ten-week series of *Making Pets Well With Marina* had been filmed in the consulting rooms at Marina and Devon's house. Eighty programmes equated to a lot of filming time. According to Ella's spreadsheet, that was an awful lot of studio fees that someone should have paid.

Ella snapped shut her laptop and nibbled at her fingernail. Marina had seemed so sincere and heartbroken the other day. Maybe she shouldn't interfere ...

Chapter Thirty-Three

'Come on, we've got a cake to finish.' Ella had spent the evening, while attaching raffle tickets to bottles, racking her brains as to how she might decorate her cake and sometime in the early hours of the morning, an idea had popped into her head. An Easter bonnet. And she had all the equipment to do it, thanks to Magda and her white witch kick. Ella frowned, looking at the box. Her decision to make a cake had been hers alone and not influenced by anyone.

She'd cover the cake in white icing and dot it with sugar paste flowers, with Cuthbert, Herbert, Englebert, Bertram and Catherine peeping out from under the petals.

The internet was a wonderful thing. When she drank her first coffee of the morning, she'd already researched several techniques to make the spring flowers. Her own mice characters she could do quite easily.

She'd rolled out the first sheet of icing when she heard a rattle and looked up to see Devon, Dex at his heels, coming down the front path with another box of bottles. Twin emotions warred; the desire to avoid him and stay safe, fighting against the inescapable lift of her spirits at the sight of him.

She opened the door to see him dump the box on the step.

'There's another one in the car,' he said over his shoulder as he took four paces down the path. Dexter wandered in through the open door to greet Tess and the two of them fussed over each other.

At least *they* were pleased to see each other.

She picked the box up and carried it into the kitchen, putting it on the table next to the laptop.

Devon appeared in the doorway with the second box, his face uncertain as he gave her a direct look. 'Where do you want it?' Dexter and Tess were chasing each other's tails with unabandoned joy which Ella felt was distinctly out of place at that moment.

'Here would be great,' she nodded and turned her back on him, indicating the table

He popped it on the table.

'Thanks, that's good.' She gave him a perfunctory smile.

'So,' Devon loitered despite her lack of welcome, 'Patrick?'

'I told him that I knew what he'd been up to, that he'd been stealing from me. My publisher sent me my royalty statements. Turns out I earn enough from the Berts to support myself. I think it's enough to rent a place in London and I can probably get my old job back at the art supplies shop.'

'You're going to go back?'

'I expect so,' said Ella firmly. 'So, we'll both be moving on.'

Devon's eyes narrowed. 'I guess you're right.' He rammed

his hands in his pockets and stood for a moment, as if he might say something else.

Ella swallowed and avoided his gaze. Letting him go was harder than she thought it would be. She didn't want them to part on bad terms but she definitely couldn't let him go back to Marina for the wrong reason.

'Devon, listen. I think I might be able to help you.'

'Help me? How?'

'I think Marina's been conning you, too.'

His head lifted sharply. 'That's a very strong word.'

Ella clenched her hands together, not quite as confident now, and then turned the laptop screen towards him.

'Look.'

He scowled down at the screen and then paused as he scanned the spreadsheet.

'Marina part owns the production company that makes her programmes,' explained Ella. He lifted his gaze to hers, his expression guarded. 'Which means she has a conflict of interest.' She gulped and raced on, 'The production company wants to make the programmes as cheaply as possible so that they can maximise their profit.'

'And what do you hope to gain by telling me this? That I'm as gullible as you were with Patrick?'

She winced, feeling the icy hauteur of his words.

'That's not it at all. I wanted to help.' His studied lack of attention made her pause, but she kept her cool even though she was shaking inside. 'She's using your joint property for filming but it's her company making the profit. At the very minimum, it, the company, should be paying a location fee or rental for the hire of the consulting rooms. Look,' she pointed to the figures in the final column, 'I did some rough estimates of how much the production company would have had to pay over eight seasons if they had to pay for studio space. It's a lot of money.'

Devon's face darkened as he studied the spreadsheet and then his eyes bored into hers.

'Ella. Did I ask for your help?' His even, reasonable tone held a hint of menace.

She swallowed at the mutinous set to his mouth. Her stomach flipped. It felt as if she'd taken one step too far over the precipice of a cliff.

She shook her head, nervous now.

He rose to his feet. 'If I wanted help, I'd ask for it. This is my problem. Not yours. Not my father's. I will sort it out. On my own.'

He was already halfway to the door.

'You're being ridiculous.' She wanted to help him, couldn't he see that?

'Ridiculous?' Devon turned and glared at her.

'Yes. I've found a possible solution. Something that will stop you working all hours. Stop your mother worrying about you. Stop Bets worrying. Your dad.'

'I don't need *anyone* to worry about me. It's no one's business but mine and I'd be grateful if you'd mind your own. Mum, Dad, Bets and you, you've all got problems of your own to deal with. I'm handling mine just fine, thank you.'

'That's just rude, Devon, and not worthy of you.' With her arms folded facing him, she sounded braver than she felt.

'I hardly think you know me well enough to be a judge of that.'

He was so wrong. 'I *do* know you.' Good, decent, kind, solid. Yeah, she might not have known him for long but she knew him. 'You're a man who does the right thing. You help other people all the time. You look after everyone else. That's what you do, Devon. So why do you find it so hard to accept help from other people?'

'I don't.'

'Yes, you do.'

He stared stonily back at her. 'When I want help, I'll ask for it. But I don't need it.'

Inside her muscles clenched. She might as well as talk to a block of granite. But she wasn't prepared to give up. 'Are you sure about that?'

Devon shot her a filthy look. 'Absolutely.'

'You're being an idiot.' OK, so finding refuge in insults wasn't the best tactic but ... grrr! Her fists bunched at her sides.

'Yeah, tell me about it.' He turned away and was already halfway to the door. 'I was an idiot. That's what got me into this mess in the first place. I'll sort myself out. And that means by myself.'

'So that's all you can say.' Ella lifted her chin. 'You *are* an idiot.'

'Tell me something I don't know. I think it's time I left.'

'Yes, I think it is.' Something in Ella's stomach soured.

Devon walked out of the room and out of the front door, pulling it shut with a decided bang.

Ella waited a beat and looked down at Dexter with a wry smile.

When the rap at the door came, she opened the door with a smug expression. 'Forgot something?'

Dexter trotted out as Devon turned on his heel and strode down the path.

'Idiot.' Ella slammed the door. Tess stood in front of her, tail wagging, her tongue hanging out with a doggy grin.

Ella patted her side. Some things you could always count on. 'Come on then, Tess, it's just you and me and another five thousand bottles to label up.'

Chapter Thirty-Four

The morning of the Spring Fayre dawned with a brilliant blue sky, just like it did in all the picture-perfect village scenes on TV. No doubt Audrey was in charge of weather arrangements too or maybe she was friends with someone who was. Ella gave the blue postcard on the pinboard a quick smile.

'Sorry, Tess,' she said, giving the kitchen a quick once-over to make sure she'd left nothing out that might cause temptation. 'I'll come back for you later.' With cakes on display and no doubt lots of other goodies, Tess might be – no scrub that, *would* be – a liability. Better to come and retrieve her later when Ella's stint on the tombola stall was over.

Bets was bang on time and already on the doorstep.

'Morning. Can you believe this weather? I swear Audrey's a witch. Now, what do you want me to carry? Has Geoffrey already been?'

'Yes, bless him. Poor man, I think he's been up since about six o'clock running around the village. He took all the bottles about twenty minutes ago.'

'Thank goodness for that. I never want to see another raffle ticket or bottle of strange-coloured liqueur again in my life.'

'Me neither, but thank you for coming to help. I don't know what I'd have done without you.' The night before, after Devon had stomped off, Ella had called in the cavalry and Bets had come round immediately to help, which was just as well as she had immediately pointed out that Ella was throwing away all the winning raffle tickets.

Bets gave her a quick hug and Ella hung on for a second. If anything, this morning she felt worse than she had done last night after Devon had left.

'You should have brained Devon with one of the bottles. Stupid bugger. Honestly, men. I still can't believe the stupid idiot wouldn't listen to you.'

'Please don't say anything to him. He was furious enough with me that I'd "interfered" – he'll be even more cross if he thinks I've told you.'

'I'm glad you did. It explains a lot.' Bets nudged her with an elbow. 'Don't give up on him. He'll come round. I thought you two ... well,' she shot a cheeky grin at Ella, 'over the last few weeks the two of you seemed to get on much better.'

Ella blushed. 'Well, we were starting to.'

Bets fixed her with a penetrating stare.

'But not any more.'

'Which explains why he's been in such a foul mood this morning. Well, aside from fielding calls from Marina; she's been on the phone every five minutes—'

'That's because she's determined to get him back and it will solve a lot of his problems. Especially as he wasn't prepared to listen to what I had to say.'

Bets' face suddenly broke into a broad grin. 'There's no way he'll go back to Marina. No matter what she's promising. The rest of the family will never speak to him again.'

'You didn't hear her the other night – she really loves him and she's making him an offer he'd be mad to refuse. It'll solve all his money worries.'

'Don't be silly. Devon's pride's taken a battering. Marina's taken him to the cleaners, emotionally and financially. The last thing he wants is someone else bailing him out.'

'I think he made that quite plain. Well, he can get on with it. Stupid man.'

'And he's going to have to, because as I was about to say before you interrupted me ... he told her to get knotted this morning.' Bets folded her arms and gave Ella a triumphant look.

'He did?'

'He did.'

'Oh.'

Ella turned away to look out of the kitchen window, feeling her cheeks flush.

'Ooh, is that the cake?' Bets' uncharacteristic attempt at diplomatically changing the subject brought a reluctant smile to Ella's face. 'Let's have a look.' She'd been intrigued the night before by the rows of sugar paste petals drying on tea towels on the kitchen side. So had Tess, but Ella had kept a close eye on her.

'Yes, but whatever you do, don't knock it.' Ella had finished it in the early hours of the morning after Bets had left.

Bets slipped the lid from the cake tin, very, very carefully.

'Oh, my. That's amazing.' She reached out a reverent finger to touch one of the sugar paste flowers.

Ella was rather pleased with it. She'd sandwiched the two slightly uneven cake layers together, and when they were covered with ready rolled icing, you couldn't tell she'd had to slice the tops off. She'd then spent ages topping the surface with lots of yellow and white flowers. Just off the centre of the cake, on top of one of the flowers, was a tiny sugar-paste Cuthbert, complete with red fez, looking out over the sea of flowers for his brothers and sister. She'd managed to bring their game of hide and seek in a flower meadow to life perfectly. To his left, Herbert peeped up at him from where he hid under a daisy while on the other side of the cake, Bertram and Englebert giggled together from behind a yellow rose and Catherine peered out from between white petals.

'You're so talented. I don't think I've got a creative bone in my body. I'm not terribly good at anything.' She sighed. 'No wonder Jack doesn't want to visit. He's meeting all those super clever girls at university.'

'Don't be silly.' Ella put the cake down and threw her arms around Bets. 'He's so lucky to have you.' She drew back, still holding on to Bets' arms. 'You are one of the nicest, kindest and loveliest people I've ever met. I can't thank you enough for all you've done for me while I've been here.'

'But I haven't—'

'Yes, you have. You made me feel welcome. You gave your friendship, unconditionally and totally without judgement. I was a stuck-up, miserable cow and it didn't stop you. You always look on the bright side. You help without being asked and when you are asked you never say no. You make me smile even when I don't want to. Being with you is always fun. You see the good things in people and you've made *me* see them. I'm a much nicer person for knowing you, so thank you for being my friend.'

'Aw.' Bets blinked and sniffed. 'Blimey, that's quite a big old speech.' She hugged Ella back. 'It's also one of the nicest things anyone has ever said to me. I know I can be a bit annoying sometimes...'

'Shush. You need to be nicer to yourself. If Jack can't see how wonderful you are, he doesn't deserve you.' Ella bent to pick up the cake tin.

Bets straightened up and Ella could see her metaphorically dust herself down. 'You're right.' She linked her arm through Ella's very gently. 'Come on. Let's go. Don't want to drop the delivery. We'd better get a wiggle on. Poor Elsie, Peter's wife. She was really hoping that with Magda out of the way, she might win best cake this year. I don't think she stands a chance.'

'Really?' Ella hugged the tin closer. 'I'm not sure about that. It is the first cake I've made since I was about ten.'

Cheerful floral bunting hung from every point of the high beamed ceiling in the village hall and the local craft group had gone yarn-bombing mad by knitting rainbow socks for the four main supporting beams. They'd also covered a bicycle, the wooden benches outside the hall and a wooden rocking chair, on which Doris sat like a queen taking the entrance money.

With her cake deposited in the marquee on the recreation ground at the back of the hall, Ella hurried to take up her post on the tombola stall. A rather harried Audrey had given her a box of change, the float, and instructions not to hand it over to anyone but Peter who was on accounting duty for the day as well as a reminder that she would be relieved at twelve by

Mrs Mason, who ran the pre-school. Ella wondered quite how that latter piece of information would help in identifying Mrs Mason when she turned up.

Arranging the bottles took quite some doing as the table was a touch on the small side but she remembered the advice from both Audrey and Bets that it would make life a lot easier to match them up with winning tickets if they were grouped in number order.

It looked as if the whole village had turned out today and the minute the doors officially opened at ten o'clock the hall was suddenly full. No light trickle of people. One minute it was empty, the next full. Obviously, the folk of Wilsgrave didn't believe in being fashionably late. Going to any event with Britta or Patrick had invariably involved a debate as to the best time to turn up. The official starting time never being an opener for ten.

'Good morning, m'dear.'

'George.' Ella beamed. 'How are you today?' She'd popped in to see him every day since he'd come home.

'Feeling better, bit stiff though.' He winced. 'You all right? That vet keeping an eye on you?'

Ella rolled her eyes. 'Yes, thank you.' George didn't miss a thing. 'He's an idiot, though.'

George looked mischievous. 'Men usually are. Good job we have women to keep us on the straight and narrow.' He patted her hand. 'And how has the cake turned out?'

He'd been very excited when she'd confessed she'd succumbed and baked a cake.

'Actually, George, I'm pretty darned pleased with it.'

'Excellent, I shall look forward to a taste. Now, I'll have five tickets. How much are they?'

'A pound a ticket. Are you sure you want five?'

'Course.'

She took his money and he made a great show of delving into the barrel and counting out his tickets. A passing family watched avidly. To George's absolute delight – he actually did a little hop skip and a jump – he won a bottle of blue curaçao. 'Grand. That's me and Doris sorted for cocktail night.' With a wave he sauntered off, clutching his booty.

The family of three stared after him.

'Would you like a ticket?' asked Ella. It was all for a good cause. They didn't look as if they had much money but there was a one in five chance of winning which was pretty good odds.

The man ignored her, but the mother and daughter shuffled closer together, the three of them closing ranks.

Ella tried to appear friendly and welcoming but it was rather like smiling down the barrel of a gun, the intensity of their stares was so fierce. After a while it started to intimidate her but thankfully Doris bowled up with a bunch of cronies, all of whom bought lots of tickets. They bore off their assorted bottles very happily, oblivious to the stony stare of the trio behind them.

Then the dad of the family stepped forward and burrowed deep into his shirt pockets before pulling out a rather tatty five pound note.

'One ticket.' He handed over the note and held out a fat pudgy hand for the change.

Ella counted out four pound coins, subject to suspicious scrutiny. 'Here you go.'

With surprising speed his hand dived into the tombola

barrel and he immediately turned away, secretively poring over his ticket, or rather, as Ella strongly suspected, tickets. Wife and daughter crowded round.

A younger family with a little girl and a toddler in a pushchair diverted Ella's attention. They were friendly and chatty, getting the little girl to take a lucky handful of tickets. They won a bottle of lager and pronounced themselves delighted to win something.

'Another,' said the man, a single pound coin pinched between his thumb and finger. Again he dipped into the barrel, keeping his hand carefully closed as he turned away.

With more customers appearing, Ella found it hard to keep an eye on the odd family but they were definitely up to something.

When Bets appeared on the other side of the room, Ella waved frantically to her, in such a way that it was obvious something was wrong.

Before Bets reached her the man approached the stall. 'I got two winners. Two-O-Five and three-O-O. Noughts and fives win, don't they?' With an aggressive thrust he waved the two raffle tickets under her nose and pointed with the other hand to a bottle of whisky and a bottle of vodka.

Ella took the tickets from him and he snatched up the two bottles before she even had a chance to check the numbers tallied. To be honest she didn't care. Now that they'd won something, hopefully they'd disappear.

Bets, having wriggled away through the crowded room, faced her across the table.

'You OK?'

'I hope I will be now,' Ella whispered. 'I think those people are cheating but they've won something now. I didn't know what to do.'

'The Bainbridges. They are a little strange. Live just outside the village in that cottage with the net curtains. All the kids call it the scary house.'

'I can see why,' muttered Ella trying to be discreet and not look at the trio who were still there whispering among themselves.

Just then the man pushed forward and waved another pound coin at her. 'Another one.'

Ella gave him a hard stare. Should she accuse him of taking more than one ticket each time?

When she looked round, Bets had gone. Trying to dredge up some bravery, Ella gave Mr Bainbridge a firm but fair smile. 'It is just one ticket for a pound.'

'Hah! Daylight robbery. One frigging ticket for a pound. Should be two. One isn't right.'

'I'm afraid I didn't set the prices and it's all for a good cause.'

Mr Bainbridge stared at her, his watery steel blue eyes locked onto hers. Goosebumps erupted on Ella's arms. She'd rather be anywhere but here. He was probably putting a curse on her or something.

'I'm having two tickets.'

'That's not very fair on everyone else, is it?' Her voice held even though inside she had no idea what to do. What the hell was village etiquette when you dealing with the local misfit family?

'Up to your old tricks are you, Bainbridge?' Devon's voice, firm and even, interjected. Her pulse reacted to the familiar timbre and with it a sudden tightening of her skin and muscles, as if her whole body had gone on full alert. With his hand on his hips and towering over the shorter, dumpy man, Devon looked like an avenging angel. Ella could have fainted with outright gratitude, except that was the last thing he would want. She stared at the stern mouth, the memory of its touch triggering a warmth inside her chest she would rather ignore.

Bainbridge glared at Devon, shrugged and without another word slid off into the crowd, his wife and daughter slinking after him without a backward glance.

Stunned into silence, Ella could only gawp stupidly at Devon. His expression didn't invite conversation. With a disdainful and long-suffering tut, he shook his head and turned on his heel and disappeared into the crowd.

Bloody typical. Apparently it was OK for *him* to come to the rescue. Despite being horribly grateful, she still wanted to shake him.

When Mrs Mason came to relieve her at twelve, Ella wasn't as desperate to leave as she thought she'd be.

'Thank you so much for holding the fort.' It was one of the ladies whom she'd met when doing her talk.

'That's OK. I enjoyed myself.' She'd had a great time, chatting to half the village she knew and lots of people she didn't, who'd all been very friendly and chatty. The time had flown by.

'I hear the Bainbridges stopped by, dear. They are such wretches. Very naughty of them. It's not even as if they drink. They just like to win.' She shook her pale pink rinse. 'But then, Mrs Bainbridge always donates the whole lot back again for next year.'

'How odd,' said Ella.

'And isn't your picture doing well?'

Ella looked blank for a second.

'Your mouse picture in the silent auction. Up to a thousand pounds!'

'Really?'

'Yes,' the older lady beamed. 'That'll go a long way to helping with the roof repairs.'

'Gosh. I'm so pleased. That's brilliant news.'

'Now, off you go. I'd get some food while you can. Pam's pulled pork burgers are a real treat. I recommend you try them. And here comes Bets.'

Ella crossed the hall to meet her.

'Thank you so much for sending Devon over.'

'That's all right. Audrey should have warned you. Did he speak to you?'

'No. Just did his knight act and buggered off sharpish.'

'Men,' they said in unison and burst out laughing.

'Come on. Let's get some food. Then you can come and watch the dog agility class.'

'Blimey, the excitement might just kill me,' teased Ella, lifting her head as the scent of food tantalised. 'Gosh, that smells delicious.'

'Pam's pulled pork burgers. They're a must. Come on.'

Replete with burger, Ella settled into the afternoon. Who'd have thought the village fayre could be so much fun? Bets' agility competition was hilarious as none of the dogs knew how to behave and only three of them managed to complete the course.

The final judging of the cakes was announced and Ella accompanied Bets to the stuffy marquee over which Audrey presided. She had two other people with her: Scott Pitman, who Ella recognised as a judge on a minor TV cookery programme from several years ago and Johannes Stern, who was a chef at the local hotel. With clipboards, looking as serious and grave as Prue Leith and Paul Hollywood, the two judges prowled along the length of the trestle table bearing an assortment of cakes. The standard varied enormously, from simple but well risen Victoria sponges to an intricate meringue with swans swimming on its surface (she guessed that was Elsie Reynolds' entry) and an elegant dark chocolate ganache-covered cake with an elaborate fascinator of white chocolate attached to one side. It was all rather impressive, although she was pleased that she could hold her head up high. Her entry was definitely up to standard.

After much heated deliberation and note taking, the judges formed into a huddle.

Out of the corner of her eye, with that second sense of awareness, she saw Devon slip into the marquee. Deliberately she turned her head away, so he didn't register on her peripheral vision, determined not to give into temptation to sneak an occasional glance his way. Unfortunately, she didn't manage to stick to that plan and as Audrey declared that they were about to announce the top five bakers, her eyes caught his. She quickly looked away, taking a sharp inward breath at the unwelcome flutter in her stomach.

'I bet you're shortlisted,' whispered Bets.

'In no particular order, we'd like to invite the bakers to come and stand with their cakes. These are our five finalists. Ella Ridgen.' Bets squealed. 'Elsie Reynolds. Brenda White. Sally Cummings and George Faber.'

Ella risked another look Devon's way, unable to stop her delight from showing. He gave her a nod of acknowledgement, bestowing a matter of fact smile. A hands off, I'm-pleased-for-you-in-a-purely-acquaintance-type-way smile.

It seemed a shame when the judges began to cut into the cakes and then got down to the serious business of tasting them.

'Nice texture. Well risen. Mmm, the chocolate has just the right balance of sweetness.'

'Light, airy meringue with just the right amount of gooey-ness in the middle. Very good indeed.'

They came to Ella's and her knees began to shake. It was as bad as being at an exhibition and waiting for *The Times* art critic to make his comments. She'd forgotten how terrifying being judged was, especially with everyone around you to hear.

'Beautifully presented. Fabulous sugar-paste work.' In tandem, Scott and Johannes lifted their forks to their mouths. There was a pregnant pause of anticipation among the crowd. As the judges chewed, people craned their necks to hear their verdict. Scott's expression changed first. Horrified disbelief. Johannes' eyes widened and his nose wrinkled. For a second it looked as if he might spit his mouthful out.

There was an agitated mutter in the crowd as everyone started talking.

'Zat is deesgusting. All I can taste is bicarbonate of soda.'

'That's a bit mean,' muttered Bets with an outraged glare.

'Oh, shit,' whispered Ella, putting her hand to her mouth in horrified realisation. She started to giggle. 'I just remembered. I guessed on the baking powder, got my teaspoons and tablespoons muddled up.'

'You noodle.' Bets shook her head, biting her lip, making an obvious effort not to laugh.

'It gets worse.' Ella's eyes danced at the memory. 'I added an extra one in because I was worried about it not rising.' Ella snorted and then burst out laughing, waving at the curious crowd who clearly thought she'd gone mad.

What a berk. No wonder they'd risen so well at first. They must taste disgusting. The more she tried to school her face to sympathise with the two judges who were valiantly trying to swallow down the cake, the funnier she found it.

The judges stared at her.

It was no good, Ella couldn't stop the tears of laugher rolling down her face. The whole room turned to look at her.

She faced them, clutching her middle, almost doubled over. 'T-tell them, Bets,' she gasped as tears ran down her cheeks.

'She got her teaspoons muddled up with tablespoons,' announced Bets in a very loud voice. 'Two tablespoons of baking powder. But it rose.'

People in the room began to smile, many laughing out loud, those nearest clapping her on the back. They weren't laughing at her, they were laughing with her. There was a difference and it felt good. No, it felt great.

When she glanced across the room towards Devon, this time he smiled properly.

Chapter Thirty-Five

'Mum! You're bright and early.' What on earth was her mother doing sitting outside her house, in her father's big Mercedes, at this time of day? 'Have you been waiting long?'

'Morning, darling.' She stepped out of the car and gave Ella a kiss on the cheek. 'Gosh, you're positively glowing. Full of beans.'

'It's a bit blustery down by the reservoir this morning. Poor Tess, I thought her ears might blow off.' They'd had a very brisk walk this morning.

Her mother looked at her expectantly. Had she missed something? 'Is everything all right?'

'Fine. Fine.' There it was, that too-bright tone. 'You didn't get my text?'

'No. Not even looked at my phone this morning.' Deliberate policy. She didn't want to see that Devon hadn't texted. Didn't want to see that he hadn't sent an apology, saying he'd over-reacted and how grateful he should have been to her. It had been a week since the village fayre and she hadn't seen him at all. The idiot.

Her mother followed her into the cottage. Tess trotted straight into the kitchen and Ella automatically grabbed her water bowl to refill it. As usual Tess lapped at the water like a desert explorer who'd just reached an oasis.

'Coffee?' asked Ella, filling up the sink with hot water to wash up her breakfast dishes.

'No, I can't stop. Good news. Mrs Bosworth is out of hospital and her sister decided to come and collect her. She's relented and said that Tess can go to Kent with them while Mrs Bosworth recuperates. So Tess can go home.'

The plate slipped through Ella's boneless fingers, sinking back into the iridescent bubbles, which suddenly blurred.

'What?' she asked, trying to process the words.

'Tess is going home.'

Tess *was* home. In her basket. In the corner of the room lying in her bed pretending to be exhausted after their walk, having hoovered up every last stray toast crumb and looking pitiful, with her usual *isn't it time for a second breakfast or a snackette* expression on her face.

Ella let out a tiny incoherent gasp at the sudden twist of pain, unable to frame any words. Her mother was talking, in jolly, upbeat, hurrying tones.

'... strike while the iron's hot and your father didn't need the car. Not first thing, although he's playing golf at eleven. So if you can just gather all the dog paraphernalia together.'

'What?' Although her mother had clearly issued a call to action, Ella struggled to process the words. It was as if her brain had frozen and she'd lost the ability to command her limbs.

'Her things, dear.'

'Her things?' echoed Ella.

'Yes, dear.' A touch of impatience crept into her mother's voice. 'Lead. Bowl. Bed. Food.'

'Right.' Ella waved a limp arm towards the larder and then another towards the hall.

'Food? Larder?'

Ella nodded. She risked a look at Tess, in her bed, her head resting on her legs watching the two of them. The amber eyes looked up at her, trust shining in their depths.

Ella stared back at the furry black face and Tess tilted her head to one side with a quizzical look, the mobile eyebrows wriggling in consternation, the tongue lolling out of one side and the black nose twitching with suspicion. Tess always seemed to know when something wasn't right. Although she probably missed her owner and Mrs Bosworth probably missed her.

Tess rose and shook herself, crossing the kitchen floor to nuzzle at Ella's hand.

'Are you OK, dear?'

'I-I just wasn't expecting you to ... You haven't given me much notice. Her things ...'

Her mother tutted. 'How much notice do you need? Honestly.' She shook her head with amused exasperation. 'It's not like packing for a trip. She's a dog, dear.'

'It still would have been useful to know,' Ella said petulantly, knowing she sounded ridiculous. 'We might have been out on a walk. She might have needed cleaning up.' Ella regretted not letting Tess jump in the water this morning.

'But you weren't,' said her mother being totally, and completely annoyingly, reasonable.

'But I might have been.'

Her mother pursed her lips. Ella knew she was pouting. It was like an unspoken tug of war.

'Ella, you're just being difficult now. I'm very grateful that you helped out with Tess. Clearly you didn't want her and in hindsight it was a lot harder work than I first imagined. I still can't believe she ate the whole of the rest of that joint. What a pickle. I know it's been really tough on you and I'm sorry, we shouldn't have asked you to have her without any warning. But it's done you some good. You look great. And now she's going back, which will make things so much easier for you. At least you've gained a bit of a glow with all that exercising her. So that's one good thing.'

Ella scowled. Why was it her mother managed to make her feel about fifteen again?

'Does she have to go now? Can't I bring her over later?'

'No. Pauline, Mrs Bosworth's sister, drove up yesterday. She's driving back to Kent this afternoon.'

'Maybe I could take Tess down later.'

'Why would you want to do that, Ella?'

'Just to give Tess time to get used to the idea.'

Her mother stared at her as if she'd gone off her rocker.

'Well ...' Ella shrugged. 'She's clever. She knows.'

Her mother raised a sceptical eyebrow. 'Really?' She tapped her watch. 'I need to get back.' She softened her voice. 'I'm sure you've got used to having her around but just think, you won't be tied any more. No more crying in the night.'

'She doesn't do that now.'

'No more stealing food, then.'

Ella looked down at Tess and raised her eyebrows at the dog. Never going to happen. Tess was always going to be an opportunist.

'You can go off and do whatever you want. Besides I should think poor Mrs Bosworth is desperate to see her.'

Tess licked her hand and Ella remembered those heart-rending howls of the first few nights. Poor baby had been scared. Missing Mrs Bosworth. Not in her own home. Lost and afraid.

'Sorry, Tess,' she whispered, her fingers stroking the velvet softness of her ears as Tess leaned against her. She was being selfish. Tess already had an owner who loved her. Ella blinked back the stupid tears. She wasn't being very fair. Mrs Bosworth had had Tess a lot longer than she had. She'd probably missed her dog terribly.

'I'll get her things,' she said, not wanting to step away from the comforting weight against her leg. 'Just let me wash these up. I bought her a new bowl. She was gulping her food down so quickly, which is why she always wanted more immediately, although she is a Lab,' She ruffled the fur on Tess's head. 'One bowl is never enough, is it?' Ella carefully rinsed the new food bowl before drying it off.

'Is that hygienic? I'd put that tea towel straight in the wash if I were you.' Her mother eyed the cloth dubiously.

'Devon recommended it. Make sure you tell Mrs Bosworth. It slows Tess down when she's eating, so there's time for her brain to send the signal that she's had some food and it's much better for her digestion.'

'Right.'

Ella crossed to the larder. 'And I bought her different dog food. She's used to it now. Devon recommended this as well. It contains more of the sort of nutrients a big dog needs. Mrs Bosworth ought to buy this one in future. The other one was really for small dogs.'

'What else?'

Ella walked in an aimless circle for a minute, trying to think.

'Lead.' Where was it? Ah, in her coat pocket. 'Poo bags. New packet. Anything else?'

The lump in her throat threatened to choke her.

'Bed?' suggested her mother looking pointedly towards the French door.

'Oh, yes. I bought her a new one. You'd better take that. She's used to it now. The old one is under the stairs. You can take that too.'

'You've spent rather a lot of money on her.' Ella's mother looked a bit worried. 'Are you sure you want me to take all this?'

'It's fine, Mum. It belongs to Tess.' She shrugged helplessly. 'I'm not going to need it, am I?'

Her mother's face tightened and then her eyes softened. 'I didn't realise you'd become so fond of her. I'm glad she's been company for you.'

There was a pause. Silence roaring for a second. Ella's stomach turned over.

'I'll take this lot out to the car. Do you want to bring Tess?'

Ella nodded, not trusting herself to speak. Her throat had closed up and her jaw hurt as she locked her back teeth together to stop any emotion escaping.

Tess wagged her tail. Ella took a deep breath. Tess was happy. That was the most important thing.

Ella followed her mother out to the car, trying not to think of all the times she'd walked along this path with Tess sniffing at every nook and cranny. Tess bounced along beside her, her nose in a flower, taking a sudden about turn diverted by the scent of something under the bush.

'This way. Come on.'

Ears pricking up, Tess pattered through the gate and followed Ella's mother who opened the boot of the car. Tess stopped, looking back. 'In you go.' Ella tugged at her collar and with an excited wag of her tail, Tess jumped into the car, turning three quick circles before looking at Ella, tongue hanging out as if to say, 'So where are we going?'

Her mother stood, one hand on the top of the boot ready to shut it. Ella pinched her lips hard, feeling the tendons in her throat straining. She wanted to throw her arms around Tess, lift her back out of the car and run back into the house. Instead, blinking furiously, she rubbed Tess's head and whispered, 'Be good,' and stepped back.

Her mother slammed the boot shut. Tess pressed her nose against the glass, her tail wagging. No doubt thinking she was going for another walk.

'Bye, Ella, see you soon.' Her mother started up the engine and Tess suddenly stilled, standing four square facing Ella, her nose up against the other side of the glass. Her eyebrows lifted up and down, almost meeting in the middle in her usual quizzical fashion as if to say, *something's different*.

Ella reached and touched the spot which had already misted up. 'Bye, Tess,' she said, her voice hoarse. As the car pulled away Ella stood motionless, watching until it turned round the bend and went out of sight.

The kitchen felt horribly empty, the spot by the French doors now stark, just a few drops of water where Tess's bowl used to be and a circle of black dog hair outlining the shape of her bed. Ella thought about sweeping them up but instead sank down into one of the kitchen chairs, laid her arms on the table, put her head down and cried.

Chapter Thirty-Six

She'd forced herself to paint for the last two days and it had been hard work. Like pulling teeth. The new picture was there – not coming quite as easily as that first painting but it was OK, the inner confidence and vision were still there. That was a huge consolation. It kept her busy, but nothing stopped her glancing round at the spot where Tess used to sit or drifting into the kitchen at six o'clock. The cottage seemed so empty. So quiet. She missed the pitter-pattering of Tess's feet on the hard stone floors in the kitchen or the jangling of her lead when she'd grown impatient with Ella's tardiness and a walk was overdue.

It was only because she was so sick of her own irritability and inability to settle at anything that Ella had decided to venture to the gallery this afternoon for something to do. Googling Margery Duffle had nearly put her off. She'd known Margery was a big deal, but not quite how big a deal her 'little' gallery in Great Missenden was.

Ella had very nearly turned tail when she walked in through the door. There were some amazing pictures on the wall. An Alison Ronson, for God's sake. She'd been shortlisted for the Turner Prize last year.

'Your pictures are superb, but especially this one.' Margery Duffle prowled around the easel upon which she'd placed Ella's reservoir picture. Looking at the finished painting with its palette of hazy greens, opalescent blues and silver lights made Ella's heart ache. Capturing the essence of a picture often seemed like knitting with mist, almost impossible to transfer the exact impression onto canvas, but this time she'd done it. And even better, she knew she could do it again.

'I love the other two as well but this is simply my favourite. What do you think, Jamie?'

Margery's nephew, who happened to be in the shop when Ella arrived, screwed up his face in silent contemplation. 'No disrespect, the secret bower one isn't really my thing but I think the picture looking in through the window of the pub is brilliant.' He laughed, dark brown eyes dancing. 'The way you've captured all the different characters. There are so many stories there.'

'Typical journalist,' said Margery with a touch of pride. 'Always the story.'

'Always,' he nodded. He dug in his pockets, rifling through several before he dug out a handful of scruffy cards. 'Jamie Milburn.' He passed her one of the small squares. 'Journalist. I write a column on pros and cons of life in the country. Whether it's all it's cracked up to be. Bucolic bad or rural idyll. Your picture of the water and this one of the pub sum up the opposites for me. I wouldn't mind doing a feature on you. Artist in the country.'

'I wouldn't mind either,' said Margery. 'Great publicity.'

'I'm not sure I'd be the best advocate,' said Ella with a half-hearted shrug. Everything seemed so much effort at the moment. 'I only moved out of London a couple of months ago. Housesitting. It's not permanent. I'm still coming to terms with not being able to get a decent cup of coffee within five metres of my house.'

'Perfect. That's exactly what I'm looking for.'

A twinge of disloyalty shot through her. 'The upside is, I do know people I can go and have a coffee with.' She thought of Bets. 'And people who would know if I hadn't been out for a coffee for a few days.' Like Doris and George. 'And that's worth a hell of a lot more.'

'Really? Where do you live? In a village? Outside? How far is the nearest town?'

'Jamie,' Margery interjected gently. 'If you could save that for another time. Ella and I have business to discuss.'

'Sorry, M. Nice to meet you, Ella. I'll liaise with M about that interview. See you next week.' He sauntered out of the door.

'Sorry about that. My nephew. Charming boy. Too charming by half but he does write clever, insightful and slightly satirical pieces. He likes to make fun of the Chelsea Tractor brigade that come out and play at being in the country. He's rather naughty sometimes.' Margery smiled indulgently. 'Now where were we?'

By the time Ella left, they'd agreed an exhibition for the autumn and in the meantime Margery would hang all three paintings in her gallery and put them up for sale. As Ella belted herself into Magda's little car, she repeated the figures out loud. Two thousand pounds! Margery had put a price tag of two thousand pounds on the reservoir picture. She really thought it was good enough.

Ella should have been elated but a sense of sadness dogged her. She didn't want to go home to an empty house.

As Ella pulled up outside Lime Tree Cottage, having done a detour to the big supermarket on the outskirts of Amersham, stopped in Chesham and visited a couple of charity shops, she spotted Bets coming along the pavement with Dexter skipping along beside her. Her heart sank. She tried to compose her face as she stepped out of the car. The last person – no, the second last person – she wanted to see at the moment.

'Hi, stranger.' Bets' grin was strained, her usual mile-wide smile dim and her cheeks a little pasty. 'Ready for our walk? Isn't it a gorgeous day? Summer is just around the corner.' All this was said with forced cheer.

Ella faltered. Damn, she'd completely forgotten that they'd arranged today. Bets was dog-sitting Dexter for Devon. Was he in London again? She couldn't remember. They were going for a walk. To Ashridge for a change.

'Ella?' prompted Bets as she ground to a halt. 'Are you OK?'

Ella couldn't say anything; it was as if something were lodged in her throat. No more walks with Tess's black body zigzagging in front of her, tail swiping ninety miles an hour. No more Tess dancing around at her feet, giving that funny little yip of excitement when she saw Dexter.

Her face crumpled. Unbidden, the tears welled up as she tried hard to stifle a sob. She didn't want to make a fuss. Embarrass herself. Be stupid. It was just a dog. It shouldn't hurt this much. But it was constant. Every time she walked into the kitchen. When she came home. When she came down in the morning. It was stupid. She'd been heartbroken when she first came here about Patrick and losing the baby. Losing her direction. Not knowing what to do. This was completely different, so how come it hurt just as much?

'Ella.' Bets immediately drew her into her arms. 'Whatever's wrong? Hey, sweetie.'

That instant kindness set her off in earnest and she began to sob while trying to muster up incoherent words. 'T-tess. Sh-she's g-g-gone. Mm-um came. T-t-o-o-ok h-her.'

Bets held her tight as noisy sobs racked her body and Ella fought against the crushing weight, heavy on her chest, trying to drag air into her lungs.

'Hey, slow down. I can't understand you. What's happened? Is Tess OK?' Bets held her arms straight and gave Ella a little a shake. 'Slow down. Breathe.'

Ella nodded, swallowing hard to try to stop the involuntary convulsions gripping her diaphragm. She felt Dex nudge her hand, as if he were trying to offer comfort too. It brought a fresh twist to her heart.

With an unladylike sniff because she had no tissues and didn't actually care, she held out her hand and let Dex nose at each of her fingers.

'What's happened?'

Ella took several deep breaths, eventually managing to slow her body's runaway emotions down. All the while, Bets rubbed her back, hugging her gently and waiting patiently without probing or hurrying her for an answer. Ella loved her for that.

'It's OK. Sorry.' She took Bets' hand and squeezed it in gratitude. She wanted to apologise to her, for thinking she was somehow inferior, she wanted Bets to know how much she valued her. 'Thank you.'

'For what?' Bets nudged her. 'I haven't done anything.' She wrinkled her freckled nose. 'Apart from stand in as hanky. I think you've made me a bit soggy.'

'Thank you for being such a good friend even when I didn't think I wanted one.'

Bets shrugged, a blush tainting her cheeks.

'Tess has gone home. Back to Mrs Bosworth.' Saying it out loud made her feel silly. Tess had gone back to where she belonged. It wasn't as if she'd died or anything. She wasn't even Ella's in the first place. It had always been temporary.

'Oh, Ella. I'm *so* sorry.' Bets hugged her again. 'Poor you. That must really suck. I'd be devastated.'

Ella smiled mistily at her.

'You don't think I'm being stupid, then?'

'Of course not.'

'I really miss her.'

'Well, of course you do. I'm so sorry. That's no consolation, is it. When did she go?'

'Day before yesterday.'

'Why didn't you call me?'

Ella pulled a face. 'I . . . don't know. I should have. I thought I was being stupid.'

'No! Never. People get so attached to their pets. When they lose them, it's so tragic. I hate it. We all do. Honestly, we should have bereavement counselling to deal with people at the practice. I might suggest that to Devon. Although he's coming round. He actually went to visit someone whose dog had to be put down. That's a first.'

'Don't talk to me about him,' sighed Ella. 'I'm still furious with him.' Which was a whole lot better than feeling sad. It helped her survive the disappointment of what might have been there. 'I am being silly because I always knew she was going to go. I got so used to her, I forgot.'

'So where's she gone? And who did she belong to?'

'Someone my mum knows.' Ella explained the full story.

'Your mum sounds a bit heartless,' said Bets with a frown.

'No. That was my fault.' Ella managed a rueful smile. 'I did lay it on a bit thick when I went home the other week about what a pain it was having a dog. I was winding them up because I'd discovered they'd been meddling. Unfortunately, Tess finishing off the beef didn't do her any favours in Mum's eyes. Bless her, Mum thought she was doing me a favour by returning Tess early.'

'Do you still want to come out for a walk with us?'

'I was going to do some painting.'

'That doesn't sound terribly enthusiastic.'

Ella shrugged.

'Some fresh air might do you good,' said Bets tentatively. 'And company.'

Ella took a deep breath. She'd spent the last two days in the studio, looking up out of the skylight imagining the fresh breeze on her skin, the brilliant spring green of the trees and the warmth of the sunshine.

'Do you know what, a walk sounds like a good idea.' She couldn't mope for ever. 'Let me grab a coat and change my shoes.' As she hurried up the path to the front door, she called over her shoulder. 'By the way, I've got some news.'

'Really? What? What?' Bets' enthusiasm was boundless. With a weak smile, Ella grabbed her coat. Bets would get a buzz from her news about the exhibition, which begged the question. Where would she be in autumn? Somehow she couldn't imagine going back to London. Ella lapsed into thought for a minute.

The garden had really blossomed since she'd first arrived. The trees and shrubs around the front gate had burst into life – light and shade, leaves and flowers all interwoven into elaborate patterns and shapes that brought to mind William Morris designs. There was always so much to see, to inspire. How had she ever thought that living out here would be stultifying? She'd gained so much by living in Magda's cottage. Far more than she'd lost.

With a lift to her spirits, she turned to Bets. 'What is it they say – better to have loved and lost than never loved at all.'

'Hmm.' Bets wrinkled her nose.

'I'm really going to miss Tess, but I gained so much by having her for a short time. Who knows, one day I might even get a dog of my own and I never thought I'd say that.'

'Blimey. You really are a country girl. Do you know what you're going to do when Magda gets back?'

A flash of inspiration hit with a punch of absolute certainty. 'Yes.' Ella beamed. 'Yes, I do. I think I'm going to stay.'

'Really?'

'Yes, I got a lawyer friend of Dad's to speak to Patrick and he's transferred quite a lot of money back to me. Apparently, he'd just signed a big merchandising deal on my behalf. I won't ever get all the money back but it's a start. I was incredibly stupid leaving everything to him, so now I'm taking charge, with a bit of help from Dad, and I don't need to worry about getting a full-time job and if Margery can sell my paintings, even better. So, I'm going to see if Geoffrey and Audrey will rent me the other barn conversion.'

'Yessss!' Bets punched the air, 'You can be my neighbour. That will be so fab.' She squealed and gave Ella a big hug, much to the bemusement of Dexter who then decided he'd had enough of being sensible and started to jump up, bumping his nose in between them as if trying to join in.

'And if that's not available, I'll try and find somewhere else round here to rent. I'm going to stay.'

Chapter Thirty-Seven

'It's happening! It's happening.' Ella put down her paintbrush and went to the top of the stairs. Bets stood at the bottom looking slightly wild, breathing hard. 'Larry's having her puppies. Devon's just left, driven straight up to London.'

'Come on in.' Ella said with only a touch of sarcasm as she started down the stairs; it was impossible to be rude to Bets. 'Want a cup of tea?' She looked at her watch. 'Or lunch?'

'Yes, please. Sorry, I was just so excited. Although why today of all days! We had two spays lined up already and then that stupid dog Buster had to go and try and eat a rugby sock again. Luckily this time they caught him, but he'd got the fibres all knotted around his teeth. I mean, seriously. It can't taste that good.'

Ella giggled. 'Depends whether it was clean or dirty, I guess. Better than knickers.'

'I don't know which is more stupid, the dog or the owner for continuing to leave the family clothing out.' Bets shook her head.

'So what is actually happening?' Ella had absolutely no

idea what was involved, although watching *Making Pets Well With Marina* had become part of her new routine for the last three mornings as the date for the puppies' arrival had grown closer.

Who'd have thought she'd ever be interested? She missed Tess desperately but watching the dogs on the programme, with their movements and distinctly doggy mannerisms, reminded her how Tess behaved and provided her with oddly masochistic comfort.

The mornings were the worst; waking up and coming down to an empty kitchen. First thing she painted for a couple of hours until the listless, lacking in energy feeling hit her. She'd taken to going for a walk, which made her miss Tess even more, but she needed the exercise and the sense of being outdoors. It definitely helped. After that she'd come back and work on her new Gurk, Burk and Turk series with the TV on in the background. The story of three aliens new to rural life had really taken root in her head and the ideas flowed thick and fast. Gurk had taken to saddling up Jonah, a male robin, to fly around exploring the village, which looked distinctly like Wilsgrave. She was able to draw and concentrate while keeping half an eye on Marina, drifting about looking glamorous and professional in her pristine white coat. Despite a vague sense of it being wrong tuning in each day to see Devon's ex, especially when she knew Marina hadn't played fair and so didn't deserve the ratings, Ella couldn't quite wean herself from the guilty curiosity of watching. Like the rest of the nation, she was hooked on the latter stages of Larry's pregnancy. The bookies were offering shorter and shorter odds on the delivery date.

'Larry's gone into labour. The first puppy could be anytime,' Bets hopped up and down, getting in Ella's way as she tried to open the fridge door.

'Sit down while I make us a sandwich,' said Ella, pointing to a kitchen chair at the table.

'I think I love you. I could murder one. It's been mad today.'

'Tuna or ham?'

'Ha—' Bets broke off with a squeal and held up her phone. 'A puppy! Look!'

Ella came to stand over her shoulder. 'Wow.'

The screen of Bets' phone showed the livestream of a tiny screwed-up puppy being licked vigorously by Larry. 'I don't believe it. God, I just love puppies. They have that cute dog smell.'

Tears welled up in Ella's eyes. 'So cute. Isn't it amazing.' Already the tiny bundle was wriggling and Larry worked hard at chewing through the umbilical cord. 'She knows what to do.'

'Maternal instinct's a powerful thing,' said Bets. 'Aren't they amazing. They just know what to do. Not sure I would.'

Ella touched her stomach with a wistful smile. 'I think you probably would. Hormones have a lot to answer for.' She thought of what she'd lost and suddenly felt a lot more hopeful about the future. She knew exactly what she wanted and it did involve settling, being bourgeois and doing what was right for her.

They craned back over the screen and Ella laid a hand on Bets' shoulder. Bets' hand crept up to give her hand a squeeze.

*

It took another half hour before any signs of the next puppy and they got on with eating their lunch.

'Here comes the next one,' said Bets, her finger tracing the screen, where the camera was focused on Larry's heaving flank.

'I'm not sure I could cope with multiple births.' Ella winced. 'And definitely not eight.'

'That's good.' Bets turned shining eyes her way. 'I hope Devon gets there in time. He was so gutted when he had to leave Larry behind.'

Ella could relate to that. Clearing away their plates, her thoughts inevitably turned to Tess as Bets watched the live feed. Hopefully she'd settled back home and was happy, although Ella worried that she might not be getting enough exercise. She'd been so overweight when she first came.

'I sometimes wonder if he was more miserable about leaving Larry than Marina. Anyway, he'll get to see the puppies. He left straight after surgery, with a very determined look about him.' She paused. 'He hasn't said anything but I did wonder if he might be having it out with her.'

'I don't care.' Ella looked unseeing out of the kitchen window. 'He made it perfectly clear it's nothing to do with me.'

'I'd love to go and see them. I love puppies. Maybe I should get one.' Bets looked fierce for a moment. 'Except Marina would probably charge me for the visit. She's such a witch. Devon needs to move on. Wonder where he'll go? I reckon he'll go back to Bristol, you know.'

Ella rather hoped he would. That would make things much easier, especially if she was able to rent the other barn conversion. It would save tripping over him every five minutes and having to be neighbourly.

Chapter Thirty-Eight

Poor Larry looked exhausted. She'd whelped four pups already and there were another four to go. Devon kept his distance. He wouldn't interfere unless it was necessary. Larry knew what she was doing and had managed beautifully with each of the pups, licking away the membrane sack and nipping through the umbilical cords like a pro. What a girl.

For once Marina had managed to curb her TV instincts and not touch any of the puppies yet, leaving nature to take its infinitely wonderful course.

'Keep the camera focused on the puppies. Don't let the audience see the dog eating the goo.' Rick's voice sounded as if he were filming an average day in the street. Devon wanted to punch him.

'The goo is the placenta and is perfectly natural for the mother to eat it. It's a source of protein and nutrients to help her rebuild her strength.'

'Devon, darling, it is a little bit revolting. Viewers don't want to see or know about that.'

'They might not, but you're giving a false impression. It's

also important to flag up that there should be a placenta for each pup. A retained placenta can make a dog very ill indeed.'

Devon worried that this nice sanitised puppy birth might encourage hundreds of viewers to start breeding their dogs, thinking this was all so easy.

He kept a careful watch on Larry nursing her four puppies. So far, so good, but occasionally there might be problems later as the bitch tired or if she rolled on a puppy and inadvertently squashed one. Her vitals seemed fine, she was alert and responsive and the puppies were all a good size. At the moment they looked more like little brown voles than Lab puppies. All their features had yet to sharpen, the heads and short stubby legs were disproportionately large and the barely-there ears just sprouting. Tucked in together next to Larry's stomach, hungrily sucking away, they made a cute, cuddly sight, but there was a way to go yet.

'Isn't it wonderful,' said Marina, slipping a hand through his arm, her recently touched-up lipstick glistening in the studio lights.

It was wonderful. Nature doing what nature did best. But just not on live television or internet or whatever it was. A litter of strong, healthy pups born with no complications ... so far.

'Fabulous television. Twitter and Facebook are going mad. The ratings will go through the roof. And there'll be weekly updates on the puppies growing. I'm so glad you came. I knew I could rely on you to help.'

He looked at her as if she'd lost her marbles. 'I came for Larry. To make sure she's OK. To be on hand if anything went wrong.'

'Yes, and that's help, isn't it?' She smiled with a coy lift of one eyebrow that once he'd found sexy and was now merely irritating. 'You always help me.' In fact, the uptilt of her lips was more a smirk. She assumed that he would help. Assumed he would step in if she needed him to.

That smug, knowing look tore something. He thought of all the times she'd run things by him and he'd had to correct her veterinary knowledge. They should have been a team, equal partners, but she'd taken more and he'd been happy to give it. When had she ever helped him? Even now, having to divide their lives, their house, her career came first. *She* came first.

He looked around at the busy room. The mic in her hand, the thing in her ear relaying Rick's direction, the heat of the lights and the cameramen, cables snaking over the floor. What had once been the consulting room of their veterinary practice was now a fully kitted-out professional studio. One that her company benefited from. Ella was right. He was an idiot. A complete idiot. Things had been going so well that evening and he'd completely ballsed it up and he didn't even know why. Ella had been trying to help and he tossed it straight back at her. His pride had been damaged when she'd been cool with him after Marina had come down. Now he realised he'd also been irritated by her assuming that he'd swallow all Marina's twaddle about him going to work on her new TV programme. So he'd been deliberately cool back to her which was a pretty stupid thing to do considering for the last few weeks he hadn't been able to stop thinking about her or those soft kisses that had been added into the memory mix, the way that they whipped up his pulse and messed with his heart. Somehow, as he'd watched Ella grow and blossom, she'd slunk under his defences. Seeing her laughing uproariously and unselfconsciously at herself at the Village Fayre, in front of everyone, had hit him with a punch of awareness. At that very moment, with her cheeks suffused with pink, her eyes dancing and her graceful artistic hands batting the air with amused disbelief at her stupidity, she'd been picture perfect. And now it hit him, a sucker punch of sudden realisation. He'd fallen in love with Ella.

'Devon. Devon, are you listening to me? I asked you what sort of nutrients there are in the placenta.' Marina tutted. 'And now I haven't got time.' With an irritated toss of her hair she strode off.

Devon stared, disbelieving, after her.

Marina had flitted off and was now doing a piece to camera. 'And after each puppy is born, the placenta comes out. Now,' she gave the camera a 'this is the important science bit' nod, 'it's not very nice but it's perfectly natural for the mother to eat it. It's a source of protein and nutrients which will help her rebuild her strength.'

Devon shook his head and pulled back out of the circle of lights. Yup, he was an A1 idiot.

At the edge of the studio, two executive-looking types in single-breasted suits and very pointy shoes with matching pointy goatee beards stood in front of a bank of three laptops.

'Going well, is it?' Devon asked, slightly bemused by them watching the video of Larry and Marina when the real event was taking place right in front of them.

'You wouldn't believe it. The hits are going through the roof. We've reached over 500,000 viewers.'

'And you are?'

'Account director for RV Pet Foods. We've sponsored the banner headline on the website today.'

'Sponsored?'

'Yeah, best sponsorship deal we've ever done. And a better position on the page than the Remove Me flea powder guys. They just got the sidebar. Cheaper than TV and as tightly targeted an audience as you could wish to find. No wastage.'

'Wastage?' Were they even speaking English?

'When you advertise on TV, there will be a lot of people watching who aren't pet owners. If you advertise around a TV programme, like *Making Pets Well With Marina*, then the ratio of pet owners to non pet owners goes up dramatically. On this site, that ratio is even better. So, less waste.'

'So how much would this sponsorship cost?'

'You don't work for Remove Me?'

'No, I'm the consultant vet for Marina.' *Unpaid* consultant, who fed her the lines. He twisted his lips. 'I don't get involved in the business side of things, just the business end.'

The two men laughed politely.

'Pretty messy business, isn't it?' The taller man shuddered. 'Although the camera guys are doing a great job of missing the really ugly bits out. That's what we're paying for.'

'You must be paying a lot to keep it clean,' said Devon, hiding his disgust. Just how much was this media circus making?

Tall goatee wearer looked around before whispering in Devon's ear.

Devon almost bit his tongue. That was no small chunk of change.

Narrowing his eyes, he looked at Larry busy licking at the latest arrival. It made the £4,000 Marina could make by selling the puppies look rather insignificant. And here he'd been sweating his balls off to try and raise the cash to buy himself out.

Yup, Ella had definitely been right. He'd been too busy protecting his pride to see her help for what it was. A genuine offer. Marina had always had an ulterior motive, another agenda.

He owed Ella an apology. More than an apology. God, he hoped after being such an idiot, she would still talk to him. Forgive him. He'd really messed up there.

'Marina, we need to talk.'

'What, now?' Marina looked over towards the camera.

'There won't be another puppy for a while and this won't take long.'

'There won't?' She looked back at the dog.

Devon had no bloody idea – pups came when they were ready – but he wasn't about to tell Marina that. 'No,' he said.

He drew her out of the studio, up the stairs, through the hallway and into the kitchen. For a second, a brief pang hit him. He'd eaten a lot of solitary meals in this kitchen. Sitting at the walnut breakfast bar, staring at his own reflection in the glossy black units that filled the opposite wall. Wiping away fingerprints from the built-in doors of the fridge where they left marks. It had always been a hopelessly impractical kitchen, even for their domestically challenged lifestyle.

'What's this about, Devon?' she asked with a kittenish purr. 'Have you made your decision?'

'Yes.'

'Devon!' She clapped her hands and leant towards him. 'That's fabulous news. You're coming back?'

He weighed up his words, studying her. Sophisticated and polished, with her perfect curves, tiny waist, long legs in high heels and sultry come-to-bed eyes and all he could think of was a slight, slender blonde who had a big enough heart to try and rescue him.

'No, but I have found a solution to our financial problems.'

Marina's lip quivered rather beautifully.

'Not coming back?'

'No.'

'B-but.' She sniffed rather elegantly and then stiffened like a cat facing off in a fight. 'If that's what you've decided. You're making a big mistake. And where are you going to find the money? We can't keep dragging it out.'

'We don't need to. It's quite simple.'

'It's a shame you didn't realise that before.'

Devon looked at her face, which had sharpened with spite.

'We agreed to split everything down the middle.'

'Yes, but sadly that's the negative equity so I have to absorb mine and you have to pay yours to me.'

'That seems fair.'

Marina put a hand on his arm. 'Of course it's fair.' She patted his arm, flirtatious charm back in place.

'Unfortunately we can't split Larry down the middle.'

'No, and we agreed she should stay in her home.'

'We did. So, I was thinking. You'll be selling the puppies.'

'Yes, Devon, I can't work and look after eight puppies. However,' she gave a saccharine sweet smile, 'we had decided that we would sell them to the highest bidders and give all the money to charity. It would be great PR.'

'"We"?'

'The production team.'

'Ah, but if we split everything down the middle, four of those puppies would be mine.'

Marina's face sharpened. 'There are costs involved. Do you want to halve those too?'

'Half of everything, that's fair. Yes.'

She looked slightly mollified. 'But it would look odd if only four of the puppies were sold for charity.'

'True. OK. Sell them all for charity, although I would like to keep one.'

Her lips pursed. 'We can talk about that later. Once they're all born.'

He folded his arms and leaned back against the breakfast bar, starting to enjoy himself. 'Today's been quite a success.'

'Amazing. Honestly. It's exceeded all our expectations. Breakfast TV have already asked me to do a slot tomorrow morning.' She sat down on one of the bar stools, arranging herself to best advantage. It was an artful pose he'd seen many a time, showing off her perfect legs and making her look up at him from under her lashes.

'What sort of expectations did you have?' Devon pretended to look puzzled. Thanks to Ella and his chat with the goatee boys, he had a much better insight into how some of this media world worked.

'It all hinged on how many people would tune in. Social media. The Facebook page. The website almost crashed at one point but luckily we'd got contingency in place.'

'A good day at the office.'

She grinned, her teeth white against her fuchsia pink lipstick. 'You bet.'

'What would half of today's profits be?' Devon crossed his feet at the ankle. 'You must have done quite well. Half the cost of the sponsorship? Facebook advertising?'

'Don't be ridiculous. That all belongs to the production company.'

'But the house doesn't. The studio doesn't. Surely the production company has to pay for hire and use of the studio.'

Marina paled. 'W-well. It's not that simple. It's more complicated than that.'

'How so? The production company films here. As half owner of the studio, I should also receive half the hire charges.'

Marina stared at him, her jaw tense. 'But I part-own the production company.'

'Hmm, that does make it messy. I think you'd better line up your accountant to talk to my solicitor. But by my calculations...' He crossed his fingers. Ella had been very thorough. 'In the last three years you've filmed eight ten-week series. That's eighty shows plus the regular breakfast show slots and of course today's events. I believe, at today's market rate...' he dredged up Ella's notes and quoted her figures for studio hire. 'And it takes a few days to film a show, so that's an awful lot of studio time owing.'

And he had an awful lot of apologising to do. He owed Ella big time. But seeing Larry today and remembering how devastated he had been when he had to leave her behind, he had an idea of how he might make things up to her.

Chapter Thirty-Nine

With fierce concentration, Ella inked in Gurk's worried little face. Worried because he was clinging to a drainpipe twelve feet up, under the beady, watchful eye of the pub cat. No, make it a friendly black Labrador who wanted to play with the strange-looking creature but the strange-looking creature saw him as a fearsome monster.

She sat back to admire the morning's work and check the time. She ought to think about getting ready. Duty called this afternoon. It was her turn to work in the shop and she'd been tasked with opening up, along with a stern warning about not being late. She was hoping she could remember how to operate the till, which on her brief induction the other day had proved tricky.

Tapping the bunch of keys on her desk, she was telling herself she'd be fine and wouldn't set off the alarm when her mobile buzzed into life, dancing along the table until she just caught it before it took a nosedive into the bin.

'Hello.'

'Hi Ella.'

'Devon,' she responded, letting the resignation show in her voice.

See, that's what you got for answering the phone without looking at the screen. Her heart started doing the impression of a Catherine wheel. Stupid thing. She sighed; she was going to have to talk to him sooner or later but she wasn't about to apologise for trying to help.

'You're mad at me.'

She rolled her eyes. No shit, Sherlock.

'And I deserve it,' he continued. 'I owe you an apology. Are you at home? I'd really like to apologise properly. In person and I've got ... got something for you.'

'As long as it's not bloody chocolates,' she said, thinking of the last diplomatic mission to her house.

'It's much better than that. I think. Do you mind if I pop over now?'

'*Now*, now?' She looked down at herself in horror.

'Yes.'

'Give me ten minutes. I'm still in my PJs. I've been working all morning. But I haven't got long because I'm working in the shop later.'

Ten minutes. Why hadn't she said fifteen? She raced down the stairs, pulling her clothes off as she darted into the bathroom and leaping into the shower before it had time to warm up. Oooh, that was cold.

What was it he needed to say in person? She was suddenly all fingers and thumbs as she struggled still damp into fresh jeans, fluffed up her hair and pulled on a clean T-shirt. With five minutes to spare, she cleaned her teeth and slapped on a touch of moisturiser and several quick strokes of mascara. That would have to do. With a pause, still mindful of the ticking minutes, she stopped and took stock of herself in the mirror. Her hair had grown out of its usual sharply styled choppy layers, they were looser and softer, and she'd stopped applying the careful eyeliner and lipstick which had been her trademark for years. There didn't seem much point these days. Not that she couldn't be bothered, but it just wasn't important any more. With a toss of her hair, she gave herself a cautious smile. She much preferred this new her.

Even though she was expecting it, the knock at the door made her jump. Trying to be casual, she took her time opening the door.

Devon stood there, empty handed and with a sheepish smile, but he made no move to come in.

Unease flickered in her stomach. Maybe he had just come to apologise and clear the air.

'Hi.' Nerves fluttered and her legs seemed to have suddenly lost their backbone.

'Hi.'

Just the low timbre of the huskily spoken word made her mouth go dry.

They eyed each other and then Devon's mouth began to curve in a slow smile. He stepped across the threshold and took her in his arms and without any further preamble kissed her. Kissed her socks off. Kissed her like there was no tomorrow. Kissed her breathless.

She clung on. Her legs gave up the last attempt to hold her upright but it didn't matter because Devon held onto her, kissing her as if he were afraid to let go.

When he finally did let go, she stared at him, dazed. No one had ever made her feel quite so important to them. It felt rather wonderful.

'I'm an idiot. I'm sorry. Will you forgive me?'

If he kept kissing her like that, most definitely.

'Are you going to come in? I'm worried we might give George another funny turn.'

'I'm sure it would take more than that to shock him. I've got something for you . . . in the car.' His face lit up like a small boy with a big secret.

She followed him to the car, almost laughing at the definite spring in his step as he confidently led her down the path.

The back window of the estate car had steamed up, apart from one wet patch, where a black nose was pressed up against the glass.

Ella's heart missed a beat as Devon opened up the boot.

A black blur leapt out and almost knocked Ella sideways, jumping up with overexcited joy, skittering about backwards and forwards, sniffing everything with unfettered delight. 'Tess!' She crouched down to hug the dog, almost knocked over by excited tail-lashing as Tess skipped about in crazy happy-dog circles.

'Hello, you.' Ella shot a teary look Devon's way. 'T-this is so kind. I've really . . . m-missed her.' Tess dropped into a sit and nuzzled at Ella, licking her hand. 'I thought she was in Kent. Has Mrs Bosworth come home?'

'No. I've been to Kent,' said Devon, gently pulling her up and putting both hands on her forearms, as if to make sure she was going to stay put.

'You've been to Kent.' Ella frowned, puzzled. 'Why?'

'I remembered the shape Tess was in when I first saw you.' He paused as Ella raised an eyebrow, still stroking the dog's ears with one hand as if unable to stop touching her. 'I apologised for that.'

She laughed. 'I know, just teasing.'

'I went to check on her, see how she was doing, when Bets told me how much you were missing Tess.' Ella looked down at the dog, who was gazing up at her with abject adoration. Her heart turned over at the expression in the amber eyes.

'So you've ... what? Borrowed her back for me?'

Devon cupped his hand under her chin and smiled gently down at her.

'No, I've brought her home.'

Ella's heart stopped.

'You mean ... ' She stifled a sob, gazing up into his eyes, her pulse tripping at his serious gaze. Devon took both of her hands, holding them in his, squeezing her fingers gently. 'Yes. She's all yours. When I told her how close you and Tess were, Mrs Bosworth was delighted – she'd been toying with the idea of staying in Kent with her sister and moving into sheltered accommodation together, but the place they really like and can afford doesn't take dogs. Tess is yours, if you want her.'

'Of course I want her,' breathed Ella, unable to tear her eyes from his.

'There are some conditions.' His face gentled and Ella bit her lip at his sudden solemnity. His pause made her heart thud louder.

'She has to live in the village.'

'She ... ' Ella stopped and for a moment couldn't say a word; she didn't think she could squeeze anything past the outsize lump in her throat, so instead she looked up at him and smiled and smiled and smiled.

'Would that be OK?' Devon's quiet question had her heart expanding, until it felt as if it might just pop.

She nodded, still unable to speak.

'I'm sure you could get a place around here.' He scrunched up his face. 'It's a shame, Dad's just let the other barn.'

'Has he?' asked Ella, with a sudden twinkle, thinking of the tenancy agreement on the kitchen table. 'I wonder who to?'

Devon raised an eyebrow. 'Ah, so that was why he was being so cagey.'

He lifted a hand and stroked Ella's face. 'I had a long chat with him. Realised I've been an idiot all round. I'm planning on staying here, too,' his mouth curved, 'if the village is big enough for the both of us.'

She gave a quick nod as he carried on. 'With the money that Marina *owes* me, I'm going to invest in the equipment and training I need, and expand the practice in partnership with Dad, who will work part-time. When Jack graduates he can join the partnership.'

'I did tell you you were an idiot.' She stepped closer to him, feeling the roughness of his favourite wool sweater graze her arms.

'You did. But I've stopped being one. Mine and Marina's solicitors are going to get together for a chat, but thanks to you, I'll come out ahead – and there's the sponsorship money I'm owed for half of my dog being a star on the internet. Plus four puppies.'

'Four puppies? That's great.'

Devon grinned. 'You've never had a puppy, have you?'

She shook her head, beaming back at him. 'How hard can it be? Look at Tess. I'm much better at this dog-owning lark. Mind you, I had some help.'

With a tremulous smile, she stood on her tiptoes and kissed him with a feather light touch on his lips. 'Thank you, Devon. For bringing her back.' Tears shimmered in her eyes.

He took her face in both his hands. 'I think I deserve another kiss ... it took me hours to drive to Kent and back.'

She dropped another kiss on his lips.

'And the traffic was absolutely dreadful.' He raised an eyebrow in challenge, his hands sliding down to rest on her shoulders.

She kissed him again.

'And it took me for ever to find Mrs Bosworth's sister's place.'

Ella rolled her eyes and stepped forward, slipping her arms around his neck and, pulling his mouth down to hers, pressed her lips with gentle insistence.

Their protracted kiss sent Tess into a tailspin of delight and Ella could feel her thrusting her head between their legs trying to squeeze through and join in.

Devon's mouth roved over hers, his hand slipping down her back to her waist to hold her closer. 'Bloody dogs,' he muttered as Tess almost pushed him over. 'Although Dexter's going to be delighted.'

'Thank goodness they get on,' teased Ella. 'It's an important consideration, you know.'

'You're an expert on canine matters now, are you?'

'I'm getting there.'

'So four Labrador puppies wouldn't faze you?'

Devon let out a shout of laughter at her horrified expression.

'Steady on!' said Ella. 'Let's just take one dog at a time.'

She stooped to pat Tess who promptly collapsed at her feet, her tongue hanging out with what Ella decided was definitely an adoring grin.

'Where did the ribbon come from?' asked Ella, spotting Magda's trademark silver-grey ribbon tied around Tess's collar.

Devon's sheepish shrug made her smile. 'Thought it made a nice touch. Although to be honest Magda gave it to me ages ago, with this.' He pulled out a crumpled piece of navy blue card. 'I've absolutely no idea why.'

Ella took it from him, smoothing out the creases as she stood in the circle of his arms.

Love and friendship come in many guises,
Steadfast and true
Loyal and honest
Pure and genuine
May you enjoy all three
Blessed be

'Blessed be indeed.' She sighed as his arms tightened around her, closing the circle to hold her fast. She closed her eyes, her breath suddenly catching as she realised this was where she belonged.

'Ahem,' The discreet cough was immediately followed up with, 'Excuse me, I'm terribly sorry to interrupt.'

Devon and she stiffened.

'Hello, Vicar,' said Devon, giving Ella a slightly panicked sidelong glance.

Richard beamed at them, standing there looking very vicarly in his dog collar and long black cassock. 'Ella. Devon. Isn't it a gorgeous day? Lovely weather for being outdoors, but I've been asked to remind you of your duties.'

'Duties?' Ella swallowed hard, feeling her cheeks turning bright red. Vicars probably frowned at public displays of affection and kissing in the middle of the street. 'Sorry, Vicar.' She looked at Devon, whose mouth twitched. He was no help at all. 'Sorry we just ... erm ... just got a little carried away.'

Richard peered over his little round glasses at her, looking very surprised, reminding her of Englebert whenever he was about to deliver news to his naughty brothers. 'No, no, my dear. The shop. Everyone's waiting for you to open up. You do have the keys, don't you?'

'Oh, sh— shoot.' Ella and Devon turned to their right. Across the green a queue had formed outside the village shop. 'Yoo-hoo,' called Audrey. 'I'd be very grateful if you could put my son down. He's supposed to be taking me to the station.'

'He'd better get a move on, then,' said George, as usual wearing his trademark mustard cardigan, 'and put her down. It's almost coffee o'clock and no one makes a cappuccino like our Ella.'

'Leave them alone,' Doris, behind George, stuck both her thumbs up. 'You're only young once and he's a handsome devil. If I were ten years younger I'd fight her for him.'

'Ten years, Doris, steady on,' giggled Bets from behind her, waving to Devon and Ella. 'Hey guys, get a room.'

'I'll have you know I was a Tiller Girl.'

'In your own time, love,' yelled Greta, 'but I have a pub full of punters and I've run out of lemons.'

Ella looked ruefully at Devon. 'I'm really sorry, would you mind taking Tess for me? Duty calls.'

'Bloody shop rota,' muttered Devon, taking her hand. 'Can't we tell them we've got a veterinary emergency?'

'Devon Ashcroft! Where's your sense of community?' she teased, waving back at the waiting crowd. 'Just coming!'

Together they crossed the green. Ella held on tight to Tess's lead with one hand, her other tucked into Devon's, feeling a warm glow as she approached them all. It was difficult to remember why she'd been so reluctant to accept Magda's offer of a bolthole in Wilsgrave. Now she couldn't imagine ever leaving.